Dave Brubeck
Improvisations and Compositions

PETER LANG
New York • San Francisco • Bern • Baltimore
Frankfurt am Main • Berlin • Wien • Paris

Ilse Storb
and
Klaus-G. Fischer

Dave Brubeck
Improvisations and Compositions

The Idea of Cultural Exchange

With Discography

Translated by
Bert Thompson

PETER LANG
New York • San Francisco • Bern • Baltimore
Frankfurt am Main • Berlin • Wien • Paris

Library of Congress Cataloging-in-Publication Data

Storb, Ilse.
    [Dave Brubeck, Improvisationen und Kompositionen. English]
    Dave Brubeck, improvisations and compositions: the idea of cultural
exchange : with discography / Ilse Storb and Klaus-G. Fischer.
      p.   cm.
    Translated from the German.
    Discography: p.
    Includes bibliographical references and index.
    1. Brubeck, Dave. 2. Brubeck, Dave—Criticism and interpretation.
    3. Brubeck, Dave—Discography. I. Fischer, Klaus-Gotthard. II. Title.
    ML410.B868S813   1994   781.65′092—dc20   92-46477
    ISBN 0-8204-2003-4   CIP
                                          MN

Die Deutsche Bibliothek-CIP-Einheitsaufnahme

Dave Brubeck: improvisations and compositions; the idea of cultural
exchange; with discography / Ilse Storb; Klaus-G. Fischer. Transl.: G.
Bertram Thompson. - Bern; Berlin; Frankfurt a.M.; New York; Paris; Wien:
Lang, 1994
    Dt.. Ausg. u.d.T.: Dave Brubeck: Improvisationen und Kompositionen
    ISBN 0-8204-2003-4
NE: Storb, Ilse; Fischer, Klaus-Gotthard

The paper in this book meets the guidelines for permanence and durability of
the Committee on Production Guidelines for Book Longevity of the
Council on Library Resources.

Foreword

Dave Brubeck: Improvisations and Compositions - The Idea of Cultural Exchange is, to my knowledge, the first book ever written about the internationally famous pianist and composer, Dave Brubeck. Besides a biography and portrayal of his stylistic development with numerous analytical examples of his complex harmonic structures—"time experiments"—and the longer compositions, it comprises a critical assessment and classification of his work as well as an extensive discography.

My interest in jazz and its research was aroused in 1969 by the First International Convention for Musicology and Jazz in Graz, Austria and by the Berlin Jazz Festival. There were three essential reasons for choosing Brubeck and his work as the subject:

1. My background as a pianist enabled me to make knowledgeable statements concerning piano compositions.
2. I was intensely motivated by the connection between "classical" music and jazz in Brubeck's works. This was later to evolve into the "cultural exchange" concept.
3. An abundance of transcriptions, piano excerpts, and scores served to simplify and reinforce the audio-analytical process.

As a traditional, classical musicologist I was first of all obliged to painstakingly acquaint myself with the methodology, analytical process, and terminology specific to jazz research. The results of this preparatory phase are on hand, though they couldn't be prefaced to a book about Dave Brubeck, since they would have exceeded the bounds of the undertaking. Needless to say, traditional "classical" musicological methods and findings as well as procedures and terminologies specific to the study of jazz have been resorted to in investigating the, in the furthest sense of the word, acculturated music of the composer and improvisor, Brubeck; and this in itself corresponds to the concept of "cultural exchange."

A long-standing contact with Dave Brubeck and his family, numerous interviews, a sojourn at the Brubeck residence in Wilton, Connecticut, and long talks with Howard Brubeck in San Diego, California yielded extensive, authentic results with respect to the life and work of the pianist and composer, Dave Brubeck. My interviews containing a storehouse of as yet unpublished information can readily be made available to the interested reader.

Special thanks to Prof. Dr. Alfons M. Dauer, who during 20 years of working together in the International Society for Jazz Research always expressed interest and encouraged me to do newer research. Special thanks also to Dave and Iola Brubeck, Howard Brubeck, Chris, Darius, and Cathy Brubeck, William O.Smith for an abundance of illuminating information, and Remy Filipovitch for the notation examples done with the utmost meticulousness according to the Hollywood Calligraphy School rules. I would also like to thank Richard S. Jeweler, San Francisco, for the copyrights of the illustrations and musical examples on pages 15-25, 28-32, 48-49, 51-54, 68, 69, 94, 120-122, 126-127, and 132.

Essen, October 1993 Ilse Storb

The first two records that transformed me, a listener to all styles of jazz, into a modern jazz buff were Dave Brubeck's albums "DAVE BRUBECK AT STORYVILLE: 1954" and "JAZZ GOES TO COLLEGE." That was already in 1955, and although the intensity has fluctuated, Dave Brubeck's music has been my constant companion ever since.

In the eighties I got to know and treasure professionally made discographies through Michael Frohne and Hans Lukas Lindenmaier. Earlier, I had of course already obtained information from "Jepsen" and "Bruyninckx" and worked with the "Bielefelder Katalog."

The discography of Dave Brubeck's recorded and published works was presented in a German version in 1991. The US version presented here has been updated and largely extended with respect to radio and television broadcasts, including several live concerts. However, a price had to be paid for extending the main body of the discography: the indices of tune titles, musicians, and records with equivalent issues had to be omitted. I am very sorry for this, as it lessens the value of the discography; but I was convinced by the publishers' argument that the book would otherwise be unaffordably expensive. I will publish the complete discography, including registers, elsewhere in a separate issue.

Neukirchen-Vluyn, October 1993 Klaus-Gotthard Fischer

Rendering of the book from its original German into English was done by G. Bertram Thompson, himself an American jazz musician and professional translator living in Germany. He has worked and recorded with, among others, Dizzy Gillespie, the ORF Big Band (Vienna), Ray Charles, Art Taylor and Charles Tolliver.

Contents

Part A

Dave Brubeck: Improvisations and Compositions
- The Idea of Cultural Exchange -
by Ilse Storb

Part B

Discography
by Klaus-Gotthard Fischer

Part A

Dave Brubeck: Improvisations and Compositions

- The Idea of Cultural Exchange -

by Ilse Storb

Chapter 1

Biography[1]

Born on December 6th, 1920 in Concord, California, Dave Brubeck received his first piano lessons from his mother, Elizabeth Ivey Brubeck. "My mother was a piano teacher who believed in prenatal influence. She played at my cradle and I heard a lot of music when I was a little child. I didn't learn to read music, and I played by hearing because my eyes were too bad."[2]

His brother Howard, too, spoke of diminished vision having spared him military service in 1944, which enabled him to begin as lecturer at Mills College. "I didn't have sight in my left eye [which made me] unacceptable for military service."[3]

Dave Brubeck's father was Howard "Pete" Brubeck, a cattle breeder and farmer who played harmonica. The piece *Dad Plays the Harmonica* from among his first compositions, *Reminiscences of the Cattle Country*, 1946, is dedicated to him. His father was also a prize-winning rodeo rider.

Elizabeth Ivey Brubeck was an extraordinary woman for her times. Initially self taught, she later graduated from King Conservatory in California and went on to study at the Universities of California and Idaho and earn her masters degree in music education. Between the ages of 35 and 40, she received music instruction from the famous piano instructor Tobias Mattey in London. She also received music instruction from the legendary Myra Hess. With all this, it is certain that the love of music was transmitted to her three sons—she was their first music teacher.

The oldest son Henry, who was ten years older than Dave, was born on January 29th, 1910. He played classical violin and jazz drums in the Del Courtney Band and in the original Gil Evans Band (Gil Evans was born in Stockton, California). "When I was 5 years old I heard my brother Henry's jazzband right in my own house every Tuesday night."[4] Henry attended the College of the Pacific in Stockton. He later became a music teacher and supervisor of the music department for the Santa Barbara, California school system. He earned a reputation with his outstanding marching bands and participated several times in the famous Rose Bowl parade.

Howard Brubeck, the second son, is four years older than Dave. He was born on November 11th, 1916. As a young man he won several piano competitions, but his main desire was to become a composer. He played exclusively classical music and graduated in music from San Francisco State College where he subsequently also lectured. Later, at Mills College in Oakland, he became assistant to Darius Milhaud. He taught at San Diego State University and became dean of the Liberal Arts Department at Palomar College in southern California. His compositions were performed at diverse universities, but presumably only a few were recorded onto disc, e.g., 1959 and 1960: *Dialogues for Jazz Combo and Orchestra* for the Dave Brubeck Quartet and symphony orchestra and *Theme For June*, 1962, for the Dave Brubeck Quartet only. These Howard Brubeck compositions were performed and recorded by the New York Philharmonic under the direction of Leonard Bernstein. Howard also arranged some of his brother Dave's piano compositions for orchestra, like *Brandenburg Gate*, *In Your Own Sweet Way* and *Summer Song*. He also transcribed many of his brother's piano improvisations and compositions for music publications. "I did a lot of arranging for Dave, retaking his work and scoring it for the orchestra, over which he would improvise again." The arranging and orchestration was taken care of by Howard until the oratorio *The Light in the Wilderness* was put together in 1968. From then on Dave Brubeck did the orchestrations himself.[5] Howard now lives retired in Escondido, California, and the contact between his and his brother's family is still close. With the Brubecks, it is foremost a matter of an integrated extended family—sort of a family undertaking in which children, grandchildren, managers and fellow musicians are all happily and systematically taken in.

The Brubeck family moved from Concord, on the East Bay near San Francisco, to a 40,000 acre cattle ranch (Arroyo Secco Rancho in Ione) in California's foothills where the father, Howard "Pete" Brubeck, became manager. Little Dave was then just twelve years old and the older brothers Henry and Howard had already left home for college. Dave felt very much alone on the big ranch. He would ride long distances on horseback, singing cowboy songs to the steady rhythm of the hoofbeats. His mother gave piano lessons in a studio in the small town of Ione near Sacramento. She played Bach, Beethoven, Chopin, and other classical composers. Howard Brubeck considers Bach and Chopin the most important classical influences in his brother's musical work,"...although he heard Beethoven morning and night because [that is what] our mother was practicing...."[6]

Ione was a city in which music was practically nonexistent. Little Dave received harmony lessons from his mother and played Bach chorales, but only as a way of becoming acquainted with musical form. Ivey Brubeck was also a choirmaster and took small Dave with her to rehearsals. Dave had already begun playing piano at 4 years of age, but he didn't practice, rather he improvised—in classical pieces as well. "In fact, in my life I did not even play one minute of good classical music.... She (his mother) played classical music...the typical European music...so I heard all the good music."[7]

At that time—he was twelve years old—Dave independently began attempting improvisations to pieces he heard on the radio. Jazz wasn't new to him, since he had gladly attended his brother Henry's band rehearsals as a child. When Dave was between thirteen and fourteen, he played, mostly Friday and Saturday nights, with local dance bands, e.g., at the Sheep Ranch or Angel's Camp. He wasn't thinking of a jazz career, but rather wanted to go into his father's cattle business. The Brubeck family then moved to Amador County (Spanish: love of gold, the town's appellation in memory of the 1849 goldrush. Dave Brubeck wrote the piece *Sentimental* in 1949 in remembrance of this golddigger country). His mother and a discerning teacher convinced Dave to go to college. In autumn 1938 he enrolled as a veterinary pre-med student. He continued, however, playing regularly with musicians in various clubs, bars and dance halls. At the end of his first year of study a science instructor at the college asked him: "Brubeck, your mind is always on music anyway. Why don't you just go over to the Conservatory next year?"[8]

And this he did, although, when he was accepted into the Conservatory in 1939, he still couldn't read music. Conversely though, he could play excellently by ear. During my week-long stay at the Brubeck residence in Wilton, Connecticut in 1980, I once played Albert Mangelsdorff's "Set'm Up." After listening to the piece only once, Dave Brubeck repeated it on piano. Howard Brubeck confirmed his brother's exceptional feel for sounds and acuteness of ear: "He has an enormous feeling and sensitivity for sounds and he would be able to know what he was hearing. One time in a college music eartraining class in Stockton, the instructor played something and asked the class what it was...and nobody in the class could answer.... Finally, he played it to Dave and said, `What do you think it was?' and Dave said, `I can't describe it for you, but I'll play it.'"[9]

The teacher was Russel Bodley who had received music instruction in Paris from Nadja Boulanger. Three years later, in the spring of 1942, Dave received his degree from the College of the Pacific in Stockton, now known as the University of the Pacific. "I played a lot of instruments like f.i. cello, clarinet, etc. When I left

High School I had to promise never to teach, because I couldn't read music. By composing I learned to read music."[10]

During his college years Dave put together a twelve-man band that he wrote arrangements for and performed with as warm-up band to boogie-woogie pianist Cleo Brown, "...a woman I worked with who had a great influence on me.... I think she was from the Midwest. She was hospitalized for a while and stayed in California where I was going to college. When she got out of the hospital she worked in Stockton and that's where the College of the Pacific is where I went to school...so I used to open for her. Sometimes I played her first set because she was always late, and I would wait and wait and wait and the people would want to hear her. Some nights she came two hours late and the people were lucky that she came at all. She was a tremendous pianist. She was the one that introduced me to Art Tatum."[11]

Dave Brubeck's band was also put on the air weekly by the College of the Pacific in Stockton's radio station. The producer and director was Iola Whitlock.

In the spring of 1942 Dave Brubeck met his wife Iola at the College of the Pacific. Since it was war time, he was inducted into an army band immediately after graduation. Shortly after his induction, in September of that year, Dave and Iola Brubeck married, while she continued her studies at the College of the Pacific in Stockton.

1942 was also the year of a short encounter between the then sixty-eight year old Arnold Schönberg and the twenty-two year old Brubeck. Schönberg was professor at the University of California, Los Angeles from 1936 to 1944. He and Brubeck were interviewed together, and afterwards Schönberg said to Brubeck: "Well, come back next week and bring me something you have written." He looked at young Brubeck's simple piano composition and remarked: "That is all right, but why did you write this note and why did you write that note?" Brubeck answered: "Well, why not?" Schönberg was insistent: "You have to have a reason for every note you write." Brubeck replied: "Because it sounds good. That's my reason." Schönberg insisted: "No, that's not a good reason. There must be other reasons, too."[12]

Schönberg then expounded his theories, composition techniques, tonal relationships with respect to specific time intervals, and the rules of the 12-tone technique. Brubeck didn't see any practical musical sense in these theoretical expositions. Schönberg, having become quite upset, pulled a key out of his pocket, prompted Brubeck to come closer, and remarked while opening the door to his studio: "There are all the Beethoven symphonies...you can ask me any piece of music and I can tell you every note of it...I know more about music than any man alive. Therefore I can tell you why you should write the way I want you to write."[13] That was the beginning and the end of lessons with Arnold Schönberg.

Debussy was another musician who knew only one standard for his music's harmonic sonority: his ear! "Certaines personnes veulent tout d'abord se conformer aux règles. Je veux, moi, ne rendre que ce que j'entends...On cherche trop à écrire, on fait de la musique pour le papier, alors quelle est faite pour les oreilles."[14]

Soon after the war's end (Brubeck was stationed in Europe including occupied Germany—Nürnberg among other places) he decided to study composition with Milhaud. The Veterans Administration made it possible for American soldiers returning from Europe to acquire inexpensive housing in the Oakland Bay area. Because Dave was studying with Milhaud, a succession of other musicians followed in his wake, and Milhaud sent them first of all to Howard Brubeck, his assistant, to study harmony and counterpoint. Bach chorales formed a fixed foundation to the studies. Besides that, a harmony book by André Gédalge was used as well as an analysis book by Walter Piston who had studied with Nadja Boulanger in Paris and who referred, for historical and harmonic analyses of, e.g., Bach, Haydn and Mozart, to the Schenker System.[15]

Mills is actually a girls college but male graduate students were allowed. Among those that studied at Mills were the arranger, composer and Stan Kenton musical partner, Pete Rugolo, as well as the experimental avant garde musician, John Cage. Alto saxophonist and composer Anthony Braxton is now heading the Department of Contemporary Music. Dave Brubeck had already met Darius Milhaud in 1941—one year, as it were, before his encounter with Arnold Schönberg—and Milhaud had been very friendly to him.

In Brubeck's view, the development of music was standing at the parting of the ways between tonality and atonality. Musically, Milhaud was moving in a polytonal direction. "And he didn't like Schönberg's music at all, and I am pretty sure, Schönberg wouldn't like his."[16] Howard Brubeck had other experiences at Mills than his brother David. According to him, "Milhaud adored Schönberg. He loved him." Milhaud also visited him in Los Angeles, on his way from the East to the West Coast, before beginning his first lectures at Mills College. After that, Schönberg lived in Beverly Hills and Milhaud was very concerned about his state of health: "Milhaud was very concerned about Schönberg's mental attitude and health, because Schönberg was so depressed all the time."[17]

Milhaud said, "I can't stand any musical system with mathematics, and if you don't have a tonal center, you rob the audience of one of the greatest things in music, modulation. They can't get anywhere, if they have never been anywhere."[18]

Dave Brubeck studied from 1946 to 1948 in Darius Milhaud's composition class. "Dave wanted very much to become a classical composer, and Milhaud would say to him, `Boo Boo, play me some boogie-woogie!—Dave, you must do what is in you...you're natural in jazz.'"[19]

He would later, too, often go back to Milhaud—for lessons or to go over new compositions with him. Milhaud was a true mentor in the classical sense of the word: he was able to instill confidence and he possessed insight. "He was fantastic, because he took each one of us as we were and tried to help us to do whatever was in us, what we wanted to do. He did not try to make us be like him. Like Hindemith who was very popular as a teacher in this country."[20]

Milhaud encouraged Dave Brubeck to continue with jazz and composition. He knew that Brubeck possessed considerable deficiencies with respect to classical European composition techniques, but he knew also that Brubeck was endowed with a vast creative imagination which made itself directly and spontaneously manifest in the realm of improvisation, and could possibly be carried over into the realm of composition. Milhaud was always very encouraging.[21]

"Don't worry about that you represent America; you are in a better position, because you don't have this European background."[22] Nevertheless, Dave was ill at ease. And there were two reasons why:

His mother was not happy that her son David was a jazz musician; and American college music professors were intensely opposed to jazz in the late '30s and '40s. Dave Brubeck, young music student, was in a very difficult position.

The Berklee College in Boston, for example, wasn't founded until 1945, and North Texas Teachers College with its jazz department only shortly before. Besides that, Dave Brubeck didn't want to submit himself to the classical style of discipline in the form of "solitary confinement at the piano."[23]

At the beginning of each scholastic year, Milhaud would ask his students about their musical background, country of origin, roots. Milhaud was also responsible for the Dave Brubeck Octet. He asked, "How many jazz musicians are here?—From now on all your compositions should be written for this instrumentation, well, for those who play jazz."[24]

Five members of the octet were taking part in Milhaud's composition class: Dave Brubeck (piano), Dave van Kriedt (tenor saxophone), Bill Smith (clarinet), Dick Collins (trumpet), and Jack Weeks (bass). They formed the nucleus of the octet. Paul Desmond (alto saxophone), Bob Collins (trombone) (Dick Collins' brother), and Cal Tjader (drums) were eventually taken into this nuclear formation.

The octet was originally supposed to be a practice group for playing through and critically discussing original compositions. Milhaud arranged a benefit concert for scholarship holders at Mills College that enjoyed great success among the students there. It was the octet's first concert—1946. The group now tried, as "The Eight," to get further engagements.

Like in an experimental workshop, the octet tried out European contrapuntal movement techniques, polytonal chords, and polyrhythmic structures. It was moving in the area between fixed compositions and free improvisation.

Among other things, they played at libraries and at the College of the Pacific in Stockton where Dave had graduated in 1942. The University of the Pacific as well as Mills College later bestowed an honorary doctorate upon Dave Brubeck.[25]

The first big concert took place in 1949 at the San Francisco Marine Memorial Auditorium. The promoter insisted on renaming "The Eight," the Dave Brubeck Octet, since Brubeck was well-known through having played for years in San Francisco's Geary Cellar.

Jimmy Lyons, for whom Gerry Mulligan composed "Line for Lyons," and who now manages the Monterey Jazz Festival, was a popular disc jockey at that time for radio station KNBC. He did broadcasts with and about the octet and subsequently arranged a concert in the San Francisco Opera House with the Dave Brubeck Octet playing as warm-up group for Woody Herman's Big Band.

Audience reaction to the experimental octet varied widely. Students and musicians, like the members of the Woody Herman Big Band, for example, were enthusiastic. Dave Brubeck's father, however, described the octet's music, after a performance at the College of the Pacific in Stockton, as "the damndest bunch of noise he'd ever heard."[26]

Gradually, other jazz musicians became interested in the octet. Charlie Parker and Charlie Mingus came to San Francisco "to check us out." Stan Kenton asked Dave Brubeck to write an arrangement for his band. Jazz journalist Barry Ulanov came to San Francisco in 1949 and wrote about the octet in *Metronome* magazine. Duke Ellington and George Shearing heard about the octet's jazz experiments, and took it upon themselves to spread the news.

"The faint stirrings of a West Coast renaissance in jazz was beginning to be felt, but too late for the survival of the octet."[27] The octet's financial difficulties had become too big. Van Kriedt began arranging for Stan Kenton, and Dick Collins became a soloist with Woody Herman. Cal Tjader, the drummer in Dave Brubeck's trio, went over to George Shearing.

The octet was able to get, as it were, only a few concert bookings—just three paid engagements; a trio was economically more feasible, so Dave Brubeck decided for Cal Tjader, drums and Ron Crotty, bass. Both Ron and Cal were attending San Francisco State College. Dave was also planning, in the meantime and for the future, to augment the trio with horns again, up to at least an octet.

The group's first engagement was at the Burma Lounge near Lake Merrit in Oakland. The trio was especially popular with the university students, and Jimmy Lyons convinced San Francisco's KNBC director, Paul Speegle, to put the trio on the air 15 minutes per week; the program, called "Lyons Busy," could be heard throughout the whole West Coast and beyond Hawaii.

The jazz critic and columnist Ralph Gleason, then with the *San Francisco Examiner*, wrote, concerning the trio's musical rise and popularity: "In the short space of two years, Dave Brubeck has risen from the obscurity of an unknown jazz pianist to a point where he is accepted in this country and abroad as one of the leaders of the modern school of musicians."[28] *Metronome* magazine named Brubeck's group "Small Band of the Year," and they were 5th place in the Down Beat Poll after George Shearing, Charlie Ventura, Red Norvo, and Louis Armstrong. The trio played small clubs in San Francisco, Los Angeles, Salt Lake City, Portland, Seattle and Chicago. When Ron Crotty had to complete his military service in 1951, Jack Weeks replaced him.

The group was engaged for a few months at the Zebra Room in Honolulu, and Iola Brubeck and two sons were living with Dave in a small apartment in Waikiki. One afternoon, during a diving demonstration for his two small sons, Dave Brubeck injured himself severely on a sandbank. That marked the temporary end of his career and the end of the trio.

His recuperation took a very long time and was like an ordeal. The new jazz club in Fan Francisco, the "Black Hawk," promised him a job. From Tripler Hospital, he wrote Paul Desmond asking him to find a bassist and drummer so that they could put together the quartet about which they had often spoken. "Thus in the summer of 1951, as the result of an accident, began the long and rather amazing life of the Dave Brubeck Quartet with Paul Desmond."[29]

During his studies at Mills College, Brubeck had taken a job in San Francisco with Darrell Cutler and Don Ratto, tenor saxophonists in his college band. Often joining the "3 D's" (Dave, Darrell, Don) was a young alto saxophonist who wanted to become a writer: Paul Breitenfeld (later Desmond). He had graduated from San Francisco State University with a degree in English literature.[30]

Brubeck's friendship with Paul Desmond went back to before the octet. In 1944, Brubeck went with his College of the Pacific roommate, Dave van Kriedt, to the Presidio in Fan Francisco to hear the Presidio Jazz Band. There Dave met Paul Desmond who described him as "a surly Sioux."[31]

The musicians agreed to play a blues in G, and Brubeck began with a B^{b} chord in one hand and G in the other: "...having never heard of polytonality, much less played in two keys at once, he [Desmond] concluded, this man is stark raving mad."[32]

Dave Brubeck and Paul Desmond were linked together by a sort of telepathic communication. Both musicians mutually knew the other's thoughts and feelings "to the uncanny extent that we would even make the same mistake together."[33]

Their ensemble playing was unique in its harmoniousness, with them imitating each other's contrapuntal ideas in a sensitive musical dialogue. Their interplay was characterized by constant cooperation and the fruitful melding of intuition and intellect.

Paul was on tour with either the Alvino Ray or the Jack Fina Band when he heard the first trio recordings. The "Black Hawk" in San Francisco had developed into a regular jazz Mecca. Paul Desmond joined Dave Brubeck's group and even followed him to Los Angeles.

A few months after the quartet was founded, radio recordings were made at the Surf Club in Hollywood. The quartet was, after the octet and trio, unique in the West Coast jazz scene. It is in keeping with the American radio system and the all-out competitiveness of American society to immediately record and air, unappraised, everything new. The ratings of the countless broadcasting companies decide whether a broadcast is to be continued. The quartet's lineup was: Dave Brubeck (piano), Paul Desmond (alto saxophone), Freddie Dutton (bass), and Herb Barman (drums). Wyatt Ruther or Ron Crotty would also play bass. In 1952 Lloyd Davis, a classical timpanist now with the San Francisco Symphony Orchestra, had replaced Herb Barman.

Jazz writers were fond of describing the quartet's music as "West Coast Jazz" or "Cool Jazz." It can't, however, be relegated to a specific category. Diversity is the special quality of Brubeck's playing. Brubeck is a collagist, impressionist, exoticist, and both classical and jazz musician in addition to being a composer and improvisor. "Cultural exchange" is his main concern. "I never wanted to be trapped into a particular style that wouldn't allow for the expression of the whole range of human emotion and an awareness of the entire history of jazz."[34]

The Brubeck Quartet received many awards in the course of time, like *Down Beat* magazine's Readers and Critics Poll Award of 1953, the year in which he was celebrated as year's best pianist. In 1954, *Time* magazine's title story was dedicated to the Dave Brubeck Quartet. (Should Duke Ellington have been the better choice?) The "pre-Columbia" phase, 1951-1953 (documented by Fantasy Records), was especially creative and already laid the foundation for later developments and openness to new sounds and rhythms.

In the fifties the Brubeck Quartet was exceptionally popular at colleges. The album *Jazz at Oberlin*, recorded in 1953 at the college of that name, contains outstanding improvisations by Brubeck and Desmond.

In 1953 Brubeck left Fantasy and was contracted by CBS. To begin with, seven albums were produced:

Jazz Goes To College, Dave Brubeck At Storyville: 1954, Brubeck Time, A Place In Time, Jazz: Red Hot And Cool, Brubeck Plays Brubeck, Dave Brubeck and Jay & Kai At Newport, and *Jazz Goes To Junior College.*

From 1954 on, Brubeck involved himself more intensely with so-called "time experiments," e.g., experiments based on heretofore, to a large extent, unusual rhythms for jazz: 3/4, 3/4 and 4/4 in alternation, 5/4, 7/4, 9/8, 11/4, etc.

Records were produced in whose every title the word "Time" was to be found: *Brubeck Time, A Place in Time, Time Out, Time Further Out - Miró Reflections, Countdown - Time in Outer Space, Time Changes, Time In,* and *Adventures in Time.*

Starting in 1955, recordings dealing with so-called foreign cultures were produced: "impressionistic" pieces springing from the perception of non-European cultures acquired during tours, spontaneously and by ear, and, intuitively arranged, released under the following titles: *Bossa Nova U.S.A., Jazz Impressions of Eurasia* (from a 1958 State Department tour of Europe and Asia), *Jazz Impressions of New York, Summit Sessions* and *Jazz Impressions of Japan* (from a 1964 tour of Japan).

In 1967 the Dave Brubeck Quartet was disbanded. "Dave wanted to write more extended works and to spend more time at home with his wife and his six children, and Paul Desmond wanted to write a book and to record on his own."[35]

The members of the quartet in 1967, besides Dave Brubeck, were Paul Desmond (alto saxophone), Eugene Wright (bass), and Joe Morello (drums).

From the end of the sixties on, Dave Brubeck devoted more and more time to the production of longer compositions. "Essentially, I'm a composer who plays the piano. I'm not a pianist first."[36] He had already written the music for two ballets—*Maiden In The Tower* (1956), *Points On Jazz* (1961)—and composed a musical, *The Real Ambassadors* (1962), with Louis Armstrong as improvisor. Now followed: an oratorio, *The Light In The Wilderness* (1968), dealing with Christ's sojourn in the wilderness; a cantata, *The Gates Of Justice* (1969), for the two most discriminated peoples on earth; and *Elementals* (1963, 1970), for jazz combo and orchestra. Then came three further cantatas: *Truth Is Fallen* (1971), for the students murdered during the anti-Vietnam War demonstrations; *La Fiesta De La Posada* (1975), a Christmas cantata which was recorded onto disc in 1979; and *Beloved Son* (1978), an Easter cantata. In 1980 came the mass *To Hope: A Mass For A New Decade.* 1983 then brought the *Pange Lingua Variations* for chorus and orchestra and the ballet *Glances* for the Murray Louis Dance Company, followed by the cantatas *The Voice Of The Holy Spirit - Tongues Of Fire* (1985) and *Lenten Triptych Easter Trilogy* (1988).

In 1973 Dave Brubeck had put together another jazz group, this time with his sons Darius (piano), Chris (trombone and bass), and Dan (drums), in addition to some friends of his sons. Two albums were produced with the group "Two Generations Of Brubeck."

"The year 1977 was a turning point for me. It began, as had every year since the dissolution of the old Quartet, with my concentration and enthusiasm dispersed. On the one hand, I wanted to devote more time to composing (after all that was the major reason the Quartet had disbanded), on the other hand, I wanted to continue to play jazz, because that's what I love most to do. That desire itself was divided between old loyalties to Paul Desmond, Gerry Mulligan, Eugene Wright, Jack Six, Joe Morello, Alan Dawson, and to the loosely knit family band we called Two Generations Of Brubeck."[37]

Paul Desmond and Gerry Mulligan were playing with "Two Generations Of Brubeck." On the other hand, Brubeck's three sons, Darius, Chris and Danny, formed their own groups. In 1976, the Dave Brubeck Silver Anniversary Tour, commemorating twenty-five years of the quartet's existence, took place. Paul Desmond played his last concert with the Brubeck family in February 1977 at the Lincoln Center in New York City. He died May 30th, 1977.

George Wein suggested that the quartet with his sons be called the "New Brubeck Quartet," and he engaged it at the 1977 Newport Jazz Festival. Its first live recording was made on July 17th, 1977 at the International Jazz Festival in Montreux. Darius, the oldest son, played synthesizer and electric keyboards, Chris Brubeck e-bass and trombone, and Dan Brubeck percussion. Dave Brubeck had never before performed at Montreux with one of his groups.

Darius and Dan were soon playing again with their own groups or various musicians. Darius went to Durban, South Africa , to build up a jazz department at Natal University.[38]

Chris Brubeck stayed in his father's quartet and Jerry Bergonzi and Butch Miles were engaged on tenor saxophone and drums respectively. The quartet took back its old name—The Dave Brubeck Quartet. The album *Back Home* was recorded April 21st, 1979 at the Concord Jazz Festival—Dave was playing in his place of birth, Concord, and the performance took place near his father's ranch.

The drummer, Butch Miles, was soon replaced by Randy Jones. In 1980, the album *Tritonis* was recorded. The interval of the tritone had occupied a key position with respect to polytonality in Brubeck's music since the early forties. "In the days of organum and Cantus, the interval of the augmented 4th was sometimes called the `devil's interval.' Rather than think of it in diabolic terms, I always thought the augmented 4th an interval of great consequence. It is the springboard of much of the polytonality that I have used through my piano playing from the early forties to today."[39]

Reminiscences, citations from earlier works, and dedications occupy a big space in *Tritonis*, like suggestions of Rachmaninoff's Prelude in C# minor, *Theme For June* from Howard Brubeck's *Dialogues For Jazz Combo And Orchestra*, *Lord, Lord* from the *Gates Of Justice* cantata, and *Mr. Fats* for Brubeck's early model, Fats Waller.

Bill Smith, the clarinetist from the octet days and one of Milhaud's composition students, and presently composition instructor at Seattle University in Washington, replaced Jerry Bergonzi in 1982. Since then, the Dave Brubeck Quartet has played in the formation: Dave Brubeck (piano), [until recently] Chris Brubeck (e-bass and trombone), Bill Smith (clarinet), Randy Jones (drums) and, of late, Jack Six (bass).

The Dave Brubeck Quartet's fame and popularity had increased more and more in the mid-eighties as a result of its countless world tours. Also, top politicians in the East and West (several performances in the White House) invited Dave Brubeck and his quartet to their summit conferences or state banquets. This was in conformity with the idea, constantly found with Brubeck, of "cultural exchange," its goal being international understanding and the mediation of peace. This idea also finds expression in the musical with Louis Armstrong, *The Real Ambassadors*. The Dave Brubeck Quartet had done, already in 1958, a State Department tour of Turkey, Iran, Iraq, India, Pakistan and Sri Lanka. The album *Jazz Impressions Of Eurasia* came out of this tour. Polish jazz journalists had described the tour, and Russian jazz fans having heard about it hoped that the Dave Brubeck Quartet would once come to the Soviet Union. At last, in 1987, the first tour of the USSR took place. The Soviet fans got their first impressions of Brubeck's music also over the "Voice of America" or by way of record rerecordings. "Brubeck for me is my youth, the 1950s, the thaw after Stalin, better relations with America," said a fifty-five year old Muscovite worker and jazz fan after a concert in 1987. "He's all that, plus, of course, his wonderful music."[40] The Dave Brubeck tour was made possible by a cultural agreement between the USA and the Soviet Union signed by Reagan and Gorbachev at a 1985 Geneva Summit Conference. "Being in the Soviet Union and playing here with my quartet is the fulfillment of a long-time dream," wrote Brubeck in the Moscow concert program.[41] Like always, the quartet played music with unusual rhythms and experimental harmonies. The grateful audience was electrified by well-known but newly arranged jazz standards like *Take Five*, "Take The A Train," "St. Louis Blues," "Summertime" and the metrically out of the ordinary *Unsquare Dance* in 7/4 time.

Brubeck's chief interest was to get his music across and not so much to appear as a political representative of America on a "goodwill tour." The enthusiasm of the listeners, musicians, fans and critics at their first live encounter with Dave Brubeck and his quartet was endless and sincere. Alexei Batshev, manager of the five Moscow concerts, said, "Welcome! It is a dream come true. I cannot believe you are really here."[42]

The Soviet regime had opened up and the Russian people were now gradually able to listen to and play jazz in freedom and without fear, a music that had previously been discriminated against and forbidden as being decadent and bourgeois. Concerts were given with the "Union of Composers" in Moscow, at the American consulate in Leningrad, and in the Tallinn (Estonia) and Leningrad jazz clubs. The president of the Tallinn jazz club declared, "Politicians meet, shake hands and smile for the cameras, and we are all used to their little white lies. But music must tell the truth and nothing but the truth. And we have heard the truth these past three nights in Tallinn."[43]

For his closing concert in the USSR, Dave Brubeck invited three Soviet musicians to play with the quartet. Seven thousand people enthusiastically greeted the American-Soviet group. "The audience is the fifth and determining member of the quartet. What you give back to us is the fuel from which we draw our energy and inspiration."[44] For Dave Brubeck, a musician's most essential talent is his joy of communication.

In the summer of 1988, the Dave Brubeck Quartet again spent time in Moscow and played at a state reception during the Reagan-Gorbachev Summit Conference. Dave Brubeck's political maxim has been borrowed from Martin Luther King Jr.: "We must live together as brothers, or die together as fools." For over thirty years, Brubeck's strongest "weapon" has been "cultural exchange."

*   *   *

Notes

Chapter 1

1   comp. interviews:
    July 7th, 1972, New York, March 6th, 1974, Cologne
    April 25th and 26th, 1980, Wilton, CT, March 17th, 1988, Burghausen
    January 9th, 1989, San Diego, CA with Howard Brubeck
    A letter dated June 8th, 1987 from Iola Brubeck
    (in the following cited as New York, Cologne, Wilton, Burghausen, San Diego, Iola
    Brubeck)
2   New York
3   San Diego
4   Wilton
5   San Diego
6   ibid
7   Wilton
8   Iola Brubeck
9   San Diego
10 New York
11 Wilton
12 ibid
13 ibid
14 Léon Vallas, "Les Idées de Claude Debussy," p.25 and p.30
15 San Diego
16 Wilton
17 San Diego
18 Wilton
19 San Diego
20 ibid
21 Iola Brubeck
22 Wilton
23 San Diego, Wehmeyer
24 Wilton
25 Iola Brubeck
26 Dave Brubeck: Early Fantasies, Book-Of-The-Month Club Records, Camp Hill,
    Pennsylvania, 1980
27 ibid
28 ibid
29 ibid
30 San Diego
31 Dave Brubeck: Early Fantasies, Book-Of-The-Month Club Records, Camp Hill,
    Pennsylvania, 1980
32 ibid
33 ibid
34 ibid
35 "Dave Brubeck: Jazz Immortal," Biography of Dave Brubeck, The Serious Composer,
    Sutton Artist Corporation
36 comp. LP: Brubeck On Campus, 1972
37 comp. LP: The New Brubeck Quartet Live At Montreux, 1977
38 comp. Ilse Storb: Jazz in Südafrika - Darius Brubeck in: "Jazzpodium," April 1988
39 comp. LP: Tritonis, 1980
40 The Dave Brubeck Quartet - News Letter, Spring 1987 Wilton, Connecticut, Volume 5,
    Number 1
41 comp. CD: Moscow Night, 1987
42 The Dave Brubeck Quartet - News Letter, Spring 1987 Wilton, Connecticut, Volume 5,
    Number 1
43 ibid
44 ibid

Dave Brubeck

With Darius Milhaud

The Dave Brubeck Octet: (left to right) Bill Smith cl, Paul Desmond as, David Van Kriedt ts, Cal Tjader dr, Ron Crotty b, Dick Collins tp, Dave Brubeck p.

The Dave Brubeck Trio: Cal Tjader dr, Ron Crotty b, Dave Brubeck p.

The "Classic" Dave Brubeck Quartet: Joe Morello dr, Dave Brubeck p, Gene Wright b, Paul Desmond as.

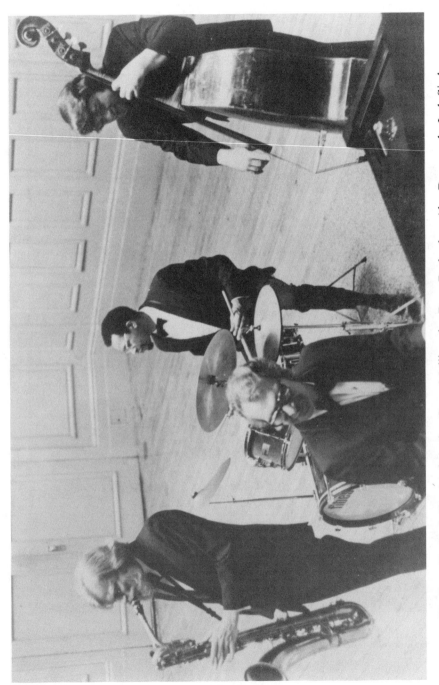

The Dave Brubeck Quartet featuring Gerry Mulligan bs, Dave Brubeck p, Alan Dawson dr, Jack Six b.

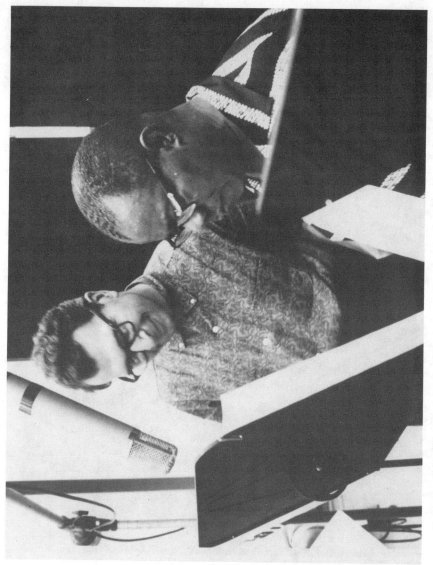

Dave Brubeck and Louis Armstrong during the recording of *The Real Ambassadors*, 1961.

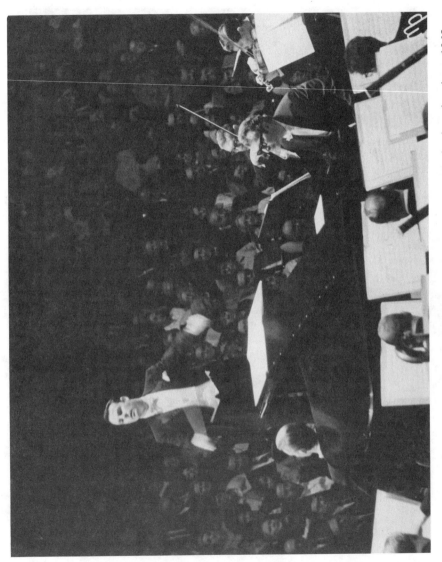

Erich Kunzel conducting the Cincinnati Symphony Orchestra; Dave Brubeck at the piano, 1968.

"Two Generations of Brubeck": Dan, Dave, Chris and Darius Brubeck, 1972.

The Dave Brubeck Quartet in the USSR, 1987: Randy Jones dr, Chris Brubeck el-b,
tb, Dave Brubeck p, Bill Smith cl.

Dave Brubeck in his house in Wilton, Connecticut.

Ilse Storb, Dave Brubeck and Klaus-Gotthard Fischer in Wilton Connecticut, 1990

Chapter 2

A Chronological Description of His Compositions
—Musical Development in the Individual Stylistic Phases—

Dave Brubeck's style of improvisation and composition is moulded from a variety of musical influences. Determinant for him are tolerance for and openness to the musical languages of all times and places; and of special concern to him is the almost messianic idea of *cultural exchange*, the concept of combining the most divergent of musical languages in order to achieve international understanding and to foster peace.

By no means does this happen scientifically and analytically, rather it manifests itself in the form of reminiscences, impressions, collages, adaptations, etc. A sensitive ear and a phenomenal memory are typical prerequisites for Brubeck's intense, "impressionistic" style of improvisation. "I'm looking for the day when all music is accepted and understood. I've always loved all music.... We're finally living in a time when we'll accept all musical cultures and know that they are all great, valid expressions of their people...."[1] The musical starting point of the young Brubeck is to be found, as we already know, between two musical languages: jazz and classical music. His mother Ivey Elizabeth played Bach, Beethoven and Chopin, his eldest brother Henry, classical violin and jazz drums, and his brother Howard composed in the classical style. Dave Brubeck has noted, however: "My roots are in jazz, and I have worked in it professionally since the age of fourteen.... My mother's classical training had given me a Bach-like harmonic approach to popular and western tunes."[2] Darius Milhaud, Brubeck's composition teacher and subsequent counsellor, confirmed and reinforced Brubeck's position in America's only original music form—jazz.

2.1. First Compositions (1946)

Dave Brubeck's first compositions, *Reminiscences Of The Cattle Country*, were written during his studies with Darius Milhaud at Mills College in Oakland, California. They do not conform to the idiomatic blues or swing forms of jazz. To read and write music were practically impossible for the young Brubeck at that time. "Very good, Boo-Boo, but not at all what you have written."[3] Milhaud nevertheless encouraged his pupil. He encouraged him to become a composer, all the while insisting, however, that he not give up the freedom jazz offers as music and life style.

Dave Brubeck's first compositions while studying with Milhaud already contain the beginnings of rhythmic and harmonic experimentation. Three of the six piano pieces are characterized by metric alternations which contribute to a rhythmical liveliness and, at times, to restlessness. Free-tonal and bitonal harmonies are encountered in several of Brubeck's first compositions, revealing somewhat of a preference for fourths, fifths and sevenths.

Sun Up

The voicings often move in opposite directions. Functional connections are rarely found. With all probability, the compositions were played on the instrument by ear and should be seen as being programmatic "impressions" of his father's ranch.

Sun Up comprises time changes between 6/8, 3/8, 5/4, 4/4 and 1/4 with 6/8 and 3/8 dominating and 5/4 and 1/4, with their sporadic appearance as structural elements providing a mosaic-like effect.

Breaking A Wild Horse is placed entirely isometrically into straight 4/4 and 2/4 meters. One single 5/4 bar, played rubato, interrupts the triplet and sixteenth note run. A constant change of tempo—rubato, faster, rubato, faster, go wild, accelerando, rubato ad libitum, easy, ritardando, tenderly, a tempo—determine the dramatic course of the piece.

The Chickens And The Ducklings is written mostly in 2/4, interrupted at certain points by elements of 1/4, 9/8 and 6/8. The piece is defined by the rhythmic motif:

Bitonal chords or passages are encountered in *Sun Up*, e.g., C and G♭ combined:

The cluster in *Sun Up*, like a pivotal point, leads from E♭m back to the beginning motif, E.

Breaking A Wild Horse (D♭ and B) is partially bitonal in its makeup.

The Chickens And The Ducklings (C and E♭ [see page 30]) as well as *Dad Plays The Harmonica* (C and E♭) also display bitonal chordality.

DAVE BRUBECK

Reminiscences of the Cattle Country

FOR PIANO SOLO

The Chickens and the Ducklings

Dad Plays the Harmonica

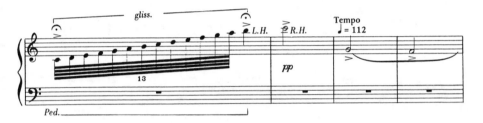

Bitonality and polytonality are principles of Milhaud's musical style. Through a vertical interweaving of diverse chords, he arrived at a richly faceted panchromatic structure[4] that must certainly have fascinated his then pupil, Brubeck. "One of the first things I wanted to do, was to write polytonal and polyrhythmic jazz. I did it and I had no other jazz musicians to talk to about that. I was doing it on my own. I had Darius Milhaud years before, but I wanted to do it in jazz. I think I was doing it before I studied with Milhaud, and I was attracted to Milhaud because of that, but there is no way to prove it."[5]

2.2. Octet (1946-1949)

The octet period is closely associated with the name and especially initiative of Milhaud. The octet was an experimental jazz-workshop ensemble. Dave Brubeck (piano), Dave van Kriedt (tenor saxophone), Bill Smith (clarinet), Dick Collins (trumpet) and Jack Weeks (bass) all belonged to Milhaud's composition class. Paul Desmond (alto saxophone), Bob Collins (trombone) and Cal Tjader (drums) rounded off the octet. Smith, van Kriedt, Weeks and Dick Collins were composers and arrangers.

The rhythmic and harmonic experiments of the first compositions were continued and extended with the octet. Innovative, heterogeneous harmonic and textural combinations arose out of the diversity of the octet's instruments. The study of counterpoint and fugue techniques with Milhaud had their effect on the octet's style. Strived for in this workshop-like group was an integration of improvisation and composition. In some of it's pieces, a polyrhythmic approach can be noted. "When you listen to the old octet, you'll hear a lot of polyrhythm...it was a very humorous situation, because the critics would say we couldn't play anything in the same tempo, so they weren't ready for what we were doing at all."[6]

The 18 pieces of the octet that have been released on record are quite varied. They comprise, among other things, jazz standards, ballads, a serenade, a rondo, a prelude and a fugue which is especially mentioned in jazz-history books. A pedagogic curiosity is the journey through the history of jazz by way of *How High The Moon* with piano introduction and speaking voice: oldtime jazz, orchestra boogie, Goodman-swing, bebop and, finally, Bach à la Brubeck, are all briefly introduced.

The pieces arranged by Dave van Kriedt, like, for example, *Love Walked In* or *Let's Fall In Love*, can be placed nearest the jazz idiom. They swing throughout and the improvisations are convincing. The themes are melodically quite catchy. The choruses utilize variation and sequence techniques.

Bill Smith's pieces are more experimental, avant-gardish, free- tonal, and, in their instrumentation, come close to Stravinsky-like collage techniques, e.g., *Schizophrenic Scherzo*. Dave Brubeck incorporated tonal contrasts into his compositions, juxtaposing, for example, unison wind passages with compact wind chords, or using sforzando wind insertions: *The Way You Look Tonight*. The five wind instruments are often employed tonally parallel or as a background layer for interactive solos; to be more precise, their style is more connected and compositionally fixed than free improvisational. Less a tonal melding is to be ascertained than a heterogeneous chordal mosaic.

Imitatory sections based on a simple nursery rhyme-like theme appear in *The Way You Look Tonight* and *Rondo*:

Strict contrapuntal rules are applied to what may possibly be the first jazz fugue, *Fugue On Bop Themes*, although only at the beginning. The piano enters with the following bop-phrased[7] theme:

From the beginning, the drums provide a rhythmical background. Already in the third bar the clarinet reinforces the piano in unison. This is followed by the alto and tenor saxophones after 8 bars respectively. Interplays, free, full of variety and sequentiality, make use of the thematic material in a purely motific, polyrhythmical interweavement. A second fugue development follows— although not, according to strict fugue rule, beginning monophonically and unaccompanied—with a subsequent free postlude and stagnating conclusion.

The octet was repeatedly compared with the Miles Davis *Capitol* orchestra; also by Brubeck himself. "I was really influenced by Tristano. And I think it was exciting to hear Miles Davis' first group. I liked it very much. I know that the octet was before this group...but they made recordings before ours did. What I mean is that Tristano and these musicians (the group of Davis) did similar things to what we were doing on the Pacific coast. It was a natural development of things in those times."[8] The integration of composition and improvisation was certainly more successful with Miles Davis. The octet recordings correspond rather to the experimental workshop character of the Mills College students, and place compositional, especially contrapuntal, techniques in the foreground.

Metric interlacements between 3/4 and 4/4 characterize Dave van Kriedt's *Prelude*. *What Is This Thing Called Love*, an arrangement by Bill Smith with an uneven meter at the beginning, is based on the following bass ostinato:

which, one time repeated, forms an introduction. Then the theme comes in on the upbeat. It has the form A A (8 bars each). The straight meter theme is set polyrhythmically interlocked with the bass ostinato. The subsequent improvisations are 4/4 throughout. The clarinet masters an intense, motific, thematic development extending into the highest register. *Playland-At-The-Beach*, by Dave Brubeck, is in simple 3/4 time. The theme is accompanied by parallel wind chords and is circus-like in character. *Laura*, a sort of "sweet music" à la Guy Lombardo, is enlivened by brilliant piano arpeggios and compact, rhythmically accentuated block chords (sound accents). The *Closing Theme*, as well, contains block chords and a suggestion of Gershwinesque thematic structuring.

Whether or not the members of the octet had already thought about Brubeck's idea of cultural exchange has to remain open. Interweavings in the form of collages, mosaics, and approaches between, in their furthest sense, classical music and jazz are experimentally explored. One especially encounters Bachian counterpoint techniques, harmonic texture characteristics à la Stravinsky, polyrhythmic approaches like Milhaud's, and, here and there, a coupling of "classical composition" and jazz improvisation. Many of the octet's experimental pieces have never in fact appeared on disc, because they were so avant garde they would have frightened the public.

2.3. Trio (1949-1951)

The trio continues some of the experiments of the octet. The diversity of the instrumental harmonic spectra is considerably limited by virtue of the trio's instrumentation. Cal Tjader, however, brings, as drummer, percussionist and vibraphonist (Milt Jackson is his role model), a few instrumental textural nuances into play. The repertoire is predominantly characterized by standard pieces, some of which are, however, novelly modified in rhythm and harmony. The workshop situation of the octet with its attempts at integrating composition and improvisation is no longer on hand. The impetus for the newly formed trio may well have been provided by the sound of the George Shearing Quintet.

Block chords—later, from the time of the quartet till now considered a characteristic of Brubeck's style—were already extensively used in the trio. Whereas Tristano, with comparably sparse chordal material, worked with linear interweavings, Brubeck utilized extended layers of thirds which have the effect on some listeners of a harmonic intensification, acquiring thereby a special intensity, as they are bound to short, easy to remember rhythmic motifs. Their utilization with respect to harmonic techniques doesn't proceed in countermovement according to classical, functional harmony, but rather parallel, and partly moving sideways over pedal-points. In this respect Hellhund makes a note of "That certain...specific warm 'lighting' of his towers of consonance."[9] The "chord towers" or chord blocks appear quite often in stylistic contrast to linear passages in the trio as well as in the quartet.

In the introduction and in the coda of the prize-winning piece *Blue Moon*, piano riff sections are set up against drum riffs in a complementary dialogue. Sequentialized block chords, heavily accented rhythmically, are tonally linked to the rhythmic repetition-motif:

The harmonic range, arrived at by parallel progressions on piano with a simultaneous harmonic base line from the bass, has a polytonal effect.

In a very long introduction, *Tea For Two* incorporates parallel sweeping thirds over ostinato pedal-points. The reharmonization of the theme through use of cycle of fifths chords leads to rhythmically fixed block chords, forming a contrast to the single note passages. A fade out with parallel thirds rounds off the piece. *Laura* begins, first of all, ballad-like, but soon experiences, like "interference factors," glaring accentuated chord interjections in the upper range. Block chords and clusters are utilized in an extremely broad harmonic spectrum. (Reminiscent of Mussorgsy's *Great Gate of Kiev* from his *Pictures At An Exhibition*?) From a Bach Chorale-like introduction, *Let's Fall In Love* goes over to block chord sequences and, finally, to chromatic major chord shifts and parallel thirds. *Avalon* starts off in the stride piano style, then shifts to block chords contrasted with long single note passages. The block chord repetitions in *Body And Soul* are extreme, almost violent, pronounced, proceeding in an ostinato rhythm

complementary to the percussion.

In *Downbeat* magazine, an article appeared in 1957 entitled "Brubeck: I did some things first."[10] With that, Brubeck meant the metric-rhythmic innovations and the breaking out of the 4/4 meter current to jazz. Already in existence, however, were Ragtime and Cake Walk music in 3/4, and, for example, jazz drummer Max Roach's 3/4 experiments.

Iola Brubeck notes that the jazz waltzes of the trio represent the first experiments in 3/4. "Fats Waller's `Jitterbug Waltz' predates Dave's use of Jazz in 3/4, but Dave had not heard it until much later. Dave feels that of the `moderns' he was the first to use the jazz waltz.... Certainly long before Bill Evans."[11] Brubeck was still referring to the jazz waltzes of the trio in general and *Alice in Wonderland* in particular.

The combination of chordal towers, i.e. block chords with asymmetrical rhythms, appears, however, to impair the "swing feeling." In the later so-called "time experiments" of the quartet, which also deal with meters of 5, 7, 9, 11 and 13 (e.g., *Take Five, Unsquare Dance, Blue Rondo A La Turk, Eleven-Four, World's Fair*), the asymmetric combinations occur with more musico-rhythmic conviction, more routine.

Always is one of the trio's jazz waltzes. It begins as a waltz with the following metric structure:

which is evidently text bound and progresses in a formal, periodic 8 bar pattern. It is joined by 3 variations followed by a transition, likewise of 8 bars, which leads to a 4/4 section with the following meter:

Singing In The Rain, also, features a change in meter, this time between 6/4 and 4/4, and, to be more precise, in the form of "chasing": 4 bars of 6/4, 4 bars of 4/4.

The comparatively strict polyphonic studies of the octet workshops are no longer to be found in the trio. The trio's public was of course also taken into consideration. Whereas the octet's listeners were mainly students, the trio was also playing for hotel and club audiences.

A polyphonic approach in the form of 2-voiced dialogues, for example between piano and vibraphone, or mutually imitatory interlacements of these instruments, is also encountered.

Bach-like sequentialized imitations are demonstrated in *Indiana* after the blocks of chords near the end. *Undecided* contains 2-voiced, mostly parallel, linear interweavements. *That Old Black Magic* employs dialogues between piano and percussion as well as rhythmically complementary interlacements or contrasts between piano and vibraphone. *Sweet Georgia Brown* proceeds in a linearly interweaving piano-vibraphone dialogue. *Squeeze Me*, at the beginning at least, has the character of an invention. The entry of instruments, at intervals of an octave, ensues in the order of bass, vibraphone and piano with the following theme:

The coda takes the initial invention up again.

The trio had achieved great success and wide-spread recognition in a short time span by virtue of the far-reaching "Lyons Busy" radio program from San Francisco, as well as because of publicity in the written media, e.g., the *San Francisco Examiner, Metronome* and *Downbeat*. The socio-cultural "secret" of this success seems to be Brubeck's outstanding ability of intense communication with the audience. Originality and innovation in the harmonic and rhythmic spheres are indeed present, but are always carried out with the audience's receptivity in mind. In the trio's case, it is mainly well-known jazz standards that are, for example, altered by harmonic enrichment, or imbued with new/old rhythmic ideas, e.g., *Jazz Waltz*.

2.4. Quartet (1951-1967)

From 1951-1967 the Dave Brubeck Quartet was made up of Dave Brubeck and Paul Desmond in addition to changing bassists and drummers. The Modern Jazz Quartet remained altogether more constant in its instrumentation. In the first radio recordings at the Surf Club in Hollywood in 1951, Freddie Dutton played bass and Herb Barman drums. Barman was replaced already in 1952 by Lloyd Davis, the classical timpanist from the San Francisco Symphony Orchestra.

The "classical" Dave Brubeck Quartet came into being when in 1956 Joe Morello (drums) and 1958 Eugene Wright (bass) joined Brubeck and Desmond. This group stayed together until 1967. The reasons for the quartet's dissolution were: Brubeck wanted to compose longer pieces and devote more time to his family; and Desmond wanted to make his own recordings and write a book. The repertoire of the quartet continued to have mostly standards as its foundation, like, for example, *Blue Moon, Tea For Two* and *Let's Fall In Love*. In an original, sometimes conservative manner, the standards were arranged, motivif- and variation-wise, into long improvisations (emergence of the LP!) and at times, as if in parody, loosened up with citations from "evergreens."

Layers of chords, parallel harmonies and polytonality had already been experimented with in the octet and trio. With Brubeck, complexity and compactness of harmonic chordal structure are   influenced to a great degree by compositional principles. Darius Milhaud and Duke Ellington, Fats Waller and Art Tatum are cited by Brubeck as having exerted a direct influence on his improvisational and compositional creations.[12] For him it is extremely retarded musically when a young musician isn't up to date with 20th century composers and, for example, plays Dixieland: "You ask me about Dixieland today. I don't see any challenge in it for a young kid. Makes me sick to see a young kid playing Dixie...if that's all he can play. From an audience standpoint, it's even worse; there's so little challenge in it. Then you're limited to tonic, subdominant, dominant chords in practically all tunes.... Now, take for example a group like Lennie Tristano's, which added onto that same feeling, made it atonal, the chord progression more intriguing and challenging. But for a kid to become a two-beat musician? Well, that's like a concert pianist studying Bach all his life, ignoring Bartok, Schönberg, Hindemith, Stravinsky, Milhaud."[13]

When the quartet played in New York in 1951 the free-jazz musician Cecil Taylor was impressed by Brubeck's harmonic-chordal textures. "When Brubeck opened in 1951 in New York I was very impressed with the depth and texture of his harmonies."[14] Charles Mingus, too, stressed that Brubeck had a special sound, an exception for a white combo. "He has the only white group that isn't copying. He has a sound of his own."[15]

2.4.1. Sonoric Structures

2.4.1.1. Block Chords

Wherein does the special stylistic feature of the "Brubeck Sound" lie? Mainly in the frequent use of so-called block chords. "An octave part with 3 inner voices.... This sound remains one of the architectural innovations in the history of jazzpiano and has become one of the permanent vernacular idioms employed by all jazzpianists today."[16]

The first attempts at block chords or "locked hands," i.e. parallel conducted chordal block progressions of identical intervallic structure, can be found already with Milt Buckner. It is possible that Buckner as well as, later, George Shearing carried Glenn Miller's saxophone section over into the piano style. Miller had inserted a 5th voice, either a 3rd tenor saxophone or a clarinet, into the voicings.

The pianist Billy Taylor sees Milt Buckner as being the inventor of the "locked hand or block chord style of piano"—having up-dated, as it were, Jelly Roll Morton's concept of orchestral imitation.[17]

Brubeckian block chords have to do with complex chordal layers which are played parallel, in octaves or repeated, and, through intense rhythmization and accentuation, have a toccata-like, explosive, percussive effect. They take up, in fact, a big place in Brubeck's improvisations and compositions.

Brubeck himself never wanted to be fixed on a specific style—West Coast or Cool. He also never wanted to be limited to a particular style of material or mode of expression. Rather, he wanted to maintain the freedom of musical choice and development, also and especially with respect to music heard on his numerous tours, music which in his opinion lends itself to association in the form of a musical collage. "If there is a Brubeckian sound as some say, it would be an identifiable harmonic approach. But I have tried to be free of musical straitjackets and to retain freedom of choice within the idiom of jazz, so that primarily my style is a summation of all experience to which I have been exposed."[18]

Even if Brubeck's style can be labeled without much difficulty, it was still possible, by numerous analyses, to ascertain that, in general, block chords represent an essential stylistic element of his improvisational work. Through their harmonic-chordal and rhythmic density they attain remarkable musical high points and convey the impression of concentrated percussive energy.

The block chords, with respect to composition technique, are never utilized abruptly or erratically in a spontaneous manner, but rather gradually developed. They appear:

1. repeated statically on the same tone,
2. diatonically or chromatically step-wise,
3. as parallel sonorities, and
4. with an ostinato bass.

The block chords, as chordal complexes, are, as a rule, bound to concise rhythmic motifs and a high degree of intensity.

At A Perfume Counter on *The Greats* album from the quartet's first year, 1951, is like a study in block chords, because of their extensive use. Double octaves and numerous chord repetitions produce an effect that is energized, toccata-like. Block chord sequences alternate with block chords proceeding step-wise and

parallel. Others, sketched on a modest motific base, are partly, over a wide tonal
space, ascendingly developed into tremendous chord complexes.

The rhythmic relationships are, among others:

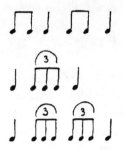

Complementary rhythms are played alternately with the right and left hands.

Many examples can be shown of the diverse application of block chords in the
quartet period, but also later in lengthier compositions, namely the improvisational
use of single themes from longer works. A systematic arrangement according to the
above mentioned aspects follows:

1. Pieces in which repeated block chords appear, statically remaining on one degree
of the scale: *How High The Moon (Jazz At Oberlin)—Jeepers Creepers (Jazz At
The Black Hawk)—Crazy Chris (Jazz At Storyville)—Balcony Rock (Jazz Goes To
College)—Why Do I Love You? (Brubeck Time)—Someday My Prince Will Come
(Countdown-Time In Outer Space)—Take Five (The Last Set At Newport)*—and
*Limehouse Blues (Dave Brubeck Trio and Gerry Mulligan Live At The Berlin
Philharmonie,* 1972).

2. Pieces displaying a step-wise diatonic or chromatic use of block chords: *Jeepers
Creepers (Jazz At The Black Hawk)—Crazy Chris (Jazz At Storyville)—One
Moment Worth Years (Jazz Goes To Junior College)—Swanee River (The Last
Time We Saw Paris)*—and *Take Five (The Last Set At Newport)*.

3. Pieces with parallel block chords (which are comparatively rare—repeated block
chords are more usual): *Cielito Lindo (Bravo! Brubeck!)—Swanee River (The Last
Time We Saw Paris)*.

4. Pieces utilizing parallel block chords with a sideways moving ostinato bass: *Blue
Rondo A La Turk (Time Out)—Bossa Nova U.S.A. (The Dave Brubeck Quartet At
Carnegie Hall)*.

Contrast to the energy- and harmony-rich block chords is obtained through:

1. a linear piano style or by the alto saxophone: *The Way You Look Tonight and
Perdido (Jazz At Oberlin)—Le Souk (Jazz Goes To College)—Bru's Blues (Jazz
Goes To Junior College)—Things Ain't What They Used To Be (Newport
1958)—Charles   Matthew   Hallelujah   (Time   Further   Out-Miró*

Reflections)—Someday My Prince Will Come (Countdown-Time In Outer Space)—Cielito Lindo (Bravo! Brubeck!).

2. a lyrical-expressive ballad-like style: *Jeepers Creepers (Jazz At The Black Hawk)—I'm Afraid The Masquerade Is Over (Jazz Goes To Junior College)—Blue Shadows In The Street (Time Further Out-Miró Reflections)—Someday My Prince Will Come (Countdown-Time In Outer Space)—These Foolish Things (The Last Time We Saw Paris).*

3. instrumental coloration: *Jeepers Creepers* (drums, *Jazz At The Black Hawk)—Crazy Chris* (bass, *Jazz At Storyville)—Lullaby In Rhythm* (drums, *Jazz At The College Of The Pacific)—Le Souk* (alto saxophone, *Jazz Goes To College)—I'm Afraid The Masquerade Is Over* (drums, *Jazz Goes To Junior College)—Stompin' For Mili* (drums, *Brubeck Time)—Upstage Rumba* (percussion, *Jazz Impressions Of New York)—Will You Still Be Mine* (drums, *Angel Eyes)—Fast Life* (drums, *Countdown-Time In Outer Space)—La Bamba* (percussion, *Bravo! Brubeck!)—Swanee River* (drums, *The Last Time We Saw Paris)—These Foolish Things (*alto saxophone, *The Last Time We Saw Paris).*

4. harmonic enrichment and intensification of the musical material, e.g., by the development of repeated single notes or melodic lines into sonoric complexes: *The Way You Look Tonight (Jazz At Oberlin)—This Can't Be Love (Jazz At Storyville)—Bru's Blues (Jazz Goes To Junior College)—Everybody's Jumpin' (Time Out)—Maori Blues (Time Further Out-Miró Reflections)—Waltz Limp (Countdown-Time In Outer Space)—Blues Roots (Blues Roots)—Take Five (The Last Set At Newport).*

Very often, a change-of-sonority interplay between piano and drums occurs, especially between piano and percussion. The rhythmic-percussive intensity produced by this instrumental dialogue is even increased for the piano, too. A linear alto saxophone line provides contrast to percussive tone blocks from the piano. An instrumental dialogue between piano and bass is seldom found.

The rhythmic interdependencies of the block chords are very diverse and distinct. Of top priority with regard to style are:
- repetitions on one level, and
- the step-wise and parallel sequencing of a "sound block."
A schematic grouping of the rhythms most used in connection with block chords yields the following overview:

simple rhythms:

triplets:

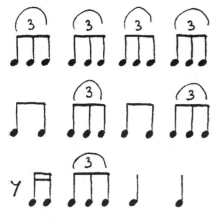

dotted notes:

offbeats:

complementary rhythms:

2.4.1.2. Polytonality

Dave Brubeck indicates polytonality and polyrhythms as being the essential stylistic vehicles for his improvisations. "For twenty years my aim has been to use more polytonality and polyrhythms in jazz."[19] The influence of his composition teacher, Darius Milhaud, is particularly evident here. The Carnegie Hall concert began with *St. Louis Blues* in G. Gene Wright played 3 choruses on the bass and ended in E instead of G. It often happened that the bassist, Gene Wright, left the original key. The remarkable thing about it was that Brubeck maintained the original key, G, and combined it with the new one, E Major. "There, that's it, Dave explained excitedly, I'm playing in E Major with my left hand and in G Major with my right."[20] Dave Brubeck often designates the tritone as having occasioned a large part of his polytonal harmonic experiments. "I always thought the augmented 4th an interval of great consequence. It is the springboard for much of the polytonality that I have used throughout my playing from the early forties to today."[21]

The tritone is in fact a harmonic "pivot" in jazz around which chord progressions can revolve, i.e. it forms a sonoric fundament. It is not to be construed as dissonance in the classical sense, but rather as tension-loaded—a sonoric center from which further harmonic tendencies spring forth. It constitutes the nucleus of blues voicings where it appears parallel in the voice leading.

Evidence of the following forms of polytonality as well as polymodality can be provided, for example, from Brubeck's improvisations and compositions out of the quartet period:

1. Layers of sound, e.g., in *When I Was Young* and *Walkin' Line*.

2.a. Changing and varied sonoric motion over a single pedal-point, e.g., in *Swing Bells*, or

2.b. Over an interval as pedal-point, e.g., in *In Your Own Sweet Way*.

3.a. "Walking lines" in connection with harmonically differentiated chord progressions, e.g., in *The Duke* and *Walkin' Line*.

3.b. Ostinati in connection with harmonically differentiated chord progressions, e.g., in *Pick Up Sticks*.

4. Polymodality, e.g., in *Swing Bells*.

5. Intervallic-sonoric structures, e.g., layers of fourths in *Swing Bells* and *When I Was Young*.

6. The twelve-tone technique combined with ostinati or parallel chords, e.g., in *The Duke* and *Upstage Rumba*.

2.4.1.3. Ostinati

Ostinati can be encountered from the octet period on and especially during the time of the quartet in different rhythmic and harmonic correlations; they bring about, because of their intrinsic element of stagnation, extreme tension relative to the remainder of the harmonic-dynamic flow.

Examples of ostinato harmonic forms are: rhythmicized or simple pedal-points, boogie woogie, riffs, "bass lines," Latin American rhythms and harmonic ostinati (interval ostinati, interchange chords).

Rhythmicized or simple pedal-points are a favorite means of improvisation and composition for Dave Brubeck. They form the pivotal center for a differentiated sonoric event and work to strengthen sound contrast. *Why Do I Love You?*, *Swing Bells*, *Calcutta Blues*, *Autumn In Washington Square*, *Countdown*, *La Bamba* and other pieces are exemplary of Brubeck's ostinato play of sounds.

He employs the boogie woogie form like a compact tonal tapestry, e.g., in *Pick Up Sticks*, *Blues In The Dark*, *Bru's Boogie Woogie*, *Countdown*, and *Back To Earth*. Riffs as a dynamizing element appear, e.g., in *Jump For Joy*, *Perdido*, *Nostalgia De Mexico*, and *Indian Song*. Pronounced bass lines are encountered in the pieces *Walkin' Line* and *Lullaby De Mexico*; Latin American rhythms in, e.g., *Heart And Soul*, *Upstage Rumba*, *Bossa Nova U.S.A.* and *Cielito Lindo*; and ostinato interchange sonorities in pieces like *At A Perfume Counter*, *Blue Rondo A La Turk* and *Out Of The Way Of The People* from the cantata *The Gates Of Justice*.

2.4.1.4. Parallel Harmonies

Parallel chords and associative sonorities represent—besides the use of block chords, polytonality and ostinato tonal forms—a further essential stylistic medium in Dave Brubeck's improvisations and compositions. Functional harmony is very often replaced or superseded by associative sonorities, rows of intervallic sounds. The tonality is, however, again clearly established at the end of the improvisation. This ultimate holding fast to the tonality is typical of Brubeck's style—Milhaud's conviction also, contrary to Schönberg's, was that music must have a tonal center lest the audience be robbed of one of music's greatest phenomena—modulation.[22]

Parallel associative intervals or sounds appear mainly in the following interval combinations:

1. Triads, also as block chords and seventh-ninth parallels,
2. Third and sixth parallels, and
3. Fourth and fifth parallels.

The first use of these parallels is already recognizable in the trio period, as in the associative sevenths in *Spring Is Here, Always* and *Heart And Soul*. In *Laura* the sevenths alternate, rich in contrast, with arpeggios. Diminished seventh chords are shifted parallel in *Two Part Connection* and *Indian Song*. Parallel seventh chords are contained in *When I Was Young, One Moment Worth Years, The Night We Called It A Day, Danse Duet, Moving Out* and many others.

Pronounced parallel thirds occur already in the trio period, too. For example, in *I Didn't Know What Time It Was*:

Numerous pieces from the quartet period contain parallel thirds or sixths, e.g., *These Foolish Things, One Moment Worth Years, St. Louis Blues* and *Audrey*:

as well as *Brother, Can You Spare A Dime?, Love Walked In, In Your Own Sweet Way, Two Part Connection, Thank You (Dziekuje), Perdido, Blue Rondo A La Turk, Blues In The Dark* (blues thirds alternating with block chords), *It's A Raggy Waltz, Three's A Crowd, Danse Duet, Blues Roots* (sixths tremolo) and *Open The Gates* (circling, ostinato parallel sixths).

The piece *Sixth Sense* is a study in sixths, with exclusively sixths being utilized, thereby giving the title a double meaning.

Sixth Sense

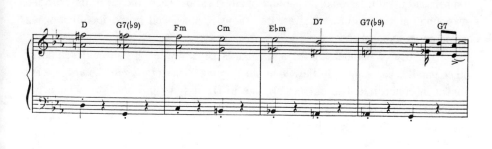

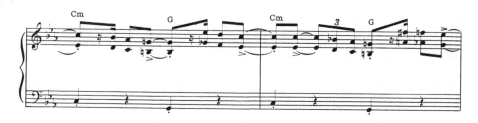

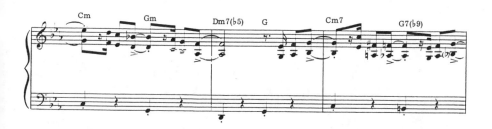

The use of parallel thirds occurs much more often than parallel sixths. It is often rooted in the blues, and also appears especially often in connection with the blues. Parallel thirds can also be encountered in some of the lyrical, ballad-like improvisations. Occasionally, parallel harmonies between the alto or baritone saxophone and piano are come across. They are very well suited for creating an introductory atmosphere.

The use of parallel fourths and fifths is generally less frequent than that of other parallel harmonies. In the album *Jazz Impressions Of Japan*, however, they appear in concentrated form, serving, like in Debussy's "Pagodes," to paint a Far Eastern atmosphere.

Parallel fifths appear, besides elsewhere, in:
I'll Never Smile Again:

Don't Worry About Me:

In Your Own Sweet Way:

Parallel fourths are utilized in, for example:
Fare Thee Well, Annabelle:

When I Was Young:

They occur with special frequency in the above mentioned Japan album—six of the eight pieces—combined, as it were, with pentatonics as a Far Eastern stylistic method in achieving a Japanese atmosphere: *Tokyo Traffic* (parallel fourths), *Toki's Theme* (exclusively parallel fourths), *Fujiyama* (sporadic fourths and fifths), *The City Is Crying* (stagnant fourths), *Osaka Blues* (pentatonic combined with fifths pedal-points) and *Koto Song* (double fifth tremolo and pentatonic).

Toki's Theme

DAVE BRUBECK

OSAKA BLUES

KOTO SONG

by DAVE BRUBECK

2.4.2. Metric-Rhythmic Structures, the So-Called *Time Experiments*

From 1954 on, an experimentation with asymmetrical rhythms makes its way to the center of Brubeck's work. "When I first started doing polyrhythms no one played those rhythms, and the people got very confused and no one expected that, because usually there is 4/4. So the other musicians didn't know what I was doing and yet I tried to explain to them that in African music there are polyrhythms.... The African music was absolutely fascinating. The first African music I ever heard was from an expedition into the Belgian Congo—and I heard it in the forties.[23] ...even before Milhaud I was thinking in polyrhythmic ways and that's why I'm so attracted to Milhaud."[24]

The numerous "Time" titles chosen by Brubeck indicate the musician's intention to experiment in the rhythmic sphere, and to be more precise, to experiment in the intercultural sense, with his incorporation of jazz, European classical concert music, and so-called non-European music (*Time In*, *Time Out*, *Time Further Out*, etc.).

The question of *swing* began being played up as a special problem with respect to Brubeck's music. Music realized not in 4/4 meter, but rather in 3/4, 5/4, 6/4, 7/4, 9/8, 10/4, 11/4, 13/4, etc., can and need not necessarily *swing*: Dauer designates bimetrics—two different meters simultaneously reoccurring with regularity—as being prerequisite to offbeat and swing, e.g.:

$$\frac{2\ 2\ 2}{3\ 3} \quad \text{or} \quad \frac{3\ 3\ 3\ 3}{4\ 4\ 4}$$

"Since bimetrical music represents, because of its at least two mutually related levels of pulsation, the prerequisite of that rhythmic effect termed offbeat or swing in Afro-American music, it must now be recognized that this sensory-motoric phenomenon is common to a great many other musical cultures."[25]

Horricks entitles his contribution on Brubeck in "Jazzmen D'Aujourd'hui" (1960): "Une Formule, Un Dilemme," that is to say, a term, a dilemma! In 1954, Brubeck gave a concert in London's Institute of Contemporary Arts at the end of which a fervent discussion ensued. A young American stated quite simply: "Certainly Dave Brubeck swings. You can see it as soon as he sits down at the piano."[26] He had evidently recognized, spontaneously and intuitively, the connection between sensory-motoric behavior and musical realization in Brubeck.

The degree to which complex, uneven meters and their combinations, through gradual, motional familiarization and rhythmic training, can lead to a nonetheless flowing, lively pulsation, would be proved by the Time Experiments. A significant and novel musical intention was the augmentation and variation of the exhausted 4/4 meter of most of the jazz standards by using meters hitherto unusual as well as asymmetrical and uneven for jazz. "I never considered what I was doing was new. I just wanted to do it. And when you listen to the old octet, you'll hear a lot of polyrhythms.... When I first did jazz waltzes I had never heard a jazz waltz before. I just wanted to do it. I recorded *Alice In Wonderland* I think in 1949, and most people think Bill Evans made the first recording. About ten years later *Someday My Prince Will Come* was a waltz, and they think Miles Davis started that, but it was very much later. But then, much later on, I discovered that *Jitterbug Waltz* of Fats Waller was waiting for me. So, it is very dangerous to think that anybody did anything first, but in my own mind I had never heard jazz in 3/4 time until I did *Alice In Wonderland*.... In the old octet, in 1946, we got into waltzes against 4/4...we were playing things in 7 in 1946—I don't think that Max Roach would have done that earlier."[27]

There had, of course, been rags in 3/4 in existence already at the end of the 19th century. Leonard Feather wrote, between 1936 and 1938, two 3/4 blues with Benny Carter for his All Star Group. In 1946, Mary Lou Williams composed a waltz boogie, and some years later Feather a bebop waltz. Duke Ellington's 3/4 *Lady Mac* from the *Such Sweet Thunder* suite appeared in 1956, and Max Roach's album *Jazz In 3/4 Time* in 1957.[28]

The development of 5/4 meter in jazz is shown by a Leonard Feather blues in 1955 and, around the same time, some experiments by Max Roach. The following albums with "Time" titles are characteristic of Brubeck's work with differentiated rhythms:

1. *Brubeck Time*, 1954, (later renamed *A Place In Time*)
2. *Time Out*, 1959
3. *Time Further Out-Miró Reflections*, 1961
4. *Countdown-Time In Outer Space*, 1962
5. *Time Changes*, 1964
6. *Time In*, 1965
7. *Adventures In Time*, 1971, (a summary of previously published titles).

The quartet became temporarily known as the "Jazz Waltz Quartet" because of its frequent use of waltzes. Dave Brubeck remarked in 1962 concerning *Jazz Impressions Of New York*: "How do you portray in 40 seconds the urbane personality of Mr. Broadway and at the same time write a signature that is immediately recognizable as Brubeck? I decided on a basic polyrhythmic approach to *Theme From Mr. Broadway* because the quartet has been long identified with the jazz waltz and unusual time signatures. Also, inherent in multiple rhythms is an inner pull which creates conflict and dramatic excitement on a sophisticated level."[29]

The phenomenal breakthrough and wide public acclaim came in 1959 with *Take Five*, a Paul Desmond composition, from the album *Time Out*. It was a million-seller and has become somewhat of an evergreen. *Take Five* became a fixed part of the Brubeck quartet's repertoire as well as its distinguishing feature. With its unusual 5/4 meter, *Take Five* proved its penetrating power also during tours with new groups like Two Generations of Brubeck and the New Brubeck Quartet, especially with the European public.

San Francisco Chronicle columnist Ralph Gleason writes concerning Dave Brubeck's *Time Experiments*: "Brubeck has already acquired a reputation as a jazz composer from the popularity of his tunes *In Your Own Sweet Way* and *The Duke* with other jazz musicians. Now applying his talents to experiments in time he is inviting them to follow his example."[30]

The album *Brubeck Time*, later retitled *A Place In Time*, was inspired by the *Time* magazine cover story. The album cover was designed corresponding to the Russian painter Boris Arzybasheff's *Time* cover photo and contained photographs of Paul Desmond, Joe Dodge and Bob Bates, as well as mini-covers of the albums *Jazz Goes To College* and *Dave Brubeck At Storyville: 1954* with their outstanding critical reviews. By re-recording well-liked standards Brubeck was always striving to reciprocate the public taste.

The so-called Time Experiments aren't yet to be found on the *Brubeck Time* album, but improvised or arranged counterpoint is—especially in the canon *Brother, Can You Spare A Dime? A Fine Romance* contains stacked, overlapping instrumental entrances, and *Pennies From Heaven* displays an occasional polytonal sound, hence, all in all, no new developments in the harmonic or rhythmic sphere. The whole quartet had, at first, a strong aversion to a studio session at Columbia Records in New York. They were all convinced that they could play better before a select live audience. Brubeck feared the engineers whom he saw as cannibals, "cold hearted ogres."[31] The photographer and film maker Gjon Mili to whom the tune *Stompin' For Mili* is dedicated was supposed to film the quartet. However, during the recording session, stone-faced and in a really bad mood, he exclaimed: "It's not jazz...you are not good!" The quartet got angry and in the true sense of the word started to cook, causing Mili to jump out of his seat yelling "You are hot! By God, you're hot! Don't stop now!"[32] The quartet's violent outbreak of temper had led to success. *Stompin' For Mili*, as well, contains imitatory, dialogue-like passages between piano and alto sax. Linear passages by the piano lead systematically and motif-wise into explosive, repeated block chords.

2.4.2.1. *Time Out*

In 1959 Dave Brubeck's album *Time Out* was released. The million-seller *Take Five*, a Paul Desmond composition and the quartet's best known number, was described in a then current *Downbeat* issue as "Chinese Water Torture": "...if this is what we have to endure with experiments in time, take me back to good old 4/4." The musicologist Dr. Willis James, on the other hand, remarked upon hearing *Time Out* for the first time that jazz should never have been limited to meters of 2 and 4, and made reference to a "Negro field holler" in 5/4.[33]

Especially with his *Time Out* album had Dave Brubeck contributed towards emancipating jazz from decades of so-called two and four beat dominance. "Bird Diz and Monk broadened its harmonic horizon. Duke Ellington gave it structure and a wide palette of colors...Dave Brubeck, pioneer already in so many other fields, is really the first to explore the uncharted seas of compound time."[34]

Even if Brubeck wasn't the first jazz musician to apply himself to so-called time experiments, he was certainly the one who carried out metric and rhythmic experiments in an intense way. He has never busied himself in an exact musicological way with meters and rhythms of different cultures, but rather worked intuitively and by ear. He tried also to combine time components from different cultures: western classical, improvisatory jazz, African, Indian, Japanese, Turkish, etc. Time and again, the American concept of the cultural melting pot comes unconventionally to the surface in Brubeck's work.

In the albums *Time Out* and *Time Further Out*, meters until then unusual to jazz come into play: 3, 5, 6, 7 and 9. The hit *Blue Rondo A La Turk* combines blues elements, rondo structures and the Turkish *aksak* meter in the sense of cultural exchange. A group of 9 is what is dealt with here: (2 + 2 + 2 + 3)

Brubeck had heard the *aksak* rhythm on the street in Istanbul on the way to the recording studio and had subsequently spontaneously played with the Turkish musicians. "Blue Rondo A La Turk is a piece that I'm working on now to put words to, which will tell the whole story of how the piece was written. But it starts:

> I was walking in the street one day
> In a Turkish village far away
> When I heard somebody start to play
> Blue Rondo, Blue Rondo A La Turk.
> They were playing in a 9/8 time
> 1 - 2 - 3 - 4 - 5 - 6 - 7 - 8 - 9."[35]

Brubeck explained further, in the Burghausen interview, that the Turkish studio musicians had improvised spontaneously on this "street rhythm" and that music in this rhythm is like the blues for them, though he didn't know what it was called.

Shortly before the start of the first improvisation, the piano, in 9/8, goes into an exchange with the alto saxophone which is playing in 4/4. This same exchange, called *chasing*, is repeated at the end of the improvisation, at the spot where the beginning theme in the *aksak* rhythm is again taken up. The improvisation is in 4/4 and characterized by punctuations:

1st improvisation

2nd improvisation

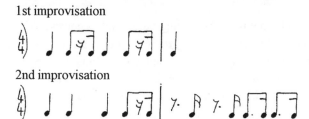

The 4/4 time signature of *Strange Meadow Lark* has little effect on the piece's rhythmical development. The tempo indicated at the beginning, free rubato, determines the piece's character. Numerous fermatas and arpeggios give support to the indefinite atmosphere until the improvisations begin, swinging in a taut counter rhythm with an abundantly punctuated steady 4/4:

At the end, a shift back to the initial rubato is achieved. The rubato tempo hinders the steady swing considerably.

The million-seller *Take Five* was composed by Paul Desmond and originated from the 10/8 meter of the bridge. Should *Take Five* therefore better be called "Take Ten"? The piece, based on an alternation between Eᵇm and Bᵇm, is quite simple and clear in its harmonic structure. Only in the sequenced B section are chord combinations deviating from those mentioned above to be found. The 5/4 meter was rather unusual for jazz at that time. The tune has asserted itself surprisingly well worldwide and does in fact swing in its uneven 5, or if you will, 10. Notated, the complementary underlying rhythm looks like this:

In addition, the following flowing rhythm appears in the melody:

In the B part of the theme, this rhythmic motif appears as a rhythmic-melodic series:

- a steady rhythm joined to a melodic sequence. In the improvisations, the basic rhythmic pattern is constantly maintained while the rhythmic-melodic cells of the theme are worked on.

Three To Get Ready, in 3/4 time, is systematically developed: it consists of 4 x 3 bars. Similar to the chasing in *Blue Rondo A La Turk* (2 x 9/8 and 2 x 4/4) the improvisations sway between meters of 3 and 4 (2 x 3 and 2 x 4), namely, they go from one meter to the other, augmenting the structure thusly to 16 bars. This principle of alternating between two different meters is maintained throughout all of the improvisations. Returning to 3/4 time, the piece then winds gently down (comp. also the structures of the rhythmical rondo *Fast Life*). Rhythmically, the individual motifs consist of combinations of: dots and triplets, continuous eighths and offbeats, complementary rhythms, e.g.:

Kathy's Waltz, dedicated to Brubeck's young and only daughter, starts with a swinging 4/4. The second improvisation is in 3/4, and in the third improvisation 6/8 and 3/4 are bimetrically superimposed over one another:

Complementary rhythms are the result:
(3rd improvisation, bar 25ff)

The closing theme is in 3/4.

Everybody's Jumpin' has an alternation between meters of 4/4 and 3/2, symmetrically 4 notated bars apart: 4 x 4/4, 4 x 3/2, 4 x 4/4. This makes 12 bars. Beginning at notated bar 13 come four bars of 3/4, six of 4/4, four of 3/2 and four of 4/4: 18 bars. We are dealing with a sort of rhythmic variation: the first improvisation corresponds to the initial 12 notated bars, the second is, by way of exception, only in 4/4, the third alternates again between 4/4 and 3/2. This sequence repeats itself again. At the end are 4 x 3/4 and 8 x 4/4. The basic rhythmic patterns in *Everybody's Jumpin'* are:

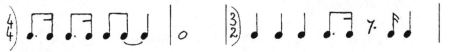

Both rhythms possess inversion characteristics which are accentuated by the ascending and descending melodic line.

The rhythmic and sonoric foundation of *Pick Up Sticks* is absolutely constant. "The chord of B^b is used throughout" coupled with a "boogie-type passacaille" rhythm:

Over the steady metric foundation, the rhythmic-sonoric progression is gradually transforming itself variationally:

Basic pattern

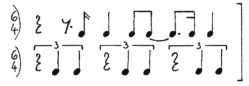

1st improvisation

2nd improvisation

(as an inversion of the basic metric pattern). A gradual transition using chains of eighth notes ensues from bar 3 of the third improvisation: "rhythm should be gradually changed to equal eighth notes!" Two static producing rhythmic layers with anticipated offbeats effect a rhythmic calming-down near the end.

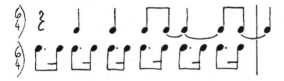

2.4.2.2. *Time Further Out*

This musical documentation (1961) is an interpretation of *Miró Reflections* from 1925. Sonorically, it is a blues suite. Each piece or musical "reflection" is in the 12 bar blues form or a variation thereof. One could carry on an intense discussion about the relationship between painting and music in general, and between Miró and Brubeck in particular. "If this should start a trend in music to look at album covers by, remember you saw it here first."[36] In the upper right corner of the Miró painting are numerals to be seen, and one can easily establish their relationship to the time signatures of the Brubeck pieces. The four alienated, mask-like faces at the bottom left of the picture are a possible allusion to the quartet.

A systematic progression can be seen in the use of time signatures which corresponds to the numerals in the Miró painting (comp. cover):

Its A Raggy Waltz	3/4
Bluette	3/4
Charles Matthew Hallelujah	4/4
Far More Blue	5/4
Far More Drums	5/4
Maori Blues	6/4
Unsquare Dance	7/4
Bru's Boogie Woogie	8/8
Blue Shadows In The Street	9/8

It's A Raggy Waltz is neither waltz nor ragtime, but rather a rhythmic variation or combination. Like the waltz, its meter is 3/4; its rhythmic grouping is 2 x 3 against 3 x 2:

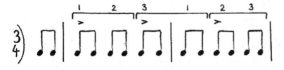

The rhythmic accents often change unexpectedly from one meter to the other giving rise to a differentiated internal rhythm. Shifts of accent (inner rhythms) also appear quite often in ragtime (secondary rag). As of the thirteenth notated bar, a waltz is manifested, alienated because of counter rhythms in the middle voicing:

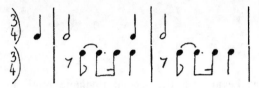

The third improvisation utilizes, besides elements of the theme, like:

the following rhythmic combinations:

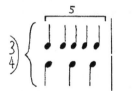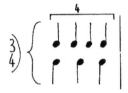

The slow waltz *Bluette*, because of its sound and lyrical character, is reminiscent of a Chopin waltz. Formally, it is a blues. Long and short periods alternate continually whereby the long periods are coupled with wide intervals and the short periods with close intervals. The first improvisation consists primarily of chains of sixteenth notes. Some Chopin-like rhythmic alterations appear in the second improvisation, like:

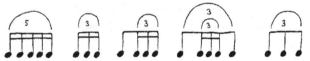

The third improvisation is sonorically static in its arrangement, and the fourth, through emphasis of the middle voicing, melodically linear in character. At the end of the piece, one encounters suggestions of Ravel's "Le Petit Poucet" from "Ma Mère L'Oye." The beginning of the third improvisation is reminiscent of Eric Satie's "Gymnopédies."

"*Charles Matthew Hallelujah* was written in a burst of joy, May 9, 1961, to celebrate the birth of my fifth son."[37] A rhythmical antithesis is created on the one hand by the flowing eighth notes:

and on the other, by shifts of accent:

The first and second improvisations begin with the second rhythmic motif in rhythmic inversion after which they change into flowing groups of eighths. The next improvisations primarily make use of melodic components, counter movement and layers of fourths.

Contrary to *Take Five*, the basic 5/4 ostinato rhythmic pattern of *Far More Blue* is occasionally breached and, for example, replaced with flowing eighths. It is possible that a settling-in period was still necessary for the 5/4 meter in *Take Five*. Likewise, the chord progression is no longer reduced to two chords. The basic rhythmic pattern of *Far More Blue*

is identical to *Take Five*'s basic rhythmic pattern. In a steady alternation the improvisations use:

The *Maori Blues* goes back to a Maori welcome greeting in 6/4 on the occasion of a tour of New Zealand in 1959 by the quartet. Only the theme and first improvisation are in 6/4; the second, third and fourth improvisations are in 4/4. The rhythm of the theme is very simple:

The first improvisation is chordally constructed, and the second intensifies the simple initial rhythm:

The third improvisation demonstrates a motional ostinato in the top voicing:

Like the first, the fourth improvisation is chord bound. Near the end, *Maori Blues* is rhythmic-sonorically reduced to a few tonic-dominant "taps of sound."

Unsquare Dance in 7/4 "is a challenge to the foot-tappers, finger-snappers and hand-clappers. Deceitfully simple, it refuses to be squared."[38] *Unsquare Dance* is a study in rhythm and at the same time an excellent concentration exercise. The 7/4 rhythm in itself was unusual for jazz; occurring complementarilly are:

The following is the first version of the Turkish 7/8 *aksak* rhythm:

Dealt with here is possibly the second version of the *aksak*:

The following variation is also added to the basic rhythm:

Subsequently, in the improvisation *Drum Sticks On Side Of Bass Drum*, come the following rhythmic modifications:

Bru's Boogie Woogie is a simple boogie in 8/8 with the typical rolling bass:

Numerous shifts of accent occur in the improvisations:

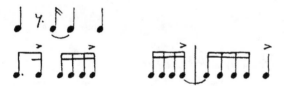

From the tenth bar of the fourth improvisation, two rhythmic layers or pulse strata are combined—an inner rhythmic superstratum with the boogie substratum:

The last piece on the *Time Further Out* album mediates, similar to *Bluette*, a Chopin-like atmosphere: *Blue Shadows In The Street* ("Slow and wistful," "expressively"). A chromatic line in 9/8 "hovers" over unchanging triadic ninth chords. Ornamental triplets, quadruplets, quintuplets, septuplets, tentuplets, etc. intensify the lyrical-romantic impression of the free rhythm.

2.4.2.3. *Countdown-Time In Outer Space*

The album *Countdown-Time In Outer Space* was 20 years in the making, which is to say, the first attempts ran parallel to those of Leonard Feather during the thirties. Innumerable test choruses went unpublished. The preferred occupation with diverse meters—the so-called *Time Experiments*—was a result of Brubeck's idea of music being the only art form that uses time (duration of time) as its central medium: "Music is as concerned with time as architecture is with space. Sound shatters time into fragments which the musician has arranged in such patterns of periodicity that we say the music has rhythm.... When these patterns fall in such precise relationships to one another that they seem to follow a natural law, we say that the music has a pulse of its own. This inner pulse belongs to the music of the world, whether expressed in common time or an exotic 9/8. Harmony and melody may stem from a musical tongue so different from ours that a knowledge of modes or scales is a prerequisite for communications. But rhythms—even complex ones—can be instinctively felt."[39]

This conviction of Brubeck with respect to a "natural" basic pulsation common to all of the world's musical languages is one of the keys to understanding his music. Connected with this, also, is his concept of cultural exchange. It is possibly the result of Brubeck's rhythmic experiences. And so it is indeed that European isometric rhythms, African asymmetric rhythms, and Asiatic, Old-European, and Arabic uneven rhythms—rhythms, in fact, from all human cultures—can be traced back to the lowest common units of energy: so-called pulsations. "The succession of units of pulsation unequal in length is, by general consensus, designated as rhythm."[40]

First of all, the 4/4 meter continued to be the group's point of departure, while it also strived for a music with unusual, uneven meters, like, for example, 3/4, 5/4, 7/4, 9/4, 11/4. The *Countdown-Time In Outer Space* album demonstrates a more intense utilization of these out-of-the-ordinary meters in its pieces.

The first number, *Countdown*, after which the album is named, starts straight away in 5/4. It is a 5/4 boogie:

The underlying bass rhythm has an offbeat structure which is not maintained in the three subsequent improvisations, but rather simplified to the following boogie pattern:

Eleven Four, a Paul Desmond composition, "possesses the feeling of free flight."[41] The grouping inside the 11/4 meter comprises the following components: (3 + 2 + 3 + 3)

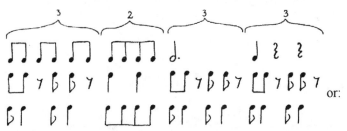

Such accentuation is oriental in origin and is already found in the Balkans. The musicians in the Brubeck quartet are trying to surmount the metric barriers of jazz, although they don't go about it with the precision of a musicologist; the public is left with little clarification. The commentaries of the journalists with respect to the metric innovations of the Brubeck quartet, especially to the *Countdown* album, sound like discoveries of revelations in the metric-rhythmic realm of jazz.

The fundamental rhythmic tapestry of *Eleven Four* looks like this:

The 11/4 progression is thusly transformed into an eighth note movement. This:

becomes

or 3 x 2 becomes 2 x 3. Both formulations are combined simultaneously.

ELEVEN FOUR

PAUL DESMOND

Why Phillis is a blues waltz by Eugene Wright, the quartet's bassist. Playing simultaneously in the 4th chorus are: Wright, in a 4/4 - 3/4 alternation, Brubeck, in a Count Basie style 4/4, and the drummer, Morello, in 3/4. In the 7th chorus Brubeck brings the bassist temporarily out of the 3/4 meter while the drummer adheres to it. In the 8th chorus Brubeck combines new polyrhythmic patterns with a swing bass. Wright ends with a solo in the original 3/4.

In *Some Day My Prince Will Come* (from the Walt Disney feature production "Snow White And The Seven Dwarfs") Desmond and Brubeck play in a free exchange between 3 and 4, the drummer Morello in 4, and the bassist Gene Wright in 3. Desmond and Brubeck deal freely and rhythmically varied with the improvisations:

CHORUS

Castilian Blues, part of a documentary film for CBS TV's 20th Century program, is in 5/4. It is mastered like a standard in 4/4 by the group, especially Desmond. The rhythm, which is "Latin" throughout, displays a basic eighth note movement—$10/8 = 3 + 3 + 2 + 2$:

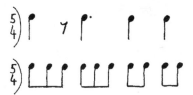

The beginning of *Castilian Blues* is based on regular eighth and quarter notes that flow into a point of repose:

The first and second improvisations are relatively complicated rhythmically in their construction with combinations of and various diminutions of, e.g.:

while the third improvisation resumes the steadily flowing initial rhythm and complicates the sonoric structure by means of alterations.

Likewise designated by Brubeck as 5/4, is *Castilian Drums*. The rhythmic foundation is identical with that of *Castilian Blues*. Morello experiments on the drums with Indian tabla rhythms; Brubeck imitates Flamenco guitar rhythms "impressionistically."

The next four pieces are from the ballet *Maiden In The Tower*. The rhythms utilized serve as, shall we say, "*leit*-rhythms": the ballet's hero is rhythmically associated with the 4/4 meter, the heroine to 3/4; and new characters are introduced by new rhythms. The cross rhythms resulting from the various combinations are also visually articulated, i.e. by way of the ballet's choreography. The titles are indicative of the situation in the ballet.

Fast Life, the hero's first solo, is characterized by frequent changes of meter: Three 4's, four 3's, five 4's, four 3's, two 4's, four 3's, one 4, four 3's, four 4's, then two times eight 3's. The two improvisations stick to 4/4, the fundamental meter of the hero. The ending, like the beginning, is fashioned from an extended 8 bar coda. A rhythmic rondo manifests itself from the continual return of the four 3's section. The middle sections are exclusively in 4, although of varying length. The main rhythmic motif is asymmetrical, its form aperiodical. In the first improvisation inner rhythms are developed by shifts of accent:

In the second improvisation the rhythmic development compresses near the end to nine- ten- and eleventuplits. Both improvisations have given up the complicated structure of the rhythmic rondo and continue throughout in 4/4.

Waltz Limp, the second piece of the ballet, has to do with the heroine who has lost her shoe. It begins with an antithetic, rhythmic theme:

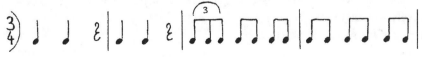

joined with a very fast tempo. The upper and lower voicings augment each other polyrhythmically. The first improvisation superimposes a 2/4 over the 3/4 meter:

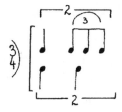

The second improvisation maintains this basic structure and diminutes the metric values to:

or

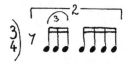

In the course of further improvisations the heroine appears in 3-, the hero in 4-, and additional characters in 2/4 meters. It has to do with the materialization of `leit-rhythms' on the basis of different metric foundations.

    The first 7/4 of the *Countdown* series appears in *Three's A Crowd*. Again it is the *leit*-rhythmization that is determinant: the heroine dances in 3, the hero in 4, and another character in 2 to a meter of 7/4 which is maintained throughout the whole piece. In the theme, simple eighth notes alternate with quarter notes:

The first improvisation simplifies on the one hand, but also diversifies on the other:

The second improvisation compresses the rhythmic structure. The middle voicing is intensively worked out.

Beginning of the second improvisation:

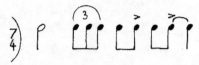

Bar 4 of the second improvisation:

Danse Duet, the fourth and last ballet number in *Countdown-Time In Outer Space*, begins with a free rubato in 4/4 that changes into a tranquil, continuous beat which, 4 bars before the first improvisation, becomes 3/4. The first improvisation in the waltz rhythm is reserved for the heroine; it begins with complementary rhythms:

The second improvisation, in 4, a solo for the hero, diversifies rhythmically through dottings and anticipations:

as well as combinations of:

 and

Danse Duet ends with the beginning section—greatly reduced: "free rubato."

The rhythmetrically illuminating album *Countdown-Time In Outer Space* concludes with the piece *Back To Earth*, a piece in normal 4/4 time. *Back To Earth* gives the impression of a triplets étude (comp. Chopin, op. 10, Nr. 12, the so-called *Revolutionsetüde*). The motoric descension ensues with Chopin in groups of sixteenths. Rhythms, structure and progression of movements all display analogies between *Back To Earth* and the Chopin étude. The first improvisation is defined by a sharply accentuated bass line:

The second improvisation, like the first piece in *Countdown*, takes place over a boogie bass line, this time in 4:

2.4.2.4. The *Time In* Album,

from 1965, again incorporates a list of rhythms unusual for jazz at that time. *Lost Waltz* sets a 2/4 meter against one of 3/4:

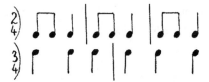

 Time In, from the oratorio *The Light In The Wilderness*, introduces a "lonely" piano line which is taken over by the alto saxophone and is intended to symbolize the feeling of Christ's abandonment in the desert. It is played over a 5/4 meter provided by the bassist Gene Wright.

 He Done Her Wrong is a sort of twist in 5/4. *Cassandra* "is a real cooking swinger."[42] The piano plays a waltz in polyrhythmic contrast to the drums which are improvising in 4/4.

2.4.2.5. *Adventures In Time*,

from 1971, is the last album with a special "Time" title and is a double album consisting of selections from:
Time Out, Time Further Out-Miró Reflections, Countdown-Time In Outer Space, Time In and *Time Changes*.

 Unisphere (in 10/4), *World's Fair* (in 13/4), *Iberia* (in 3/4), *Cable Car* (in 3/4) and *Shim Wha* (in 3/4) are taken from the *Time Changes* LP.

 Fast And Happy Unisphere moves in an unusual 10/4 which is difficult to bring to materialization in a continuous, rhythmic unity:

The improvisations are characterized by triplets and dotted notes as well as by flowing eighths: "...that's the one my brother said was a 10. I agree with him. With *Take Five* I can't see your point."[43] Brubeck is of the opinion that *Unisphere* truly builds from a meter of 10, contrary to *Take Five*.

World's Fair, in 13/4, is conceivably comprised of 3 + 3 + 4 + 3 in a constant, yet sequentialized, repeating alternation between 3/4 and 4/4. Duplets and quadruplets diversify the inner, rhythmic structure:

Iberia combines meters of 3 and 6: a new grouping emerges as a result of internal accentuation:

Cable Car divides the 3 meter into units of 2 and 6, then combines the two groupings:

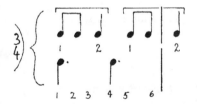

Shim Wha, by the drummer Joe Morello, is termed a "Fast Waltz": ♩ = 176 Quadruplets and quintuplets appear in polyrhythmic contrast to a differentiated 3/4 meter:

A Schematic Overview: Rhythmic-Metric Structures in the So-Called Time Experiments: "A word loosely used for meter and sometimes also applied in other contexts to do with rhythm and tempo."[44]

Time Out

Blue Rondo A La Turk	9/8 - *aksak* and 4/4 (comp. *A La Turk* from the ballet *Points on Jazz*)
Strange Meadow Lark	4/4 free rubato
Take Five	5/4
Three To Get Ready	3/4 and 4/4
Kathy's Waltz	4/4 and 3/4 as well as 6/8 and 3/4 (simultaneously)
Everybody's Jumpin'	4 x 4, 4 x 3, 4 x 4 rhythmic variation; later, 4 x 3, 6 x 4, 4 x 3, 4 x 3
Pick Up Sticks	6/4 (3/2) "boogie type passacaille," two rhythmic layers at the end (boogie & offbeat)

Time Further Out-Miró Reflections

It's A Raggy Waltz	rhythmic variations and combination of waltz and ragtime in blues form
Bluette	3/4; quintuplets, triplets, suggestions of Chopin
Charles Matthew Hallelujah	4/4; rhythmical antithesis, rhythmic inversion
Far More Blue	5/4
Far More Drums	5/4
Maori Blues	6/4; "Maori welcome greeting"
Unsquare Dance	7/4, study in rhythm, exercise in concentration, "Challenge to the foot tappers, finger snappers and hand clappers"[45]
Bru's Boogie Woogie	8/8; 2 rhythmic layers: boogie rhythm & inner rhythm
Blue Shadows In The Street	9/8; Chopin-like ornamentation: triplets, tentuplets, etc.

Countdown-Time In Outer Space

Countdown	5/4 boogie
Eleven Four	11/4
Why Philis	3/4 blues waltz
Someday My Prince Will Come	3/4 & 4/4 combined simultaneously
Castilian Blues	5/4
Castilian Drums	5/4
Fast Life	3/4 and 4/4 rhythmic rondo: three 4/4s, four 3/4s, five 4/4s, four 3/4s, two 4/4s, four 3/4s, one 4/4, four 3/4s, four 4/4s, 2 x eight 3/4s
Waltz Limp	hero in 4/4; heroine in 3/4; third person in 2/4; rhythmic *Leitmotifs*
Three's A Crowd	7/4
Danse Duet	4/4 & 3/4
Back To Earth	4/4, triplets étude with suggestions of Chopin

Time In

Lost Waltz	3/4 against 2/4; comp. *Bluette, Far More Blue, Blue Shadows In The Street*
Time In	4/4 against 3/4, rhythmically free, recitative, rhythm section in 3/4 meter
40 Days	5/4 bass, free piano line taken up later by alto saxophone
He Done Her Wrong	5/4 twist
Cassandra	piano waltz over drums in 4/4

Adventures In Time
(among other things, with the following titles from *Time Changes*)

Unisphere	10/4
World's Fair	13/4 (3 + 3 + 4 + 3)
Iberia	3/4 & 6/8
Cable Car	3/4
Shim Wha	3/4

2.4.3. Cultural Exchange and Musical Impressions

Growing up between jazz and classical music, in childhood, adolescence and also while at college, Brubeck always tried to join diverse musical languages with each other—intuitively, by ear, "impressionistically," seldom scientifically. His teacher Milhaud and his brother Howard, the "professor," counselled him over a long period of time: "My brother is a professor. He knows everything. What do I know!"[46]

The multicultural milieu of America and later the numerous world wide tours layed the foundations for and strengthened Brubeck's idea of *cultural exchange* through the working out of "impressions" of foreign musical languages. His opinion that the rhythms of all peoples can be experienced instinctively has already been expounded.

2.4.3.1. European Concert Music and Jazz

To call Dave Brubeck a "classically" influenced musician meets with intense protest from the pianist himself. The first question of my 1972, New York interview, immediately before a concert at the Newport Jazz Festival, was: "You passed a lot of classical studies. You have been a student of Arnold Schönberg and Darius Milhaud. Did you originally want to be a classical musician?": "I have never been a classical musician."[47]

Brubeck had a decided distaste, not for classical music, but for the method of classical training at official institutions. "He wanted to do what he would hear in his own mind and what came from him."[48]

Reasons for a direct and decisive rejection of a "classical" Brubeck are certainly quite justified. Brubeck has frequently been accused of intellectualism, constructivism, etc.—dispositions which were knowingly directed at or reinforced by his compositional training in counterpoint and harmony. On the cover of his 1956 album *Brubeck Plays Brubeck - Original Compositions For Solo Piano*, he expresses himself thusly: "I am aware that I have become a controversial figure in jazz. In the course of one concert tour I can read such contradictory comments as cerebral-emotional, delicate well constructed lines - pile driver approach - technically facile - chaotic pounding - contributor to jazz - defiler of jazz - this is jazz?"[49] His rejection of being classified as "classical" is understandable, since, for the critics, it was open to doubt whether "Brubeckian music" was in fact jazz.

Brubeck told me in April of 1980 in Wilton, Connecticut—on our way to the "Dave Brubeck Tenth Contemporary American Composers Festival" in Bridgeport (27-28 April 1980)—that Bach and Chopin had had a great influence on him. Brubeck's mother Ivey was an accredited classical pianist who played and taught baroque, classical, and romantic piano music. His brother Howard is a "classical" composer. Brubeck also reserves special praise for his esteemed former teacher, Darius Milhaud, to whom he, as a composer ("I am a composer who plays the piano," LP cover: *Brubeck On Campus*, 1972) gives infinite thanks, especially with respect to his openness to all musical languages of every time and place.[50]

The oft discussed problems in connection with Brubeck's music—
Is this jazz?
Does this music swing?[51]
aren't of the utmost priority for the composer-pianist Brubeck, since, as a musician and human being, he is characterized by tolerance and openness and not fixed on one musical language or style. "It has been said that I have attempted a marriage between classical music and jazz. If by this phrase, it is meant that I employ certain classical composition techniques in arranging or within improvisations, it is true. In all modesty, I hasten to add that this is not MY innovation."[52]

The "classical" influence is doubtlessly evident and altogether audible in Brubeck's music. It reaches expression especially in the early octet, trio and quartet periods where titles like *Fugue On Bop Themes, Prelude, Fugue, Scherzo, Waltz, The Duke Meets Darius Milhaud and Arnold Schönberg*, etc. reveal a direct European influence, especially with regard to sonoric and formal structures. It is for this reason that Brubeck has been assigned to the so-called West Coast jazz school, a new category of style listened to primarily by a white audience.

Brubeck's "classical approach" lends itself to subdivision into three points of focus:

• **The Bach and baroque approach** (contrapuntal-linear style),
• **The Chopin and romantic approach** (lyric-sonoric style),
• **The influence of the music of the 20th century**.

The Bach and baroque approach

The whole early octet-quartet period is characterized again and again by a contrapuntal-linear style. The influence of the counterpoint instruction from Mills College was possibly still very much in effect. Paul Desmond, whose particular improvisatory ability lay in the production of "infinite" motificly varied lines, had also certainly encouraged Dave towards linear playing, to be more precise, proved to be the ideal partner for dialogue-rich imitatory improvisations. Desmond very often takes the lead in this respect. His technique of perpetual weaving, sequenced or freely associated, is constantly surprising in its superb motific construction. "Then too, Paul and I have tried to create a great deal of improvised counterpoint between the two of us...."[53]

Diverse contrapuntal form principles were brought to materialization in the early fifties. Contrapuntal-linear arrangements, partially in the form of a canon, invention or fugue, appear in the following pieces:

Fugue On Bop Themes (Van Kriedt, Octet, 1948), composed throughout in a fast tempo, is strictly composed as such only at the beginning. It is followed by a free play with fragments of the theme. The theme's beginning reappears constantly. This composition is one of the first jazz fugues.

A series of horn pieces appear on the same album that don't always have a jazz character, but rather give the impression of being composition projects of students of Milhaud. *How High The Moon* (octet arrangement) was chosen to demonstrate a miniature history of jazz and serves as a theme for rag, boogie, swing, bop, and a fugue which is strictly adhered to only at the beginning. *The Way You Look Tonight* (*Jazz At Oberlin*) is imitatory in its approach and concerns a dialogue in the form of counterpoint; the middle part contains block chords; near the end, linearity is reinstituted. The *Jazz At Oberlin* version of *How High The Moon* has the character of an invention—the linear principle is utilized especially near the end where a typical concerto grosso ending is conspicuous. At the end of *Perdido* (*Jazz At Oberlin*), just before returning to the theme, an imitatory dialogue takes place between the alto saxophone and the piano in combination with a compression of the rhythmic texture. *Let's Fall In Love* (*Jazz At The Black Hawk*) features fugato approaches and an ostinato bass line.

In 1953 Brubeck gave some concerts at the College of the Pacific where the audience was completely different from that of the clubs. The students didn't think of the music as being a pleasant background, on the contrary, they really listened to the complicated rhythmic structures. Iola Brubeck then sent hundreds of letters to the West Coast colleges. Successfully. It gave rise to a series of concerts and the records *Jazz Goes To College* and *Jazz Goes To Junior College*.

I'll Never Smile Again (*Jazz At The College Of The Pacific*) is improvisational in character with a contrapuntal interplay with the alto saxophone being developed. The piece is an outstanding compositional and improvisational success. Desmond's infinite linear development is again masterly and his intonation is very differentiated. Brubeck begins at first extremely restrained, in the style of Bach's inventions. His talent at composing becomes evident with the contrapuntal development. The imitatory work in the fugato technique alternates with motoric passages realized with block chords especially in the left hand. Increasing dynamics, constantly changing harmonic aspects, and intense, rhythmical impulses lead steadily to a tension loaded climax. The ending is formed by a contrapuntal interweavement of alto saxophone and piano. The imitations happen successively and simultaneously in a unique interplay, and the balancing of improvisation and composition is convincingly achieved. Imagination and technique, expression and structure, the rhythmic vitality of jazz and the structural methods of baroque chamber music are all sovereignly joined together.

 Too Marvelous For Words (*Jazz At Wilshire-Ebell*) contains a linear dialogue between alto saxophone and piano near the end of the piece. *Stompin' For Mili* (*Brubeck Time*), too, just before the end, has alto saxophone and piano lines on display. *Brother, Can You Spare A Dime?*, also from *Brubeck Time*, is a canon. The alto starts with a simple, ascending, C minor line within an octave that is at first answered note for note by the piano, but already in the third bar takes over an accompanying function:

Fare Thee Well, Annabelle (*Jazz: Red Hot and Cool*) imitates the theme at the beginning in the order of piano, alto saxophone. Resounding near the end is the Bach citation "Wohl mir, daß ich Jesu habe," from the cantata "Herz und Mund und That und Leben," BWV 147:

and

Afterwards, more imitatory dialogues between alto saxophone and piano follow.

Sometimes I'm Happy (*Jazz Red Hot And Cool*) is remarked on thusly: "a bit of contrapuntal hocus pocus to old school country piano to an oriental duet."[54] In other words, contrapuntal playing around; country music and oriental ornamentation are collage- and citation-like combined. *Love Walked In* (*Jazz Red Hot And Cool*) contains, just before the end of the piano chorus, a sort of chorale prelude. *In Your Own Sweet Way* (*Brubeck Plays Brubeck*): the first improvisation has the character of an invention and stands in stark contrast to the romantic, ballad-like sonority (seventh and ninth chords, alterations, chromatics) of the style at the beginning. The invention scheme is chromatically descending step-wise in its arrangement, and complementary rhythms define the dialogues. *Two Part Contention* (*Brubeck Plays Brubeck*, comp. also the recordings on *Dave Brubeck And Jay & Kai At Newport*) begins like a two voice invention; near the end, the rhythmic and sonoric compression again give way to the two voice simplicity. Seventh chords, shifted chromatically and parallel, are inserted into the blues section. *When I Was Young* (*Brubeck Plays Brubeck*) contains a contrapuntally constructed very heavily rhythmicized section. *Two Part Contention* (*Dave Brubeck And Jay & Kai At Newport*, comp. *Brubeck Plays Brubeck*): Alto saxophone-bass or alto saxophone-piano dialogues alternate, the differentiation of sound being determined by the texture of the instruments. The melding of sound with the piano is quite pronounced. The beginning and ending are contrapuntal-linear in construction. *Bru's Blues* (*Jazz Goes To Junior College*) is from the *College* series which could count on a musically educated public. Contrastive effects are arrived at through two-voiced lines between the alto saxophone and piano on the one hand and through pronounced block chords on the other.

Brandenburg Gate (*Jazz Impressions Of Eurasia*, comp. *Brubeck In Amsterdam*) comprises different principles of baroque form: invention, fugue, chorale, concerto grosso. "The German phrase *danke schön* is the basis for the Bach-like theme of Brandenburg Gate. The root progressions of this piece are similar to those of a Bach Chorale, with some modern alterations of the chord structure. We used the device of imitation and simple counterpoint in the development of the theme—in a manner reminiscent of Bach. *Brandenburg Gate* is a title with many connotations for me. I think of Bach and the Brandenburg Concertos."[55] *Jump For Joy* (*Newport 1958*) is a play in counterpoint, the group's fondness for which has already been shown, this time with an Ellington theme. *Pick Up Sticks* (*Time Out*, 1959) is a passacaille over the ostinato rhythm:

The B♭7 chord is maintained throughout as sonoric basis. *Fugue* and *Chorale* (*Points On Jazz*) conform to Bachian models. *Bluette* (*Time Further Out-Miró Reflections*) is composed in the style of a Chopin waltz. Linear-contrapuntal sections are interwoven with a richness of contrast in the interplay with the alto saxophone. *Charles Matthew Hallelujah* (*Time Further Out-Miró Reflections*) is reminiscent of the B♭ Major Prelude from Johann Sebastian Bach's Well-Tempered Piano, Part I. *Forty Days* (*Time In*, comp. *The Last Time We Saw Paris*) was planned for the oratorio *The Light In The Wilderness*. Certain methods of the Bachian oratorio style are displayed via choral entries and the Bachian ornamentation technique. *Lonesome* (*Time In*): The improvisations proceed prelude-like; the final segments suggest of chorales. *Winter Ballad* (*Jazz Impressions Of New York*) is a waltz with two-voice linear segments and choralic concluding elements. *Danse Duet* (*Countdown-Time In Outer Space*) resembles a Bach Chorale. The improvisations are more active rhythmically and harmonically. Towards the end, a return to the chorale character is effected. *Pennies From Heaven* (*The Dave Brubeck Quartet At Carnegie Hall*) utilizes again the familiar contrapuntal interplay between alto saxophone and piano, albeit just at the end.

Man Of Old (*Summit Sessions*), like *Forty Days*, was conceived for the oratorio *The Light In The Wilderness*, but was not, however, used in it. It is chorale-like in construction. *Because All Men Are Brothers* (*Summit Sessions*) conforms with the Bach Chorale "*O Haupt voll Blut und Wunden.*" *Crossed Ties* (*Blues Roots*, with Gerry Mulligan): The title says something about the musical content in which linear voices sequentially intersect one another. *Broke Blues* (*Blues Roots*) contains a citation out of the c minor fugue from Bach's Well-Tempered Piano, Part I. *World's Fair* (*Time Changes*) has a free-tonal melodic development and imitations between alto saxophone and piano.

In short: the much argued "discriminating," "classical," in this case Bachian, influence is clearly in evidence with Brubeck. Composition technique, thoroughly learned from Milhaud, is utilized in later years for jazz symphonic works, jazz ballets and jazz cantatas. The technique of linear counterpoint, always only evident from time to time, is never employed with consequence throughout a whole piece, but mostly at the beginning and/or end. A significant musical and communicative factor is the outstanding interplay with the alto saxophonist, Paul Desmond, which is at times relieved by dialogues with the bass or drums. The differentiation of the lines, instrument-wise, is guaranteed by virtue of their diverse textures.

Some of the Bach citations (fugue, chorale...) are literal, but, in general, the case is one of approach, style similarities, reminiscences, suggestions, impressions of the linear-contrapuntal style, all of which are brought to materialization via the following principles of style: canon, invention, fugue, chorale, passacaille, toccata and concerto grosso.

Two phenomena play an important musical role in connection with the linear style:

1. the creation of contrast using block chords: sonoric events are set against linear interweavings, and
2. the compression of the linear tapestry into complex sonoric constructions with a simultaneous increase of rhythmic complexity.

The principle of a collage-like cultural exchange between classical music and jazz is later carried over to other musical cultures—not in a scientifically exact manner, but rather as the outcome of the spontaneous, intuitive reception of foreign musical elements. The numerous albums with the title "Impressions" are the result.

The Chopin and romantic approach

As regards style in Brubeck's improvisations, linear-contrapuntal methods are more frequently used than romantic ones. It is perhaps for this reason that in jazz circles he was often accused of a designed-intellectual academicism, lacking in spontaneity and elemental swing. The influence of romantic harmony and its sonoric atmosphere is, nonetheless, clearly evident. Parallel chords, chromatics, alterations, density and complexity of sound—which also Cecil Taylor[56] admired in Brubeck—are essential determinants of the Brubeckian style. "Cecil Taylor told me that he came to all my concerts."[57] The influence exerted upon him by Chopin waltzes is unmistakable and manifold, for, later, when crossed with even meters or themselves in even meters, the Chopin waltz impression is conveyed nevertheless. Miles Davis admired also Brubeck's ballads.[58]

A special case is the piece *Thank You (Dziekuje)* from the 1958 *Jazz Impressions Of Eurasia* album. The word is Polish and is dedicated to the memory of Chopin. "I thought I had insulted the audience by linking the memory of Chopin to jazz. Then came the applause and I realized with relief that the Polish audience had understood that this was meant as a tribute to their great musical tradition and as an expression of gratitude."[59] Unfortunately Brubeck didn't specify what was meant by Poland's great musical tradition. Many of the 19th century composers incorporated national elements into their music as Chopin did, too, with indigenous Slavic elements in the form of, for example: polonaises, mazurkas. *Thank You (Dziekuje)* was heard in New York by the Polish choreographer and dancer Dania Krupska who subsequently asked him to compose a ballet for the Metropolitan Opera. And so it was that *Points On Jazz* with the "Dziekuje" theme at its foundation and pieces reminiscent of Chopin in character, like Prelude, Scherzo and Waltz, came into being.

The following pieces are demonstrative of Chopin stylisms or are suggestive of his music by virtue of their sound character or rhythmic-melodic form: *September Song* (*Dave Brubeck Trio*) conveys the mood of a Chopinian prélude. *Always* (*Dave Brubeck Trio*) is a waltz with a pronounced melodic voice which later goes into 4/4 while maintaining the waltz character. *Laura* (*Jazz At The College Of The Pacific*), through arpeggios and a "wave-like" melodic formation, is reminiscent of Chopinian impromptus. *Swing Bells* and *Weep No More* (*Brubeck Plays Brubeck*) exhibit marked melodic ornamentation and rubato tempi. *Thank You (Dziekuje)* (*Jazz Impressions Of Eurasia*) contains suggestions of Chopin and has the character of a waltz—despite its being in 4/4 meter. *Strange Meadow Lark* (*Time Out*) begins with a rubato introduction and virtuosic arpeggios. *Bluette* (*Time Further Out-Miró Reflections*) is a slow waltz with sevenths and sixths alternating with chromatic lines in the upper voice. *Blue Shadows In The Street* (*Time Further Out-Miró Reflections*), "slow and wistful" in 9/8, has the character of a Chopin prélude. *Lost Waltz* (from *Time In*) along with *Softly, William, Softly* and *Lonesome* are defined by arpeggios and ornamentation. *Jazz Impressions Of New York* contains four waltzes: *Autumn In Washington Square*, *Spring In Central Park*, *Summer On The Sound* and *Winter Ballad*. *Back To Earth* (*Countdown-Time In Outer Space*) is a triplet étude "à la manière de Chopin" with a wide sound spectrum, chromatic melodic development, flowing movements in the right hand and short, rhythmic impulses in the left. The piece is reminiscent of Chopin's "Revolutionsetüde." *Someday My Prince Will Come* (*Countdown-Time In Outer Space*) is a waltz with a bimetric touch, effected by the 4/4 of the bass. *Southern Scene* (*The Dave Brubeck Quartet At Carnegie Hall*) exhibits rich ornamentation and complicated, altered harmonies.

In summary: Suggestions of Chopin and a linear contrapuntal style exert a strong influence in the early quartet period. The Dave Brubeck Quartet had even been temporarily given the appellation "Jazz Waltz Quartet" by the jazz critics.[60] Chromatics and ornamentation characterize the melodic structure. Contrast is frequently provided by sevenths and sixths. The voice leading is taken over by the upper voice. Harmony and sound are determined by alterations and bitonality. A wide spectrum of sound and extended, unexpected modulations betray the influence of "romantic" piano music. In the rhythmic sphere a utilization of triplets and quintuplets, change of meter, and metric combinations are to be found. Tempos are changeable, frequently "slow" and "rubato." Principles of form are not strictly adhered to, the style of playing being determined by prélude improvisations or arpeggio warm-ups and a gradual transition to firmer structures.

The titles of many "romantically influenced pieces"[61] seem to play an essential role with regard to expression and atmosphere: *Autumn In Washington Square*, *Blue*

Shadows In The Street, Winter Ballad, I'm Afraid The Masquerade Is Over, Some Day My Prince Will Come and many more.

The influence of 20th century music

"I was digging Stravinsky and Brubeck had been studying with Milhaud!"[62] Composition instruction with Milhaud doubtlessly gave the jazz musician Brubeck occasion to utilize—in his improvisations and, more frequently and in greater concentration, in his compositions—composition techniques and sound structures of the so-called avant garde. On the other hand, it was Milhaud who reinforced Brubeck in his desire to play jazz. Besides the influence of Milhaud, Brubeck indicates the effect of Bartók and Stravinsky as well.[63] Especially the rhythmic components of these two composers had surely interested him.

Twelve-tone compositions are seldom encountered in Brubeck's works, since he is of the opinion that much is still to be learned from Mozart, Bartók and Stravinsky.[64] The intellectual-rational element in twelve-tone and electronic music is too predominant for his sensibilities. An estrangement from jazz, which should primarily be expressive and emotional, is the result. "...I've now come to believe that any music that expresses emotion is the only music that's going to live. And jazz certainly does that."[65]

The two lessons with Schönberg were not without controversy. Brubeck, the intuitive improvisor playing by ear, seldom proceeded according to strict rules of composition. With the exception of certain compositions, the twelve-tone technique was not used very much—i.e. in *Truth Is Fallen* or *Love Your Enemies*. Brubeck sees the application of the twelve-tone system to jazz as, indeed, one of many possibilities, without, however, seeing any special stimulation for himself in this composition technique, since, of its nature, tonal centers and possibilities of modulation are eliminated. "I had two lessons with Arnold Schönberg. When I came to the second lesson I showed him a composition that I had written in the meantime. He said, `That's very good. Now go home and don't write anything like that again until you know the reason each note is there. Do you know now?' he asked. I said, `Isn't it reason enough if it sounds good?' He said, `No, you have to know why.' That was my last lesson with Schönberg."[66]

The use of Debussyesque sonorities is relatively frequent. *Jazz Impressions Of Japan* utilizes a great deal of associative sonorities and fourth layers, pentatonic and "genderless suspended chords." Similar to in "Pagodes" from Debussy's "Estampes," the Japanese atmosphere is authentically reproduced. A parallel, associative sonoric arrangement is also evident in some of the earlier pieces: *Laura* (*Jazz at the College of the Pacific*) contains parallel chordation with a "bell-like" character. In *Fare Thee Well, Annabelle* (*Jazz: Red Hot and Cool*) parallel fourth sonorities alternate with linearity. At the end of *Swing Bells* (*Brubeck Plays Brubeck*) fourth layers change into parallel chords. Parallel chords are also found in *When I Was Young* (*Brubeck Plays Brubeck*).

Nearly the whole *Jazz Impressions of Japan* (1964 tour of Japan) album is a musical reproduction of the Far Eastern atmosphere. There is never an exact citation from or arrangement of Japanese music, rather, as already reflected in the title, "impressions" and "exoticisms" are dealt with. *Rising Sun* incorporates parallel sonorities and third-related chords. *Toki's Theme* contains pentatonics, fourth- and parallel sonorities. *Zen Is When* is materialized through an associative, parallel alternating-harmony in the rhythm:

as well as parallel "impressionistic" triads. *Osaka Blues* contains an extensive employment of the pentatonic.

The Duke is dedicated to Schönberg and Milhaud. Its complete title is *The Duke Meets Darius Milhaud and Arnold Schönberg.*[67] The composition is completely written out, with an incomplete twelve-tone series appearing as a sort of ostinato in the bass at the beginning and end of the piece. The middle section is characterized by a complicated sonoric harmony. *Upstage Rumba* (*Jazz Impressions of New York*) combines an ostinato rumba in the left hand with a twelve-tone series in the right, which frequently, of its nature, effects bitonality or indefinite tonality.

Consequent and extended applications of the twelve-tone system are found in the compositions: *Love Your Enemies* from the oratorio *The Light in the Wilderness* in which three twelve-tone series are combined; *Truth Is Fallen*, from the cantata of the same name whose underlying material rests throughout on a twelve-tone series. Following are a few examples of Stravinsky citations: *Purple Moon* by Paul Desmond (*The Greats*), which was originally to have been called "Sacre Blues":

Too Marvelous For Words (*Jazz at Wilshire-Ebell*), with a "Sacre" citation in the piano solo, *Bru's Blues* (*Jazz Goes To Junior College*), with a "Sacre" citation in the theme:

Intense, heavily profiled, Béla Bartók inspired rhythms appear in the following pieces: *These Foolish Things* (*Jazz at Oberlin*), with heavily rhythmicized double intervals, which, toccata-like, give the effect of rhythmic "shreds":

Tea For Two (*Jazz at Storyville*), with rhythmicized accents of sound accompanying a frequently interrupted forward movement; *The Golden Horn* (*Jazz Impressions of Eurasia*), with fourth toccati and an aggressive rhythm; *Blessed Are The Poor* (*Dave Brubeck Trio & Gerry Mulligan Live at the Berlin Philharmonie*), with a toccata-like rhythm combined with block chords; *Indian Song* (*Dave Brubeck Trio & Gerry Mulligan Live at the Berlin Philharmonie*), with folk song variations reminiscent of Bartóks "Microcosm."

By way of summary, with regard to the so-called "classical" influence of European concert music on Brubeck, it can be said that Bach and Chopin, as well as their principles of style, play an essential, documentable role for the structuring of Dave Brubeck's improvisations. The complex sonoric harmony can be traced back to, besides others, romantic and impressionistic influences. The rhythmic component is partly influenced by Bartók or Stravinsky. Twelve-tone improvisations are only seldom encountered. The twelve-tone composition technique is used all the more in his cantatas and oratorios.

In closing, a remark from Brubeck with regard to the position of jazz in America and the significance of so-called "serious" music, namely, the twelve-tone technique in particular: "In their intellectuality, most of the contemporary composers, including most of the twelve-tone system writers, are getting too far from the roots of our culture. And for American composers, our roots should be in jazz. So I hope that what I do eventually write has more of a jazz influence in it than any other influence. But I do not think there is any necessary dichotomy between jazz and what is called `serious music.' I think jazz can be as `serious' as any `serious music.'"[68]

2.4.3.2."Non-European" Musical "Impressions"

"I'm looking for the day when all music is accepted and understood. I've always loved all music.... We're finally living in a time when we'll accept all musical cultures and know that they are all great, valid expressions of their people. If you look at the first *Downbeat* interview with me, by Ralph Gleason, in 1948, I'll probably be talking about this. At the time, I was listening to music from the Belgian Congo (the Dennis Roosevelt Expedition),[69] and most Afro-Americans didn't know what I was talking about. I've seen many of the things I predicted happen. The first

African music I heard, just knocked me so far out—it was unbelievable that anything could be this fantastic, complex, simple, swinging...—and jazz wasn't reflecting it at the time."[70]

Brubeck's assumption that the Afro-American jazz musicians at that time would not have understood the contents of the interview is astonishing. Apparently, both the consciousness of the African origins of jazz and the turning towards all possible musical cultures of the world were to manifest themselves with full intensity first with the free jazz of the sixties.

Tolerance and openness with regard to music of all times and places is grounded in Brubeck's musical development, since he grew up with jazz as well as European music. A non-purist point of view should be, especially for jazz musicians, a matter of course, since jazz of its nature is an acculturated music which continually opens itself to new musical influences. "Jazz is a huge sponge...jazz is perfectly capable of assimilating all types of influences. There are no racial limits that determine jazz interpretation. Musicians of the most diverse races and nationalities have been and are now playing jazz."[71]

The concern of some musicologists with the authenticity of the originating cultures, the fear of being swamped in and alienated by musical melting pot cultures, is answered by Brubeck in an interview from March 6th, 1974 in Cologne thusly:
Question: "The idea of cultural exchange, world music, acculturation, etc. seems to exert a strong influence on your music. Some musicologists think that the mingling of different kinds of music brings about the end of authentic music. What would you answer to this objection?"
Answer: "Who is to say this?—The end of the cycle must be: all men understand all men. Did you understand the meaning? It has to start with only one man—it ends with all men. Think of the Tower of Babel! People speak different languages, but can reach to common understanding. The end of the development is like a MOSAIC."[72]

The various musical cultures that are dealt with in Dave Brubeck's piano improvisations and appear only as "impressions" (*Jazz Impressions of New York*, *Jazz Impressions of the U.S.A.*, *Jazz Impressions of Eurasia*, *Jazz Impressions of Japan*) have been taken up, spontaneously, sporadically and attempt-wise, during the quartet's many tours. The South American appeal: "the cool wave from Brazil"[73]—widespread in the jazz of the fifties and sixties—manifested itself with Brubeck in albums like *Bossa Nova U.S.A.*, *Brubeck-Mulligan: Compadres*, and *Bravo! Brubeck!*

Later, the idea of cultural exchange is distinctly represented in his compositions: *The Real Ambassadors* was written for "cultural exchange" and for Louis Armstrong as ambassador for jazz in the music world. Over a Gregorian-chant background choir, he sings the blues: *They Say I Look Like God*. In the cantata *The Gates of Justice* the voices of an Afro-American baritone and a Hebrew tenor, as representatives of the two most oppressed races, are interwoven with one another.

A tour of Europe and Asia resulted in *Jazz Impressions of Eurasia*, 1958, containing elements from the musical cultures of the following countries: England (folk music), Germany (Bachian principles of form), Poland (suggestions of Chopin), Turkey (modal, Turkish theme), Afghanistan (pastoral flute imitation) and India (sitar and tabla imitations). Especially attractive to Brubeck is the Turkish music because of its specific meters and rhythms. For the *Time Experiments*, 9/8 seems fascinating (*Blue Rondo A La Turk* and *A La Turk* from the ballet *Points On Jazz*). One record is dedicated to Japan, *Jazz Impressions of Japan*. It sprang from a Japanese tour in 1964. Some pieces that were inspired by Indian music came about in connection with the musico-ethnological studies of his son Darius at Wesleyan University, and through his personal friendship with the Indian musician Palghat Raghu.

Finally in 1974—even if after some hesitation—Brubeck occupied himself with rock music.[74] This was the time of his European tour with his sons, with the group called "Two Generations of Brubeck." The attempt to join jazz, symphonic music and rock goes already back to 1971 with the cantata *Truth Is Fallen* which was premiered in 1972.

Criticism in the direction of "world music," the mixing of different musical cultures, is, in part, quite heavy. Fears are articulated which assert the adulteration and eventual fall of the individual authentic musical cultures. Brubeck, questioned in Cologne during his "Two Generations" tour, sees in the different cultural convergences and crossing of borders a mutual enrichment and development towards new musical forms with a simultaneous continuation of the old cultures. The individual musical languages will continue as they are, but a musical dialogue between alien cultures should also come about—relationships, understandings in the form of collages. In Brubeck's musical and socio-cultural perception, it has to do with a sort of "musical international understanding" with auditory means. Music has an important socio-psychological task, according to Brubeck: communication with the people who inspire the quartet.[75] In Brubeck's view, the quartet is actually a quintet: the fifth member is the audience.

The South American or Latin American influence

The bossa nova is a South American jazz form whose center of gravity is Brazil. South American folklore, formed by Spanish guitar music, has mixed itself with jazz elements, elements in the percussive/rhythmic sphere and their relevant instruments. The basic rhythm is:

for the bossa nova

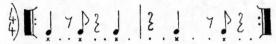

(16 pulse and 5 beats, asymmetrical rhythm)

for the samba[76]

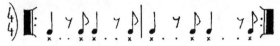

(16 pulse and 8 beats, symmetrical rhythm)

The bossa nova, a "sophisticated" form of the samba, is defined thusly in the *Grove Dictionary*: "A musical style of Brazilian origin blending elements of the samba and cool jazz."[77] North American jazz was heavily influenced by the bossa nova, especially by its specific rhythm. The first bossa nova compositions were written by Antonio Carlos Jobim, best known of which are "Desafinado," "The Girl From Ipanema" and "Samba de Una Nota So." The bossa nova achieved wide dissemination through the film "Orfeo Negro." Stan Getz recorded an album with the title "Samba Jazz."[78]

The USA, as "melting pot of the world," gladly accepted the bossa nova as a musical enrichment and "cross fertilization." Says Brubeck: "I would be surprised to hear a jazz musician who had been exposed to Chinese music use devices from the oriental system while improvising a chorus....new and complex rhythm patterns more akin to the African parent is the natural direction for jazz to develope in....contemporary jazz [is] concentrating a great deal of its effort [on] rhythmic improvisation, [and is] borrowing heavily from South American music."[79]

The aspect of South American music that is especially interesting to Brubeck is naturally the rhythmic one. Simple samba rhythms are represented in every piece in the series, e.g., in *Bossa Nova U.S.A.*:

basic rhythm

upper voice

variation

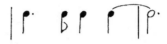

whereby the drums play the bossa nova rhythm:

Also in *Vento Fresco*:
basic rhythm

or

Coraçao Sensivel:
basic rhythm

Irmao Amigo:
basic rhythm

above which is played, e.g., the following rhythm:

Cantiga Nova Swing:
basic rhythm

   Jazz Impressions of New York contains two improvisations in the South American style: *Broadway Bossa Nova* and *Upstage Rumba*. The former is based on the following rhythmic pattern:

which is supported by the percussion instruments. The melody lines, too, are influenced by this rhythm:

which is not a bossa nova rhythm.[80] The drums, however, again play the bossa nova.
   Upstage Rumba uses an ostinato rhythm in the bass line which doesn't conform to the rumba:

Claves, congas and other percussion instruments provide for a Latin American atmosphere as well as a percussion solo. The claves play a simplified rumba-like rhythm:

instead of a rumba:

Numerous bimodal sonorities result from the interplay of the bass line in G with a twelve-tone upper voice: g, f$^\#$, d, e, a, b^b, f, a^b, e^b, d^b, b, c:

Upstage Rumba

Sporadic, Latin American influenced pieces surface again and again: *Perfidia* (*Dave Brubeck Trio*), *Camptown Races* (*Gone With The Wind*), *Trolley Song* (*Bossa Nova U.S.A.*) and *Theme for Jobim* (*Summit Sessions*). The following rhythm dominates the improvisations in *Theme for Jobim* with Gerry Mulligan which is dedicated to the bossa nova composer Antonio Carlos Jobim:

or the inversion

The drums again play a bossa nova, with the piano functioning in the second improvisation percussively as an ostinato rhythm instrument to the baritone solo.

The album entitled ***Jazz Impressions of Eurasia*** deals with musical elements from Europe and Asia. "I did not attempt to capture these various musical languages by exact notation as would a musicologist. Instead I tried to create an impression."[81]

These "impressions" extend from Middle Eastern polyrhythms to Bachian counterpoint. Brubeck's method of introducing exotic and innovative modes consists in intensive listening and the spontaneous application thereof in a jazz improvisation. Brubeck doesn't care very much for notation, since it is his intention to work out things heard as "impressions" and mix them with jazz elements. "How does one go about writing such themes? One way is to listen to the voices of the people."[82]

The album comprises three European and three Asiatic influenced improvisations. Germany, Poland, England, Afghanistan, Turkey and India are the countries represented. As a rule, the word for "thank you" in the respective languages is used as a metric starting point.

Brandenburg Gate is played in the contrapuntal-linear style of Bach, and is reminiscent of chorales and *concerti grossi*. Very long, linear sequences and dialogues materialize in the interplay with the alto saxophone. The motif:

is to have sprung from the German, "danke schön."

Dziekuje, an *hommage à* Chopin, is Polish for "thank you." The piece is in 4/4 and nevertheless waltz-like in character because of the shift in accent. Arpeggios, chromatics and ornamentation, as well as "espressivo" for the attack, are suggestive of a Chopin waltz.

English folklore is mirrored in *Marble Arch*, the entrance to Hyde Park; folk song-like melodies and music hall sounds intermingle with jazz rhythms in the London "impressions."

The piece *Nomad* is written in memory of Afghanistan. "One night in Kabul, I was awakened by the weirdest sound I ever heard. It actually made my hair stand on end. The muffled beat of drums and the eerie tones of a lone flute came closer and closer...."[83] A 3/4 meter intended to remind one of the rhythm of the nomads joins up with a 4/4 jazz meter:

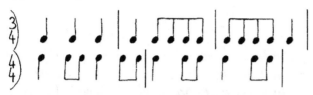

The alto saxophone entry is rhythmically free, and drum swirls interrupt the individual choruses. The piano solo contains cutting, accentuated rhythms. Shortly before the end, a drum solo resounds, leading back to the initial nomad motif.[84]

Brubeck is partial to using Turkish meters, especially the *aksak*: 2 + 2 + 2 + 3 (comp. *Blue Rondo A La Turk*). Turkey, as a bridge between Europe and Asia, is treated musically in the piece *The Golden Horn*, in which a modal, Turkish theme joins European harmonic progressions.

The Indian musical culture differs succinctly from that of Europe through different tonal systems—ragas—and metric structures—talas. A characteristic of essential import for Brubeck, held in common by both cultures, was the element of improvisation. In Calcutta, Brubeck was presented with the opportunity to play with the sitarist Abdul Jaffar Khan and various tabla musicians. These "jam sessions" with the Indian musicians resulted in a successful musical cross-fertilization. *Calcutta Blues* is a reminiscence of this Indo-Jazz. The piano, in imitation of a sitar, is used only melodically, with the bass imitating the Indian instrument, tamboura, in a background ostinato.

On the *Summit Sessions* album are two improvisations influenced by Indian music: *Raga Theme for Raghu* and *Our Time of Parting*. The former is dedicated to Palghat Raghu, the teacher of Brubeck's oldest son, Darius. Raghu was born in Rangoon, Burma and went to Madras, India in 1941 where he played and instructed karnatic music two years long in the country's south. The instruction received by Darius Brubeck in 1967 was part of a "world music program" at Wesleyan University. Dave Brubeck, having heard of Palghat Raghu on the occasion of his India tour, arranged a studio session with the Indian tabla player as well as Eugene Wright and Joe Morello at his house in Wilton, Connecticut. Joe Morello, the

American specialist for unusual meters, and Palghat Raghu, the Indian tabla expert competed with each other: "Hey Raghu, what about 8 against 5? What about 7 against 4? Man, did you hear that?"[85] The raga used in the improvisation reads: c, d, e^b, f$^\#$, g, a^b, b, c. The rhythmic structure comes from the "tasra eka" tala: 3 beats, 1 beat.

In *Our Time of Parting* Darius Brubeck plays the Indian stringed instrument, vina, as well as piano; Chris Brubeck, bass guitar; Dan Brubeck, percussion; Jim Montgomery, rhythm guitar; and a neighbor, Amos Jessup, sings. The vina comments over a seven beat tala: 3-2-2.

A recording from 1964 was entitled *Jazz Impressions of Japan* and came about in connection with a Japanese tour made by the quartet in that year. "The music we have prepared tries to convey these minute but lasting impressions somewhat in the manner of classical Haiku, wherein the poet expects the reader to feel the scene himself as an experience. The poem only suggests the feeling."[86] "Jazz meets Japan" as a musical experiment! A "feeling" for Japanese musical phenomena is suggested; the Japanese harp, koto, is imitated on the piano.[87]

Tokyo Traffic brings a New York rush hour to mind, and was inspired by the verse:

Hurry, hurry, trady crow!

Your house is on fire,

You're far too slow.[88]

A Japanese atmosphere is created by parallel fourth layers and the pentatonic.

Rising Sun stands in stark contrast to the pieces preceding it. From his hotel room window Brubeck could look out onto a serene Japanese garden and the rising sun. The following Haiku provided additional inspiration:

A lovely morn! The summer night is gone!

How hushed and still is all the world,

In wonder at the dawn.[89]

The morning mood of a Japanese sunrise is conveyed by a tender, "impressionistic" sonoric harmony; the rhythm is freely suspended or flowing.

Toki's Theme was conceived before the Japanese tour as TV music—*Jazz Impressions of New York*. It deals with the visit of a Japanese girl to New York. Brubeck had heard Japanese rock music in cafés and on the radio: "After the initial shock of hearing Japanese pop music...the Toki theme combination of western beat and pseudo-oriental sounds no longer seemed incongruous."[90] The Japanese produce a lot of Japanese rock that utilizes parallel fourths which effectuate an "oriental sound." *Toki's Theme*, too, has a corresponding text at its base:

Is it a flower? Is it a butterfly?

Butterfly or flower?

When you come flickering like that you charm me,

When you come twinkling like that I'm bewitched.[91]

The parallel fourths of Japanese rock music resound in *Toki's Theme*, as well, almost continuously. The Far East impression is, furthermore, intensified by the pentatonic.

Fujiyama. It is said that Fujiyama is the soul of Japan; for centuries it has been painted or sketched by Japanese artists. Its majesty and serenity are impressive:

The snail does all he can,

But oh, it takes him quite a while

To climb great Fuji-San.[92]

The widely sweeping, serene, linear theme is reminiscent of Japanese pen-and-ink drawings. Subtle linear interweavements between alto saxophone and piano intensify the impression of the grandeur, serenity and delicacy of Fujiyama landscape portrayals.

Zen Is When. One night there is a discussion with the Japanese artist Faure Hareda and some American students enthused over Zen meditation and Haiku verse. The Zen Buddhist Hareka asks Brubeck if he is acquainted with the Zen philosophy. Brubeck's answer:

Zen is when you're thinking to think,

Or not thinking to think.

Zen is when you hunger, eat—when you're thirsty, drink.

A meditative climate is created by a wood drum solo. The parallel, associative harmony of sound brings the solemnities of Debussy's "Danseuses De Delphes" to mind.[93] A Japanese gong conveys, by a reverberation effect, a mysterious background. The melody is defined by oriental *kleinmotivik*.

The City Is Crying. Kyoto, the city of 2000 shrines, is meant:

Above and all around

The thunder rolls and poppies drop

Their petals on the ground.[94]

Sound and rhythm have a complicated structure here. Altered and bitonal sounds are combined with triplet variations. Triple appogiaturas in the bass voice, reinforced by the bass drum, are a programmatic imitation of a thunderstorm over the city. The peals of thunder portrayed by the drums are like a tone painting. Bitonal layers of sound, altered sonoric progressions, free rhythms, rhythmic combinations—all characterize the musical impression of *The City Is Crying*.

Osaka Blues. The city Osaka was the last stop in the Japanese tour. Pentatonic lines are combined with blues harmonies. Fourth layers are motionless in the second improvisation while melody and rhythm are applied "aimlessly," freely suspended.

Koto Song. The thirteen stringed harp, koto, is an especially typical Japanese instrument, if not in fact the most typical. *Koto Song* is a blues dedicated to two female koto players in Kyoto. "*Koto Song* is the most consciously Japanese of these pieces."[95] At the beginning the piano imitates the koto with astonishing similarity by a fast, fortissimo, doubled-fifth tremolo, pedally veiled. A pentatonic melodic development melds with blues harmonies.

> For me who goes
> For you who stay
> Two autumns.[96]

Koto Song is counted among Brubeck's "Greatest Hits" and was performed in a new arrangement at the 1982 North Sea Jazz Festival with William O. Smith, the clarinetist that played with Brubeck in 1946 during the octet period. Smith, with a great deal of audio-technical proficiency, uses an oscillator to electronically alienate the clarinet sound and create thereby an "impressionistic" Far Eastern atmosphere.

Seen as a whole, the Latin American, Euro-Asiatic and Japanese "impressions" are spontaneous-intuitive-auditory in construction, and, from the improvisational-technical aspect, are based on the collage principle and the idea of "cultural exchange."

2.4.3.3. The Integration of Improvisation and Composition

"Essentially I'm a composer who plays the piano. I'm not a pianist first. Therefore my piano playing is shaped by the material, the ideas I'm trying to express, not by a system or a search for an identifiable sound. Inevitably, because of my own approach to harmony and rhythm, a Brubeckian sound has come into being, but I never went looking for one. I've always tried to stay free of musical straitjackets. I try to retain freedom of choice within the idiom of jazz so that, primarily, my style is a summation of all experience to which I've been exposed."[97] Since his composition lessons with Milhaud Brubeck had also aspired to be a composer. He wasn't able to exhibit the comprehensive, "classical" training of a European composer in harmony, counterpoint, twelve-tone technique, etc. Nor did he, as an intuitive, auditive type of musician, want to subjugate himself to the "iron" discipline of many a conservatory. On top of that, the numerous, world tours of the Dave Brubeck Quartet left precious little time for composing. This was to change after the quartet's dissolution in 1967. The idea of "cultural exchange" and the "impressionistic" adaptations or collage-like combinations of diverse musical citations was preserved. Brubeck's musical identity is richly facetted and of a sparkling diversity.

"I have neither worked nor studied from any theory books you have listed (Schillinger, Russo, Slonimsky, Grove). Some I recognize as authorities, but I never studied jazz or improvisation. I studied composition and counterpoint with Darius Milhaud and he used a book by Walter Piston as his basic harmony text book. I don't know if Russo studied with Milhaud. Pete Rugolo did, but I'm not sure about Bill Russo."[98] As Milhaud's assistant, Howard Brubeck used a counterpoint book by Gédalge for his students, of which his brother David was one.

Brubeck's recognition as a "serious composer" in the USA is widespread. Performances of his lengthier compositions take place time and again—his mass *To Hope*, the cantatas *La Fiesta De La Posada* and *The Voice Of The Holy Spirit* as well as the variations for chorus and orchestra *Pange Lingua* are frequently performed.[99]

Taking place in Bridgeport on the 27th and 28th of April, 1980 was "The Tenth Annual Contemporary American Composers Festival DAVE BRUBECK." It was dedicated exclusively to compositions of Dave Brubeck—excerpts from the oratorio *The Light In The Wilderness* and the cantata *The Gates of Justice*. The workshop on April 28th was dedicated to Dave Brubeck and his honored teacher Darius Milhaud, and consisted of the following chamber music works: *Tritonus*, for flute and guitar, by Dave Brubeck; *Scaramouche*, for two pianos, by Darius Milhaud; a suite for violin, clarinet and piano, by Milhaud; and the ballet *Points on Jazz*, for two pianos, by Brubeck.

The mass *To Hope* was performed on 24 April 1980 in Providence, Rhode Island's St. Peter's and Paul's Cathedral. I was able to attend both the "Composers Festival" in Bridgeport and the mass performance in Providence, as I was spending a week at the Brubeck residence in Wilton, Connecticut.

The mass also included a jazz quartet. With respect to an eventual performance at the Catholic Convention in 1982 in Düsseldorf or in the Dome of Essen, Brubeck remarked: "If that doesn't correspond to the German taste, leave off the jazz quartet."[100] My recommendation to perform the mass, *To Hope*, at a later date at one of the Catholic Conventions, eventually without the jazz quartet, fell through because of the objection of the Bavarian Diocesan Music Directors Conference. "The members are of the opinion, because of the English language, choice of text, musical style and instrumentation, that a performance during the liturgy would not be possible. As the mass is of a good calibre, a concert performance is conceivable; however, due to the high degree of difficulty and indispensability of specialized jazz musicians, even an accomplished church choir would be overtaxed."[101]—It would seem that the actual reason for the refusal is the notion that jazz and church music are incompatible—in addition to an unadmitted aversion to jazz.

The idea of cultural exchange and the incorporation of foreign musical elements under the influence of many musical languages is just as alive in his compositions as in his improvisations; it is characteristic of Brubeck's multifarious style.

The relationship between composition and improvisation has shifted in the course of Dave Brubeck's musical development. The early years are characterized by a closer relationship to composition. "Before...I thought I *had* to compose to fully express myself.... [I only realized later that] there is as much possibility to say what I want to say through jazz as there is through composition."[102] This probably came from the early jazz quartet period.

After an almost twenty year orientation towards jazz improvisation, a sort of return to composition came about in the late sixties, with improvisation continuing parallel to it, although on a reduced scale because of the quartet's dissolution in 1967. With the death of Paul Desmond, Brubeck's "alter ego," on May 30th, 1977, a further watershed in Brubecks musical career is reached. The ensuing compositions are almost exclusively from the realm of spiritual music. Desmonds death marks the unequivocal end of the old Brubeck quartet. "The year 1977 was a turning-point for me. It began as had every year since the dissolution of the old quartet, with my concentration and enthusiasm dispersed. On the one hand I wanted to devote more time to composing—after all, that was the reason the quartet had disbanded. On the other hand I wanted to continue to play jazz, because that's what I love most to do. That desire itself was divided between old loyalties to Paul Desmond, Gerry Mulligan, Eugene Wright, Jack Six, Joe Morello, Alan Dawson and to the loosely knit family band we called `Two Generations of Brubeck'.... Paul Desmond and I planned another duet album, and he had intended, on his next recording, to use Danny on drums. He played his last concert with the family at Lincoln Center, New York City in February 1977. He died three months later. Paul's death was the final and painful wrench with the past."[103]

From Brubeck's written and oral remarks one always gets the impression that he doesn't make a sharp distinction between the terms composition and improvisation, but rather strives towards an integration. He uses the superterm creativity, and differentiates, with respect to creativity in jazz, between three root categories:
1. Imagination as the highest level of creativity, which comes from the subconscious and flows like a continuous, creative current. 2. The use of models, personal or derived "patterns," which are combined with creative ideas. 3. The use of repertoire, a sort of "frozen improvisation" with fixed "patterns," cadenzas, etc., which offer the

The term, composition, is defined by Brubeck following Stravinsky as "selective improvisation." "This is a definition with real significance for me, because it states the primary difference between composition and improvisation. The element of contemplation—a higher degree of selectivity and, consequently, an organically more intricate and more distilled form of musical expression."[105]

Dave Brubeck's Compositions Systematically Ordered

1946   First piano compositions: *Reminiscences of the Cattle Country*
1956   Piano Compositions: *Brubeck Plays Brubeck*

Three ballets:
1956   *Maiden In The Tower*
1961   *Points On Jazz*
1983   *Glances*

Two Jazz Symphonic Compositions:
1959   *Dialogues for Jazz Combo and Orchestra* (by Howard Brubeck)
1963   *Elementals for Jazz Combo and Orchestra* (with Paul Desmond)
1970   *Elementals for Jazz Combo and Orchestra* (with Gerry Mulligan)

A musical:
1962   *The Real Ambassadors* (with Louis Armstrong)

An oratorio:
1968   *The Light In The Wilderness*

Six cantatas:
1969   *The Gates of Justice*
1971   *Truth Is Fallen*
1975   *La Fiesta De La Posada*
1978   *Beloved Son*
1985   *The Voice Of The Holy Spirit - Tongues Of Fire*
1988   *Lenten Triptych - Easter Trilogy*

A mass:
1980   *To Hope: A Mass For A New Decade*

Variations and further compositions:
1976   *They All Sang Yankee Doodle*
1978   *Tritonis for Guitar and Flute*
1983   *Pange Lingua Variations for Choir and Orchestra*
1989   *An die Musik*, for piano, cello, viola, violin and oboe
1989   *Variations of Litanies: Praise of Mary*

Dave Brubeck's Compositions in Chronological Order

1946   *Reminiscences of the Cattle Country*
1956   *Brubeck Plays Brubeck*
1956   *Maiden In The Tower*
1959   *Dialogues for Jazz Combo and Orchestra* (by Howard Brubeck)
1961   *Points on Jazz*
1962   *The Real Ambassadors*
1963   *Elementals for Jazz Combo and Orchestra* (with Paul Desmond)
1968   *The Light In The Wilderness*
1969   *The Gates of Justice*
1970   *Elementals for Jazz Combo and Orchestra* (with Gerry Mulligan)
1971   *Truth Is Fallen*
1975   *La Fiesta De La Posada*
1976   *They All Sang Yankee Doodle*
1978   *Beloved Son*
1978   *Tritonis for Guitar and Flute*
1980   *To Hope: A Mass For A New Decade*
1983   *Pange Lingua Variations for Choir and Orchestra*
1983   *Glances*
1985   *The Voice Of The Holy Spirit - Tongues Of Fire*
1988   *Lenten Triptych - Easter Trilogy*
1989   *An die Musik,* for piano, cello, viola, violin and oboe
1989   *Variations of Litanies: Praise of Mary*
1991   *Joy in the Morning,* for chorus and orchestra based on 30th Psalms
1991   *When the Lord is pleased,* choral composition based on Proverbs 8: 10, 19, Proverbs 15: 16, Psalms 37:16
1992   *Earth is our Mother,* for baritone solo and mixed chorus

The origin and contents of the ballet suite *Points on Jazz*

Points on Jazz is composed for two pianos, and deals with rhythmic variations on a Polish theme. The variations are based on jazz compositions and/or classical conceptions, that is to say, on the influence of European concert music:
- the prelude, scherzo and waltzes have the imprint of romantic piano music, especially of Chopin's style.
- the fugue and chorale have the imprint of baroque music, especially of Bachian voice leading techniques.
- the blues and rag are stamped by jazz.
- The piece *A La Turk* is, like *Blue Rondo A La Turk*, in 9/8 and defined by the Turkish *aksak* rhythm.

The story of the ballet suite *Points on Jazz* began on a cold March day in 1958 on the train from Llodz to Poznan. The romantic, melancholy theme was a reflection on the bleak, grey winter landscape. In the evening during a concert pause Brubeck played the theme for his quartet. He suggested to his friend and concert master as well as interpreter, Roman Waschko, that the piece be introduced as a dedication to Poland and as an encore. It should be a reciprocation of the warmheartedness with which the group was received in Poland. For this reason the piece is called *Dziekuje*, i.e. thank you in Polish. It was especially after a visit to the Chopin museum that the piece developed into a lyrical jazz version with suggestions of Chopin.

The audience reacted with astonished quiet - then with applause mixed with tears. The theme was very frequently played by the Brubeck Quartet as well as by Polish jazz musicians, and subsequently appeared on the *Jazz Impressions of Eurasia* album.

When the Polish-American choreographer Dania Krupska heard *Dziekuje* she asked Brubeck if he would like to use the theme to compose a ballet for the Metropolitan Opera. She told him the ballet's story and explained the "variations in rhythm" she had designed.

"The Boy is the theme. He is all alone on the stage - detached. Gradually movement begins. The Girls make their entrances. He tries to reach out and make contact with them, but cannot. Even with other people on the stage he is all alone, Dania would say, and the basis for the first variation, PRELUDE, was improvised. Now The Girl enters. She is fresh, gay, bubbling with life. I improvised the SCHERZO with bright arpeggios and a pounding, rhythmic pulse. Here comes The Temptress. I played a slow BLUES. She entices The Boy, then leaves him to summon other men to gather around her. They fight for her in a primitive dance and she is tossed wildly from one man to another. The BLUES tempo quickens. Then

The Temptress snaps her fingers and walks out on the men. End of BLUES variation. Now The Girls and The Boys are happily together again. They are wacky, happy Couples. The Rag. Their happiness makes The Boy feel even more alone. The Boy's theme is a CHORALE. The Girl reaches out for The Boy. She wants to comfort him. Introduction to WALTZ variation. He recognizes her as The Girl of the SCHERZO. They dance a romantic pas de deux. The SCHERZO theme in 2/4 and The Boy's theme in 3/4 meet in the WALTZ variation. The Girl is overjoyed. She must call everyone to share her happiness. A LA TURK variation and FINALE. In the confusion of their celebration The Boy and The Girl are separated. After a climactic search they find each other, embrace and walk away arm in arm."[106]

Brubeck's first musical reactions to this story were spontaneous improvisations. In New York, Dania Kruspka went about completing her choreography with Brubeck's improvisations in mind, while he occupied himself in California with working the spontaneous improvisations out and revising them into compositions.

Unfortunately, Brubeck had only ten days in which to complete the ballet, so he sent piano transcriptions of the "BLUES" and the 9/8 "A LA TURK" to New York and played the rest in later. On a world tour that took him first of all to Honolulu, he composed further. He then telephoned his brother Howard from Australia to give him the final details for the conclusion of the ballet. Howard, as so often was the case, took over the notation. It was only near the end of the tour that Brubeck found out that the performance at the Metropolitan Opera in New York had been cancelled.

Brubeck remembers that the piano duo Gold and Fizdale asked him in December 1958 during a mutual concert with the New York Philharmonic Orchestra to write a piece for them, though they hadn't yet played any jazz. It was also not intended that *Points on Jazz* be reserved exclusively for jazz musicians. The ballet was supposed to reflect a form of 20th century jazz that conformed to the "Third Stream Idea." Brubeck fit a fugue into the ballet and the duo performed the whole suite under the title, *Points on Jazz*.

Because Dania Krupska never gave up the idea of having the ballet performed, it finally did premiere in January 1961 in Hartford, Connecticut. The orchestration was done by Howard. Since then there have been numerous performances of it in different American cities.

Carmen McRae sang the theme "Dziekuje" under the title "There'll Be No Tomorrow" in the USA and Europe. Iola Brubeck wrote the text. The piece appeared on the album *Points on Jazz* with trio accompaniment. On the album *Bossa Nova U.S.A.* it is played by the quartet and had become a fixed part of the repertoire for all of the world tours. The catchy theme, based on interval diminution (octave, minor seventh, minor sixth), has experienced many rhythmic variations extending from jazz rhythms to Chopin ballads and Bach chorales, as well as to the Turkish *aksak*.

European "classical" concert music and the American jazz tradition are melded together in *Points on Jazz* and have a further effect on other cultural forms of expression, e.g., jazz dance. The problem for the composer was to maintain the improvisational character of the ballet despite the necessary commitment to jazz choreography. It was a problem for the dancers and both pianists, Gold and Fizdale, to bring their "classical" training to terms with the execution of jazz sonorities and rhythms. The composition *Points on Jazz* was eventually to become part of the piano and ballet literature. Its purpose was to span a bridge between jazz and European concert music. The ballet suite is comprised of 8 pieces: *Prelude, Scherzo, Blues, Fugue, Rag, Chorale, Waltz* and *A La Turk*.

The *Prelude* is dedicated to Chopin and the Polish people, and comprises the main part of the ballet. The waltz character stays within view despite the 4/4 meter. The central key of B$^\flat$ is rarely left. A chromatic influence is on hand, and numerous ornamental variations are called forth by the varied utilization of triplets:

The *Scherzo*, like the *Prelude*, is Chopinesque in character. B$^\flat$ minor and F Major as well as diminished fifths and sixths define the harmonic landscape. The tonal sphere is efficiently designed. Triadic arpeggios are rhythmically bound to the following motif:

and "shoot like a rocket" upwards. The theme is found in the lower voice; in the middle voice is a sort of sonoric pedal-point:

triadic arpeggios

sonoric pedal-point

linear theme

Blues. Blue notes as well as numerous anticipations determine the blues character. Compressions are created by: parallel sevenths, series of thirds, block chords. The differentiated rhythmic structure of the theme stabilizes itself, through an increasing sonoric compression, into the following rhythmic formula:

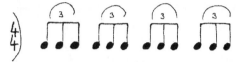

For the resumption of the theme, a progression based on the following rhythmic elements manifests itself:

The *Fugue*, in the style of Bach and "in a swinging style," is four-voiced and in the key of C minor. The first entry occurs on the fifth. The theme is drawn from that of *Dziekuje*. A synoptical comparison makes clear its relationship with the original theme:

Dziekuje

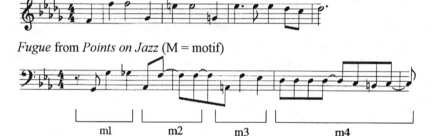

Fugue from *Points on Jazz* (M = motif)

The principle of chromatic melody-diminution is maintained in the original theme and in the fugue with few divergences. *Dziekuje*: octave - augmented sixth - minor sixth. *Fugue*: octave - major sixth - minor sixth.

The fugue gets its actual profile from the rhythmic diminution. Already the eighth note upswing on the upbeat and avoidance of the half note hold effectuate the energetic character of the fugue theme. The offbeat accentuation—and1, and2—and the ostinato repetition of the tone d give the fugue theme the appearance of a striking, catchy line that lends itself to subdivision into four rhythmic-melodic motifs which are sustained by the contrast between leap and repetition as well as by the upbeat-offbeat phrasing.

The second entry (bar 4, answer) occurs in actuality on the tonic; the third entry again on the dominant, g (bar 3); the fourth entry again on the tonic (bar 11). The order of voices is bass, tenor, alto, soprano. The entries are aperiodical in duration. The contrapuntal goings-on take place in the diatonic sphere via the construction of sequences of eighth note chains (bars 4-5) whereby a contrast (counterpoint) to the leaping theme is created.

The counterpoint to the third thematic entry in the tenor is comparable to the counterpoint in the bass to the second thematic entry (transposition, retained counterpoint). A further counterpoint to the third thematic entry occurs in the bass in the form of a chromatically ascending quarter note countermovement (bars 8-9).

The fourth and last thematic entry is fitted with the following counterparts: the alto is comprised of sixth, seventh and octave leaps, executed mainly with eighth notes, and enriched by offbeats; the tenor, diatonically ascending and descending, is bound to an eighth note movement; the bass is chromatically varied and retains mainly a quarter note movement (bar 11ff).

About the overall form of the "fugue":

The second development appears from bar 22 in E^b—in the tonic parallel, namely on the 3rd degree. The third development, from bar 40, is thematically and structurally augmented. With the soprano in D^b, the theme enters in a state of rhythmic augmentation. The head of the theme is subsequently introduced in the soprano with the rhythmically augmented theme in the bass (bars 45-46ff). Soprano D^b = bII.

From bar 62 a triple augmentation of the theme occurs, beginning in D^b. Motif 4 is left out. From bar 71ff a sort of 4th development takes place—or, in fact, a sort of interlude (?)—which utilizes, however, only motif 4 (tone repetition) of the theme. Key: Fm = IV. The 5th and last development (from bar 101) strives again towards the central key, Cm. A further diminution occurs in half bar intervals in the order: soprano, alto, tenor, bass.

The primary musical elements given expression in the *Points on Jazz* fugue are:
 - naturally, the theme—also doubled, and four times augmented and diminished,
 - parallel thirds, sixths and tenths, progressing diatonically or chromatically,
 - motif 4 of the theme, repeated partial motif, especially in the 4th development.

As relatively few elements are utilized, and as these in turn are combined with each other, the fugue makes a unified, transparent and concentrated impression. The linear, contrapuntal principle of the fugue is, through the extended use of parallel intervals, no longer ensured. Near the fugue's end the rhythmic-sonoric principle of repeated block chords forcibly "slugs" its way through and briefly conveys a toccata-like impression.

Scheme of the fugue

1st development (bar 1)
(beginning in G, key = C)

Interlude using counterpoint 1, 2nd entry, 1st development.

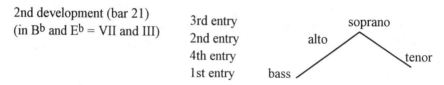

2nd development (bar 21)
(in B♭ and E♭ = VII and III)

Interlude using counterpoint 1 as well as parallel thirds and tenths.

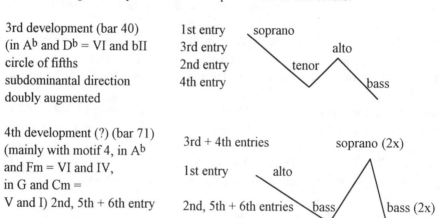

3rd development (bar 40)
(in A♭ and D♭ = VI and bII
circle of fifths
subdominantal direction
doubly augmented

4th development (?) (bar 71)
(mainly with motif 4, in A♭
and Fm = VI and IV,
in G and Cm =
V and I) 2nd, 5th + 6th entry

The 5th entry in the bass is additionally combined with the theme, augmented four times, in the alto voice.

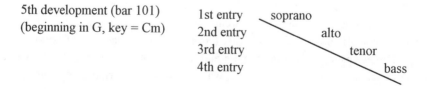

5th development (bar 101)
(beginning in G, key = Cm)

There is a repeated thematic entry in the soprano only (bar 110). The conclusion then ensues with repeated, inner-rhythmically accented block chords and a "genderless" change of meter into C.

In the 1st development the entry of voices proceeds in ascending order from bass to soprano, and in the last development the order is reversed. The 2nd, 3rd and 4th developments become increasingly varied with regard to the order of voice entries.

Rag. The beginning offers a frequent metrical alteration between 5/4 and 3/4. The 4/4 rag begins at bar 4. A rhythmical hammering and a "stride piano style" reminiscent of Fats Waller connect with chromatically modified chains of thirds or fourth-sixths in counter movement.

Chorale. A step-wise harmonic development typical for chorales is utilized. Bitonal sonorities are produced from the combination of G Major and E^b Major.

Waltz (in 3/4 and 9/8), like the prelude and scherzo again in the central key of B^b, is Chopin-like. The following rhythmic motif:

is applied in ostinato. The ending is bitonal: C/D.

A La Turk. The rhythmic, mostly octaved, motive pedal-point is maintained up to the finale. Like in *Blue Rondo A La Turk* from the *Time Out* album, the Turkish *aksak* meter is dominant:

After a symmetrical transition the finale changes the meter as follows:

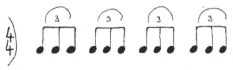

Numerous septuplets create a rhythmic contrast, and the principle of sonoric compression is again applied: melodic lines are relieved by octave and seventh intervals. Triads and quadrads, e.g., seventh chords and compact block chords, follow. The block chords are combined with polyrhythmic structures:

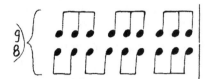

The ballet *Glances* comprises "Five Movements." I had piano excerpts from Movements I and V at my disposal. Movement I begins with a fast symmetrical rhythm in 4/4:

that is accompanied by steady strings of eighth notes in the bass which soon change into groups of sixteenths. From bar 11, metric and tonal changes occur: 6/4, 5/4, 6/4, 4/4 in combination with the keys C, B^{b7}, D^b, C^7, F, C. An initial high point is reached in bar 25 by powerfully ascending parallel block chords in the sphere of B^b over F and C triadic arpeggios.

Brief changes of meter between 5/8 and 4/8 transpire as of bar 26. The sonoric expression is especially linked to thirds, triads and sixths. From bar 34 the meter remains constant, with the motive progression being loosened by an occasional triplet or 6/8. From bar 46, alternating block chords in fortissimo are encountered in the realm of C. Bar 62 is introduced with a glissando leading to D^b, rich in modulation and rhythmically modified with conciseness:

A sonoric and rhythmic quieting-down ensues from bar 70—F chords with a simple rhythm:

which lead over to a section marked "tenderly" (bar 76) and "espressivo" (bar 82) in an uneven 3/8 meter. Flowing sixteenth notes then enter over E^9 sonorities, and in bar 88 comes a return to 4/8 meter combined with dottings in the domain of B^b.

The initial key of C is again reached in bar 102 via a chromatic cellular motific structure and the dominant G. Bouncing triplets and dottings as well as offbeats now determine the sonoric texture. A shift of tonality to B^7 is occasioned from bar 118, and the rhythm is simple and succinct:

Then comes another metric and sonoric change to 3/8 and C^7 in bar 130 with the following bimeter playing a roll:

With the 4/8 meter in bar 136, the rhythm again becomes symmetrical, the sound bitonal: F and B sonoric compressions (e.g., D + E or C + G^b) follow, along with toccata-like, complementary rhythms:

Near the end of the piece, the blocks of sound move in a massive counter movement around C, D^b, and E^b with a catchy rhythm (bar 174ff):

and end accented thusly:

on the complex bitonal chord $C(m)^{7/9/11/13}$.

The two symphonic jazz compositions are from 1959 and 1963: ***Dialogues for Jazz Combo and Orchestra*** was composed by Howard Brubeck, ***Elementals for Jazz Combo and Orchestra*** by Dave Brubeck.

The designation ***Dialogues for Jazz Combo and Orchestra*** becomes clear especially in the 4th movement, as here is where a true musical equilibrium between jazz group and orchestra is offered. To combine jazz and symphonic music has always been problematical, for being dealt with here are two clearly different forms of music possessing very different modes of expression and structures. As a rule, a succession rather than a coupling or permeation of jazz and symphonic music takes place. In the case of composers of symphonic music, jazz rhythms and sounds are frequently utilized to depict alienation. As for jazz musicians, insufficient knowledge of difficult occidental composition techniques often leaves a convincing integration to be desired. With such adaptations, interpretation acquires an increased relevance.

Dialogues for Jazz Combo and Orchestra had its première on December 10, 1959 at Carnegie Hall under the direction of Leonard Bernstein. The movements are designated as Allegro, Andante Ballad, Adagio Ballad, Allegro Blues. The first and last movements were completely rewritten by Howard Brubeck. Bernstein wanted more orchestral sections, especially in the second movement, *Theme For June*, which is dedicated to Howard's wife. *Dialogues* was Howard's first and last composition in the jazz-symphonic Third Stream domain. He had always done a great deal of arranging and instrumentation for his brother Dave.

The 1959 composition was preceded by a simple version in 1956 with whose performance in San Diego none of the participating jazz and symphonic musicians were really happy. "Well, I wrote `Dialogues' because I was on the board of directors of the San Diego Symphony Orchestra and Robert Shaw was the conductor.... The orchestra president asked me if I would get Dave to come and play `Rhapsody in Blue' with the San Diego Symphony Orchestra, and I said, well, he really is not that kind of musician."[107] What was meant was that Dave is an improvisor not an interpreter. Both brothers, Howard and Dave, got together many times and agreed on the following basic structures for the composition *Dialogues for Jazz Combo and Orchestra*:

- a 16 or 32 bar chordal progression would be the point of departure for the jazz improvisations,
- jazz solos and orchestral sections should alternate,
- the jazz improvisations should be combined with a simple or complicated orchestral background.

The Dave Brubeck Quartet was interwoven with a large orchestral apparatus. The strings were heavily represented. An integration and, in part, addition of jazz and symphonic music was on hand.

In the first movement—an allegro—extended, tonally bound piano and alto saxophone improvisations occur along with orchestral sonorities in a countermovement of sonoric entities. An additional compression is provided by complementary rhythms between the piano and orchestra.

The second movement, "Andante Ballad"—*Theme For June*—is characterized by lyrical-linear, *kleinmotivic* piano improvisations. Dramatic brass contrasts penetrate the lyrical style. A dialogue between oboe and piano with a background of strings proves to be a successful integration of jazz piano improvisation and symphonic instrumentation.

The third movement, "Adagio Ballad," is distinguished by new sonoric aspects and combinations: sound spacing and differentiation between high flutes and deep horns are used with rich contrast. A gradual, instrumental-sonoric compression is developed by way of a sonoric stratification:
- alto saxophone and strings begin,
- bass and drums supplement the texture,
- almost unnoticed, the piano improvises with a background of strings.

The dialogue principle is especially noticeable in the fourth movement, "Allegro Blues," as the jazz group and symphony orchestra alternate with one another. Following one orchestral section is a drum solo, then a bass solo. The orchestra and combo play simultaneously, with an instrumental penetration especially by the horns, jazz piano and jazz drums. A blues and a classical fugato bring the composition to a close.

"In this work an attempt is made to construct a score giving the orchestra an important part to play which adheres strictly to written notes, while the particular combination or `combo' of jazz instruments is free to improvise on the material of the movement."[108]

The première of *Elementals for Jazz Combo and Orchestra* took place on August 1, 1963 at the Eastman School of Music in Rochester, New York for an arrangement course graduates commencement concert. Playing were the Dave Brubeck Quartet with Paul Desmond, as well as a symphony orchestra conducted by Rayburn Wright. It was recorded again in May 1970 with the Cincinnati Symphony Orchestra under Erich Kunzel, along with "guest star" Gerry Mulligan and the Dave Brubeck Trio. Why the designation "Elementals"? An abundance of divergent musical elements are incorporated into this jazz-symphonic work, and the instrumentation alternates between symphonic music and jazz. The binding factor is the continuous drumming. Utilization of the brass is given prominence, save for a few woodwind intermezzos and the initial pizzacatoed string background over which piano interjections, of a rhythmically stark profile, resound, later followed by the tonally bound motifs of the baritone saxophone. A substantial, sonoric compression gradually embracing the complete orchestral apparatus is one of the compositional vehicles used. Another is the alternating mutual replacement of orchestra, jazz trio or piano, and baritone saxophone. Baroque structural elements are realized in a fugato head and concerto grosso suggestions.

A motific, linear development in the piano frequently alternates in rich contrast with intense, toccata-like block chords. The baritone saxophone uses, step-wise, a tight, lyric-like cellular melodic structure as well as sound "shreds" and rhythmically "hammering" note repetitions. After a piano-baritone saxophone dialogue, a gradual integration into the orchestra takes place.

All in all, the piece gives somewhat the impression of a symphonic work. Near the end, after a playing time of 15' 35", the orchestra reaches the state of swing, so that one is given the impression that the symphonic musicians are also accustomed to playing jazz. The numerous baroque, romantic and jazz elements, as regards instrumentation and structure, give the work a mosaic-like character, rich in contrast.

The musical *The Real Ambassadors* was composed by Dave Brubeck from 1959 to 1962. The lyrics were conceived by Iola and Dave Brubeck together. The first concert performance took place on September 23, 1962 during the Monterey Jazz Festival. Costumes were worn only by the vocal group which provides commentary in the style of the Greek chorus. The players for the first performance at Monterey included:

Hero	Louis Armstrong
Girl Singer	Carmen McRae
Side Man	Trummy Young
The Chorus	Vocal Group of:
(Ambassadors, Priests,	Dave Lambert, Jon Hendricks,
Citizens)	Yolande Bavan
Narrator	Iola Brubeck
Band I (Modern)	Dave Brubeck, Joe Morello,
	Eugene Wright
Band II (Traditional)	Louis Armstrong, Trummy Young,
	Joe Darensbourg, Billy Kyle,
	Willy Kronk, Danny Barcelona

Howard Brubeck was the general musical coordinator.

Before the first number, *Everybody's Comin'*, the narratress, Iola Brubeck, announces that a special sort of music drama is taking place, one requiring a lot of imagination and spontaneity: "Words and notes on pieces of paper suddenly coming to life." The story, as well as time, place and costumes, is in the realm of fantasy. "We must paint a view of the world from an airplane window, build an African village...."[109]

The text and music—both only sketched—are supposed to be more or less spontaneously improvised. The rhythmical specialities comprise triplets, dottings—offbeats. As a rule, the rhythm is determined by the text. Polyrhythmic phenomena materialize in Nr. 7, *King For A Day*, e.g.:

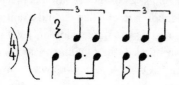

The sonoric structures are simple. Chord construction is characterized by simple triads, alterations ($5^\#$ or $11^\#$, 9^b, $m7^\#$), bitonality and occasionally layers of fourths. The chord progressions are enriched by chromatics, modulations and parallel voice leadings. Nr. 11, *One Moment Worth Years*, exhibits a more complex harmony because of frequent alterations. Nr. 12, *They Say I Look Like God*, combines a Gregorian background chorus with a blues vocal done by Louis Armstrong. Nr. 15, *Finale*, utilizes, with conspicuous frequency, parallel fourth sonorities.

The musical drama—or better—Broadway Musical—*The Real Ambassadors* is dedicated in its entirety to the idea of cultural exchange. Appointed as musical ambassador for cultural exchange in the enterprise jazz, Louis Armstrong is the musical's "hero." The composition was directly occasioned by Armstrong's trip to the Congo, Léopoldville, in 1960 where he visited the Babotas, Ekondas and Nkongos. He wrote at that time in a telegram to his manager: "Like myself you and I just have no business dying. That's all. We are put here on earth for humanitarily purpose."[110]

In the musical *The Real Ambassadors* Louis Armstrong and his band find themselves in an unknown African country that has recently achieved independence—Talgalla. Armstrong's music joins the African inhabitants in friendship with the Afro-American ambassador, Louis Armstrong. The man and the musician, Louis Armstrong, becomes, as a politician, "King For A Day"; and he gives expression to his worldwide musico-political intentions: "From a swinging band with all the leaders from every land.... All I do is play the blues and meet the people face to face. I'll explain and make it plain. I represent the human race."[111] An Afro-American jazz musician as representative of the whole human race is in 1962 still an idea packed with a lot of explosives!

A musical reciprocity is realized in just one number, namely, *They Say I Look Like God*. As mentioned previously, Gregorian Chants and blues are resounding here simultaneously. Armstrong sings a blues over a Gregorianic background chorus. This piece appears to be an out of the ordinary experiment. Louis Armstrong finds himself in Talgalla on the steps of the church with Gregorian motifs emerging from within, and he interjects his religious-humanistic thoughts in the form of a blues vocal. From a musical perspective, a collage out of the first European musical language and the source of jazz, the blues, is manifested. The text and content concern the timorous question of black people as to God's skin color. God is the god of the whites, though, according to Christian teachings, existent for all people. "Could God be black, my God?—If all are made in the image of Thee. Could Thou perchance a zebra be?"[112] The way out of the problem gives the impression of being somewhat naive, humorous. A subsequent discussion of racial discrimination leads to hope for the future: all people are equal. "Everyone Is One"—only in this way can all people peacefully achieve freedom.

The oratorio *The Light In The Wilderness - An Oratorio For Today* had its première on 29 February 1968 under the direction of Erich Kunzel. The participants were:

Orchestra	Cincinnati Symphony Orchestra
Piano	Dave Brubeck
Baritone	William Justus
Mixed Chorus	Miami University A Capella Singers directed by George Barron
Organ	Gerre Hancock
String Bass and Del Rhuba	Frank Proto
Jazz Drums and Tablas	David Frerichs

Text: Selections from the bible and original texts by Dave and Iola Brubeck.

The original title of the oratorio was to have been "The Temptations and Teachings of Christ." One would naturally ask a jazz musician why he would write an oratorio, and at the same time be interested in his religious convictions: "I'm not affiliated with any church. I am a product of Judaic-Christian thinking.... Three Jewish teachers have been a great influence in my life—Irving Goleman, Darius Milhaud and Jesus."[113]

The Light In The Wilderness portrays Christ's temptation in the desert, which elucidates the existential problem everyone faces. The spiritual rebirth of mankind can only come about under the commandment of charity. If one wants to revolutionize the world without destroying it, how does one begin?—Human avarice must be done away with, for man lives not from bread, i.e. money, alone. And—what good is it to man if the whole world is won, yet his soul is afflicted. The twelve disciples of Jesus are symbolized by a 12-tone theme. Each of the disciples is called up by a specific tone in the series: "Follow me!" The core of Christian teachings, charity—even and especially in the sense of love thy enemy—becomes the main concern of the oratorio. Fratricide is to be replaced by fraternization. In God's eyes there is no enemy.[114]

themes:

1. *Love Your Enemies* in 3/4 meter, with *Do good to those who hate you* in 4/4 (p. 72/73 of the piano score).

2. *And as you wish that men would do to you, do so to them* (p. 78 of the piano score).

3. *If you love those that love you, what credit is that to you?* (p. 78 of the piano score).

Matthew 5: 44; 39-47
Luke 6: 27-38
(Matt. 7: 1, 12)

VII. Love Your Enemies
(Chorus and Baritone Solo)

DAVE BRUBECK

*Perc. play first 7 measures 4 times: (1) and (3)- as written, (2) and (4)-Each player plays war-like sounds of choice.

** Throughout the opening section of this anthem, (to ①), the 3/4 measures should be sung with harshness and stridence, while the answering 4/4 measures are softer, smoother, and more peaceful in character.

If desired, chorus may speak rather than sing to ①, each section using the rhythms and general pitch inflections of its part. Final notes of phrases should be shortened to more nearly resemble natural speech. (Soloist and accompaniment parts remain as shown.)

*Maintain this relationship between ¾ and ⁴₄ to letter ①

As Christ's teachings should speak to everyone, every possible style is wielded towards the musical realization in the sense of a collage: "Quick jumps from modern to modal, Middle Eastern to country hoe-down, jazz, rock and roll, martial drums."[116] Hope can perhaps be placed in coming generations which would judge and act sociocritically. It could be that the 21st century will be the new age of love.

The sonoric structure encompasses empty fifths—especially to represent the desert, in the orchestra and chorus—bitonality (frequent: F/G combinations), simple triadic harmonies, clusters, parallel fourths against parallel fifths in counter-movement, and combinations of three 12-tone themes in the *Love Your Enemies* section.—The progressions of sound are differentiated through the use of chromatics, parallel fourths and fifths series, series of sixths and thirds joined to sextuplets, block chords over an octaved pedal-point or pedal-points, and ostinati as well as rhythmicized pedal-points.

In Sections I and IIc the rhythmic structures are determined by 5/4 meter, Section IVb by 6/8. In Section VII, the text "Even sinners" (p. 80 of the piano score) is characterized by changes of meter. A metric extension takes place at the end of Section VII: Meters of 2/4 - 3/4 - 4/4 up to 12/4, each lasting one bar, are joined with rhythmic variations like:

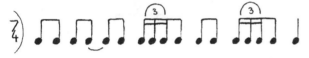

and a diatonically ascending bass line in the organ. *Love Your Enemies* constitutes the "heart" of the oratorio.

The cantata ***Gates of Justice*** was composed in 1969. "The essential message of `The Gates of Justice' is the brotherhood of man.... When I had completed writing `The Gates of Justice' I found in Micah (Ch. 6, v. 8) a summation of my thinking: `It hath been told thee, O man, what is good and what the Lord does require of thee: only to do justice, and to love mercy and walk humbly with thy God.'—Only? !!"[117]

Justice, mercy, humility—three abstract ideals whose realization seems a challenge. The "Brotherhood of Man" already mentioned in the oratorio is the decisive message of the cantata. Race, religion, nation...should no longer be allowed to lead to discrimination. Minorities, too, should be recognized with respect to human rights. Because of their long history of suffering, Jews and blacks know best the consequences of hate and alienation. Martin Luther King Jr. once said: "If we don't live together as brothers, we will die together as fools."[118] The extremely one-sided technical-civilizational development of mankind will lead to a final chaos if man doesn't learn to desist from his "stone aged" mentality of force. A new mentality must evolve, one that generates moral energies for the development of quality of life.

Brubeck's "generally human" sense of mission is mirrored in the music of the cantata. The Jewish tenor appears as representative of Hebrew tradition and Hebraic modes—the black baritone represents Afro-American development and music which are especially articulated in spirituals and blues. The structural character of the cantata on the whole, textually as well as musically, can again be termed a collage. The texts are from Isaiah, Martin Luther King Jr., Hillel, the Psalms.

The music is influenced by the Beatles, Chopin, Israeli, Simon and Garfunkel, and incorporates Mexican and Russian folklore, spirituals and blues, jazz and rock, classical and modern styles in the sense of the idea of cultural exchange. It has to do with a complex musical collage intended to symbolize the diversity and plurality of peoples, races, groups and individuals.

The première of *The Gates of Justice* cantata took place on October 19, 1969 in Cincinnati's Rockdale Temple.[119] The players in the first performance were:

Jazz Trio	Dave Brubeck, piano, combo organ; Jack Six, bass; Alan Dawson, drums
Bass Baritone	McHenry Boatwright
Tenor	Cantor Harold Orbach
Chorus	The Westminster Choir, under the direction of Robert Carwithen
Brass Ensemble	Members of the Philharmonia Orchestra - University of Cincinnati College Conservatory of Music
Organ	Robert Delcamp "With optional keyboard improvisation"
Conductor	Erich Kunzel
Text	adapted by Dave and Iola Brubeck (Psalms, Isaiah, M. L. King Jr., Hillel)

The cantata's twelve pieces are carried by three "pillars" which support the whole of the structure like a bridge, these being the three corresponding choruses:
- *Oh, Come Let Us Sing Unto The Lord*, from Nr. II, a veneration in the traditional chorus style with a few harmonic and rhythmic innovations,
- *Shout Unto The Lord*, from Nr. VII, a complex consisting of free, jazz improvisations, rock, blues and traditionals; full of ecstasy and joy, but containing Martin Luther King's sobering admonition towards "brotherhood,"

- *Oh, Come Let Us Sing A New Song*, from Nr. XII, a reminder of the power of God and of man, with an integration of the 12-tone technique.

The other pieces serve as "connecting cables" between the pillars of the bridge. The "heart" of the cantata is Nr. III, *Open The Gates*.

I. *Lord, The Heavens Cannot Contain Thee*, for solo tenor, begins with a rams horn signal, a fanfare in fifths, and signifies a call to a battle of conscience. Triplet ostinati in alternation with groups of sixteenths reinforce the penetrating call compounded with the sharp bitonal background sound (C/D^b). The melodic development—since it deals with the Hebraic representative—has an "oriental" hue: augmented steps, a melodic flowing and descending over neutral "genderless" chords. The melodic progression reaches its climax with the cry "The people Israel." Bitonal, free rhythmically immobile sonorities usher in the transition to:

II. *Oh, Come Let Us Sing Unto The Lord*, one of the three carrying choral pieces, which only appears in abridged form on the album. Especially noticeable is the descending ostinato pedal-point line in the organ, which, as regards movement technique, stands in considerable contrast to the ascending unisonic choral voices which reach out with vitality. The polyrhythmic formula:

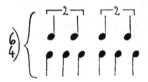

which has a very powerful effect, is bound to parallel triads which find themselves in countermovement.

III. a) *Open The Gates*, for solo tenor, solo baritone and chorus "with optional improvisation," is the cantata's "heart." The bitonality (C/G^b) in the closing section of Nr. I is taken up again, replaced after four bars and continued with fourth layers in combination with a 12-tone row in the bass (p. 21/22 of the piano score):

IIIa. OPEN THE GATES

(Solo Tenor, Solo Baritone, and Chorus, with optional Improvisation)

The tenor solo with choral accompaniment, *Open The Gates*, is of a penetrating rhythmic intensity and is maintained for over thirty bars in the bass voicing of the chorus and in the timpani's ostinato. *Clear you the way for the people* uses parallel fifths in the bass and tenor. The following ostinato rhythm in *Out Of The Way Of The People* is coupled to "genderless" static C sonorities combined with the following meters of 3 and 4:

The static "genderless" C sonorities are subsequently executed in a diatonic countermovement and then reduced to parallel fifths:[120]

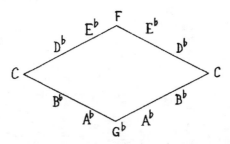

This provides the impulse and source material for a piano improvisation carried by a static cellular motific structure and supported by hammering basses. Ostinato melodic phrases alternate with blues influenced motifs. Frequently, "genderless" chords are inserted percussively. Clearly to be felt in the ostinato rhythms is the suggestion of Ravel's "Bolero." After the improvisation, the static C ostinato and polymetrie (combinations of 3 and 4) are again resumed.[121] The "violent" rhythmical hammering is accentuated by heavy dynamics and intensified to a forte fortissimo. *Open The Gates* concludes with a powerful musical exertion of strength and urgency.

III. b) *Open The Gates Chorale*, for solo tenor, solo baritone and chorus stands in stark contrast to Nr. IIIa of the same name. A calmly progressing, chorallic step harmony in D♭ relieves the hammering, urgent rhythm. The 12-tone bass voice with the layer of fourths countermovement, in progress since IIIa, is taken up again in IIIb shortly before the hammering static C chordistry—as well an element from IIIa—concludes the piece.[122]

IV. a) *Except The Lord Build The House*, for solo tenor, solo baritone and chorus, is a piece influenced by blues tonalities. The basic rhythm is:

and, with slight modification, is maintained. Layers of fifths—in part statically repeated—determine the tranquil sostenuto character of the piece.

IV. b) *Except The Lord Build The House* is set for choral background and improvisation. The choral background and the sensitive piano improvisation hold essentially to the central key, Cm. In the improvisation linear motifs alternate with impressionistically veiled sounds and blues chords. A short fourths sequence in the bass leads chromatically back again to Cm.

V. *Lord, Lord*, for solo tenor, solo baritone, "chorus and optional improvisation," is tonally bound to Fm, and begins chorale-like: "with great feeling." At the place in the text, "Lord, Lord, I felt an arrow stinging in a place so deep," series of thirds in the soprano are found moving over a calm choral underground. The initial tranquility is in one fell swoop explosively interrupted by the screaming of "Nigger—Whitey! Jew!" The section "What Will Tomorrow Bring"[123] is a fugato with an ascending theme of fifths; the soprano, tenor, alto and bass enter successively, each on the prime. "When will the ill wind change?" follows in the fashion of a tonal painting, with parallel fifths alternately in the soprano, alto, tenor and bass. "What Will Tomorrow Bring?"[124] is again resumed as a fugato, this time with diminished note values, "with growing excitement," and in the order: soprano on f, bass on e, alto on d^b, tenor on g. The place in the text "Except The Lord Build The House" seems to offer a combined—theological as well as musical—resolution of "cultural exchange." The fundamental idea of racial and folk understanding is realized musically by a contrapuntal interweaving of a blues-like baritone voice and Hebraic tenor vocal over a tranquil choral underground, Bachian in character.

VI. *Ye Shall Be Holy!*, for solo tenor, solo baritone and chorus, takes the already often used bitonal sonorities (C/G^b) up again as a static sonoric pedal-point, where they are combined with the rhythmic pedal:

In contrast to the static sonoric rhythms, the tenor and baritone move in grand melodic arcs characterized by a stepped melodic structure and chromatics. "For Ye Were Strangers In The Land Of Egypt"—a text bound *kleinmotivik* in a 3 tone area concludes Nr. VI.

VII. *Shout Unto The Lord*, for solo tenor, solo baritone, "chorus and optional improvisation," begins with a blues influenced chorus melody over triads, four-six and seventh chords, alternating in 6/4 meter. "Shout For Joy"[125] is accompanied by parallel triads. "Let Us Shout" consists of fugato heads which are connected with the parallel triads until the word "trumpet" which is profiled by a multiple layer of fourths.

The rock-jazz improvisation which now follows[126] over a 32 bar background scheme takes over the layer of fourths treating them parallel or statically. "With The Sound Of The Trumpet" is taken up by the chorus again in the style of a rock-jazz improvisation. "Thou Has Kept Us" corresponds to "Ye Shall Be Holy" at the beginning of Section VI. The high point of this section is dedicated to Martin Luther King's saying: "If we don't live together as brothers, we will die together as fools,"[127] and a concentration of the following musical elements is at hand: the solo baritone vocal in e^b dorian is combined with parallel triads in the chorus, parallel fourths in the brass and hammering fifths in the drums.

"We are living in a land of freedom" is parallel voiced until the word "free" which is bitonally anchored (E^bm/D^b). "Make Peace Not War" stands in rhythmic contrast to the extreme calmness of the preceding "Peace" section. Polymetrie—combinations of 4 and 6—is coupled with ostinato, static five-seven chords. The parallel triads appear once again at "Let Them Beat Their Swords." "Give Us Peace, Make A Joyful Noise, Shout!," in forte fortissimo with multiple layers of fourths, forms the conclusion.

VIII. *When I Behold Thy Heavens*, for solo baritone and chorus, starts with a double tone motif, g-a^b, for a horn solo. The baritone solo is influenced by blues in C, but is also chromatically varied, as is the chorus. "How Glorious Is Thy Name In All The Earth" contains an impressive coloration in the C blues for baritone vocal, and ends with pizzicato fifths in the bass.

IX. *How Glorious Is Thy Name*, for chorus, has a text-bound rhythm at its disposal:

In the chorus fugato, the entrances ensue at intervals of a fifth—G, d, a and e'—ascending from the bass over the tenor and alto to the soprano. To interpret the word "glorious," numerous offbeats coupled with repeated ninth chords are utilized:[128]

X. *The Lord Is Good,* is for solo tenor, solo baritone, chorus and optional improvisation. The admonitory double tone motif of the horn solo from Nr. VIII reappears in the bass and all of the choral voices. A dense interweavement of voices is created. "The days of thy mourning should be ended" is realized as an urgent challenge with empty, static fifths combined with hammering rhythms:

"Unto all of His beautiful people" combines, collage-like, well known folk melodies with a Bachian fugue *Thematik* (comp. Fugue II in C minor, WTK Part I). "How beautiful His people are," in the oriental "sing song style," is relieved by "Go through the Gates of Justice" in the spiritual and work song style of the Afro-American baritone singer.

XI. *His Truth Is A Shield,* for solo tenor, solo baritone, chorus and optional improvisation begins with a rock-jazz organ improvisation: "with knife and sharpening steel." The chorus is called upon to clap to the instrumental improvisation. After the rock-jazz improvisation the baritone enters in the blues style. Ostinato rhythms are connected to the sonoric pedal in the tonal sphere of the F blues scale. The following rhythmic-sonoric structure becomes manifest: a motific structure of fourths is combined with static four-six chords, and falling sphere of fourths motifs with octaved pedals. The harmonic, formal progression reveals itself in total as an enlargement of the blues scheme: 8 bars F, 4 bars Bb, 4 bars F, 2 bars C, 2 bars Bb, 4 bars Ab Ab Gb with f phrygian for the transition.

XII. *Oh, Come Let Us Sing A New Song,* for chorus, is constructed from the material of a 12-tone row: d-g-c-f-e-eb-ab-db-cb-gb-bb-a (p. 117 of the piano score):

XII. OH, COME LET US SING A NEW SONG
(Chorus)

*Adapted from
the Psalms*

DAVE BRUBECK

The linear fourth, fifth, seventh construction is taken up corresponding to sound, e.g., in "The Lord our God is righteous."[129] The chorus' 12-tone theme is later taken over by the horns. At the spot in the text "Serve The Lord," clusters are utilized: four-six and four-five chords combined with 12-tone lines in the chorus. Hammering fifths and the rhythmical "Open The Gates" citation from Nr. III end the cantata:

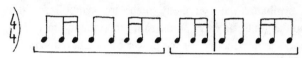

The cantata *Truth Is Fallen* was composed in 1971 in memory of the members of Kent University killed during the student revolts. "In memory of the slain students of Kent University and Mississippi State and all other innocent victims caught in the crossfire between repression and rebellion."[130] "Freedom of choice is narrowing so quickly that I sometimes feel that the sane heads, trying to solve real problems in a real way, have all been pushed on to a small island in a stormy sea of violence."[131] Participants for the recording on 30 and 31 August 1971 were:

Soprano	Charlene Peterson
Rock Group	New Heavenly Blue (led by Chris Brubeck)
Choir	St. John's Assembly (Gordon Franklin)
Piano	Dave Brubeck
Orchestra	Cincinnati Symphony Orchestra
Conductor	Erich Kunzel
Special Effects	Dave Brubeck: Oscillator
	Lowell Thompson: Bongo Drums

The première took place on 1 and 2 May 1971 with the Midland Symphony Orchestra and the Midland Music Society Chorale. There were three further performances in 1971:
- on 1 July 1971 with the Aspen Festival Orchestra and the Denver Classic Chorale, in Aspen for the opening of the Colorado Council on the Arts and Humanities,
- on 27 and 29 August 1971 with the Cincinnati Symphony Orchestra under the direction of Erich Kunzel, at Coney Island during the summer concerts.

The cantata's texts are taken, for the most part, from Isaiah, and adapted and extended by Iola and Dave Brubeck. "We wait for light, but behold obscurity".... In a time of the dissolution of firmly anchored senses of value, senseless wars—like, for example, the one in Vietnam—the one-sided build-up of the technical world...the Isaiah texts are of urgent actuality.

The substance of the cantata, "Truth is fallen in the street and equity cannot enter," summarizes the personal shock and dismay of Brubeck in light of the inordinate brutalities of our times, like the murder of J.F. Kennedy or the slaying of the students of Kent and Jackson Universities. The musical reasons for the cantata's sonoric set-up were highly symbolic: the symphony orchestra symbolizes "the establishment," the rock group the youth, an extra percussion group the military. The organ, realizing a baroque choral style symbolic for the power of the church, can act in place of the orchestra. The rock group is supposed to improvise freely and encompass a variable spectrum of popular styles corresponding to a campus scene. A series of electronic instruments (e-bass, e-piano) and special effects (hummer, oscillator, siren, wa-wa) comes mainly out of a rock group's possibilities of realization.

I. The prelude for rock group can be played as written or improvised. On the album at hand, the prelude is improvised by the rock group New Heavenly Blue. The group is led by Chris Brubeck, one of Dave Brubeck's sons, who plays trombone and e-bass. Rock group and orchestra maintain their respective identities during their interactions. The military drums symbolize war and destruction. The young and old generations recognize in the chaotic sounds violence and the disunity between nations and cultures, races and religions.

Fundamental to the whole cantata is the descending 12-tone scale:

which is played in unison by rock group and orchestra. The oscillator is utilized cyclically in the style of Terry Riley; flutes and violins make their entrance in a country-western style. The horns, especially the trombones, connect themselves to the harmonica. Now, the 12-tone series is resounding unisonically in the horns. A section of hard rock rhythms in ostinato follows; then comes a solo piano improvisation. The 12-tone series is then taken up by the symphony orchestra in conjunction with the military drums. A chaotic struggle develops through a sonoric and dynamic intensification. The trombone solo utilizes the central d^b - c interval, a Major seventh. The transition to Nr. II follows.

II. *Merciful Men Are Taken Away*, for solo soprano, is reminiscent of Cassandra's mission in Troy. The soprano soloist appears as a visionary, seeing right through the turbulences of war and confusion to reality: "The righteous perisheth and no man layeth it to heart." Yet she has trust in the ability of mankind to find truth and with it to persevere. Over a thrifty sonoric basis, bound mainly to a A$^{b9\#}$ chord, the 12-tone series appears in inversion and differently rhythmicized:

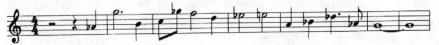

The harp occasionally underlines the sensitive sonoric character of the piece with "tender" glissandos.

III. *Truth Is Fallen*, for chorus and solo soprano, is the core of the cantata. The oscillator, sounding like a police siren, leads from Nr. II to Nr. III. Violin glissandos and e-viola create the effect of fluctuation. Fifth, seventh and ninth intervals play a determinant role for the sound of the chorus. "We wait," statically construed in a narrow area, is rhythmically urgent and at the same time monotonous.[132] The fugue "Truth Is Fallen"[133] again makes use of the 12-tone scale in the succession of voices: tenor - alto - soprano - bass. The voicings are compressed immediately thereafter in the same order of succession. The descending course taken by the voices is to be seen symbolically. A musical rending asunder of the American national anthem follows, with jerk-like, "brutal" orchestral percussion syncopations.[134] The hymn is played by the strings and trombones, as rock and symphonically, with the intense involvement of all groups! Representing the hymn musically is the "intact" world of triads. The counter sonorities are sharply accented rhythmically. "Destructive" dissonances, constructed from tones out of the 12-tone series, are combined with blocks of sound from the organ, woodwinds and brass. Following the "destruction" of the national anthem, a "free and wild"[135] improvisation takes place. The 12-tone fugue is again taken up: "sprightly, macabre," sharp staccato—and, in a doubly raised tempo, has the effect of a caricature of the original fugue. The piece concludes "choraliter-espressivo" with the descending, "despairing" 4-note soprano motif:

IV. *Oh, That My Head Were Waters*, for solo soprano, is a pianissimo-espressivo piece. Modified anew, the 12-tone series is taken by the soprano and combined with clusters from the rock group and orchestra.

V. *Speak Out* was composed for chorus, rock group, solo rock vocalist and solo soprano. Through a rhythmical speaking without a definite pitch, the truth is to be expressed. Intended is the idea of a "rational humanism." The young generation is divided between militant revolutionaries: "We're breaking down the walls"—and visionary idealists: "We've got to live together peacefully." The two opposing

notions correspond closely to the respective conceptions of the Black Power and Black Panther proponents:
- Malcolm X, Eldridge Cleaver, Stokley Carmichael, on the one hand, and the passive resistance ideas of
- Martin Luther King Jr., on the other.
"Yeah, yeah, yeah, we're breaking down the walls" is in a markedly bluesy rock style. The keyboard, lead guitar and e-bass play a forceful ostinato. A constant change of meter between 3 and 4 and numerous offbeats illustrate the urgent demand. The second "idealistic" rock group tries to placate the militant spirit of rock group number one: "We've got to live together peacefully." "Jefferson and Lincoln wrote the words to our song"—Over a calm Am—D^7 exchange, the text is, unchanging, steadily repeated. The simple rhythmic motif:

♪ 𝄾 𝄾 ♪

is intended to confirm this conviction. Through a gradual sound texture compression[136] in the instruments, diverse sonoric phenomena become interconnected:
- the ostinati of rock group nr. 1,
- parallel triads in the organ and keyboard,
- glissandos in thirds from the horns and whole orchestra with a constant metric change between 3 and 4. The free improvisation begins with the piano and drums with other instruments gradually being added. At 8 bar intervals, the harmonica, guitar, violins, piano, bass and other rock instruments successively fill out the sonoric-textural structure. By this compositional principle is a wide sonoric diversity and orchestral compression created. The revolutionary rock group once again briefly strikes up "We're breaking down the walls" with "machine gun" and "rim shots." The conclusion is formed by a combination of a blues vocal and classical soprano solo. The blues text reads: "I called and no one answered, I cried and no one came." The blues is intoned very expressively with an extensive use of blue notes.

The classical soprano sings: "The harvest passed, the summer is ended and we are not saved"—with a phrygian influence accompanied by e-bass and contra bass playing empty fifths: "slow and sad."

VI. *Yea, Truth Faileth*, for chorus, is executed "choraliter" with a step-wise melodic development and a calm *Isorhythmik*. Numerous alterations lead to 12 tonality. Linear countermovement, seventh and ninth chords determine the choral structure.

VII. *Truth*, for chorus, rock group and rock vocal duo, is composed over a far reaching "planet" motif: f - c' - g" - a^b - g": "Planets Are Spinning." The movement is a filigree of complementary voicings, mosaic-like in fashion. Texturally conspicuous are the chromatic, fourth chord triplet glissandos in the woodwinds; they give the effect of briskness to the planetary goings-on. The fundamental 12-tone series is instituted again and again. The orchestra and rock group unite in parallel, chromatically ascending, coupled layers of fourths:

VIII. *Is The Lord's Hand Shortened?*, for soprano solo, again utilizes the 12-tone series over "genderless," reposing sonorities in the rock group and orchestra. Stagnating blocked seventh chords over E^b follow "like a dividing wall" in the compact sonoric combination of organ, rock group, trombone. "Your iniquities have separated between you and your God. Your sins have hid His Face from you and He will not hear" is realized, above all, through parallel triads directed step-wise downward, and then parallel Major seventh chords—D^b, C, Bm, B^{b}m, A^b, G^{7j}, F^{7j}, E^{b7j}—directed step-wise downward, thereby accentuating the impression of separation.

IX. "Arise," for chorus, soprano solo and rock group, closes the cantata *Truth Is Fallen*. It is filled with violence and sadness about violence. The last piece is intended to make a cheerful recovery possible. "We wait, we wait, we wait" is taken from the core piece Nr. III, "Truth Is Fallen," and coupled with an urgent two tone motif, g - a^b. For the text "For we are in desolate places," an attempt at a last ditch stand is undertaken: lines full of vitality proceed chromatically up and down in countermovement. Woven into the sound of the symphony orchestra is again the 12-tone series—diminished, melodically and rhythmically varied, fragmented and inverted. "And the glory of the Lord" is a chorale in G^b with numerous alterations and fragmentations of the 12-tone series. "For ye shall go out with joy and be led forth with peace" represents the finale.[137] Powerful fortissimo triads "tread" chromatically upwards to the final chord in D^b on the word "Peace." Fragments of the 12-tone series combined with triplet variations:

reinforce the impression of musical density and intensity.

In December 1975 the world première of the festival *La Fiesta De La Posada* (A Christmas Choral Pageant) took place in Honolulu. The cantata was composed for solo soprano, -tenor, -baritone, and -bass, children's voices (unison), mixed chorus and piano, 2 guitars, 2 trumpets, bass and percussion.

"La Posada" (The Inn) is an old Latin American custom which is also encountered in the American South West. It deals with the biblical story of Joseph and Mary's search for lodgings shortly before the birth of Christ. In Mexico, religious and profane traditions are amalgamated with one another. Children play an important role in the torch and lantern processions of the "posada." The participants of the procession sing litanies and knock here and there on doors where they receive the answer, "There is no room!" Subsequently the procession reaches the church where the doors are opened wide and Maria is elevated to her position as celebrated central figure. Numerous guests kneel in front of the manger. The Christchild is greeted on earth. Finally the piñata, a figure full of color and symbolism in the form of a pine cone, is brought in and hung over the heads of the children. Some young people break it open whereupon sweets and small gifts fall down on the children.

Dave Brubeck stresses the fact that he has had contact with Mexican folk music since his childhood. He has a special admiration for the religious and group feeling of the Mexicans. In the cantata *La Fiesta De La Posada* he tries to convey musically this atmosphere of collective partnership.

The cantata comprises 15 sections and begins with a "Prelude":

1. *La Posada* (manger setting, instrumental)
2. *Processional* (chorus)
3. *In The Beginning* (solo soprano and chorus)
4. *Where Is He?* (solo soprano, -tenor, -baritone, -bass, and chorus)
5. *Gloria* (solo soprano and chorus)
6. *We Have Come To See The Son Of God* (solo tenor, -baritone, -bass, and chorus)
7. *Behold! The Holy One* (chorus and children's choir)
8. *Run, Run, Run* (chorus)
9. *Gold, Frankincense And Myrrh* (solo tenor, -baritone and -bass)
10. *My Soul Magnifies The Lord* (Mary, soprano solo)
11. *Sleep, Holy Infant, Sleep* (chorus)
12. *In The Beginning* (Mary, three wise men and chorus)
13. *Neither Death Nor Life* (tutti)
14. *God's Love Made Visible* (tutti)
15. *La Piñata* (instrumental)

The cantata's musical elements are folksy and simple. Rhythmically, triplets, continuous eighth notes, even quarter notes and an occasional sextuplet appear. The different rhythms remain constant in their allotted section—3/4, 6/8, 4/4, 2/4—and remain bound syllabically to the text. *Behold The Holy One* is in an uneven 7/4 meter. Melodically, as a rule, singable, step-wise diatonically composed themes are used. *In The Beginning* is, by the way, pretty much 12-tone in arrangement. With respect to interval and harmony, parallel thirds and sixths, occasional seventh and ninth chords or clusters are encountered; for the most part, tonality predominates. The forms are symmetrical and distinct. The sonoric textures providing a Mexican atmosphere are: trumpets, guitars, claves, Maracas, wood block, castanets. Versions of the cantata for Mariachi orchestra or symphony orchestra were also made.

The cantata *The Voice Of The Holy Spirit - Tongues Of Fire* from 1985 is Dave Brubeck's eighth spiritual work.

The texts rest on the dramatic Pentecostal reports as portrayed in the stories of the apostles. The Spirit of God descends to the earth from heaven in the form of tongues of fire and roaring winds. The cantata was composed in 1985 in commemoration of Johann Sebastian Bach's 300th birthday. From a musical perspective, each of the cantata's voices, instrumental or vocal, represents the Holy Ghost which invests unstructured sound with harmony and order. Philosophy and language are taken from the bible text. The baritone sings words from Jesus, Peter, Paul or the prophet Joel. In alternation with the baritone, the chorus occasionally takes a central role. The Wonders of God are represented in many languages, as was the case then in Jerusalem. The confusion and apartheid of the Tower of Babylon situation is renewed. The description of God's Wonders is built on a text from John, chapter 3, verse 16: "For God so loved the world."

The cantata comprises the following sections:

1. "Preface: I will ask the Father and He will give you another counsellor to be with you forever...the spirit of truth!" This is a tranquil, tonally free baritone solo over a piano background of pianissimo tremoloed clusters.

2. "Full Authority" is represented by a four voiced choral fugue with a flowing rhythm in c minor with real (i.e. tone for tone, interval for interval) reply: "The eleven disciples went into Galilee."

3. "Witnesses" rests on "unwieldy" fourth-fifth leaps and parallel fourth-fifth-octave sonorities to the text: "The former treatise I have made."

4. "Pentecost" resumes the fugue from Nr. 2 and modifies it, especially where the text reads "...and suddenly there came a sound from heaven as of a rushing mighty wind," with Gm^7, offbeat, chord whacks, and extended trills—and where it reads "After that the Holy Ghost will come upon you...Tongues of Fire," with chromatically ascending $7^{5\#}$ chords.

5. In "Tongues of Fire" the following languages are utilized for the text from John: Libyan-Mysterioso

Det Ja————Ra   Mes - en   Eh

Libyan, Coptic, Old Arabic, Hebrew, Ancient Greek, Sahidic Coptic, Armenian, Latin and Aramaic. The respective lingual rhythm determines the melodic unfolding of the recitation. The organ accompaniment is precise, transparent, frequently defined by parallel fifths or repetitions, especially in the Aramaic section.

6. "New Wine," beginning bitonally (E^{13}/B^{b7}), is a fierce, strongly accented piece in fortissimo.

7. "Peter's Sermon" is convincing as a tranquil, suspended section with an octaved pedal-point on E:

with a mixolydian touch. "Then Peter stood up with the Eleven...these men are not drunk as you suppose—No!!" The negation is fixed by a forte-fortissimo declamation with cluster-pedal-point reinforcement.

8. "My Children" provides contrast by way of its baritone solo in a calm 3/4 meter with a chorale-like melody:

The organ accompanies in a tripletted, *klein*motific manner:

9. "Silver and Gold" depicts the healing of a cripple by Peter in the name of Jesus. Baritone solo and chorus unite in a praise to God: "All the people ran together unto them in the porch"; repeated and parallel fourth-fifth sonorities convey the impression of convincing power.

10. "Greater Gifts": "You must know that your body is a temple of the Holy Spirit"—starts with a baritone solo and piano accompaniment in the style of a Bach chorale. The chorus enters with "There are different gifts" in a Bachian dialogue with the baritone. A strong rhythmic differentiation is achieved through an extensive utilization of triplets:

11. "Though I Speak With The Tongues Of Men And Of Angels" is composed like a Bach chorale. "Love suffereth long, love is kind" in 5/4 Meter: "slow lyrically"—is language bound, "gently," arranged step-wise over triads.
12. "When I Was A Child" has the character of a children's song. Major thirds alternate in a 6/8 rhythm.
13. "For Those Who Love God" is a lightly swinging baritone solo in 3/4 with a simple sixth accompaniment over a resting F pedal:

14. "Be Strong In The Lord." Bach chorales have again served as a model.
15. "Benediction" as well, is influenced by the Bachian chorale technique. The bass line progresses for the most part chromatically.

The composition *To Hope: A Mass For A New Decade* was completed in 1980. As Dave Brubeck told me during my 1980 stay in Wilton, Connecticut, *To Hope* is a composition he was commissioned to do for "Our Sunday Visitor, Inc." The community—the congregation—should be able to spontaneously sing along with it, namely, the voicings—at least for the congregation, and consequently for the chorus and orchestra, too—should be very simple. The improvisations of the jazz quartet form a stylistic and soloistic contrast to the chorus and orchestra. At the performance in Providence, Rhode Island the congregation consisted mostly of Catholic church musicians who had come to Providence from all over America for their annual convention. Brubeck was nevertheless of the opinion that "Alleluia" in 5/4 meter could best be sung by a student chorus. The difficulty of the whole composition lay in developing a musically simple yet impressive mass. Extended liturgical and Gregorian studies with his brother Howard Brubeck had preceded the composition of the mass. Fundamental to these studies was the "Liber Usualis."[138] The second performance of the mass took place on 24 April 1980 at St. Peter's and Paul's Cathedral in Providence, Rhode Island; the première was in Philadelphia. The participants in Providence were:
The Peloquin Chorale
The University Chorale of Boston College (Direction: Dr. Alexander Peloquin)
The Brown University Chamber Singers (Direction: William Ermey)
The Dave Brubeck Quartet:

Dave Brubeck, piano; Chris Brubeck, bass;
Jerry Bergonzi, tenor saxophone; Randy Jones, drums
Cantors: Laetitia Blain, Lucien Olivier
Priest Celebrant: Rev. Enrico Garzilli
Reader: Christine Kavanagh
Organ/piano - accompaniment
Celeste
Orchestra
Congregation
Text from the Roman ritual with selected text by Iola Brubeck.

"The heart of the mass is found in the words themselves, living language full of deep meaning, born from the very human need to know God. ...hoping to translate into music the powerful words which have grown through the centuries.... Emotions that are life, from sorrow to exaltation, were part of my experience in writing `To Hope.' When the work was completed, I felt a strong sense of wholeness and affirmation. I pray that those who experience the work will share my feelings."[139]

To Hope can be looked upon and performed as a liturgical as well as concert work. For an abridged concert version with glockenspiel, piano or organ passages, Brubeck suggests the following pieces: "Lord Have Mercy," "The Desert And The Parched Land," "Alleluia," "Holy, Holy, Holy," "Lamb Of God," "All My Hope" and "Gloria."

The newspaper company "Our Sunday Visitor, Inc.," which commissioned the mass, did not expect any close association with Catholic mass liturgy; and the end product was a mixture of Latin and Greek, Middle Eastern and Middle European, American and Spanish liturgies, i.e. musical forms. This mixture is typical for American Christians, and again corresponds to the idea of cultural exchange.

The mass *To Hope* offers a fill of concert material for the most varied of formations, depending on requirement or feasibility.

The unabridged version of the mass *To Hope* consists of 15 sections:
1.   "Processional"
2.   "Lord Have Mercy" (Kyrie)
3.   "The Desert And The Parched Land" (Isaiah 35, 1-4)
4.   "The Peace Of Jerusalem" (Responsorial)
5.   "Alleluia" (Gospel Acclamation)
6.   "Father All Powerful" (Preface)
7.   "Holy, Holy, Holy"
8.   "While He Was At Supper" (Institutional Narrative)
9.   "When We Eat This Bread" (Memorial Acclamation)
10. "Through Him With Him" (Doxology)

11. "Great Amen"
12. "Our Father" (and Doxology)
13. "Lamb Of God"
14. "All My Hope"
15. "Gloria"

Following "Lord Have Mercy," "The Peace Of Jerusalem," "Alleluia," and "Gloria" are jazz quartet improvisations on the material of the respective pieces.

"Lord Have Mercy," the kyrie of the mass *To Hope*, begins with an exchange of responsory calls between the soloists and congregation (b. 1-9) in English and, subsequently, Greek. The thrice repeated exclamation: "Lord, Christ, Lord"—follows the Greek kyrie. The voices are treated recitatively, repeating on one note which descends a half step chromatically from b to b♭, from a to a♭, and from g to g♭.

The harmonic structure follows the step-wise downwards moving *Melodik* with triad related chords from the organ: Bm - Gm, Am - Fm, Gm - E♭m. The VIth degree, on the fourth bar in each case, provides a "sensitive," deceptive cadence-like effect of alienation. In bars 2, 4 and 6 the same harmonic progression resounds, octaved and having an echo effect through the doubling, and thereby intensification, of the call. The celeste plays just in the bass position: a sensitive, ascending line which is interrupted in each case by a full bar pause, thereby leaving room for the echo of the organ and the call of the congregation. The last three bars strive melodically upward in a vigorous mezzo forte using the following sonorities and countermovement of the left hand and organ pedal: G♭ - G♭7 - F♭7 - G♭ - C♭ - G♭ - A♭m - G♭7 - C♭. This provides room for a liturgical conclusion.

After the exchange between the soloistic and congregational calls, the chorus enters. The material from the first section is used in condensed form—the responsorial vocal exchange is omitted. The plea becomes more intense through the simultaneous entreaties of the soloists, congregation and chorus. The alto voice forms a *kleinmotivisch* contrast to the remaining voices: a half tone—whole tone exchange as well as use of the augmented seconds, c♯ - b♭, b - a♭, which convey an "oriental" impression. This section closes with a unison ending.

The next four bars contain a transposition of the voices of the soloists, chorus and organ in intervals of a fifth from b to e. The bass takes over the *kleinmotivisch* material of the alto voice, and the alto extends its melodic tonal sphere with the text "Christe Eleison" to a fourth. Also, the rhythmic formula:

is extended to

♩. ♪

The next section, "Lord Have Mercy," resounds again in the chord progression emanating from Bm. A further compression of the material takes effect: the *kleinmotivisch*, "orientalizing" line is now taken over, after alto and bass, by the tenor; the bass takes over the augmentational alto voice, the alto receives a new voice which moves evenly between the other rhythms, step-wise, diatonically:

♩♩ ♩ ♩♩ ♪ ♪

The organ voices, as well, become denser and more intense, especially through octavation in the left hand and pedal.

The renewed English "Christ Have Mercy," combined with the Greek "Christe Eleison," is again in Em. The whole chorus is now engaged at full volume, and, again, the previous voice material is utilized—the soprano now takes over the "*kleinmotivisch*" line that had previously emerged in the alto, bass and tenor; the alto gets a new voice characterized by fourths and tonal repetitions.

The conclusion and climax—fortissimo—is formed by the Greek exclamation "Kyrie Eleison" in all the voices, that is to say, 2 soloists, congregation, and the whole chorus sing together. Numerous octavations reinforce the impression of a powerful call. The voice leading progresses parallel, this time diatonically upwards, from C, over $D^{7/9}$ to Em.

Graphic Representation of the Vocal Leading and Motif Construction in the Mass Section:
Lord Have Mercy (Kyrie Eleison)

Measures 1-9
(reduced scale)
2 Soloists
(reduced
"wave motif")
Congregation

Measures 10-13
2 Soloists and
Congregation

Chorus: Alto

Measures 14-17
2 Soloists and
Congregation

Chorus: Alto

             Bass

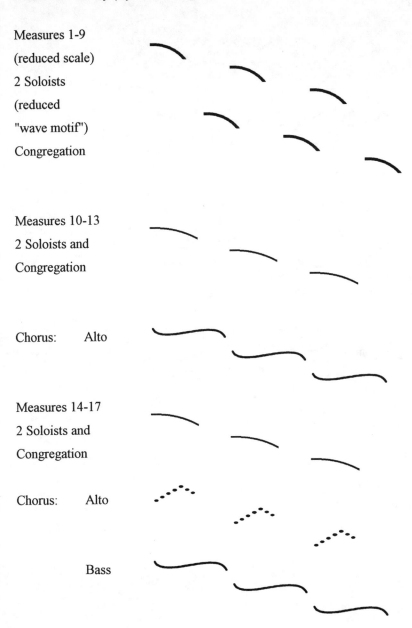

Measures 18-21
2 Soloists and
Congregation

Chorus: Alto

            Tenor

            Bass

Measures 22-25
2 Soloists and
Congregation

Chorus: Soprano

            Alto

            Tenor

            Bass

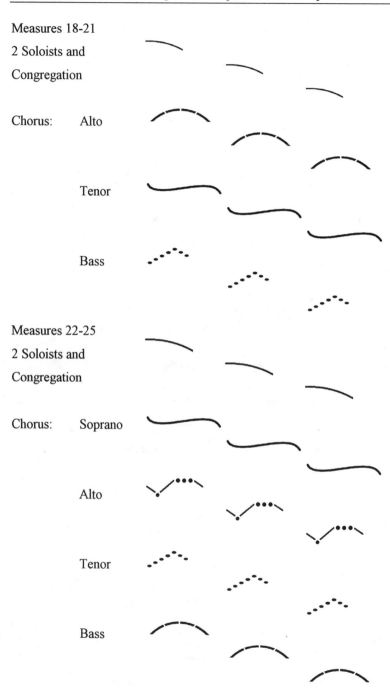

Commentary:

1. "Wave Motif"

 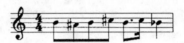

2. Dotted Third-Fourth Motif

3. "Arc Motif"

4. Repeated Fourths Motif

While the soloists and congregation provide contrast by holding fast to their repeated original motif, the motifs in the choral voices change systematically from the alto to other voices in the following manner:
- the "wave motif" wanders from alto to bass, to tenor, to soprano
- the dotted third-fourth motif from alto to bass, to tenor
- the "arc motif" from alto to bass
- the repeated fourth motif appears in the alto only.
Motifs 1 and 3 as well as 2 and 4 display, in their linear direction, an associative relationship. The "wave motif" wanders with consequence through all of the voices. The remaining motifs follow in the same sequence with a reduction in choral entrances. Later, they no longer appear in every voice. The gradual compression of the linear material is brought about by the entry of more and more choral voices, and is combined with an instrumental sonoric doubling in the organ, forming thereby a contrast to the continuous, simple initial motif of the soloists.

*   *   *

Notes

Chapter 2

1 Dan Morgenstern Interview, "Downbeat," May 25, 1972
2 Reminiscences Of The Cattle Country
3 op.cit.
4 Stuckenschmidt, p.208
5 Wilton
6 ibid
7 Hellhund, p.248
8 Polillo, p.190
9 Hellhund, p.254
10 Ralph Gleason in "Downbeat," September 5, 1957
11 Letter of Iola Brubeck, November 11, 1988
12 New York, Wilton
13 Shapiro, p.402-403
14 Spellman, p.61
15 comp. LP: Brubeck On Campus
16 Mehegan, p.128 ff
17 Billy Taylor, p.107
18 comp. LP: Brubeck Plays Brubeck
19 comp. LP: The Dave Brubeck Quartet At Carnegie Hall
20 comp. ibid
21 comp. LP: Tritonis
22 Wilton
23 Dennis Roosevelt's Expedition into the Belgian Congo, Commodore DL 30 005
24 Wilton
25 "Jazzforschung" 20, pp. 147-148
26 Horricks, p. 233
27 Wilton
28 Feather, p. 213
29 comp. LP: Jazz Impressions Of New York
30 comp. LP: Countdown-Time In Outer Space
31 comp. LP: Brubeck Time
32 ibid
33 comp. Countdown synopsis
34 comp. LP: Time Out
35 Burghausen
36 comp. LP: Time Further Out-Miró Reflections
37 ibid
38 ibid
39 comp. LP: Countdown-Time In Outer Space
40 comp. A.M. Dauer in "Jazzforschung" 20, p. 117 and p. 147 ff
41 comp. LP: Countdown-Time In Outer Space
42 comp. LP: Time In
43 Burghausen
44 see: "The New Grove Dictionary Of Jazz"
45 Brubeck on Brubeck in piano transcriptions of Time Out and Time Further Out-Miró
   Reflections
46 Burghausen
47 New York
48 San Diego
49 comp. LP: Brubeck Plays Brubeck
50 Wilton
51 comp. Horricks, p. 223ff
52 comp. LP: Brubeck Plays Brubeck
53 comp. LP: The Dave Brubeck Quartet At Carnegie Hall
54 comp. LP: Jazz Red Hot And Cool

55 comp. LP: Brubeck On Campus
56 Spellman, p.61
57 New York
58 comp. LP: Brubeck On Campus
59 comp. LP: Jazz Impressions Of Eurasia
60 comp. LP: Time In
61 comp. romantic piano pieces and Debussy's "Préludes"
62 Cecil Taylor in Spellman, p. 61
63 Shapiro, p. 251
64 Wilton
65 Shapiro, p. 394
66 Shapiro, p. 393
67 New York
68 Shapiro, p. 394
69 Wilton
70 Dan Morgenstern interview in "Downbeat," May 25, 1972, p. 32
71 comp. LP: Bravo! Brubeck!
72 Cologne
73 comp. LP: Bossa Nova U.S.A.
74 New York
75 New York and Newsletter, Spring 1987
76 Birger Sulsbrück, p. 151 and 160; also Gerhard Kubik, p.121ff
77 The New Grove Dictionary of Jazz
78 Birger Sulsbrück, p. 160
79 comp. Brubeck on Bossa Nova U.S.A.
80 comp. the tango rhythm
81 comp. piano transcriptions of Jazz Impressions of Eurasia
82 ibid
83 ibid
84 comp. also Le Souk on Jazz Goes to College
85 comp. LP: Summit Sessions
86 comp. LP: Jazz Impressions of Japan
87 comp. Debussy's Pagodes from Estampes
88 comp. Little Pictures of Japan, edited by Olive Beaupre Miller, Chicago, 1925
89 comp. Haiku Translations of Basho, Issa and Buson in "An Introduction to Haiku," Harold
     G. Henderson, Doubleday Anchor Books, 1958, Garden City, New York
90 comp. LP: Jazz Impressions of Japan
91 comp. Little Pictures of Japan
92 comp. Haiku Translations
93 comp. Debussy: Préludes I, 1: Danseuses de Delphes
94 comp. LP: Jazz Impressions of Japan
95 ibid
96 comp. Haiku Translations
97 comp. LP: Brubeck On Campus, 1972
98 a letter to the authoress from 4-19-1978—Piston's book contains musical analyses.
99 comp. itinerary for the DBQ '86-'87
100 comp. correspondence with Dave Brubeck
101 letter from the Bavarian Minister of Education and Culture, Hans Maier, Munich, dated 3-2-
     84
102 Shapiro, p. 394
103 comp. LP: The New Brubeck Quartet Live At Montreux
104 comp. LP: Brubeck Plays Brubeck
105 ibid
106 comp. LP: Points on Jazz
107 San Diego
108 comp. LP: Bernstein Plays Brubeck Plays Bernstein
109 comp. the piano scores of The Real Ambassadors
110 ibid
111 ibid

112 ibid
113 comp. LP: The Light In The Wilderness
114 ibid
115 ibid
116 ibid
117 comp. LP: The Gates of Justice
118 see Section VII of the cantata
119 I was able to attend a performance on April 27th, 1980 in Bridgeport, Connecticut
120 comp.piano score - The Gates of Justice, p. 29
121 ibid p. 30
122 ibid p. 21 and p. 37
123 ibid p. 52
124 ibid p. 55
125 ibid p. 65
126 ibid p. 67
127 ibid p. 75-76
128 ibid p. 92
129 ibid p. 120
130 comp. score to Truth Is Fallen
131 comp. LP: Truth Is Fallen
132 comp. the score to Truth Is Fallen, p. 32
133 ibid p. 41
134 comp. Jimi Hendrix's performance at Woodstock, 1969
135 comp. score of Truth Is Fallen, p. 45
136 comp. ibid, p. 63ff
137 comp. ibid, p. 122-124
138 San Diego
139 Dave Brubeck in the piano score of the mass To Hope

Chapter 3

Critical Evaluation and Classification

The idea of *cultural exchange* is the basic concept underlying Brubeck's music and philosophy of life. Dave Brubeck sees his roots as being in the classical music of America, jazz. He has also, however, studied European composition techniques and counterpoint with Milhaud, and in the course of his numerous world wide concert tours he has incorporated musical "impressions" of Europe, Asia, Latin America and Japan into his music. This does not happen in a musicologically exact manner, but rather in the form of collages, reminiscences, adaptations, fusions, mosaic-like in character. And it is for this reason that Brubeck's style is not to be pinned down—it derives its being from diversity and variety.

Brubeck is convinced that the sonorities and modes of the various world musical cultures are very different from one another and stand in need of thorough study, but that the diverse rhythms, because of their basic pulsations, instinctively and emotionally affect all people. Rhythm is the common denominator and spontaneous connecting factor of all musical languages which enables the musical understanding of foreign musical cultures. This could well be the reason for his occupation with so-called "time experiments" or with various meters.

His deep religious-humanitarian attitude—which is almost like a call to "missionize," to want to mediate between nations and races—provides an ideal motivation. This is especially the case in the lengthlier compositions like, for example, the musical *The Real Ambassadors*, the oratorio *The Light In The Wilderness*, the cantatas like *The Gates Of Justice* and *Truth Is Fallen*, and the mass *To Hope*.

On the occasion of his first tour of the Soviet Union in 1987 Dave Brubeck indicated the idea of cultural exchange as being his best, musical "weapon" for peace. He casts in his lot with the struggle of Martin Luther King for inter-cultural understanding through non-violent resistance, in the sense of a world wide brotherhood. Musically, this idea corresponds to a diversity and plurality of styles of as many cultures as possible. "My style is the summation of all experience to which I have been exposed."[1]

The plurality of styles used in Brubeck's music can only be realized at the cost of intensity and exactness. Whether complex rhythmic structures can be experienced instinctively needs to be proved through extensive, empirical research into receptivity. Brubeck handles his improvisations spontaneously, intuitively, auditively; his European, Asian, Latin American, Turkish, Japanese and Gregorian "impressions" are just that—musical impressions, not authentic compositions or musicologically grounded constructions.

Brubeck also rejects categorization in any one style or the other: "I prefer what's going on now, which is a summation, because when I first started playing, people classified me as West Coast School, and I didn't believe we were West Coast School or Cool. I don't think that has anything to do with it. I just listened to some of my old recordings, and they sound hot, swinging—and they call me cool. I will never know why!"[2]—Presumably, the numerous contrapuntal experiments from the octet and early trio and quartet periods led the critics to believe Brubeck's music to be chamber musical cool jazz. *Look For The Silver Lining*, one of the first quartet recordings, is indicated by Brubeck as being exceptionally "hot."

Already in 1956, from reactions to his diverse, pluralistic, not always jazzy enough style, does Brubeck come to a realization: "I am aware that I have become a controversial figure in jazz. In the course of one concert tour I can read such contradictory critical comments as cerebral-emotional—delicate well constructed lines—pile driver approach—technically facile—chaotic pounding—contributor to jazz—defiler of jazz—this is jazz??? No style—except the style of the idea performed."[3]

Fats Waller influenced especially the early years of Dave Brubeck's musical development: "I went to Ellington and to Fats Waller. Waller was my favorite influence when I was a kid. The first record I ever bought was `There's Honey On The Moon Tonight.'"[4]

George Wein, longtime organizer of the Newport Jazz Festival, considers Brubeck's "mainstream jazz" effective and successful: "Whenever we need to break new ground for jazz, Dave Brubeck is the first man we put in the programme."[5] The well-known jazz writer Leonard Feather stresses the contrary nature in Brubeck's musical personality structure, but recognizes as well that he has exercised a great influence, not only as a pianist, but as a composer, too: "Dave Brubeck, a controversial figure, has been accused of `senile romanticism,' but has also been called by the distinguished British pianist-composer Steve Race `the most uniquely significant jazzman of our time.' Though his touch seems very heavy at times, he is capable of building solos to a pitch of climactic excitement. Whether he swings or not has been angrily debated. Certainly he is an accomplished pianist and composer and has exerted a powerful influence."[6]

The positive views of the trend setting free jazz pianist Cecil Taylor about Brubeck were to take an about turn with the passing of time: "When Brubeck opened in 1951 in New York I was very impressed with the depth and texture of his harmony which had more notes in than anyone else's that I had ever heard. It also had a rhythmical movement that I found exciting. I went over and told him what I had heard, and he was amazed that anyone could see what he was doing...I was digging Stravinsky and Brubeck had been studying with Milhaud."[7]

Cecil Taylor aptly recognized that Brubeck represented a sort of stylistic "counterpart" to Lenny Tristano. With Brubeck the sonoric structure is more developed, with Tristano the linear texture. "Brubeck was the other half of Tristano; Tristano had the line thing and Brubeck had the harmonic density that I was looking for, and that gave a balance."[8]—Later, Taylor heard Horace Silver, Charlie Parker, Percy Heath and Milt Jackson, whose music seemed, to him, incomparably better: "...and I noticed Brubeck imitating Horace. Then came Bird with Percy and Milt and man, like they demolished Brubeck for me. And it ended my emotional involvement with his music and my intellectual involvement too."[9]

Charlie Parker, on the other hand, commented positively about Brubeck's music. Parker spoke of the awareness in Brubeck's jazz: "He's a perfectionist—he knows what he wants to do, which is a lot more than a lot of the other guys, the followers, do."[10]

Incidents of both—awareness and originality—can be furnished extensively in the music of Brubeck. He gives instructive hints and revealing explanations concerning his music again and again on the album covers or in the forewords to the piano transcriptions (note the *Brubeck Plays Brubeck* album piano solos); for example, with regard to the connection between classical music and jazz in his music: "...if by this phrase it is meant that I employ certain classical composition techniques in arranging or within improvisations, it is true." His clear-sighted discussions of creativity, improvisation and composition, too, bear witness that he belongs to that cadre of jazz musicians who reflect on what they produce. Creativity, for him, embraces three categories of value: improvisation from the subconscious, the playing of patterns, and the playing of repertoire.

The influence of Art Tatum on Brubeck must have been quite singular. No one in the whole jazz scene had this exceptional significance for him. Especially fascinating to Brubeck was the complexity of Tatum's harmonies: "To me he was the closest to being the complete expression of music. In '38 when I first heard Tatum there was no Big Band putting out such complex harmonies. There was no Big

Band, no small band, playing the tempos he was playing. He was everything. He had the whole thing locked up. There's just nothing in the complete jazz experience that can equal what Art Tatum was to me. I have never known a pianist I respected who didn't think that Tatum was the boss."[11]

Brubeck seems to have a particular fondness for Duke Ellington, too. His performance at Newport in 1958 was a tribute to him. Of the 7 pieces that he played, 5 were from or for Ellington: "Things Ain't What They Used To Be," "Jump For Joy," "Liberian Suite (Dance No. 3)," "C Jam Blues" (with a "Take The A-Train" closing): "...for Dave not only respects Ellington and understands him as few musicians do, he seems to parallel Duke in many ways. I find in his attitude toward music, his performance and composition of jazz, many points that remind me of Duke...for both Dave and Duke have little interest in doing what has already been done well. This is the attitude that compels progress."[12]—In 1980, during my interview in Wilton with Dave Brubeck, he stressed: "He always helped me and wanted me to be a Duke Ellington fellow."

His encounter with the avant garde precipitates especially in the later compositions. The completely written out piece *The Duke*, which utilizes an incomplete 12-tone scale, attempts to span a bridge between jazz and avant garde. The original title reads: *The Duke Meets Darius Milhaud And Arnold Schönberg*. Brubeck had received instruction for a long time from Milhaud—instruction with Schönberg had been terminated after the second lesson.[13]

Brubeck emphasizes that, besides the African influence in jazz today, the importance of the influence of contemporary composers—Bartok, Stravinsky, Milhaud—must also be given its due.[14] Milhaud's influence was of course especially pronounced, as Brubeck was his student for some years. "It was Milhaud who reinforced me in my desire to play jazz. He was of the opinion that jazz was an expression of the American culture. He thought that a musician born in America should be influenced by jazz. Every time he stood in front of a new class at the beginning of the semester, his first question was—`Which of you is a jazz musician?'"[15]—The combining of jazz and 12-tone music by Brubeck is achieved especially in the 1971 cantata *Truth Is Fallen*. At the beginning of the sixties he was still maintaining a cautious position regarding the combining of jazz and 12-tone techniques: "Yes, there is a possibility to create jazz based on the 12-tone scale, but I won't be the man to work in that direction. However, if I were to completely master the language of 12-tone music, I would possibly make use of it. As it is, I wouldn't be able to name, off hand, a jazz musician who is already capable at present of doing it."[16]

From the beginning, Brubeck's musical development has been shaped by the most diverse of musical influences. In his childhood and adolescence he was exposed to classical piano music, choral music and jazz. While a student under Milhaud at Mills College in Oakland, 1946-1948, he studied counterpoint and harmony; at the same time he played with fellow students in jazz bands, combined European concert music and jazz—mainly in the octet's experimental workshop—and utilized theretofore unusual, uneven meters like, e.g., 7/4. Dave Brubeck wrote already in 1946 a piece for two pianos with a movement in 5/4: *Centennial Suite.* It was written for a Mills College piano duo.[17] The experimental octet was already, then, making use of pre-recorded tapes and prepared pianos.

The trio (1949-1951) continued some of the contrapuntal works in baroque style. The block chords typical of Brubeck were already now being increasingly utilized. A series of so-called "jazz waltzes" came into being.

The sonoric harmony became more differentiated during the quartet period (1951-1967). Rhythmic-metric experiments, the so-called "time experiments," were continued, and the "impressions" stimulated by the numerous tours were arranged and used as source material for improvisations. The associative, collage-like "impressions" correspond to a high degree with Brubeck's fundamental musical concept and life philosophy of world wide communication and *cultural exchange.*

The essential musical elements of his sonoric harmony comprise, especially, block chords contrasted with an ostinato, linear-contrapuntal, linear-melodic, instrumental-sonoric playing technique; and block chords in combination with toccata-like, repeated, stagnating rhythms, or rhythms sequenced step-wise.—Polytonality, ostinati and parallel sonorities are further sonoric-harmonic particularities of Brubeck's improvisations. Harmonic complexes are gradually built up through compressing the line by intervals up to triads, quadrads, quintads, in a way that is rich in tension.

The so-called "time experiments" with rhythmic-metric structures, done more intensely from the mid-50s, contain numerous uneven meters: 3, 5, 7, 9, 11, 13; rhythmical sequences, rhythmical antitheses, a "rhythmical rondo," rhythmical "leitmotivik," rhythmic inversions and ostinati, rhythmical ornamentation, rhythmic diminution and augmentation.

The idea of "cultural exchange" is seen again and again to play a significant role—from the first improvisations, i.e. compositions in the form of European concert music and jazz, to the "non-European" musical "impressions" and the integration of improvisation and composition in the later compositions.—In the early improvisations/compositions of the octet period and student period at Mills College under Darius Milhaud, a strong connection with the influence of European concert music is evident. The contrapuntal-linear style was developed especially through working together with the alto saxophonist Paul Desmond.—Two stylistic elements were significant for the phase evocative of baroque and Bach structures: 1. the development of contrast between line and sonority, and 2. the compression of the linear interweavement into sonoric complexes, combined with rhythmic differentiation. The effect of romantic piano music bears a relation mainly to Chopin. Waltzes and ballads of melodic expressiveness and harmonic density undergo a variety of diversification through alterations, chromatics and ornamentation. The piece *Dziekuje* from the *Eurasia* album is an "hommage à Chopin."

The influence of "serious" 20th century music was augmented by his study with Milhaud. A series of pieces from the early and late periods is compositional in character. Sonoric phenomena like layers of fourths and associative parallel chords are utilized quite frequently and are stylistically suggestive of Debussy. Twelve tone techniques combined with jazz and jazz-rock elements are more extensively incorporated into the compositions of the later years, e.g., in *Love Your Enemies* or *Truth Is Fallen*. The piece *The Duke Meets Darius Milhaud And Arnold Schönberg* rests on an incomplete 12-tone scale or "gamme métatonale."[18]

"Non-European" music and jazz are combined in the numerous works with the "Impressions" title, e.g., *Jazz Impressions Of Eurasia, Jazz Impressions Of Japan*. In the harmonic and rhythmic spheres, European, Turkish, Indian, Japanese, Brazilian and Mexican influences can be documented, and are mostly tour related. "I've always loved all music."[19] Dave Brubeck's whole musical attitude is defined by an openness and receptivity to all musical languages of foreign cultures or times past. The music jazz has been characterized by him as a "huge sponge"[20] and New York City as the "melting pot of the world."[21] "Impressions" are arranged into collages and mosaics, and alien musical material incorporated as an innovative potential towards cultural exchange.

Brubeck's relationship to composition and improvisation varies. "Essentially I'm a composer who plays the piano!"[22] During the octet period and in 1967 after the quartet period, compositional work, namely the integration of improvisation and composition, took precedence.—The musical *The Real Ambassadors* with Louis Armstrong as ambassador of jazz is expressly dedicated to the idea of cultural exchange.—The section "They say I look like God" combines blues and Gregorian Chant in a symbolic fraternization of Afro-American and Christian feeling and thought.—*The Gates Of Justice* unites a Hebrew Tenor with an Afro-American baritone as representatives of the two most oppressed peoples.—In *Truth Is Fallen*, a rock-blues singer and a "classical" soprano are coupled as representing revolutionary youth and "the establishment" respectively.

A socio-cultural classification of the musician Dave Brubeck must also end in controversy. It is frequently asserted by jazz musicians, critics and managers alike that Dave Brubeck is an "elitist," conservatory trained academician who plays for an "elitist" college and university public: contrapuntal-linear or 12-tone techniques and complicated sonoric and rhythmic experiments allegedly make his music difficult for the average listener to understand.

Dave Brubeck has indeed played in many colleges and universities and worked with symphony orchestras (College of the Pacific, Mills College, Oberlin College, University of Cincinnati, Cincinnati Symphony Orchestra, Aspen Festival Orchestra, Denver Classical Chorale, etc.), and two albums carry the special "College" title:

- *Jazz Goes To College*[23] and
- *Jazz Goes To Junior College.*

However, as well as having composed spiritual music for church related performances, Brubeck has also played blues in "black" clubs and at the Apollo Theater in Harlem.

An audience of listeners with an understanding of music has been consciously sought after by Brubeck. Iola Brubeck, his wife and authoress, wrote hundreds of letters to colleges and universities to make concerts there possible. Brubeck could not and no longer had the desire to play in clubs for nocturnal drinkers and table hoppers—a noisy and inattentive public. His complex sonoric-rhythmic structures deserved listening to; the audience should be relaxed and listen with a critical consciousness. "Dave had his own ideas of the way he wanted his music listened to. The atmosphere of the club was not it. He was playing complicated harmonies. He took pride in the quartet's ability to produce intelligent counterpoint ad lib and to use eccentric rhythms and combinations of rhythms. He wanted his audiences to pay attention, to relax and listen in comfort. He also wanted to get away from the table hoppers, from loud, interrupting noise...."[24]

As a white jazz musician with an education in western art-music, however, Brubeck had greater chances of social integration, though the initial stages of his career, with the octet and especially with the trio, were connected with financial difficulties: "Already decades ago, I saw myself forced to establish my own record company, namely `Fantasy,' simply because no one wanted to record my group."[25]

The group nevertheless enjoyed early success and stayed together uninterruptedly for 16 years (1951-1967). They played up to 250 one-nighters per year, and were soon assured of concerts, studio recordings for record companies, radio and television contracts, and tours of other continents, like, for example, the 1958 tour of Europe and Asia. Managers and magazines also contributed to his success: In 1954 Dave Brubeck appeared as the first jazz musician on the cover of *Time* magazine. He was spared the fears of, for example, a Charlie Parker: "I was always in a sort of panic. I had to sleep nights in garages. I became completely confused. The worst part of it was that nobody understood my music."[26]

The oratorio *The Light In The Wilderness*, 1968, brought little success to Brubeck. There was no public interest in 1968 for this oratorio that dealt with the biography of Jesus—it originally bore the title "The Temptations And Teachings Of Christ"—like there would be years later for Andrew Lloyd Webber's rock musical "Jesus Christ Superstar."

The musical *The Real Ambassadors*—1962, for and with Louis Armstrong as Afro-American ambassador for "cultural exchange" and intercultural understanding—as well, couldn't find a place on Broadway, despite good reviews. Racial and political problems as content of a musical were rejected by an entertainment expecting American public.

The social locations for his quartet's performances were as a rule intended for western art-music: Carnegie Hall in New York, the University of Hawaii, the Salle Pleyel in Paris, the Berlin Philharmonie, Cologne's Gürzenich, the Rheinhalle or Tonhalle in Düsseldorf, the Palm Springs Desert Museum, Princeton's Theological Seminary, the Municipal Auditorium in New Orleans, etc., whereby the performance at New York's Yankee Stadium, which can capacitate 60,000 spectators, is an exception to the rule.

Brubeck, The Serious Composer, reads the title of a short biography from Sutton Artists Corporation. Here, the superficial "entertainer" role of the musician is rejected. A part of Brubeck's music is in fact either influenced by western art-music or composed in that style (cantatas, ballets, an oratorio, a musical, jazz-symphonic works). The Europeanization of his music appears, among other things, to have been a determinant factor in Brubeck's success.

The combination of stars like Bernstein and Brubeck at Carnegie Hall performing excerpts from "West Side Story" and *Dialogues For Jazz Combo And Orchestra* is also certainly conducive to success with the public: *Bernstein Plays Brubeck Plays Bernstein* !! - *Greatest Hits* albums, as well, with tunes like *Take Five*, *Blue Rondo A La Turk*, *The Duke*, etc., work to intensify the dissemination of Brubeck's music and increase mass distribution. Tours to South America, Eurasia, India and Japan give rise to albums with a music that renders "the exotic," through "Jazz Impressions," engaging. The world tour with his sons, "Two Generations of Brubeck," presents a music that unites jazz and rock elements—newer, youth engaging currents, as it were—like the cantata *Truth Is Fallen* for jazz combo, rock band and symphony orchestra.—The album *All The Things We Are*, 1976, joins such stylistically divergent saxophonists as Anthony Braxton and Lee Konitz with the Brubeck trio.

A "perfect example" for a mass success, i.e. million-seller, is the best known piece associated with Brubeck, *Take Five*, a Paul Desmond composition.: "Mass production of music can only be secured when definite formal frameworks of form and instrumentation are altered as little as possible.... Each of its products must...combine, as it were, the catchyness of the familiar with the conspicuousness of the unknown...."[27] Hellhund describes this controversial improvisation and composition technique used by Brubeck as "*trivialesoterik.*"[28] Well-known standards are enriched with new sound and rhythmic "experiments," and culturally foreign "impressions" incorporated into the repertoire. This is communicative, consumable jazz—melodically catchy, formally clear. "This music's success with the public is foremost the result of its partial incorporation of the contemporary, musical popular culture; its success with the critics, however, is based on the indisputable, substantial alteration of the popular material through a grasp of things rooted in jazz as well as European music, and, moreover, on the group and individual originality which is not to be denied."[29]

In the example of *Take Five*, the catchyness of the familiar and popular is characterized in the constant harmonic alternation of just two chords, an easily grasped melody, and the simple structure. What was innovative and original as well as comparatively unknown in jazz was the 5/4 meter, which was conveyed in its turn with a catchy ostinato rhythm. Stylistically typical for Brubeck is, frequently: to combine novelty or complexity in one musical sphere, with simplicity in another, e.g., rhythmic complexity with harmonic simplicity, or harmonic complexity with easily grasped rhythms. This appears to be a recipe for audience appeal.

Brubeck's world embracing success is due also, to be sure, to his attention—or concessions—to the public.—*Take Five* is played upon request especially often in European concerts.—*Dziekuje* was a token of thanks to the Polish audience and Chopin.—*To Hope*, as a commissioned work, was not to be too difficult for a spontaneous performance with a congregation.

Brubeck refers again and again to the importance of communication with the audience: "Our group seems to depend upon audience response for its inspiration."[30] He confirmed this outlook in my first interview in 1972 in New York on the way to the huge Yankee Stadium in whose surroundings the concert became an inassessable adventure for him.[31] During the 1987 tour of the USSR as well, contact with the people takes priority. He expands the group from a quartet to a quintet—the audience is its fifth member. Brubeck's intercultural sense of mission, as an American in Moscow, results in a resounding success.[32]

Brubeck's group, the Dave Brubeck Quartet, the most successful jazz group in history,[33] always bespoke an impressive continuity. Sixteen years long, though with different drummers and bassists, it remained together (1951-1967). It was called by one American critic, an "American institution."[34] The only jazz group that played together longer and displayed a greater group consistency with regard to bass and drums is the Modern Jazz Quartet.—The Brubeck-Desmond relationship was especially fruitful and harmonious; the numerous musical dialogues were conducive to mutual inspiration. An internal tension, as between John Lewis and Milt Jackson of the MJQ, did not exist, although it did occasionally surface between the drummer Joe Morello, and the bassist Gene Wright. Brubeck would mediate and smooth out the discrepancies. Morello was heavily polyrhythmic in his playing; Wright—an exponent of the Chicago blues—provided a steady beat as foundation for the rhythmic experiments. Brubeck's sensitivity during interplay or as accompanist is also noteworthy in combination with Gerry Mulligan, the quartet's frequent guest star, or with Desmond and Mulligan. That Brubeck is a good blues player was proved in recordings with Jimmy Rushing. His joint ventures with "non-European" musicians like, for example, the Indian, Palghat Ragu, already in 1958, show Brubeck to be an understanding partner and interpreter.

Jazz is the only contemporary art form for Brubeck that combines individual freedom and a group feeling. Every musician in his groups is given time and space to improvise, including the sometimes neglected members of the rhythm section. He didn't part with his black bassist, Gene Wright, even when whole tours came to nothing; because he has always been against racial discrimination.[35] The generation conflict—Brubeck's difficulty in adapting to the rock sound—was settled in cooperation with his sons. "Two Generations," the formation formed in combination with his son Chris' rock group, "Heavenly Blue," is the vehicle with which Dave Brubeck presented himself in 1974 during a tour of Europe and the world. The New Brubeck Quartet, founded in 1977, the year of Desmond's death, played, with the participation of Dan Brubeck (percussion), Darius Brubeck (synthesizer, electric keyboard) and Chris Brubeck (electric bass, trombone), "Live At Montreux." Dave Brubeck had not planned to make his sons jazz musicians; so when working together, he tried to treat them as partners, musical colleagues. They quickly became accustomed to seeing the band bus, studio and stage as their home. In 1979, Jerry Bergonzi was engaged as tenor saxophonist and Butch Miles as drummer. Now the quartet is called "The Dave Brubeck Quartet." Chris Brubeck stayed in his father's quartet for a long time, even in 1982 when a re-formation was undertaken and Bill Smith, a former member of the octet, now a professor at the University of Seattle, took over the clarinet part and Randy Jones the drum part. The quartet again resumed its old name, Dave Brubeck Quartet.

Tolerance instead of protest: with respect to the musicians with whom he plays, the music of other peoples, races, times—this appears to be Brubeck's endeavor and contribution towards communication between musician and audience, and between people themselves. "I was content with every sort of music that I could make, regardless of the group. The only thing important to me was the communication. Only when you are unable to make any contact at all with your music to the audience are you really unsatisfied."[36]

Dave Brubeck has, for the sake of communication, consistently strived for a musical equilibrium between innovative experimentation and tradition—and herein lies the explanation of his musical and financial success.

Contact and communication, and also true "musical communion" were what I experienced at the performance of the mass *To Hope* in 1980 at St. Peter's and Paul's Cathedral in Providence, Rhode Island. The participants of an international church musician convention formed an interactive, harmonious unit with the groups performing the mass: choruses, orchestra, organ and jazz quartet. The spiritedness and warmheartedness of all the participants, including the congregation, was comparable to the Afro-American church service with its call and response technique, use of drums, and participation of all.

Dave Brubeck's most driving concern is, through music—in the path of *cultural exchange*—to attain a "brotherhood of men" in the spirit of Martin Luther King, Jr.:

If we don't live together as brothers—we will die together as fools!

*   *   *

Notes

Chapter 3

1   comp. LP: Brubeck Plays Brubeck
2   Wilton
3   comp. LP: Brubeck Plays Brubeck
4   comp. LP's: The Dave Brubeck Quartet At Carnegie Hall and Jazz Impressions Of New York
5   "Biography of Dave Brubeck, Jazz Immortal"
6   Feather, pp. 68-69
7   Spellman, p. 61
8   ibid, p. 62
9   ibid, p. 63
10   comp. LP: Brubeck On Campus
11   in "Different Drummer," pp. 13-14
12   comp. LP: Newport 1958
13   Wilton
14   Shapiro-Hentoff, p. 251
15   ibid, p. 252
16   ibid, p. 253-254
17   Letter from Dave Brubeck, November 11, 1988
18   comp. Claude Ballif, "Introduction à la Métatonalité"
19   Downbeat, May 25, 1972
20   comp. LP: Brubeck On Campus
21   comp. piano transcriptions of Bossa Nova U.S.A.
22   comp. LP: Brubeck On Campus
23   It is especially through this album that Dave Brubeck became known in Germany.
24   comp. LP: Brubeck On Campus
25   Jazzpodium, May 1975
26   Miller in: Jazz Aktuell, p. 89
27   Miller in: Jazzforschung, vol. 1, p. 153
28   Hellhund, p. 259
29   ibid, p. 261
30   comp. LP: Brubeck Time
31   New York
32   comp. Newsletter DBQ, Spring 1987
33   comp. LP: Dave Brubeck Trio & Gerry Mulligan Live At The Berlin Philharmonie
34   Biography of Dave Brubeck, Jazz Immortal
35   Jazzpodium, May 1974
36   ibid

Appendix

1. Musicography

Concerning the "time experiments":

Time Out - Time Further Out
Hansen, New York, 1962

Time Changes
Shawnee Press, Delaware, USA, 1968

Countdown - Time in Outer Space
in: *Dave Brubeck, De Luxe Piano Album Number Two*
Hansen, New York, 1973

Concerning the "impressions" and the idea of "cultural exchange":

Themes From Eurasia
Feldman, London, 1959

Bossa Nova U.S.A.
Hansen, New York, 1962

Jazz Impressions of the U.S.A.
Hansen, New York, 1963

Jazz Impressions of New York
Cinephonic Music, London, 1964

Jazz Impressions of Japan
Shawnee Press, Delaware, USA, 1967

Watussi Drums
Manuscript from Dave Brubeck

Bru's Blues
Manuscript from Dave Brubeck

Concerning the compositions:

Reminiscences Of The Cattle Country (For Piano Solo)
Ass. Music Publishers, New York, London, 1980 (composed in 1946)

Brubeck Plays Brubeck
(Original Themes and improvised Variations for Solo Piano, Vol. I, II)
Feldman, London, 1956

Themes From Elementals (Jazz-symphonic compositions)
in: *Time Changes*
Shawnee Press, Delaware, USA, 1964

Points On Jazz (Ballett)
in: *Dave Brubeck, De Luxe Piano Album*
Hansen, New York, 1965

The Light In The Wilderness (Oratorio)
Shawnee Press, Delaware, USA, 1968

The Gates Of Justice (Cantata)
Shawnee Press, Delaware, USA 1970

Truth Is Fallen (Cantata)
Shawnee Press, Delaware, USA, 1971

Maiden In The Tower (Ballet, in acts)
in: *Dave Brubeck, De Luxe Piano Album, Number Two*
Hansen, New York, 1973

The Real Ambassadors (Musical)
in: *Dave Brubeck, De Luxe Piano Album, Number Two*
Hansen, New York, 1973

La Fiesta De La Posada
Shawnee Press, Delaware, USA, 1976

Tritonis (For Guitar And Flute)
Manuscript from Dave Brubeck, 1978

To Hope: A Mass For A New Decade
St. Francis Music, Huntington, Indiana, 1979

Glances (Ballett)
Manuscript from Dave Brubeck, 1983

The Voice Of The Holy Spirit - Tongues Of Fire (Cantata)
Preprint from Dave Brubeck, 1985

Lenten Triptych - Easter Triology (Cantata)
Hinshaw Music, Derry Music, San Francisco, 1988

2. Bibliography

Adorno, Theodor W.
Zeitlose Mode. Zum Jazz.
in:" Prismen, Kulturkritik und Gesellschaft."
Nomos, Baden-Baden, 1969

Aebersold, Jamey
"A New Approach To Jazz Improvisation"
New Albany, Indiana, 1975

Baker, David
"A Method For Developing Improvisational Technique"
(Based On The Lydian Chromatic Concept)
Today's Music, National Educational Service, 1968

Baker, David
"Jazz Improvisation"
Music Workshop Publications, Maher Printing Co., Chicago, 1969

Baker, David
"Arranging And Composing"
Music Workshop Publications, Maher Printing Co., Chicago, 1970

Baker, David
"Techniques Of Improvisation"
Music Workshop Publications, Maher Printing Co., Chicago, 1971

Ballif, Claude
"Introduction A La Métatonalitée"
Revue Musicale, Paris, 1956

Bebey, Francis
"La Musique De L'Afrique"
Horizons de France, Paris, 1969

Benary, Peter
"Rhythmik und Metrik"
Eine praktische Anleitung (A Practical Introduction)
Gerig, Köln, 1967

Berendt, Joachim-Ernst
"Das große Jazzbuch, Von New Orleans bis Jazzrock"
Fischer, Frankfurt, 1982

Bergson, Henri
"Les Données Immédiates De La Conscience, l'Idee De La Durée"
Presses Universitaires De France, Paris, 1948

Bresgen, Caesar
"Am Anfang war der Rhythmus"
Heinrichshofen, Wilhelmshafen, 1977

Boulez, Pierre
"Penser La Musique Aujourd'hui"
Couthier, Mayence, 1963

Bower, Bugs
"Chords and Progressions," Vol. I and Vol. II
Charles Colin, New York, 1952

Chailley, Jacques
"Traité Historique D'Analyse Musicale"
Leduc, Paris, 1947

Coker , Jerry
"Improvising Jazz"
Prentice Hall Inc., Englewood Cliffs, New Jersey, 1964

Coker, Jerry
"The Jazz Idiom"
Prentice Hall Inc., Englewood Cliffs, New Jersey, 1975

Coker, Jerry
"Listening To Jazz,"
Pentrice Hall Inc., Englewood Cliffs, New Jersey, 1978

Cowell, Henry
"Mein Weg zu den Clusters"
in: Melos, 1973, H.5

Dahlhaus, Carl
"Musikästhetik"
Gerig, Köln, 1967

Dahlhaus, Carl
Analyse und Werturteil
in: "Musikpädagogik, Forschung und Lehre"
Schott, Mainz, 1970

Dauer, Alfons M.
"Der Jazz, seine Ursprünge und seine Entwicklung"
Erich Röth, Kassel, 1958

Dauer, Alfons M.
"Jazz, die magische Musik"
Schünemann, Bremen, 1961

Dauer, Alfons M.
Klassifikation von Rhythmen
in: "Jazzforschung," 20
ADEVA, Graz, 1988

Delamont, Gordon
"Modern Arranging Technique"
Kendor Music Inc., Delevan N.Y., 1965

Doruzka, Lubomir
Anmerkungen zur musikalischen Analyse von Jazz und Rock

in: "Jazzforschung," 8
ADEVA, Graz, 1977

Endress, Gudrun
Ein halbes Jahrhundert am Klavier: Dave Brubeck
in: "Jazzpodium," Mai 1974
Endress, Gudrun
Zwischen Jazzclub und Kirche - Dave Brubeck
in: "Jazzpodium," Februar 1990

Eggebrecht, Hans Heinrich
Musikverstehen und Musikanalyse
in: "Musik und Bildung," H.3, 1979

Feather, Leonhard
"Jazz From Then Till Now"
Bonanza Books, New York, 1956

Flechsig, Hartmut
Studien zur Theorie und Methode musikalischer Analyse
in: "Beiträge zur Musikforschung," Bd. II
München, Salzburg, 1977

Glawischnig, Dieter
Motivische Arbeit im Jazz
in: "Jazzforschung," I
UE, Wien, 1969

Gonda, Janos
Problems Of Tonality And Function In Modern Jazz Improvisation
in: "Jazzforschung," III/IV
UE, Wien, 1971/72

Gridley, Marc C.
"Jazz Styles"
Prentice Hall Inc., Englewood Cliffs, New Jersey, 1978

Grove, Dick
"The Encyclopedia Of Basic Harmony And Theory Applied To
Improvisation On All Instruments"
First Place Music Publication Inc., Cal., 1975

Grove
"The New Grove Dictionary Of Jazz," (Edited by Barry Kernfeld)
Macmillan Press Limited, London, New York, 1988

Haerle, Dan
"Jazz Improvisation For Keyboard Players"
Studio Publications/Recordings Inc., Lebanon, Indiana, 1978

Haerle, Dan
"Jazz Language"
Studio Publications/Recordings Inc., Lebanon, Indiana, 1978

Häusler, Josef
"Musik im 20. Jahrhundert"
Schünemann, Bremen, 1972

Hellhund, Herbert
"Cool Jazz"
Schott, Mainz, 1985

Hindemith, Paul
"Unterweisung im Tonsatz"
Schott, Mainz, 1940

Howard, Joseph A.
"The Improvisational Techniques Of Art Tatum"
Case Western Reserve University, 1978

Hunkemöller, Jürgen
Analytische Untersuchungen zur Kontinuität des Big-Band-Jazz
in: "Jazzforschung," II
UE, Wien, 1970

Hunkemöller, Jürgen,
Zur Terminologie afroamerikanischer Musik
in: "Jazzforschung," 9
ADEVA, Graz, 1978

Hunkemöller, Jürgen
Zur Gattungsfrage im Jazz
in: "Archiv für Musikwissenschaft," H.1, 1979

Hodeir, André
"Jazz, Its Evolution And Essence"
Grove Press, New York, 1956

Horricks, Raymond
"Jazzmen D'Aujourdhui"
Buchet/Castel, Paris, 1960

Jones, A.M.
"Studies In African Music"
Oxford University Press, London, 1959

Jost, Ekkehard
"Free Jazz, stilkritische Untersuchungen zum Jazz der 60er Jahre"
Schott, Mainz, 1975

Jost, Ekkehard
Zur jüngsten Entwicklung des Jazz
in: "Musik der 60er Jahre"
Schott, Mainz, 1972

Jungbluth, Axel
"Jazzharmonielehre"
Schott, Mainz, 1981

Kerschbaumer, Franz
"Miles Davis - Stilkritische Untersuchungen zur Entwicklung seines Personalstils"
ADEVA, Graz, 1978

Kofsky, Frank
"Black Nationalism And The Revolution In Music"
Pathfinder Press, New York, 1970

Kolneder, Walter
Visuelle und auditive Analyse
in: "Der Wandel des musikalischen Hörens,"
Published by the Institute for New Music and Music Education (Institut für neue Musik und Musikerziehung), Bd. 3
Darmstadt, Berlin, 1965

Kostelanetz, Richard
"John Cage"
Dumont, Köln, 1973

Kubik, Gerhard
Afrikanische Musikkulturen in Brasilien
in: "Brasilien, Weltmusik"
Schott, Mainz, 1986

Legido, Alvaro
Les Harmonies Du Jazz,
in: "Jazz Magazine," Nrs. 263, 264, 265, Paris, 1978

Maler, Wilhelm
"Beitrag zur Durmolltonalen Harmonielehre"
Leuckart, München/Leipzig, 1931

Mehegan, John
"Jazz Improvisation"
Watson Guptill Publications, New York, 1959

Mecklenburg, Carl Gregor, Herzog zu
Zur Theorie: Definition und Gegenüberstellung der Begriffe
"after beat" und "two beat," "beat" und "Takt," "off beat" und "Synkope," "swing" und "drive"
in: "Jazz Aktuell"
Schott, Mainz, 1968

Mecklenburg, Carl Gregor, Herzog zu
"International Jazzbibliography"
Editions Heitz, Strasbourg, Baden-Baden, 1969

Mecklenburg, Carl Gregor, Herzog zu
"Stilformen des Jazz," 1
reihe Jazz: e1, ue, Wien, 1973

Mecklenburg, Carl Gregor, Herzog zu
"Stilformen des Modernen Jazz - Vom Swing zum Free Jazz"
Koerner, Baden-Baden, 1979

Messiaen, Olivier
"Technique De Mon Langage Musical"
Alphonse LeDuc, Paris, 1944

Messiaen, Olivier
Musikalisches Glaubensbekenntnis
in: "Melos," Dezember 1958

Milhaud, Darius
"Noten ohne Musik. Eine Autobiographie"
Prestel, München, 1962

Miller, Manfred
Der moderne soziologische Hintergrund
in: "Jazz Aktuell"
Schott, Mainz, 1968

Miller, Manfred
Die zweite Akkulturation
in: "Jazzforschung," I
UE, Wien, 1970

Morgenstern, Dan
Two Brubeck Generations : A Talk with Dave, Darius and Chris
in: "Downbeat," May 25, 1972

de la Motte, Diether
"Musikalische Analyse"
Bärenreiter, Kassel, 1968

de la Motte, Diether
"Harmonielehre"
Bärenreiter, Kassel, 1976

de la Motte, Helga
Musik und Informationstheorie
in: "NZ," H.7, Februar 1974

Autoren-Team
"Neue Wege der musikalischen Analyse"
Merseburger, Berlin, 1967

Nketia, Kwabena
"The Music Of Africa"
Victor Gollancz, London, 1975

Noll, Dietrich J.
"Zur Improvisation im deutschen Free Jazz"
Karl Dieter Wagner, Hamburg, 1977

Owens, Thomas
"Charlie Parker - Techniques Of Improvisation"
University of California, Los Angeles, 1974

Panassié, Hugues
"Die Geschichte des echten Jazz"
Signum, Gütersloh, 1962

Persichetti, Vincent
"20th Century Harmony"
W.W. Norton Inc., New York, 1961

Polillo, Arrigo
"Jazz, Geschichte und Persönlichkeiten"
Goldmann-Schott, München-Berlin, 1975

Pressing, Jeff
Towards An Understanding Of Scales In Jazz
in: "Jazzforschung," 9
ADEVA, Graz, 1978

Ramsey, Doug
Dave Brubeck
in: "Different Drummer," July 1974

Rauhe, Hermann
Der Jazz als Objekt interdisziplinärer Forschung
in: "Jazzforschung," I
UE, Wien, 1970

Ricigliano, Daniel
"Popular And Jazz Harmony For Composers, Arrangers, Performers"
Donato Music Publishing Company, New York, 1967

Russell, George
"The Lydian Chromatic Concept of Tonal Organization For Improvisation"
Concept Publishing Company, New York, 1959

Russo, Bill
"Jazz Composition And Orchestration"
University of Chicago Press, Chicago, 1968

Schaeffer, Cohn
"Encyclopedia Of Scales"
Charles Cohn, New York, 1965

Schillinger, Josef
"Schillinger System Of Musical Composition" (Vol I, II)
Da Capo Press, New York, 1946

Shapiro, Nat and Hentoff, Nat
"Hear Me Talkin' To Ya"
Dover Publications, Inc., New York, 1966

Simon, Artur (Publisher)
"Musik in Afrika"
Museum für Völkerkunde, Berlin, 1983

Slave, Jan
"Einführung in die Jazzmusik"
Kleine Jazzbibliothek, Basel, 1948

Slonimski, Nicolas
"Thesaurus Of Scales And Melodic Patterns"
Duckworth, London, 1975

Spellman, A.B.
"Black Music"
Schotten Books, New York, 1971

Stearns, Marshall
"The Story Of Jazz"
Mentor Books, New American Library, New York, 1958

Stewart, Milton Lee
Structural Development In The Jazz Improvisational Technique of Clifford Brown
in: "Jazzforschung," VI/VII
UE, Wien, 1974/75

Strawinsky, Igor
"Musikalische Poetik"
Schott, Mainz, 1949

Stuckenschmidt, H.H.
"Schöpfer der Neuen Musik"
Suhrkamp, Frankfurt, 1958

Sulsbrück, Birger
"Latin-American Percussion Rhythms And Rhythm Instruments From Cuba And Brazil"
Den Rytmiske Aftenskoles Forlag, Copenhagen, 1980

Taylor, Billy
"Jazz Piano, A Jazz History"
Wm. C. Brown Company Publisher, Dubuque, Iowa, 1982

Ulanow, Harry
"Handbook Of Jazz"
The Viking Press, New York, 1980

Vallas, Léon
"Les Idées de Claude Debussy"
Librairie de France, Paris, 1927

Viera, Joe
"Grundlagen der Jazzrhythmik"
Blaue Reihe Jazz
UE, Wien, 1982

Viera, Joe
"Grundlagen der Jazzharmonik"
Blaue Reihe Jazz
UE, Wien, 1983

Viera, Joe
"Improvisation und Arrangement"
Blaue Reihe Jazz
UE, Wien, 1984

Waeltner, Ernst Ludwig
Metrik und Rhythmik im Jazz
in: "Terminologie der Neuen Musik"
Merseburger, Berlin, 1965

Wehmeyer, Grete
"Carl Czerny und die Einzelhaft am Klavier"
Bärenreiter, Atlantis Musikbuch, 1983

Willems, Edgar
"Le Rythme Musical"
Presses Universitaires de France, Paris, 1954

Winter, Keith
Communication Analysis In Jazz
in: "Jazzforschung," 11
ADEVA, Graz, 1979

3. Time Table

1920	December 6: Dave Brubeck born in Concord California
1925	Dave Brubeck listens to his brother Henry's jazzband
1932	Arroyo Secco Ranch, Ione: first attempts at improvisation to pieces on the radio; instruction in harmony from his mother, a classical pianist
1933-34	Plays with local dance bands
1938	Enrollment as veterinary pre-med student; simultaneously plays jazz in clubs, bars and dance halls
1939-42	Studies at the College of the Pacific—graduation, spring '42
1941-42	Forms a 12-piece band as warm-up group to boogie woogie pianist Cleo Brown
1942	Marries Iola in September
1942	Two lessons with Arnold Schönberg
1942-46	Service in the U.S. Army
1946	First compositions: *Reminiscences of the Cattle Country*
1946-48	Studies at Mills College, Oakland with Darius Milhaud
1946-49	Octet
1949-51	Trio
1951-67	Quartet with Paul Desmond (Joe Morello from 1956, Eugene Wright from 1958)
1953	*Downbeat* Critics Poll's best pianist of the year
1954	*Time* magazine runs Dave Brubeck Quartet title story
1954	Contract with Columbia—7 albums produced: *Jazz Goes To College* *Dave Brubeck At Storyville: 1954* *Brubeck Time* *Jazz: Red Hot And Cool* *Brubeck Plays Brubeck* *Dave Brubeck And Jay And Kai At Newport* *Jazz Goes To Junior College*

from 1954:	**Time Experiments**
1954	*A Place In Time (Brubeck Time)*
1956	*Countdown - Time In Outer Space* *Time Out*
1961	*Time Further Out*
1962	*Time In*
1964	*Time Changes*
1972	*Adventures In Time*

from 1955:	**Cultural Exchange**
1955	*Bossa Nova USA*
1958	*Jazz Impressions Of Eurasia*
1962	*Jazz Impressions Of New York*
1962-67	*Summit Sessions*
1964	*Jazz Impressions Of Japan*

from 1956:	**Compositions**
1956	*A Maiden In The Tower* (Ballet)
1961	*Points On Jazz* (Ballet)
1962	*The Real Ambassadors* (Musical with Louis Armstrong)

1963-64	*Elementals For Jazz Combo And Orchestra* (performed again in 1970 with Gerry Mulligan)
1968	*The Light In The Wilderness* (Oratio For Today)
1969	*Gates Of Justice* (Cantata)
1971	*Truth Is Fallen* (Cantata)
1975	*La Fiesta De La Posada* (Cantata)
1976	*They All Sang Yankee Doodle* (200 Jahre USA)
1978	*Beloved Son* (Cantata)
1978	*Tritonis* (For Guitar And Flute)
1980	*To Hope: A Mass For A New Decade*
1983	*Pange Lingua* (Variations for Choir und Orchestra)
1983	*Glances* (Ballet)
1985	*The Voice Of The Holy Spirit - Tongues Of Fire* (Cantata)
1988	*Lenten-Triptych - Easter Triology* (Cantata)
1991	*Joy in the Morning* based on 30th Psalms, for chorus and orchestra—dedicated to Dr Lawrence Cohen, commissioned by the Hartford Symphony to commemorate the 30th anniversary of the University of Connecticut Health Center.
1991	*When the Lord is pleased*: based on Proverbs 8: 10, 19, Proverbs 15: 16, Psalms 37: 16—choral composition premiered December 5th in Steubenville, Ohio.
1992	*Earth is our Mother*: for baritone solo and mixed chorus—presented by the University of Northern Michigan.

from 1972:   New Groups

1972	Two Generations (with sons: Darius, Chris, Danny)
1977	February, Lincoln Center, New York: last concert with Paul Desmond
1977	May 30: Paul Desmond's death
1979	The New Brubeck Quartet (with sons, Darius, Chris, Danny) Live at the Montreux-Jazz Festival
1979	The Dave Brubeck Quartet (Chris Brubeck, Jerry Bergonzi, Butch Miles)
1982	The Dave Brubeck Quartet (Chris Brubeck, Bill Smith, Randy Jones)
1987	May: first tour of the USSR
1989	7 February: heart operation and a months-long break in performances Work on compositions: *An die Musik*, for piano, cello, viola, violine, oboe *Variations Of Litanies: Praise of Mary*
1990	November 27th: Dave Brubeck 70th Birthday Concert London Symphony Orchestra (patron: HM The Queen)

The Dave Brubeck Quartet: Dave Brubeck, piano
                               Bill Smith, clarinet
                               Jack Six, bass
                               Randy Jones, drums
With special guest Stephane Grappelli, violin; also presenting:
                               Darius Brubeck, piano
                               Matthew Brubeck, cello
                               Dan Brubeck, drums
        Russell Gloyd: conductor

| 1991 | Leverkusen Jazz Festival |

The Dolphins (fusion group with Daniel Brubeck)
Family Quartet (with Matthew, Dan and Chris)
The regular Dave Brubeck Quartet (with Bill Smith, Randy Jones and Jack Six)
Nürnberg Jazzfestival—Jazz Ost-West: the Dave Brubeck Quartet with Gerry Mulligan

Part B

Discography

by Klaus-Gotthard Fischer

Introduction

The purpose of this discography is to publish a listing of music recorded by Dave Brubeck on records and compact discs. Without claiming to be complete, a chronological listing of radio broadcasts, television broadcasts, and live concerts is given after the basic discography in cases where these were recorded and available to us. We are aware, of course, that much of Brubeck's music also has been released in various countries on audiotape-cassettes, 8-track, and reel-to-reel format. Because limited information is available to us about commercially-released tapes, a comprehensive discography including tapes must await a future revision of this work.

The arrangement of dates in this chronological discography presents difficulties for different reasons: In the early years (late 1940s and early 1950s), partly contradictory information is available from different sources as well as from Dave Brubeck himself, who often provided his comments at later times. In later years one must be aware of incorrect information or none at all, especially in the case of bootleg issues and issues of sampler and compilation albums of obscure companies.

The recorded music of Dave Brubeck is reasonably well surveyable compared to other jazz artists who have enjoyed international popularity over a long period of time. In only rare cases did he act as a guest star. Moreover, Brubeck was contracted by only a few companies for comparatively long times: Fantasy, Columbia, Atlantic and Concord produced the overwhelming majority of his records. In addition to being a jazz musician it must not be forgotten that Dave Brubeck is a very proficient composer of ballet music, cantatas, oratoria, and even a musical. These compositions were recorded by Brubeck and his various groups, or at least with substantial participation by members of his groups. Accordingly, these have been included in this discography. Various themes of these compositions have become part of the jazz repertoire of the Dave Brubeck Quartet and been recorded in jazz versions.

Compact discs are a relatively new trend and have resulted in a great number of re-issues with sometimes unissued titles. Regrettably, a number of obscure labels issue sampler series including tracks from Dave Brubeck, generally no information on recording date, personnel and copyright. It is also difficult to obtain these CD's as they are locally released in limited numbers.

Complete coverage is impossible, but where information is available, it is included in this discography.

Dave Brubeck has made many concert tours throughout the world - we are awaiting his first concert tour through the People's Republic of China. Because millions of people are familiar with his music, and because he is widely regarded as a cultural ambassador, Brubeck has remarkable rapport with his audiences everywhere. According to his own statements, Brubeck regards the audience as the fifth member of the quartet.

It is quite possible that a vast amount of Dave Brubeck recordings exist which have not yet been released. This discography will be updated with any relevant data in subsequent editions. Every researcher in this field knows that errors, omissions, and misinterpretations of information are commonplace to a work involving so many details. It is a truism that musical discographies are "living documents" and thus it is understood that none is likely to be totally accurate or totally complete. Every comment, correction, and addition is valuable. Please communicate with Dr. Klaus-G. Fischer, Haydnstr. 9, D-47506 Neukirchen-Vluyn, Germany, Phone 049-(0)2845-31665; Fax 049-(0)203-379-2913.

To conclude this introduction I should point out that this discography would never have been possible without the preliminary work of Jorge Grunet Jepsen of Denmark, Walter Bruyninckx of Belgium, and Erik Raben of Denmark. In addition, I thank Johan Wilhelm Schiebaan for his significant help in archival and computer work and also his active friends Jaap van de Berge and Dick Kruys of the Netherlands. In Germany I received assistance from Michael Frohne, Rolf Kleinert, and Udo Neubauer. In Austria, I thank Andreas Felber. In France, I thank Gérard Dugelay. Appreciation is expressed to Muriel Schiebaan for her help with the English text. I would like to mention gratefully the assistance of some American collectors like Mathias C. Hermann and William H. Schrickel, and especially Willmon L. White from Evanston, Illinois. Finally, I thank the Brubeck Quartet management and Juliet Gerlin for valuable information - and my profound gratitude goes to Iola and Dave Brubeck not only for information but also the encouraging and stimulating interest in this project.

Explanations

Information on the recording sessions is given in chronological order. Every session has been provided with the following data:

1. The recording date is given (in most cases) as a six digit number (i.e. **57.02.08**). The year (19)**57**, the month February **02**, and the day **08** of the recording session are abbreviated meaning February 8, 1957. If the exact information on the month or day of the session is not known, **00** will appear.

2. The recording location is cited as precisely as is known.

3. The participating musicians are given indicating the tunes and the different instruments they

played. In session **51.12.15**, for example, Paul Desmond as (a,c) does not play on tune b whereas Herb Barman dr, perc (b) plays drums on all tunes and doubles on percussion on tune b.

4.   The recorded titles are indexed by means of lower case letters. Master numbers are shown where available as well as playing times, record labels, and numbers of the first release on long playing (LP) record. The playing time is given according to the LP issue, even when there are small deviations to our own measurements, to facilitate the comparison with later issues.

5.   Under issues we list 78 rpm, 45 rpm, and extended play (EP) records as well as Brubeck contributions to sampler and compilation albums. Equivalent issues will not be given.

6.   The notes start with the titles of the first issues. The titles and further information on subsequent issues are given, when they appear for the first time. Otherwise we give reference to the relevant session. Remarks on interesting points are added.

The recorded music will be found in the section "Chronological List of Recorded and Broadcasted Music". The subsection "Chronological Discography: Records and Compact Discs" lists all basically different records (78 rpm, 45 rpm, EP's, LP's) and Compact Discs. The subsection "Radio and Television Broadcasts, Live Concerts" lists all radio and television broadcasts known to us, when a recording on any audiovisual medium is at our disposal. Some live concerts are included with the same general restriction.

Abbreviations of Record Labels

AFF	Affinity, Charly Records (GB)
AM	America (F)
AMI	Amiga VEB (DDR)
AOH	Ace of Hearts (GB)
ATL	Atlantic Recording Corporation
ATM	All-Time Music (EU)
A&M	A & M Records Inc.
BBCTV	BBC Video Productions (GB)
BELL	Bellaphon (D)
BLU	Blue Vox (CH)
BOMC	Book-Of-The-Month-Club Records
CAN	Canyon (J)
CBS	Columbia Broadcasting System Inc. (EU)
CBS/SONY	Columbia Broadcasting System / Sony (J)
CHA	Charter Line (I) / Atlantic
COL	Columbia Broadcasting System Inc., U.S.A.
COL/SONY	Columbia / SONY Music
CON	Concord Jazz Inc.

COR	Coronet (AUS / NZ)
CORO	Coronet, San Francisco
CRO	Crown
CSP	Columbia Special Products
CUR	Curcio I Giganti Del Jazz (I)
CUS	Custom
DD	Direct Disk Labs
DEC	Decca
DEJA	Deja Vu (I)
DEN	Denon (J)
DRIVE	Baur Music Production (CH)
EAS	Eastworld (J)
EMB	Ember (GB)
EMBA	Embassy / CBS (GB / NL)
EPIC	Epic Records / Columbia
EUJ	Europa Jazz (I / D)
FAN	Fantasy
FES	Festival Distribution Musidisque (F)
FON	Fontana (NL / GB)
GDJ	I Grandi Del Jazz, Fabbri Editori (I)
GOJ	Giants Of Jazz (I / F)
GRP	Grusin / Rosen Production
HAL	Hallmark (GB)
HAR	Harmony / Columbia
HOR	Horizon / A & M
JBR	Jazz Band Records (F)
JCO	Jazz Connoisseur (I)
JMY	Jazz Music Yesterday (I)
JOK	Joker (I)
JSE	Jazz Selection (F)
JVC	Japanese Victor Company (J)
JW	Jazz World (EU)
JZT	Jazztone
KAR	Karusell (S)
KAY	Kay Productions
KIN	Kingdom Jazz (GB)
KING	King (J)
KOJ	Kings Of Jazz (I)
LIM	Limelight (EU)

LON	London (GB)
MCA	MCA Records
MEL	Melodija (SU)
MGM/UA	Metro Goldwyn Mayer / United Artists
MIDI	Midi / Atlantic (F / D)
MM	MusicMasters
MOD	Mode International (F)
MOON	Moon Records (I)
MUZA	Muza (PL)
OJC	Original Jazz Classics / Fantasy
OXF	Oxford (I)
OZO	Ozone
PHI	Philips (NL / GB)
PHIL	Philology (I)
PINN	Pinnacle (GB)
PION	Pioneer (J)
PLA	Platinum (D)
PLAY	Playboy
RMN	Jazz Round Midnight (EU)
ROC	Rocking Chair (CH)
ROJ	Romance Of Jazz (EU)
SAH	Sandy Hook Records
SONY	Sony Music Entertainment
SSO	Street Sounds (EU)
SUP	Supraphon (CZ)
SW	Swing (F)
TEL	Telarc
TOB	Tobacco Road
TOM	Tomato
UN	United Superior
VOC	Vocalion (GB)
VOG	Vogue (F / GB)
WYN	Wyndup (GB)

Abbreviations of Countries:
(according to the denomination of the nationality on automobiles)

AUS/NZ	Australia / New Zealand
B	Belgium
CAN	Canada
CH	Switzerland
CZ	Czechoslovakia
D	Germany
DDR	German Democratic Republic
DK	Denmark
E	Spain
EU	Europe
F	France
GB	England
I	Italy
J	Japan
NL	The Netherlands
PL	Poland
S	Sweden
SA	Republic of South Africa
SU	Soviet Union
USA	No designation
YU	Yugoslavia.

Abbreviations of Instruments

arr	arranger
as	alto saxophone
b	bass
bar	baritone saxophone
bjo	banjo
b-mar	bass marimba
b-tb	bass trombone
cl	clarinet
clav	clavichord
cond	conductor
cor	cornet

dir	director
dr	drums
el-b	electric bass
el-org	electronic organ
el-p	electric piano
fl	flute
g	guitar
harm	harmonica
keyb	keyboards
mell	mellophone
org	organ
osc	oscillator
p	piano
perc	percussion instruments including Latin American instruments such as bongo drums and conga drums
ss	soprano saxophone
synth	synthesizer
tamb	tambourine
tb	trombone
tp	trumpet
ts	tenor saxophone
vib	vibraphone
viol	violin
voc	vocal

General Abbreviations

ann.	announcer
CD	compact disc
ed.	edited
EP	extended play
inc.	incomplete
LP	long playing record
SP	single play
unkn.	unknown
unn.	unnumbered issue

Literature

1. Jepsen, Jorge Grunet: Jazz Records 1942-62/69.
    K. E. Knudsen (Editor), Copenhagen (DK), 1969.
2. Bruyninckx, Walter: 6o Years Of Recorded Jazz :
    Be-Bop // Hard Bop // West Coast : Vol. 1 A-D.
    Mechelen (B), 1984-87.
3. Raben, Erik (Editor): Jazz Records 1942 - 80.
    A discography, Vol. 3 BRO - CL.
    Copenhagen (DK), 1991.
4. Storb, Ilse; Fischer, Klaus-Gotthard: Dave Brubeck
    Improvisationen und Kompositionen - Die Idee der
    kulturellen Wechselbeziehungen.
    Mit einer Diskographie.
    Frankfurt am Main; Bern; New York; Paris: Lang, 1991.

Chronological List of Recorded and Broadcasted Music

Chronological Discography: Records and Compact Discs

46-48.00.00   **Dave Brubeck Octet**

San Francisco, California.
Dick Collins tp; Bob Collins tb; Bob Cummings as (a-e,h); Paul Desmond as (f,i,k); Dave Van Kriedt ts; Bill Smith cl, bar; Dave Brubeck p; Jack Weeks b or Ron Crotty b; Cal Tjader dr; Jimmy Lyons narr (i).

a.	The Prisoner's Song (Arr. Weeks) (1946)	1:04	FAN 3-16
b.	Rondo (1946)	1:30	-
c.	You Go To My Head (Arr. Smith) (1946)	2:54	-
d.	Laura (Arr. Brubeck) (1946)	2:05	-
e.	Closing Theme (1946)	0:30	-
f.	I Hear A Rhapsody (Arr. Van Kriedt) (1946)	2:10	-
g.	Serenades Suite (1946-47)	4:30	-
h.	Schizophrenic Scherzo (1946-47)	2:15	-
i.	How High The Moon (1948)	7:28	-
k.	Playland-At-The-Beach (1948)	1:27	-

Issues: FAN 3239; FAN 8094; FAN OJCCD-101-2; **g,i,k** FAN EP 4019; **a-f,h** FAN EP 4020; **e** BOMC 80-5547; COL C4K 52945.

Notes: FAN 3-16 is a 10" record with the title "DAVE BRUBECK: OLD SOUNDS FROM SAN FRANCISCO". BOMC 80-5547 is a set containing three albums entitled "DAVE BRUBECK: EARLY FANTASIES", released in 1980 by the Book-Of-The-Month-Club, Inc., Camp Hill, Pennsylvania. COL C4K 52945 is a 4-CD box set from the Columbia / Legacy project "COLUMBIA JAZZ MASTERPIECES" with the title "DAVE BRUBECK: TIME SIGNATURES A CAREER RETROSPECTIVE", released in 1992. FAN OJCCD-101-2 is a CD re-issue with digitally remastered tapes entitled "THE DAVE BRUBECK OCTET", released in

1991. The earliest recording date is given by Dave Brubeck himself in the booklet packed with the CD box set as 1946. Possible recording dates and locations are:

1946	Mills College, Oakland,
1948	College of the Pacific, Stockton,
August 7, 1948	War Memorial Opera House, San Francisco,
March 6, 1949	Marines Memorial Theatre, San Francisco,
November 19, 1950	Black Hawk, San Francisco.

The liner notes as well as Jepsen /1./ and Bruyninckx /2./ do not specify which tunes are played by Bob Cummings and Paul Desmond, respectively. A similar problem arises with the bass players Ron Crotty and Jack Weeks. In this respect we mention the information on the label of FAN 3-16 where the title f is not mentioned. The title "How High The Moon" is an "account of the evolution of jazz ... for entertainment". Narrator is Jimmy Lyons, the jazz disc jockey and promoter who was the first to give Brubeck exposure on his radio show in San Francisco in the late 1940s.

49.09.00   Dave Brubeck Trio
San Francisco, California, Sound Recorders Studio.
Dave Brubeck p; Ron Crotty b; Cal Tjader dr.

a.	551	Blue Moon	2:56	FAN 3-2
b.	552	Tea For Two	2:36	-
c.	553	Indiana	2:33	FAN 3-1
d.	554	Laura	2:41	-

Issues: BOMC 80-5547; FAN 3204; FAN 8073; FAN F-24726; FAN FCD-24726-2; **a,c,d** ROC unn.; **a,b** CORO 104; FAN 505; FAN EP 4001; SW 378; VOC LAE-F 12008; VOG LAE 12008; VOG V 2095; **c,d** CORO 103; FAN 504; FAN EP 2-802; VOC EPV-F 1275; VOG EPV 1275; **c** COL C4K 52945.

Notes: FAN 3-1 and FAN 3-2 are both 10" records with the title "THE DAVE BRUBECK TRIO: DISTINCTIVE RHYTHM INSTRUMENTALS". FAN F-24726 and FAN FCD-24726-2 contain the music of the three 10" records FAN 3-1, FAN 3-2 and FAN 3-4 have the same title as FAN F-24726 "THE DAVE BRUBECK TRIO - DISTINCTIVE RHYTHM INSTRUMENTALS";released in 1982. ROC unn. is an unnumbered compilation CD with the title "DAVE BRUBECK TRIO & QUARTET" , released in 1991 and distributed by Jazz Workshop S.L. BOMC 80-5547, COL C4K 52945 cf. **46-48.00.00.**

50.03.00   Dave Brubeck Trio
San Francisco, California.

Dave Brubeck p; Ron Crotty b; Cal Tjader dr (b-d,f), perc (a,e), vib (b,d).

a.	3006	You Stepped Out Of A Dream	2:52	FAN 3-1	
b.	3008	Lullaby In Rhythm	3:30	-	
c.	3010	Singin' In The Rain	2:34	-	
d.	3025	I'll Remember April	3:20	-	
e.	3039	Body And Soul	3:43	-	
f.	3042	Let's Fall In Love	2:40	-	

Issues: FAN 3204; FAN 8073; FAN EP 2-802; FAN F-24726; FAN FCD-24726-2; VOC LAE-F 581; **c,e,f** BOMC 80-5547; **a,b** FAN 501; FAN 501-X; **b,c** VOG V 45-25; **c,d** FAN 502; 502-X; **d,f** VOG V 45-26; **e,f** FAN 503; **c** VOG V 2204; VOG V 2264; VOG V 3366; **e** COL C4K 52945; FAN 3372; FAN 8372; JZT J 1272.

Notes: FAN 3-1 is a 10" record with the title "THE DAVE BRUBECK TRIO: DISTINCTIVE RHYTHM INSTRUMENTALS". FAN 3372, FAN 8372 are compilation albums with the title "DAVE BRUBECK'S GREATEST HITS FROM THE FANTASY YEARS 1949-1954", released in 1966. JZT J 1272 is a compilation album with the title "THE BEST OF BRUBECK: TRIOS, QUARTETS AND OCTETS", released in 1957. BOMC 80-5547, COL C4K 52945 cf. **46-48.00.00**; FAN F-24726; FAN FCD-24726-2 cf. **49.09.00**.

50.06.00   **Dave Brubeck Trio**

San Francisco, California.

Dave Brubeck p; Ron Crotty b; Cal Tjader dr (a,b,d), perc (e,f), vib (a-d).

a.	6031	'S Wonderful	2:42	FAN 3-2	
b.	6034	Sweet Georgia Brown	2:42	-	
c.	6037	Undecided	2:20	-	
d.	6041	September Song	3:25	-	
e.	6045	Spring Is Here	2:26	-	
f.	6048	That Old Black Magic	2:30	-	

Issues: FAN F-24726; FAN FCD-24726-2; VOC LAE-F 12008; VOG LAE 12008; **a,b,c,f** BOMC 80-5547; **a,b,d,e** AM 6095; FAN 3205; FAN 8074; FAN EP 4002; **a,b** ROC unn.; **a,e** FAN 508; VOG V 2091; **b,d** FAN 507; VOG V 2096; **b,e** SW 387; **c,f** FAN 506; FAN 3204; FAN 8073; FAN EP 4001; VOG V 2089; **c** COL C4K 52945; **e** VOC EPV-F 1275; VOG EPV 1275.

Notes: FAN 3-2 is a 10" record with the title "THE DAVE BRUBECK TRIO: DISTINCTIVE RHYTHM INSTRUMENTALS". AM 6095 is entitled "BRUBECK - TJADER : THE DAVE

BRUBECK TRIO". BOMC 80-5547, COL C4K 52945 cf. **46-48.00.00**; FAN F-24726; FAN FCD-24726-2 cf. **49.09.00**; ROC unn. cf. **49.09.00**.

50.07.00   Dave Brubeck Octet

San Francisco, California.

Dick Collins tp; Bob Collins tb; Paul Desmond as; Dave Van Kriedt ts; Bill Smith cl, bar; Dave Brubeck p; Jack Weeks b or Ron Crotty b; Cal Tjader dr.

a.	7013	Love Walked In (Arr. Van Kriedt)	2:45	FAN 3-3
b.	7021	IPCA	2:45	-
c.	7027	What Is This Thing Called Love? (Arr. Smith)	2:40	-
d.	7031	The Way You Look Tonight (Arr. Brubeck)	2:05	-
e.	7036	September In The Rain (Arr. Van Kriedt)	2:55	-
f.	7042	Prelude	2:15	-
g.	7047	Fugue On Bop Themes	2:45	-
h.	7052	Let's Fall In Love (Arr. Van Kriedt)	2:22	-

Issues: BOMC 80-5547; FAN 3239; FAN 8094; FAN OJCCD-101-2; JSE LP 705; **a,c-h** VOC LAE-F 12008; VOG LAE 12008; **a,c-e** FAN EP 4003; **b,f-h** FAN EP 4004; **a,d** FAN 509; SW 377; VOG V 2090; **a,h** JSE JS 4008; **b,h** FAN 512; SW 374; VOG V 2094; **c,e** FAN 510; SW 376; VOG V 2093; **f,g** FAN 511; SW 375; VOG V 2092; **d** COL C4K 52945; JZT J 1272.

Notes: FAN 3-3 is a 10" record with the title "THE DAVE BRUBECK OCTET: DISTINCTIVE RHYTHM INSTRUMENTALS". BOMC 80-5547, COL C4K 52945; FAN OJCCD-101-2 cf. **46-48.00.00**; JZT J 1272 cf. **50.03.00**.

50.10.00   Dave Brubeck Trio

San Francisco, California.

Dave Brubeck p; Ron Crotty b; Cal Tjader dr (a,c,d), perc (e), vib (b-d).

a.	10004	I Didn't Know What Time It Was	2:32	FAN 3-4
b.	10010	Squeeze Me	3:44	-
c.	10020	Too Marvelous For Words	3:07	-
d.	10026	How High The Moon	3:05	-
e.	10041	Heart And Soul	2:20	-

Issues: AM 6095; FAN 3205; FAN 8074; FAN F-24726; FAN FCD-24726-2; ROC unn.; VOC

LAE-F 581; **b-e** FAN EP 4006; **b,c** BOMC 80-5547; **b,d** FAN 515; SW 432; VOG V 2170; **c,e** FAN 516; **a** FAN 514; FAN EP 4005.

Notes: FAN 3-4 is a 10" record with the title "THE DAVE BRUBECK TRIO: DISTINCTIVE RHYTHM INSTRUMENTALS". AM 6095 cf. **50.06.00**; BOMC 80-5547 cf. **46-48.00.00**; FAN F-24726; FAN FCD-24726-2, ROC unn. cf. **49.09.00**.

50.11.00   **Dave Brubeck Trio**
San Francisco, California.
Dave Brubeck p; Ron Crotty b; Cal Tjader dr (a,b), perc (c).

a.	11010	Always	2:47	FAN 3-4
b.	11015	Avalon	2:10	-
c.	11036	Perfidia	2:22	-

Issues: AM 6095; FAN 3205; FAN 8074; FAN EP 4005; FAN F-24726; FAN FCD-24726-2; **a,b** BOMC 80-5547; ROC unn.; **b,c** FAN 513; **a** FAN 514; VOC LAE-F 581; **b** FAN 3372; FAN 8372; **c** VOC EPV-F 1275; VOG EPV 1275; VOG V 2264; VOG V 3366.

Notes: FAN 3-4 is a 10" record with the title "THE DAVE BRUBECK TRIO: DISTINCTIVE RHYTHM INSTRUMENTALS". AM 6095 cf. **50.06.00**; BOMC 80-5547 cf. **46-48.00.00**; FAN F-24726; FAN FCD-24726-2, ROC unn. cf. **49.09.00**; FAN 3372, FAN 8372 cf. **50.03.00**.

51.08.00   **Dave Brubeck Quartet**
San Francisco, California.
Paul Desmond as; Dave Brubeck p; Fred Dutton b, bassoon (a,b,d); Herb Barman dr.

a.	8127	Crazy Chris	3:19	FAN 3-5
b.	8130	A Foggy Day	3:07	-
c.	8134	Lyons Busy	3:07	-
d.	8137	Somebody Loves Me	3:22	-

Issues: AM 6068; FAN 3229; FAN 8092; FAN EP 2-803; FAN F-24728; FAN FCD-24728-2; JVC VDJ 1595; **a,d** FAN 517; FAN 517-X; FAN X-517; SW 390; VOG V45-48; **b,c** FAN 518; SW 393; VOG V 45-47; **c,d** VOG V 2280; **a** CRO CLP 5056; CRO CST 470; FAN 558-X; FAN FS-654; MODERN 827; MODERN 7027; PLAY PB 7473; **b** BOMC 80-5547; **c** CRO CLP 5361; CUS CS 1097; EMB CJS 814; JZT J 1272; UN US 7803; **d** FAN 3372; FAN 8372.

Notes: FAN 3-5 is a 10" record with the title "DAVE BRUBECK QUARTET". AM 6068 is entitled "THE GENIUS OF DAVE BRUBECK". CRO CLP 5056, CRO CST 470 are samplers entitled "JAZZ CONFIDENTIAL", containing only one tune with the Dave Brubeck Quartet mistitled "Crazy Time" for "Crazy Chris". For the release (1983) of FAN F-24728 and FAN FCD-24728-2 with the title "THE DAVE BRUBECK QUARTET FEATURING PAUL DESMOND / STARDUST", which contain the music of the 12" albums FAN 3229 and FAN 3230, the tapes were re-mastered in the Fantasy Studios, Berkeley. CUS CS 1097 is entitled "DAVE BRUBECK & PAUL DESMOND: MOODS AND GROOVES". EMB CJS 814 is entitled "THE GREATS!!! DAVE BRUBECK QUARTET / PAUL DESMOND QUARTET / CAL TJADER". FAN FS-654 is entitled "FANTASY RECORDS HI-FI SAMPLER". MODERN 827, MODERN 7027 are samplers with the title "JAZZ ALL STARS". PLAY PB 7473 is a three LP sampler set entitled "THE PLAYBOY MUSIC HALL OF FAME WINNERS", released in 1978 celebrating Playboy's Silver Anniversary. UN US 7803 (= CRO CLP 5361) is entitled "THE GREATS! DAVE BRUBECK * PAUL DESMOND * BOBBY CONELL * BOB KINDLE * FRANK BLAKE". BOMC 80-5547 cf. **46-48.00.00**; FAN 3372, FAN 8372 and JZT J 1272 cf. **50.03.00**.

51.11.00   Dave Brubeck Quartet
San Francisco, California.
Paul Desmond as; Dave Brubeck p; Wyatt "Bull" Ruther b; Herb Barman dr.

a.	11103	At A Perfume Counter	2:50	FAN 3-5
b.	11113	Mam'selle	2:50	-
c.	11119	Me And My Shadow	2:26	-
d.	11133	Frenesi	2:35	-

Issues: AM 6068; FAN 3229; FAN 8092; FAN EP 2-803; FAN F-24728; FAN FCD-24728-2; JVC VDJ 1595; VOC EPV-F 1063; VOG EPV 1063; **a,c** VOC V-F 2171; VOG V 2171; **a,d** FAN 520; FAN 520-X; JSE JS 830; VOG V 45-49; **b,c** EMBA 180; FAN 519; FAN 519-X; JSE JS 829; VOG V 45-50; **b,d** VOC V-F 2206; VOG V 2206.

Notes: FAN 3-5 is a 10" record with the title "DAVE BRUBECK QUARTET". AM 6068 and FAN F-24728; FAN FCD-24728-2 cf. **51.08.00**.

51.12.15   Dave Brubeck Quartet
New York City, New York, Birdland.
Paul Desmond as (a,c); Dave Brubeck p; Wyatt "Bull" Ruther b; Herb Barman dr, perc (b).

a.		(At A) Perfume Counter	2:32	ALTO 711
b.		That Old Black Magic	2:24	-
c.		How High The Moon	3:49	-

Issues: SAH SH 2064; SAH CD SH 2064; **b** DEJA DVRECD 58.

Notes: ALTO 711 is entitled "DAVE BRUBECK: MODERN COMPLEX DIALOGUES". DEJA DVRECD 58 is a compilation CD entitled "THE DAVE BRUBECK STORY" released in 1991. SAH SH 2064 is entitled "THE DAVE BRUBECK QUARTET", SAH CD SH 2064 is a CD with the title "THE DAVE BRUBECK QUARTET: RARE RADIO RECORDINGS 1953, 1954". The information on the cover of the CD referring to the personnel and the recording dates is incorrect.

51.12.22   Dave Brubeck Quartet
New York City, New York, Birdland.
Paul Desmond as (a,b,d-g); Dave Brubeck p; Wyatt "Bull" Ruther b; Herb Barman dr, perc (c).

a.	Jeepers Creepers	2:09	ALTO 711
b.	Crazy Chris	2:46	-
c.	Spring Is Here	2:00	-
d.	Stardust	3:28	-
e.	This Can't Be Love	3:20	-
f.	These Foolish Things	2:49	-
g.	Jingle Bells	2:49	-

Issues: SAH SH 2064; SAH CD SH 2064; **e** DEJA DVRECD 58.

Notes: ALTO 711 is entitled "DAVE BRUBECK: MODERN COMPLEX DIALOGUES". SAH SH 2064; SAH CD SH 2064; DEJA DVRECD 58 cf. **51.12.15**.

52.01.22   Dave Brubeck Quartet
New York City, New York, Birdland.
Paul Desmond as; Dave Brubeck p; Wyatt "Bull" Ruther b; (prob.) Lloyd Davis dr.

a.	Tea For Two	4:45	ALTO 711

Issues: SAH SH 2064; SAH CD SH 2064.
Notes: ALTO 711 is entitled "DAVE BRUBECK: MODERN COMPLEX DIALOGUES". Raben /3./ gives further unissued titles of this session. SAH SH 2064; SAH CD SH 2064 cf. **51.12.15**.

52.01.24   Dave Brubeck Quartet
New York City, New York, Birdland.
Paul Desmond as; Dave Brubeck p; Wyatt "Bull" Ruther b; (prob.) Lloyd Davis dr.

a.   I'll Remember April   4:32   ALTO 711

Issues: SAH SH 2064; SAH CD SH 2064.

Notes: ALTO 711 is entitled "DAVE BRUBECK: MODERN COMPLEX DIALOGUES". Raben
/3./ gives further unissued titles of this session. SAH SH 2064; SAH CD SH 2064 cf. **51.12.15.**

52.09.00   Dave Brubeck Quartet
San Francisco, California.
Paul Desmond as; Dave Brubeck p; Wyatt "Bull" Ruther b; Lloyd Davis dr.

a.	9205	My Romance (p-solo)	2:32	FAN 3-7
b.	9217	I May Be Wrong	2:50	FAN 3210
c.	9232	Just One Of Those Things	3:07	FAN 3-7
d.	9237	Lulu's Back In Town	2:20	-
e.	9244	On A Little Street In Singapore	2:39	FAN 3210
f.	9252	All The Things You Are	3:20	FAN 3-7
g.	9253	Alice In Wonderland	3:55	-
h.	9339	Stardust	2:55	-

Issues: a,c,d,f-h FAN 3230; FAN 8093; FAN F-24728; FAN FCD-24728-2; **a,c** FAN 523; FAN
523-X; **b,e** FAN 527; FAN 527-X; FAN 8081; FAN EP 4053; FAN F-24727; FAN FCD-24727-
2; **c,h** SW 433; **d,h** BOMC 80-5547; FAN 524; FAN 524-X; **f,g** FAN 526; 526-X; **b** MUSICA
JAZZ (I) MJP 1018; **h** AM 6068; FAN 3372; FAN 8372; OJC-18004.

Notes: FAN 3-7 is a 10" record with the title "THE DAVE BRUBECK QUARTET". FAN 3210
is entitled "BRUBECK - DESMOND: JAZZ AT THE BLACKHAWK". For the release (1982) of
FAN F-24727; FAN FCD-24727-2 with the title "DAVE BRUBECK PAUL DESMOND" which
contains the two albums FAN 3210 and FAN 3240 the tapes were remastered at the Fantasy
Studios, Berkeley. AM 6068 and FAN F-24728; FAN FCD-24728-2 cf. **51.08.00**; BOMC 80-
5547 cf. **46-48.00.00**; FAN 3372, FAN 8372 cf. **50.03.00.**

52.10.00   Dave Brubeck Quartet
Los Angeles-Hollywood, California, Surf Club
Paul Desmond as; Dave Brubeck p; Wyatt "Bull" Ruther b; Herb Barman dr.

a.	9202	This Can't Be Love	4:13	FAN 3-7
b.	9204	Look For The Silver Lining	3:40	-

Issues: BOMC 80-5547; FAN 521; FAN 521-X; **a** AM 6091; FAN 3240; FAN 8080; FAN F-24727; FAN FCD-24727-2; FES ALB 254; JVC VDJ 1596; **b** AM 6068; COL C4K 52945; FAN 3229; FAN 8092; FAN F-24728; FAN FCD-24728-2; JVC VDJ 1595.

Notes: FAN 3-7 is a 10" record with the title "THE DAVE BRUBECK QUARTET". AM 6091 is entitled "DAVE BRUBECK AT THE BLACK HAWK IN SAN FRANCISCO FEATURING PAUL DESMOND". FES ALB 254 is entitled "DAVE BRUBECK THE BEST LIVE SESSIONS". JVC VDJ 1596 is entitled "THE COMPLETE JAZZ AT STORYVILLE". AM 6068, FAN F-24728, FAN FCD-24728-2 cf. **51.08.00**; BOMC 80-5547, COL C4K 52945 cf. **46-48.00.00**; FAN F-24727; FAN FCD-24727-2 cf. **52.09.00**.

52.10.12   Dave Brubeck Trio
Boston, Massachusetts, Storyville.
Paul Desmond as; Dave Brubeck p; Lloyd Davis dr (c,d).

a.	Over The Rainbow	5:05	FAN 3-8
b.	You Go To My Head	7:55	-
c.	Oh, Lady Be Good /	4:10	-
d.	Give A Little Whistle	2:41	-

Issues: FAN 3240; FAN 8080; FAN F-24727; FAN FCD-24727-2; JVC VDJ 1596; **a,b,d** BOMC 80-5547; **a,b** FAN EP 4011; **c,d** FAN EP 4012; VOC EPV-F 1240; **a** COL C4K 52945; FAN 3372; FAN 8372.

Notes: FAN 3-8 is a 10" record with the title "BRUBECK - DESMOND". **c** and **d** were published on FAN 3-8 as a single tune. The date of the session is given following the liner notes of FAN F-24727. BOMC 80-5547, COL C4K 52945 cf. **46-48.00.00**; FAN F-24727; FAN FCD-24727-2 cf. **52.09.00**; FAN 3372, FAN 8372 cf. **50.03.00**; JVC VDJ 1596 cf. **52.10.00**.

53.02.00   Dave Brubeck Quartet
Los Angeles-Hollywood, California, Surf Club.
Paul Desmond as; Dave Brubeck p; Ron Crotty b; Lloyd Davis dr.

a.	Tea For Two	6:58	FAN 3-8
b.	Blue Moon	8:10	FAN 3210
c.	Let's Fall In Love	7:25	-

Issues: AM 6091; FAN F-24727; FAN FCD-24727-2; FES ALB 254; **a,b** DEJA DVCD 2036; **b,c** FAN 8081; FAN EP 4014; **a** FAN 3240; FAN 8080; FAN EP 4012; JVC VDJ 1596; VOC EPV-F 1240; **c** VOG EPV 1184.

Notes: FAN 3-8 is a 10" record with the title "BRUBECK - DESMOND". FAN 3210 is entitled "BRUBECK - DESMOND: JAZZ AT THE BLACK HAWK". AM 6091, FES ALB 254, JVC VDJ 1596 cf. **52.10.00**; FAN F-24727; FAN FCD-24727-2 cf. **52.09.00**.

53.03.02   Dave Brubeck Quartet
Oberlin, Ohio, Oberlin College, Finney Chapel.
Paul Desmond as; Dave Brubeck p; Ron Crotty b; Lloyd Davis dr.

a.	These Foolish Things	6:30	FAN 3-11
b.	The Way You Look Tonight	7:47	-
c.	Perdido	7:45	-
d.	Stardust	6:25	-
e.	How High The Moon	9:03	FAN 3245

Issues: AM 6073; ATL SD 2-317; FAN 3245; FAN 8069; FAN-OJCCD 046-2; FES ALB 254; JVC VDJ 1597; **a-d** FAN FCD-60-013; **a,b** FAN EP 4007; KAR KSEP 3075; **a,c** VOC EPV-F 1216; VOG EPV 1216; **c,d** FAN EP 4013; **a** FAN 3372; FAN 8372; **c** COL C4K 52945; FAN EPF 5805; **e** FAN EP 4062.

Notes: FAN 3-11 is a 10" record with the title "THE DAVE BRUBECK QUARTET: JAZZ AT OBERLIN". FAN 3245 is the 12" record with the same title. AM 6073 is entitled "JAZZ AT STORYVILLE THE DAVE BRUBECK QUARTET". ATL SD 2-317 is a double album with the title "THE ART OF DAVE BRUBECK" which contains the two albums FAN 8069 and FAN 8078 and was released in 1976. FAN-OJCCD 046-2 is a re-issue with the title "THE DAVE BRUBECK QUARTET: JAZZ AT OBERLIN" , released in 1987 with digitally remastered tapes. FAN FCD-60-013 is a Compact Disc with the title "THE DAVE BRUBECK QUARTET FEATURING PAUL DESMOND: IN CONCERT". COL C4K 52945 cf. **46-48.00.00**; FES ALB 254 cf. **52.10.00**; FAN 3372, FAN 8372 cf. **50.03.00**.

53.06.20   Dave Brubeck Quartet
Los Angeles, California, Wilshire-Ebell.
Paul Desmond as; Dave Brubeck p; Ron Crotty b; Lloyd Davis dr.

a.	All The Things You Are	6:43	FAN 3249
b.	Too Marvelous For Words	7:49	-
c.	Stardust	6:17	-
d.	I'll Never Smile Again	7:24	-
e.	Let's Fall In Love	4:14	-
f.	Why Do I Love You	2:37	-

Issues: AM 6083; FAN 8095; **a,b,d,e** FES ALB 254; **a,b** FAN EP 4066; **c,d** FAN EP 4065; FAN EPF 5806; **f** FAN 3372, FAN 8372.

Notes: FAN 3249 is entitled "DAVE BRUBECK & PAUL DESMOND AT WILSHIRE - EBELL". AM 6083 is entitled "THE DAVE BRUBECK QUARTET FEATURING PAUL DESMOND RECORDED LIVE AT THE NEWPORT FESTIVAL".
FES ALB 254 cf. **52.10.00**; FAN 3372, FAN 8372 cf. **50.03.00**.

53.09.00   Dave Brubeck Quartet
San Francisco, California, The Black Hawk.
Paul Desmond as; Dave Brubeck p; Ron Crotty b; Lloyd Davis dr.
a.   Jeepers Creepers   7:24   FAN 3210

Issues: AM 6091; FAN 8081; FAN EP 4053; FAN F-24727; FAN FCD-24727-2; JZT J 1272.

Notes: FAN 3210 is entitled "BRUBECK - DESMOND: JAZZ AT THE BLACK HAWK".
AM 6091 cf. **52.10.00**; FAN F-24727, FAN FCD-24727-2 cf. **52.09.00**; JZT J 1272 cf. **50.03.00**.

53.12.00   Dave Brubeck Quartet
Boston, Massachusetts, Storyville.
Paul Desmond as; Dave Brubeck p; Ron Crotty b; Joe Dodge dr.
a. CO51849   On The Alamo   10:43   COL CL 590
b. CO51850   Don't Worry 'Bout Me   6:50   -

Issues: COL B 465; COL CL 6330; **a** COL B 2016; COL (J) EM 43; **b** PHI 429.116 BE.

Notes: COL CL 590 is entitled "DAVE BRUBECK AT STORYVILLE: 1954". COL CL 6330 is a 10" record with the title "DAVE BRUBECK AT STORYVILLE: 1954 (VOL. 1)".

53.12.00   Dave Brubeck Quartet
Los Angeles, California, Home Studio of Bill Bates.
Paul Desmond as; Dave Brubeck p; Ron Crotty b; Joe Dodge dr.
a.   (The) Trolley Song (Rehearsal)   2:15   FAN 3210
b. 1501   My Heart Stood Still (p-solo)   3:27   -

Issues: FAN 8081; FAN EP 4055; FAN F-24727; FAN FCD-24727-2; **a** FAN 535; FAN 535-X;

FAN 3372; FAN 8372; **b** BOMC 80-5547; FAN 530; FAN 530-X; VOC EPV-F 1184; VOG EPV 1184.

Notes: FAN 3210 is entitled "BRUBECK - DESMOND: JAZZ AT THE BLACK HAWK". BOMC 80-5547 cf. **46-48.00.00**; FAN F-24727, FAN FCD-24727-2 cf. **52.09.00**; FAN 3372, FAN 8372 cf. **50.03.00**.

53.12.14   **Dave Brubeck Quartet**
San Francisco, California.
Paul Desmond as; Dave Brubeck p; Ron Crotty b; Joe Dodge dr.
a.   1502   (The) Trolley Song   3:15   FAN 3210

Issues: FAN 530; FAN 535; FAN 530-X; FAN 535-X; FAN 558-X; FAN 3372; FAN 8081; FAN 8372; FAN EP 4055; FAN F-24727; FAN FCD-24727-2; OJC-18004.

Notes: FAN 3210 is entitled "BRUBECK - DESMOND: JAZZ AT THE BLACK HAWK". FAN F-24727, FAN FCD-24727-2 cf. **52.09.00**; FAN 3372, FAN 8372 cf. **50.03.00**.

53.12.14   **Dave Brubeck Quartet**
Stockton, California, College of the Pacific.
Paul Desmond as; Dave Brubeck p; Ron Crotty b; Joe Dodge dr.
a.   I'll Never Smile Again   5:30   FAN 3-13
b.   All The Things You Are   9:20   -
c.   For All We Know   5:40   -
d.   Laura   3:07   -
e.   I Remember You   9:10   FAN 3223
f.   Lullaby In Rhythm   7:23   FAN 3-13

Issues: ATL SD 2-317; FAN 3223; FAN 8078; FAN-OJCCD 047-2; **a-c,e,f** FAN FCD-60-013; **a-d,f** BEL BJS 40176; VOG VG 304.40013; VOG DP 13; VOG LD 559-30; **a,d,f** VOC EPV-F 1108; VOG EPV 1108; **a,f** FAN EP 4054; **c** MOD MDINT 9144; PYE CGL 0307; VOG VG 603.000103; **d** FAN 3372; FAN 8372; FAN EP 4055; VOG 670072; VOG DP 64; VOG VG 304.400064; **f** JZT J 1272.

Notes: FAN 3-13 is a 10" record with the title "JAZZ AT THE COLLEGE OF PACIFIC". FAN 3223 is the 12" record with the same title. FAN-OJCCD 047-2 is a re-issue with the title "DAVE BRUBECK QUARTET: JAZZ AT THE COLLEGE OF PACIFIC" , released in 1987 with digitally remastered tapes. BEL BJS 40176 is a compilation album from the series "JAZZTRACKS" entitled "DAVE BRUBECK" released in 1977. MOD MDINT 9144 is a sampler entitled "LES GEANTS DU JAZZ MODERNE". VOG 670072, VOG DP 64 are samplers with the title "25 GEANTS DU JAZZ PIANO". VOG DP 13 is a double album with the title "JAZZ SUMMIT: STAN GETZ - DAVE BRUBECK" with one record by Stan Getz and the other one by the Dave Brubeck Quartet. ATL SD 2-317, FAN FCD-60-013 cf. **53.03.02**; FAN 3372, FAN 8372 and JZT J 1272 cf. **50.03.00**.

54.00.00   **Dave Brubeck Quartet**

Cincinnati, Ohio.

Paul Desmond as; Dave Brubeck p; Bob Bates b; Joe Dodge dr.

a.	CO51803	Don't Worry 'Bout Me, Part 1	COL 4-PE 12
b.	CO51804	Don't Worry 'Bout Me, Part 2	-

Issues: COL PE 12.

Notes: According to Raben /3./ and W. H. Schrickel these versions are different from those with master numbers CO51327 (cf. **53.12.00**) and CO51850 (cf. **54.03-04.00**). They were part of Columbia's "Priceless Editions" series; this disc was never sold, but was part of a promotion during summer, 1954 (W. H. Schrickel).

54.00.00   **Dave Brubeck Quartet**

Los Angeles, California, Hollywood.

Paul Desmond as; Dave Brubeck p; Bob Bates b; Joe Dodge dr.

a.		Camille	3:02 COL XLP 36210

Notes: The above title was recorded at a party in Hollywood, given by composer Paul Weston and wife Jo Stafford, and was published on a Columbia promotion LP with the title "COLUMBIA HOUSE PARTY" (W.L. White).

54.03.00   **Dave Brubeck Quartet**

Boston, Massachusetts, Storyville.

Paul Desmond as; Dave Brubeck p; Ron Crotty b; Joe Dodge dr.

a.		Crazy Chris	6:45 FAN 3-20

Issues: AM 6091; FAN 3240; FAN 8080; FAN EP 2-801; FAN F-24727; FAN FCD-24727-2; JVC VDJ 1596; JZT J 1272.

Notes: FAN 3-20 is a 10" record with the title "PAUL AND DAVE: JAZZ INTERWOVEN". In the liner notes of FAN F-24727 the recording location and date are given as Storyville, Boston and **54.03.30**. It is not clear whether this information is correct (cf. next session). FAN F-24727, FAN FCD-24727-2 cf. **52.10.00**; JZT J 1272 cf. **50.03.00**.

54.03.30   Dave Brubeck Quartet
Boston, Massachusetts, Storyville.
Paul Desmond as; Dave Brubeck p; Bob Bates b; Joe Dodge dr.
a.	CO51851	Gone With The Wind	8:15	COL CL 590
b.	CO51852	Back Bay Blues	6:28	-

Issues: COL B-466; COL B-1834; COL CL 6331; **a** CBS 52703, HAR HS 11336; PHI 429116 BE; PHI BBE 12052; PHI BBL 7498.

Notes: COL CL 590 is entitled "DAVE BRUBECK AT STORYVILLE: 1954". COL CL 6331 is a 10" record with the title "DAVE BRUBECK AT STORYVILLE: 1954 (VOL. 2)". The album partly consists of material recorded off the air. The announcer John McLellan closes the late air show with a few words over the last part of the "Back Bay Blues". CBS 52703, HAR HS 11336 cf. **54.03-04.00**.

54.03-04.00   Dave Brubeck Quartet
Berkeley, California, University of California.
Paul Desmond as; Dave Brubeck p; Bob Bates b; Joe Dodge dr.
a.		Stardust	6:49	FAN 3-20
b.		At A Perfume Counter	14:40	-
Cincinnati, Ohio, University of Cincinnati.				
c.	CO51323	Out Of Nowhere	8:07	COL CL 566
(**54.03.09**) Oberlin, Ohio, Oberlin College.				
d.	CO51324	Le Souk	4:46	-
Ann Arbor, Michigan, University of Michigan.				
e.	CO51322	Balcony Rock	11:50	-
f.	CO51325	Take The "A" Train	6:10	-
g.	CO51326	The Song Is You	5:47	-
h.	CO51327	Don't Worry 'Bout Me	8:50	-
i.	CO51328	I Want To Be Happy	6:43	-

Issues: a,b FAN EP 2-801; FAN F-24728; FAN FCD-24728-2; JVC VDJ 1597; **c-i** CBS 465682-1/-2; COL CJ-45149; COL CK-45149; COL CS 8631; COL KG 31298; **c,f,g,h** CBS 52703, HAR HS 11336; **c-e** COL B-435; COL CL 6321; **f-i** COL B-436; COL CL 6322; **c,e** COL 5-1941; COL B-1941; **c,f** PHI BBE 12024; PHI 429018 BE; **d,e** COL B-1940; **d,g** COL (J) PL 2033; **f,g** COL B-1942; **f,i** COL (J) EM-13; **h,i** COL 5-1943; COL B-1943; **a** FAN 3229; FAN 8092; JVC VDJ 1595; JZT J 1272; **b** CRO CLP 5288; CRO CLP 5406; CRO CST 288; FAN 3230; FAN 8093; **d** CBS 466314-1/-2; COL CB-12; COL CK-45146; COL C4K 52945; COR KEP 173; PHI 429793 BE; PHI B 07109 L; PHI BBE 12285; **f** CBS 80775; PHI D 99796 Y; **g** CBS 54490; PHI 429462 BE; **h** PHI BBE 12052; PHI 429116 BE; **i** PHI 429746 BE.

Notes: FAN 3-20 is a 10" record with the title "PAUL AND DAVE: JAZZ INTERWOVEN". COL CL 566 is entitled "THE DAVE BRUBECK QUARTET: JAZZ GOES TO COLLEGE". CBS 52703 and HAR HS 11336 are both compilation albums with the title "GONE WITH THE WIND". CBS 54490 is a compilation album with the title "DAVE BRUBECK 1954-1972", which was sold exclusively by the German company "Zweitausendeins"; in contradiction to information indicated on the cover and given by Bruyninckx /2./ the record contains previously released material. CBS 80775 - CBS 80777 is a boxed set of three compilation albums entitled "THE ORIGINAL DAVE BRUBECK QUARTET: TAKE FIVE". COL KG 31298 is a double album, released in 1972 with the title "BRUBECK ON CAMPUS - THE DAVE BRUBECK QUARTET" and contains the albums COL CS 8631 "JAZZ GOES TO COLLEGE" and COL CL 1034 "JAZZ GOES TO JUNIOR COLLEGE". CBS 465682-2, COL CJ-45149 and COL CK-45149 are albums from the series "COLUMBIA / CBS JAZZ MASTERPIECES" , released in 1989 with the title "DAVE BRUBECK: JAZZ GOES TO COLLEGE" with digitally remastered tapes. CBS 466314-1/-2, COL CK-45146 are samplers from the series "COLUMBIA / CBS JAZZ MASTERPIECES" entitled "COLUMBIA / CBS JAZZ MASTERPIECES VOLUME VI" with digitally remastered tapes. COL CB-12 is a sampler with the title "JAZZ AT COLUMBIA - MODERN" and was a free bonus record for members of the Columbia Record Club. CRO CLP 5288, CRO CLP 5406, CRO CST 288 are samplers with the title "DAVE BRUBECK QUARTET * PAUL DESMOND QUARTET * CAL TJADER". PHI B 07109 L is a sampler entitled "THIS IS JAZZ NO. 2". PHI D 99796 Y is a demonstration sampler with the title "HI-Z STEREOPHONIC DEMONSTRATION RECORD", released in New Zealand by Philips Electrical Industries of New Zealand Ltd. COL C4K 52945 cf. **46-48.00.00**; FAN F-24728, FAN FCD-24728-2 cf. **51.08.00**; JZT J 1272 cf. **50.03.00**.

54.07.22   Dave Brubeck Quartet
Los Angeles, California.
Paul Desmond as; Dave Brubeck p; Bob Bates b; Joe Dodge dr.
a. HCO33177   When You're Smiling   9:50   COL CL 590

b. HCO33179   Here Lies Love   5:48   -

Issues: COL B-1894; **a** CBS 52703; COL B-466; COL CL 6331; COL (J) PL 2033; HAR HS 11336; PHI BBE 12285; PHI BBL 7498; **b** COL B-465; COL B-2016; COL CL 6330; PHI 429746 BE.

Notes: COL CL 590 is entitled "DAVE BRUBECK AT STORYVILLE: 1954". CBS 52703, HAR HS 11336 cf. **54.03-04.00**; COL CL 6330 cf. **53.12.00**; COL CL 6331 cf. **54.03.30**.

54.10.12   Dave Brubeck Quartet
New York City, New York.
Paul Desmond as; Dave Brubeck p; Bob Bates b; Joe Dodge dr.

a.	CO52615	Jeepers Creepers	4:57	COL CL 622
b.	CO52616	Audrey	3:34	-
c.	CO52617	A Fine Romance	3:50	-

New York City, New York, Basin Street Club.

d.	CO52618	Take The "A" Train		COL 4-42447 (?)
e.	CO52619	Sometimes I'm Happy	5:17	COL CL 699
f.	CO52620	Indiana	5:48	-
g.	CO52621	Fare Thee Well, Annabelle	7:20	-
h.	CO52622	Love Walked In	8:43	-

Issues: a-c,e,f,h COL CK-47032; COL/SONY 467917-2; **a-c** HAL HM 553; HAR HS 11253; **e-h** COL B-699; COL CS 8645; **a,b,e** PHI BBL 7498; **a,c** CBS 80777; **b,c** PHI 429601 BE; PHI BBE 12353; **e,g** CBS 52703; COL 5-2282; HAR HS 11336; **f,g** PHI 429727 BE; **a** CBS 88120; COL B-1946; PHI B 07148 L; **b** COL B-1947; COL JPA 52114 (ed.); GDJ 82; GOJ LPJT 3; PHI B 07606 R; PHI B 07148 L; ZOUNDS 27200446 B; **c** CBS 467148-2; COL B-473; COL B-1967; COL 5-2067; COL B-2067; COL B-2287; COL CL 777; COL (J) PL 2033; COR KLP 500; PHI B 07735 R; **d** COL 3-42447 (ed.) (?); **e** COL B-2552; COR KEP 173; PHI 429793 BE; **f** COL 5-2281; **h** COL 5-2280.

Notes: COL CL 622 is entitled "THE DAVE BRUBECK QUARTET: BRUBECK TIME". COL CL 699 is entitled "THE DAVE BRUBECK QUARTET: JAZZ RED HOT AND COOL". CBS 467148-2 is a compilation album with the title "THE ESSENTIAL DAVE BRUBECK" released in 1990. COL/SONY 467917-2 and COL CK-47032 are compilation albums from the series "COLUMBIA / CBS JAZZ MASTERPIECES" with the title "DAVE BRUBECK FEATURING PAUL DESMOND: INTERCHANGES '54", released in 1991. COL CL 777 is a sampler entitled "$ 64.000 JAZZ". COL JPA 52114 is a promotion record for Helena Rubinstein Cosmetics Co.

with the title "JAZZ COMBO HOT / COOL" and contains an edited version (1:00) of "Audrey" (W.L. White). GDJ 82 is a compilation album from the series "I GRANDI DEL JAZZ" with the title "DAVE BRUBECK", released in 1968. GOJ LPJT 3 is a compilation album with the title "DAVE BRUBECK & PAUL DESMOND". HAL HM 553 is a re-issue of COL CL 622 with the title "INSTANT BRUBECK". PHI B 07148 L is a sampler with the title "JAZZ". PHI B 07735 R is a sampler with the title "A VISIT TO BIRDLAND NO. 3". ZOUNDS 27200446 B is an album with the title "DAVE BRUBECK" from the series "JAZZ PORTRAIT", compiled in 1992 for the German Vereinigte Motor-Verlage GmbH & Co KG by SONY Music Entertainment (D) GmbH. CBS 52703, CBS 80777, HAR HS 11336 cf. **54.03-04.00.**

54.10.13   Dave Brubeck Quartet
New York City, New York.
Paul Desmond as; Dave Brubeck p; Bob Bates b; Joe Dodge dr.

a.	CO49849	Makin' Time	3:49	COL JZ-1
b.	CO52634	Lover		(unissued)
c.	CO52635	The Duke		(unissued)
d.	CO52636	Stompin' For Mili	5:18	COL CL 622

Issues: a CBS 52703; COL CL 1036; COL JZP-1; MR. PICKWICK (GB) MPD 238; PHI 429727 BE; PHI B 07754 R; PHI B 07100 L; RTB (YU) LPV 4301; d CBS 54490; COL B-699; COL B-1947; COL CB-12; COL CK-47032; COL C4K 52945; COL/SONY 467917-2; GOJ LPJT 3; HAL HM 553; HAR HS 11253; ZOUNDS 27200446 B.

Notes: COL CL 622 is entitled "THE DAVE BRUBECK QUARTET: BRUBECK TIME". COL JZ-1 is a sampler with the title "I LIKE JAZZ!". CBS 52703 is a sampler with the title "JAZZ PANORAMA". PHI B 07100 L is a sampler entitled "THIS IS JAZZ NO. 1".
CBS 54490, COL CB-12 cf. **54.03-04.00**; COL/SONY 467917-2, COL CK-47032, GOJ LPJT 3, HAL HM 553, ZOUNDS 27200446 B cf. **54.10.12**; COL C4K 52945 cf. **46-48.00.00.**

54.10.14   Dave Brubeck Quartet
New York City, New York.
Paul Desmond as; Dave Brubeck p; Bob Bates b; Joe Dodge dr.

a.	CO52637	Brother, Can You Spare A Dime?	5:20	COL CL 622
b.	CO52638	Why Do I Love You	5:13	-
c.	CO52639	Pennies From Heaven	6:11	-

Issues: COL B-473; COL CK-47032; COL/SONY 467917-2; HAL HM 553; **b,c** COL 5-2068;

COL B-2068; **a** COL 5-2067; COL B-2067; PHI B 07059 L; **b** COL K3L-326; PHI 429462 BE; **c** PHI 429601 BE; PHI BBE 12353; ELITE 009 CD.

Notes: COL CL 622 is entitled "THE DAVE BRUBECK QUARTET: BRUBECK TIME". COL K3L-326 is a 3 LP sampler entitled "BASIC LIBRARY OF GREAT JAZZ". ELITE 009 CD is a sampler entitled "TAKE ... THE GREATEST HITS". PHI B 07059 L is an album entitled "LYRIK UND JAZZ: GOTTFRIED BENN".
COL/SONY 467917-2, COL CK-47032, HAL HM 553 cf. **54.10.12.**

54.11.10   **Dave Brubeck Quartet**
Los Angeles, California.
Paul Desmond as; Dave Brubeck p; Bob Bates b; Joe Dodge dr.
a.   HCO33282   Keepin' Out Of Mischief Now   5:04   COL CL 622

Issues: COL/SONY 467917-2; COL B-1946; COL CK-47032; HAL HM 553; PHI B 07183 L; PHI BBL 7498.

Notes: COL CL 622 is entitled "THE DAVE BRUBECK QUARTET: BRUBECK TIME". PHI B 07183 L is a sampler entitled "THIS IS JAZZ NO. 3".
COL/SONY 467917-2, COL CK-47032, HAL HM 553 cf. **54.10.12.**

55.00.00   **Dave Brubeck Quartet**
Paul Desmond as; Dave Brubeck p; Norman Bates b; Joe Dodge dr.

a.	Shish Kebab	4:13	BLU B/90174
b.	Fairy Day	5:09	-
c.	Don't Worry 'Bout Me	6:50	-
d.	Lover, Come Back To Me	6:24	-
e.	Royal Garden Blues	3:45	-
f.	Love Walked In	3:28	-
g.	How High The Moon	2:24	-

Issues: BANDSTAND (I) BDCD 1538; JOK SM 3804; PHONIC (E) PHL 5517; TOB B/2620; TOB MB/9620.

Notes: BLU B/90174 is entitled "LIVE TOGETHER DAVE BRUBECK FEATURING PAUL DESMOND". BANDSTAND (I) BDCD 1538 is a compilation CD entitled "DAVE BRUBECK QUARTET LIVE FEATURING PAUL DESMOND". JOK SM 3804 is entitled "DAVE BRU-

BECK FEATURING PAUL DESMOND". TOB B/2620 is an album from the series "American Jazz & Blues History", Vol. 120 entitled "DAVE BRUBECK: LIVE IN CONCERT". "Fairy Day" is "Fare Thee Well, Annabelle"; "Royal Garden Blues" is "Balcony Rock".

55.03.19   **Dave Brubeck Quartet**
Philadelphia, Pennsylvania, Penn State University, Recreation Hall.
Paul Desmond as; Dave Brubeck p; Norman Bates b; Joe Dodge dr.

a.	Give A Little Whistle	8:33	PENN STATE JAZZ
b.	Here Lies Love	7:45	CLUB F80P 7083-84
c.	The Trolley Song	3:18	-
d.	Jeepers Creepers	8:09	-
e.	These Foolish Things	11:17	-
f.	All The Things You Are	11:14	-
g.	For All We Know (inc.,ann.)	6:30	-

Notes: PENN STATE JAZZ CLUB F80P 7083-84 is a special release LP by the University of Pennsylvania, entitled "A UNIVERSITY LISTENS TO DAVE BRUBECK" (W. H. Schrickel).

55.07.16   **Dave Brubeck Quartet plus Chet Baker, Clifford Brown and**
                 Gerry Mulligan
Newport, Rhode Island, Newport Jazz Festival.
Chet Baker tp; Clifford Brown tp; Paul Desmond as; Gerry Mulligan bar; Dave Brubeck p; Norman Bates b; Joe Dodge dr.

a.	Tea For Two (incompl.)	9:44	PHIL W 51

Issues: PHIL W 51-2.

Notes: PHIL W 51 is an album with the title "CHET BAKER QUARTET PLUS ... THE NEWPORT YEARS, VOL. 1" , released in 1989; the CD PHIL W 51-2 was released in 1991. The sheet notes for this session additionally give Max Roach dr (M. Frohne). The Dave Brubeck Quartet played two more tunes (see next section) and another set the next day.

55.07.23   **Dave Brubeck Quartet**
New York City, New York, Basin Street Club.
Paul Desmond as; Dave Brubeck p; Bob Bates b; Joe Dodge dr.

a.	CO52634	Lover	4:56	COL CL 699

b.   CO52635   The Duke   2:38   -

Issues: COL B-699; COL CS 8645; **a** CBS 52703; CBS 80777; CBS 467148-2; COL 40776; COL 4-40776; COL 5-2280; COL B-2552; COR KEP 241; HAR HS 11336; PHI 332004 BF; PHI 362012 ARF; PHI 429273 BE; PHI BBE 12118; PHI BBL 7498; PHI JAZ 106; **b** COL 5-2282; COL CK-47032; COL C4K 52945; COL D-2(?); COL/SONY 467917-2; PHI 429793 BE.

Notes: COL CL 699 is entitled "THE DAVE BRUBECK QUARTET: JAZZ RED HOT AND COOL". COL D-2 is a Columbia Record Club demonstration record.
CBS 52703, CBS 80777, HAR HS 11336 cf. **54.03-04.00**; CBS 467148-2, COL CK-47032, COL/SONY 467917-2 cf. **54.10.12**; COL C4K 52945 cf. **46-48.00.00.** ·

55.08.08   **Dave Brubeck Quartet**
New York City, New York, Basin Street Club.
Paul Desmond as; Dave Brubeck p; Bob Bates b; Joe Dodge dr.
a.   CO52743   Little Girl Blue   10:32   COL CL 699

Issues: COL B-699; COL CS 8645; COL 5-2281.

Notes: COL CL 699 is entitled "THE DAVE BRUBECK QUARTET: JAZZ RED HOT AND COOL".

56.02.00   **Dave Brubeck Quartet**
New York City, New York, Basin Street Jazz Club, Broadcast.
Paul Desmond as; Dave Brubeck p; Norman Bates b; Joe Dodge dr.

a.	Theme (The Duke)-Introduction	1:02	JBR EBCD 2102-2
b.	Stardust	6:50	-
c.	Gone With The Wind	6:36	-
d.	Stompin' For Mili	5:04	-
e.	Out Of Nowhere (inc.)	4:29	-
f.	Theme (The Duke)	2:18	-
g.	Love Walked In	7:24	-
h.	Here Lies Love	6:47	-
i.	All The Things You Are	4:45	-
k.	A Minor Thing	6:25	-
l.	In Your Own Sweet Way	4:27	-
m.	The Trolley Song	2:50	-

Issues: f-m JBR EB 402.

Notes: JBR EB 402 is an album with the title "THE DAVE BRUBECK QUARTET FEATURING PAUL DESMOND: LIVE FROM THE BASIN STREET N.Y.C.", released in 1987. JBR EBCD 2102-2 is a Compact Disc with the title "THE DAVE BRUBECK QUARTET LIVE IN 1956-57 FEATURING PAUL DESMOND", released in 1991. It is likely that the material originates from at least three broadcasts.

56.03.12   **Dave Brubeck**
New York City, New York.
Dave Brubeck p.
a.   CO55556   When I Was Young   3:15   COL CL 878
b.   CO55557   I'm In A Dancing Mood   COL 4-40776

Issues: a PHI 429530 BE; PHI BBE 12118 (?); PHI BBL 7356; **b** COL 40776; MEL S 60-07229/30; PHI BBL 7208.

Notes: COL CL 878 is entitled "BRUBECK PLAYS BRUBECK". Raben /3./ gives another version of "I'm In A Dancing Mood" issued on an unnumbered Columbia 7" disc produced for The Music Educators National Conference in 1956.

56.03-04.00   **Dave Brubeck Quartet**
New York City, New York.
Paul Desmond as; Dave Brubeck p; Norman Bates b; Joe Dodge dr.
a.   When I Was Young   2:24   COL CL 1020

Issues: PHI BBL 7184; COR KLP 687; PHI R 13602 L; RTB (YU) LPV 4300.

Notes: COL CL 1020 is a sampler entitled "JAZZ OMNIBUS". PHI R 13602 L is a sampler entitled "THIS WONDERFUL WORLD OF JAZZ".

56.04.18+19   **Dave Brubeck**
Oakland, California.
Dave Brubeck p.
a.   In Your Own Sweet Way   4:57   COL CL 878

b.	One Moment Worth Years	4:50	-
c.	The Duke	2:51	-
d.	Two-Part Contention	5:36	-
e.	Swing Bells	3:36	-
f.	Walkin' Line	2:43	-
g.	The Waltz	3:47	-
h.	Weep No More	3:55	-

Issues: a,d,f PHI 429530 BE; **a** CBS 88061; CBS S 67257; CBS S2VL 1006; COL CL 2484; COL CS 9284; COL KG 32355; COL PG 32355; **d** COL C4K 52945.

Notes: COL CL 878 is entitled "BRUBECK PLAYS BRUBECK". COL CL 2484 is a compilation album entitled "DAVE BRUBECK'S GREATEST HITS", released in 1964. CBS S 67257, COL KG 32355 are sampler albums with the title "A JAZZ PIANO ANTHOLOGY: FROM RAGTIME TO FREE JAZZ", released in 1972. COL C4K 52945 cf. **46-48.00.00.**

56.07.06   Dave Brubeck Quartet
Newport, Rhode Island, Newport Jazz Festival.
Paul Desmond as; Dave Brubeck p; Norman Bates b; Joe Dodge dr.

a.	CO56788	In Your Own Sweet Way	8:01	COL CL 932
b.	CO56789	Two-Part Contention	11:44	-
c.	CO56790	I'm In A Dancing Mood	2:59	-
d.		The Duke		(unissued)
e.		Take The "A" Train	5:05	COL CL 932

Issues: a CBS 54703; COL C4K 52945; **b** CBS S 68288; COL KG 32761; **c** COL 3-42444 (ed.) (?); COL 4-42444 (ed.) (?); COL Spec. Prod. unn.; PHI 332004 BF; PHI 362012 ARF; PHI 429273 BE; PHI 429315 BE; 429530 BE; PHI BBE 12118 (?); PHI BBL 7208; **e** COL 3-42447 (ed.) (?); COL 4-42447 (ed.) (?).

Notes: COL CL 932 is entitled "DAVE BRUBECK AND JAY & KAI AT NEWPORT". The album was recorded live at the Newport Jazz Festival and contains three additional tracks by the J. J. Johnson-Kai Winding Quintet. According to Raben /3./ the above titles are taken from the Voice of America transcription (J 75 / 76); probably the issue of "Take The 'A' Train" on COL 4-42447 with master number CO52618 was recorded during the session **54.10.12.** CBS 54703 is a compilation album with the title "GOLDEN HIGHLIGHTS, VOL. 5 DAVE BRUBECK". COL KG 32761 is a compilation album with the title "DAVE BRUBECK'S ALL-TIME GREATEST HITS", containing two records, released in 1972. COL C4K 52945 cf. **46-48.00.00.**

56.08.03   **Dave Brubeck Quartet**
Stratford, Ontario, Canada.
Paul Desmond as; Dave Brubeck p; Norman Bates b; Joe Dodge dr.
a.   Pilgrim's Progress   9:16   PLAY 1957

Issues: COL (GB) 33CX1530; COL (D) C90977178; PLAY PB 7473; PLAY PJCS 1 & 2.

Notes: PLAY 1957, COL (GB) 33 CX 1530 are samplers with the title "THE PLAYBOY JAZZ ALL STARS", containing two records. PLAY PJCS 1 & 2 is a sampler entitled "1957 PLAYBOY JAZZ POLL WINNERS", re-issued in 1978. PLAY PB 7473 cf. **51.08.00.**

56.08.25   **Dave Brubeck Quartet**
New York City, New York.
Paul Desmond as; Dave Brubeck p; Norman Bates b; Joe Morello dr.
a.   Two-Part Contention   OZO 14
b.   One Moment Worth Years   -

Notes: OZO 14 is entitled "DAVE BRUBECK - LEONARD BERNSTEIN: DIALOGUE FOR JAZZ COMBO & ORCHESTRA".

56.11.16   **Dave Brubeck Quartet**
New York City, New York.
Paul Desmond as; Dave Brubeck p; Norman Bates b; Joe Morello dr.
a. CO56745   Yonder For Two   4:58   COL CL 984
b. CO56746   Curtain Time   4:44   -
c. CO56747   History Of A Boy Scout   4:32   -
d. CO56748   Summer Song   6:02   -

Issues: c COL C4K 52945; PHI 429407 BE; PHI BBE 12188; **d** PHI 429517 BE; PHI BBE 12230.

Notes: COL CL 984 is entitled "DAVE BRUBECK QUARTET: JAZZ IMPRESSIONS OF THE U.S.A.". COL C4K 52945 cf. **46-48.00.00.**

56.11.26   **Dave Brubeck Quartet**
New York City, New York.

Paul Desmond as; Dave Brubeck p; Norman Bates b; Joe Morello dr.

a.	CO57101	Plain Song	3:53	COL CL 984
b.	CO57102	Sounds Of The Loop	7:25	-
c.	CO57103	Ode To A Cowboy	4:57	-

Issues: a PHI 429517 BE; **b** PHI 429407 BE; PHI BBE 12188.

Notes: COL CL 984 is entitled "DAVE BRUBECK QUARTET: JAZZ IMPRESSIONS OF THE U.S.A.".

57.02.00   Dave Brubeck Quintet
San Francisco, California.
Dave Van Kriedt ts; Paul Desmond as; Dave Brubeck p; Norman Bates b; Joe Morello dr.

a.	Chorale (Arr. Van Kriedt)	4:13	FAN 3268
b.	Prelude	3:53	-
c.	Divertimento	5:14	-
d.	Shouts	6:05	-
e.	Leo's Place	5:17	-
f.	Darien Mode	4:31	-
g.	Pieta	5:48	-
h.	Strolling	3:18	-

Issues: FAN OJCCD-150-2; **d,e** FAN EP 5813; KAR KSEP 3187; **d,f** VOC EPV-F 1272; VOG EPV 1272; **a** FAN FS 655.

Notes: FAN 3268 is entitled "BRUBECK DESMOND VAN KRIEDT: RE-UNION". FAN FS 655 is a sampler with the title "INTRODUCTION TO STEREO".

57.02.04   Dave Brubeck
Oakland, California.
Dave Brubeck p.

a.	CO57361	Home At Last	3:49	COL CL 984

Issues: PHI 429517 BE; PHI BBE 12230.

Notes: COL CL 984 is entitled "DAVE BRUBECK QUARTET: JAZZ IMPRESSIONS OF THE U.S.A.".

57.02.08   **Dave Brubeck**

Oakland, California.

Dave Brubeck p.

a.	In Search Of A Theme	2:24	FAN 3259
b.	Sweet Cleo Brown	3:55	-
c.	You'd Be So Nice To Come Home To	2:25	-
d.	Imagination	6:06	-
e.	They Say It's Wonderful	2:40	-
f.	I'm Old Fashioned	4:55	-
g.	Love Is Here To Stay	2:46	-
h.	Indian Summer	3:42	-
i.	I See Your Face Before Me	4:55	-
k.	Two Sleepy People	3:30	FAN OJCCD-716-2

Issues: FAN OJCCD-716-2; **b,d-f** BOMC 80-5547; **b** FAN 3372; FAN 8372.

Notes: FAN 3259 is entitled "DAVE BRUBECK PLAYS AND PLAYS ...SOLO PIANO...". FAN OJCCD-716 is the CD issue including one bonus track with the same title, released in 1992. BOMC 80-5547 cf. **46-48.00.00**; FAN 3372, FAN 8372 cf. **50.03.00.**

57.03.00   **Dave Brubeck Quartet**

Chicago, Illinois, Blue Note.

Paul Desmond as; Dave Brubeck p; Norman Bates b; Joe Morello dr.

a.	Theme (The Duke) - Introduction	0:53	JBR EB 402
b.	I'm In A Dancing Mood	2:54	-
c.	The Song Is For You	2:54	-

Issues: JBR EBCD 2102-2.

Notes: JBR EB 402 is entitled "THE DAVE BRUBECK QUARTET FEATURING PAUL DESMOND LIVE FROM THE BASIN STREET N.Y.C.". "The Song Is For You" is "The Song Is You". For one other title see the next section. JBR EB 402 cf. **56.02.00.**

57.05.01   **Dave Brubeck Quartet**

Los Angeles, California, Fullerton College.

Paul Desmond as; Dave Brubeck p; Norman Bates b; Joe Morello dr.

a.	CO58211	Bru's Blues	11:28	COL CL 1034

b. CO58212   These Foolish Things (Remind Me Of You)   10:02-
c. CO58213   One Moment Worth Years   8:52   -

Issues: COL KG 31298; **a** COL B 10341; FON 462028 TE; FON TFE 17032; **b** COL B 10342; FON 462029 TE.

Notes: COL CL 1034 is entitled "DAVE BRUBECK QUARTET: JAZZ GOES TO JUNIOR COLLEGE". COL KG 31298 cf. **54.03-04.00.**

57.05.02   Dave Brubeck Quartet
Los Angeles, California, Long Beach Junior College.
Paul Desmond as; Dave Brubeck p; Norman Bates b; Joe Morello dr.
a. HCO40231   St. Louis Blues   8:17   COL CL 1034
b. HCO40234   (I'm Afraid) The Masquerade Is Over   6:06   -

Issues: CBS 467148-2; COL B-10343; COL KG 31298; COR KEP 156; FON TFE 17021; FON 462030 TE; **a** CBS 80776; CBS/SONY 26 AP 1321.

Notes: COL CL 1034 is entitled "DAVE BRUBECK QUARTET: JAZZ GOES TO JUNIOR COLLEGE". CBS/SONY 26 AP 1321 is a compilation album from the "GOLD DISK SERIES" entitled "DAVE BRUBECK". CBS 467148-2 cf. **54.10.12**; CBS 80776, COL KG 31298 cf. **54.03-04.00.**

57.06.29   Dave Brubeck Quartet
New York City, New York.
Paul Desmond as; Dave Brubeck p; Norman Bates b; Joe Morello dr.
a. CO58214   Alice In Wonderland   9:25   COL CL 1059
b. CO58215   Give A Little Whistle   7:31   -

Issues: COL B-10591; COL CS 8090; COM 6187382 **a** FON 462092 TE; FON TFE 17230; **b** FON 462062 TE; FON TFE 17074.

Notes: COL CL 1059 is entitled "THE DAVE BRUBECK QUARTET: DAVE DIGS DISNEY". COM 6187382 is a compilation album on CD entitled "DAVE BRUBECK: GREATEST HITS".

57.06.30   Dave Brubeck Quartet
New York City, New York.

Paul Desmond as; Dave Brubeck p; Norman Bates b; Joe Morello dr.

a. CO58243   Someday My Prince Will Come   8:15   COL CL 1059
b. CO58245   One Song   (unissued)

Issues: a CBS 80776; CBS 467148-2; CBS/SONY 23 AP 663; CBS/SONY 32 DP 785; COL 3-42444 (ed.) (?); COL 4-42444 (ed.) (?); COL B-10593; COL C4K 52945; COL CS 8090; COM 6187382; FON 462062 TE; FON 662039 TR; FON TFE 17074; FON TFL 5136.

Notes: COL CL 1059 is entitled "THE DAVE BRUBECK QUARTET: DAVE DIGS DISNEY". CBS 80776 cf. **54.03-04.00**; CBS 467148-2 cf. **54.10.12**; COL C4K 52945 cf. **46-48.00.00**; COM 6187382 cf. **57.06.29**.

57.08.03   **Dave Brubeck Quartet**
Los Angeles, California.
Paul Desmond as; Dave Brubeck p; Norman Bates b; Joe Morello dr.

a. HCO40178   One Song   4:55   COL CL 1059
b. HCO40179   Heigh-Ho   3:53   -
c. HCO40183   When You Wish Upon A Star   4:48   -

Issues: COL CS 8090; COM 6187382; **a,b** CBS 80775; CBS 467148-2; **b,c** COL B-10592; **a** COL B-10593; **b** FON TFL 5136; **c** FON 462092 TE; FON TFE 17230.

Notes: COL CL 1059 is entitled "THE DAVE BRUBECK QUARTET: DAVE DIGS DISNEY". CBS 467148-2 cf. **54.10.12**; COM 6187382 cf. **57.06.29**.

57.10.24   **Dave Brubeck Quartet**
Chicago, Illinois.
Paul Desmond as; Dave Brubeck p; Norman Bates b; Joe Morello dr.

a.   Two Sleepy People   5:40   PLAY 1958

Issues: COL (J) SL 3010.

Notes: PLAY 1958 is a sampler with the title "PLAYBOY JAZZ ALL STARS VOL. 2".

57.12.30   **Dave Brubeck Quartet**
New York City, New York, CBS-TV "TIMEX All Star Jazz Festival No. 1".

Paul Desmond as; Dave Brubeck p; Gene Wright b; Joe Morello dr.

a.   St. Louis Blues   4:11   KOJ KLJ 20030

Louis Armstrong and His All Stars plus Guests

Louis Armstrong tp, voc; Trummy Young tb; Edmond Hall cl; Billy Kyle p; Arvell Shaw b; Barrett Deems dr; Bobby Hackett cor; Jack Teagarden tb, voc; Peanuts Hucko cl; Marty Napoleon p; Cozy Cole dr; Dave Brubeck p; Paul Desmond as; Gene Krupa dr.

b.   When The Saints   2:27   -

Issues: a,b MUSIC FOR PLEASURE (GB) 4M 126-23594/5; SOUNDS GREAT SG 8005; TIMEX CS-1; **a** JASMINE (GB) JASM 2530.

Notes: KOJ KLJ 20030 is a sampler with the title "HERE ARE FROM THE 50s RARE OF ALL RAREST JAZZ PERFORMANCES VOL.1 FEATURING : LESTER YOUNG * DAVE BRUBECK * DUKE ELLINGTON * JACK TEAGARDEN * BOBBY HACKETT * CARMEN MCRAE * GENE KRUPA * WOODY HERMAN * JUNE CHRISTY * LOUIS ARMSTRONG" , released in 1981. Herman Wright b is incorrectly given on the cover. MUSIC FOR PLEASURE (GB) 4M 126-23594/5 is a sampler double album entitled "THE JAZZ GIANTS". SOUNDS GREAT SG 8005 is entitled "ALL STAR JAZZ SHOW".

58.02.22   **Dave Brubeck Quartet**

Berlin, Germany, Sportspalast.

Paul Desmond as; Dave Brubeck p; Gene Wright b; Joe Morello dr.

a.   These Foolish Things (inc.)   9:13   PHIL W 72-2

b.   St.Louis Blues   13:01 -

c.   Two-Part Contention   15:38 -

d.   Take The "A" Train   18:14 -

Notes: PHIL W 72-2 is a CD with the title "SWEET PAUL, VOLUME 1", released in 1992.

58.02.28   **Dave Brubeck Quartet**

Hannover, Germany, Niedersachsenhalle.

Paul Desmond as; Dave Brubeck p; Gene Wright b; Joe Morello dr.

a.   Out Of Nowhere   9:56   PHIL W 72-2

b.   These Foolish Things   8:15   -

Notes: PHIL W 72-2 is a CD with the title "SWEET PAUL, VOLUME 1", released in 1992.

58.03.05   **Dave Brubeck Quartet**

Copenhagen, Denmark.

Paul Desmond as (a-c,e-f); Dave Brubeck p; Gene Wright b; Joe Morello dr.

a.	Tangerine	9:32	COL CL 1168
b.	Wonderful Copenhagen	4:48	-
c.	The Wright Groove	6:37	-
d.	My One Bad Habit Is Falling In Love	3:51	-
e.	Like Someone In Love	7:10	-
f.	Watusi Drums	7:48	-

Issues: COL CS 8128; **a,b,e** CBS 462403-1/-2; COL CK-44215; COL JC2-44215; **a,b** COL CK-47931; **b,c** FON E 76805; **b,e** FON TFE 17196; FON 467030 TE; **b,f** COR KEP 210; **a** COL 3-42445 (ed.); COL 4-42445 (ed.); COL C4K 52945; **b** CBS 465192-1/-2; COL CK 45037; COL J2C-45037; FON TFL 5136; **d** FON 662039 TR; **e** ELITE 009 CD.

Notes: COL CL 1168 is entitled "THE DAVE BRUBECK QUARTET IN EUROPE". CBS 462403-1/-2, COL CK-44215, and COL JC2-44215 are compilation albums from the series "COLUMBIA / CBS JAZZ MASTERPIECES" with the title "DAVE BRUBECK QUARTET: THE GREAT CONCERTS ... AMSTERDAM, COPENHAGEN, CARNEGIE HALL", released in 1988 with digitally remastered tapes. CBS 465192-1, COL J2C-45037 are 2 LP sampler sets from the series "COLUMBIA / CBS JAZZ MASTERPIECES" with the title "THE JAZZ MASTERS". CBS 465192-2, COL CK 45037 are 2-CD sampler boxes with the same title. COL CK-47931 is a compilation CD with the title "THE ESSENCE OF DAVE BRUBECK". COL C4K 52945 cf. **46-48.00.00**; ELITE 009 CD cf. **54.10.14**.

58.07.03   **Dave Brubeck Quartet**

Newport, Rhode Island, Newport Jazz Festival.

Paul Desmond as; Dave Brubeck p; Joe Benjamin b; Joe Morello dr.

a.	Jump For Joy	5:15	COL CL 1249
b.	Perdido	12:40	-
c.	Things Ain't What They Used To Be	7:00	-
d.	C-Jam Blues/	4:12	-
	Take The "A" Train	0:26	-
e.	The Duke		CBS (GB) 31769

Issues: a-d COL CS 8082; **a,c** FON 467210 TE; **c,d** CBS 80775; **a** COL C4K 52945; **b** CBS 52976; CBS SPR 55; **c** CBS S 63517; COL JJ 1 (ed.); COL JS 1 (ed.); FON 467119 TE; FON 662039 TR; FON TFE 17245; **d** CBS S 52988; CBS 88136; JW 77010.

Notes: COL CL 1249 is entitled "THE DAVE BRUBECK QUARTET: NEWPORT 1958". CBS 52976 is a sampler with the title "HORIZONS DU JAZZ". COL JJ 1, COL JS 1 are samplers entitled "COLUMBIA JAZZ FESTIVAL". JW 77010 is a sampler on CD with the title "DAVE BRUBECK: TAKE FIVE", released in 1987. CBS 80775 cf. **54.03-04.00**; COL C4K 52945 cf. **46-48.00.00**.

58.07.28 **Dave Brubeck Quartet**

New York City, New York.

Paul Desmond as; Dave Brubeck p; Joe Benjamin b; Joe Morello dr.

a.	CO61316	The Duke	6:20	COL CL 1249
b.	CO61317	Dance No.3 From "The Liberian Suite"	6:30	-
c.	CO61318	Flamingo	6:15	-

Issues: COL CS 8082; **a,b** FON 467211 TE; **a,c** JW 77010; **a** ATM 032; CBS 54703; CBS/EMBA 31769; COL 3-42445 (ed.); COL 4-42445 (ed.); COL CL 2484; COL CS 9284; COL KG 32761; MEL S60-07229/30; **b** FON 467119 TE; FON TFE 17245; FON TFL 5136; **c** CBS 80775; CBS 467148-2.

Notes: COL CL 1249 is entitled "THE DAVE BRUBECK QUARTET: NEWPORT 1958". CBS/EMBA 31769 is a compilation album entitled "TAKE FIVE". CBS 54703; COL KG 32761 cf. **56.07.06**; CBS 80775 cf. **54.03-04.00**; CBS 467148-2 cf. **54.10.12**; COL CL 2484 cf. **56.04.18+19**; JW 77010 cf. **58.07.03**; MEL S60-07229/30 cf. **56.03.12**.

58.08.23 **Dave Brubeck Quartet**

New York City, New York.

Paul Desmond as (a, c-f); Dave Brubeck p; Joe Benjamin b; Joe Morello dr.

a.	CO61320	Nomad	7:18	COL CL 1251
b.	CO61321	Thank You (Dziekuje)	3:29	-
c.	CO61322	The Golden Horn	4:58	-
d.	CO61323	Brandenburg Gate	6:52	-
e.	CO61324	Marble Arch	6:54	-
f.	CO61325	Calcutta Blues (Oriental Rag)	9:50	-

Issues: CBS/SONY 25 DP 5315; COL CK-48531; COL CS 8058; COL/CBS 471249-2; **b,c,e** COL B-12511; **a,e** FON TFE 17135; **c,d** FON 467071 TE; FON TFE 17999; **c,e** COL C4K 52945; **d,e** CBS EP 5533; FON 467031 TE; **b** CBS 1122; CBS CA 281122; FON 662034 TR; **c** PLAY 1959B; **e** COL D 288; COL DS 288.

Notes: COL CL 1251 is entitled "THE DAVE BRUBECK QUARTET: JAZZ IMPRESSIONS OF EURASIA". COL D 288, COL DS 288 are compilation albums with the title "DAVE BRUBECK! RIGHT NOW!", released by the Columbia Record Club. COL/CBS 471249-2, COL CK-48531 are albums from the series "COLUMBIA / CBS JAZZ MASTERPIECES" with the title "THE DAVE BRUBECK QUARTET: JAZZ IMPRESSIONS OF EURASIA", released in 1992. PLAY 1959 is a sampler with the title "PLAYBOY JAZZ ALL STARS: VOLUME 3". COL CK-48513, COL/CBS 471249-2 cf. **58.07.25**; COL C4K 52945 cf. **46-48.00.00**.

59.04.22   Dave Brubeck Quartet
Los Angeles, California, American Legion Hall.
Paul Desmond as; Dave Brubeck p; Gene Wright b; Joe Morello dr.

a.	HCO46192	Gone With The Wind	6:22	COL CL 1347
b.	HCO46193	The Lonesome Road	7:38	-
c.	HCO46194	Swanee River	5:53	-
d.	HCO46195	Basin Street Blues	4:30	-
e.	HCO46196	Georgia On My Mind	6:37	-
f.	HCO46198	Ol' Man River	2:26	-

Issues: CBS 450984-1/-2; COL CG 33666; COL CJ-40627; COL CK-40627; COL CS 8156; **a,b** CBS EP 5544; **a,c** COL B-13471; **a,e** FON TFE 17305; FON 467130 TE; **b,c** FON TFE 17304; FON 467129 TE; **c,d** ZOUNDS 27200446B; **c,e** CBS EP 5545; **d,e** CBS 80776; **a** CBS 460063-1/-2; COL 3-42446 (ed.); COL 4-42446 (ed.); COL CJ-40798; COL CK-40798; COL CK-47931; **c** COL D 288; COL DS 288; COL JS7-4S7 30719; **d** FON 467131 TE; FON 780004 TV; FON TFE 17303; **e** CBS/SONY 26 AP 1321; COL C4K 52945; **f** CBS 80777; COL JS7-4S7 30722..

Notes: COL CL 1347 is entitled "THE DAVE BRUBECK QUARTET: GONE WITH THE WIND". COL CG 33666 is a double album with the title "THE DAVE BRUBECK QUARTET: GONE WITH THE WIND AND TIME OUT" containing both records COL CS 8156 und COL CS 8192. CBS 450984-1/-2, COL CJ-40627 and COL CK-40627 are albums from the series "COLUMBIA / CBS JAZZ MASTERPIECES" with the title "THE DAVE BRUBECK QUARTET: GONE WITH THE WIND" containing digitally remastered tapes, released in 1987. CBS 460063-1/-2, COL CJ-40798 and COL CK-40798 are samplers from the series "COLUMBIA / CBS JAZZ MASTERPIECES" with the title "COLUMBIA / CBS JAZZ MASTERPIECES VOLUME II", released in 1987. CBS 80776, CBS 80777 cf. **54.03-04.00**; CBS/SONY 26 AP 1321 cf. **57.05.02**; COL CK-47931 cf. **58.03.05**; COL C4K 52945 cf. **46-48.00.00**; COL D 288, COL DS 288 cf. **58.07.25**; ZOUNDS 27200446B cf. **54.10.12**.

59.04.23   Dave Brubeck Quartet

Los Angeles, California, American Legion Hall.

Paul Desmond as; Dave Brubeck p; Gene Wright b; Joe Morello dr.

a	HCO46213	Camptown Races	1:55	COL CL 1347
b		Camptown Races	2:06	-
c	HCO46214	Short'nin' Bread	2:27	-

Issues: CBS 450984-1/-2; COL CG 33666; COL CJ-40627; COL CK-40627; COL CS 8156; **a,c** COL 4-41485; FON 271121 TE; FON TFE 17303; FON 467131 TE; FON 780004 TV; **a** CBS CA 201102; COL 3-42447; COL 4-42447; COL 4-42675; COL CL 2484; COL CS 9284; COL KG 32761; ELITE 009 CD; FON AAG 1202; FON 662039 TR; MEL S60-07229/30; **a or b** COL B-13471; COL JS7-4S7 30719; **c** PHI B 07059 L.

Notes: COL CL 1347 is entitled "THE DAVE BRUBECK QUARTET: GONE WITH THE WIND". CBS 450984-1/-2, COL CG 33666, COL CJ-40627, COL CK-40627 cf. **59.04.22**; COL CL 2484 cf. **56.04.18+19**; COL KG 32761 cf. **56.07.06**; ELITE 009 CD, PHI B 07059 L cf. **54.10.14**; MEL S60-07229/30 cf. **56.03.12**.

59.06.25   Dave Brubeck Quartet

New York City, New York.

Paul Desmond as; Dave Brubeck p; Gene Wright b; Joe Morello dr.

a.	CO62555	Kathy's Waltz	4:52	COL CL 1397
b.	CO62556	Three To Get Ready	5:25	-
c.	CO62558	Everybody's Jumpin'	4:19	-

Issues: CBS 460611-1/-2; COL CG 33666; COL CJ-40585; COL CK-40585; COL CK-52860; COL CS 8192; JW 77035; **a,b** COL G 30625; **a** CBS 54703; CBS EP 5528; CBS/EMBA 31769; COM 6187382; FON 780013 TV; FON TFL 5136; RMN 73002; **b** CBS EP 5527; COL C4K 52945; COL D 288; COL DS 288; FON 467162 TE.

Notes: COL CL 1397 is entitled "THE DAVE BRUBECK QUARTET: TIME OUT". COL G 30625 is a double compilation album with the title "DAVE BRUBECK: ADVENTURES IN TIME", released in 1971. CBS 450984-1/-2, COL CJ-40585 and COL CK-40585 are albums from the series "COLUMBIA / CBS JAZZ MASTERPIECES" with the title "THE DAVE BRUBECK QUARTET: TIME OUT" containing digitally remastered tapes, released in 1987. COL CK-52860 is a 24-karat gold limited re-issue of COL CK-40585. JW 77035 is a compilation Compact Disc with the title "DAVE BRUBECK GREATEST HITS VOL. 2", released in 1990.

RMN 73002 is a sampler with the title "JAZZ ROUND MIDNIGHT VOL. 2". CBS 54703 cf. **56.07.06**; CBS/EMBA 31769 cf. **58.07.28**; COL CG 33666 cf. **59.04.22**; COL C4K 52945 cf. **46-48.00.00**; COL D 288, COL DS 288 cf. **58.07.25**; COM 6187382 cf. **57.06.29**.

59.07.01 **Dave Brubeck Quartet**
New York City, New York.
Paul Desmond as; Dave Brubeck p; Gene Wright b; Joe Morello dr.

a.	CO62578	Take Five	5:25	COL CL 1397
b.	CO62578	Take Five (alt. take)		COL 4-41479
c.	CO62580	Strange Meadow Lark	7:18	COL CL 1397

Issues: a,c CBS 460611-1/-2; COL CG 33666; COL CJ-40585; COL CK-40585; COL CK-52860; COL C4K 52945; COL CS 8192; ELITE 009 CD; **a** AFF AFFD 180; CBS 1103; CBS 4662; CBS 54703; CBS 54490; CBS 80775; CBS 450979-1/-2; CBS 453041-1; CBS 465429-2; CBS 467148-2; CBS AGG 320026; CBS EP 5527; CBS EP 5608; CBS S 66238; CBS/EMBA 31769; CBS/SONY 23 AP 663; CBS/SONY 26 AP 1321; CBS/SONY 32 DP 785; CIRCLE 344-3350; COL 4-33036; COL 13-33036; COL CJ-40474; COL CK-40474; COL CK-47931; COL CL 2484; COL CS 9284; COL CSP 217 M; COL CSP 217 S; COL CSP 13230; COL G 30625; COL JS7-4S7 30720; COL KG 32761; COL SONX 60138; COL SOPM 47; COL XSV 86015; COL XTV 86088 (?); COL ZSV 62123; COM 6187382; FAVOURITES (NL) FAV 002; FON 467162 TE; FON 467177 TE; FON TFE 17307; JW 77010; MEL S60-07229/30; SUP 015/115.1029; UNIVERSE UN 1046; ZOUNDS 27200446B; **b** FON 271168 TF; FON H 339; **c** FON TFL 5136; JW 77035.

Notes: COL CL 1397 is entitled "THE DAVE BRUBECK QUARTET: TIME OUT". Entry b is given following Raben /3./. AFF AFFD 180 is a sampler with the title "JAZZ DANCE KICKS", released in 1987. CBS 450341-1 is a sampler entitled "JAZZ A TOUS LES ETAGES". CBS 450979-1/-2, COL CJ-40474 and COL CK-40474 are samplers from the series "COLUMBIA / CBS JAZZ MASTERPIECES" with the title "COLUMBIA / CBS JAZZ MASTERPIECES VOLUME I", released in 1986. CBS 465429-2 is a sampler CD entitled "JAZZ FEELINGS", released in 1989. CBS/SONY 23 AP 663 is a compilation album entitled "HEY BRUBECK! TAKE FIVE". CBS/SONY 32 DP 785 is the CD issue with the same title. CIRCLE 344-3350 is a 2 LP sampler entitled "SWING AND SWEET". COL CSP 217 M, COL CSP 217 S are samplers entitled "ZENITH JAZZ SET", released by Columbia Special Products as a Zenith Collector's Item. COL CSP 13230 is entitled "REALISTIC JAZZ GREATS, VOL. 2" and was produced by Columbia Special Products for Realistic, Radio Shack, a Tandy Corp. division. COL XSV 86015 is a 2 LP sampler with the title "GENERAL ELECTRIC PRESENTS ... A STEREO OF STARS", released by Columbia Special Products. COL XTV 86088 is a 2 LP set produced as a

"DIAMOND JUBILEE SHOWCASE: REXALL'S 60TH ANNIVERSARY". FAVOURITES (NL) FAV 002 is a sampler CD entitled "JAZZ FAVOURITES". UNIVERSE UN 1046 is a box of three sampler CD's with the title "SWINGTIME VOL. 1", released in 1992. CBS 54490, CBS 80775 cf. **54.03-04.00**; CBS 467148-2, ZOUNDS 27200446B cf. **54.10.12**; CBS/EMBA 31769 cf. **58.07.28**; CBS/SONY 26 AP 1321 cf. **57.05.02**; COL CG 33666 cf. **59.04.22**; CBS 460611-1/-2, COL CJ-40585, COL CK-40585, COL CK-52860, COL G 30625, JW 77035 cf. **59.06.25**; COL CK-47931 cf. **58.03.05**; COL CL 2484 cf. **56.04.18+19**; COL C4K 52945 cf. **46-48.00.00**; CBS 54703, COL KG 32761 cf. **56.07.06**; COM 6187382 cf. **57.06.29**; JW 77010 cf. **58.07.03**; MEL S60-07229/30 cf. **56.03.12**.

59.07.02   **Dave Brubeck Trio**
New York City, New York.
Dave Brubeck p; Gene Wright b; Joe Morello dr.
a. CO62590   King For A Day   3:41   COL OL 5850

Issues: CBS 467140-2; COL OS 2250; COL JS7-69S7-31589.

Notes: COL OL 5850 is entitled "THE REAL AMBASSADORS: AN ORIGINAL MUSICAL PRODUCTION BY DAVE AND IOLA BRUBECK". Jepsen /1./ and Raben /3./ indicate that the vocal parts of Armstrong and Young in the final issue were recorded at a later date (cf. **61.09.19**).

59.07.05   **Dave Brubeck Quartet**
Newport, Rhode Island; Newport Jazz Festival.
Paul Desmond as; Dave Brubeck p; Gene Wright b; Joe Morello dr.
a.   Gone With The Wind   5:10 MOR MLP 028-1
b.   Lonesome Road   8:16 -
c.   Three To Get Ready   4:30 -
d.   Blue Rondo A La Turk   5:15 -

Issues: BANDSTAND (I) BDCD 1538; MOR MCD 028-2.

Notes : MOR MLP 028-1, MOR MCD 028-2 are entitled "DAVE BRUBECK FEATURING PAUL DESMOND: ST. LOUIS BLUES" , released in 1990. MOR MLP 028-1 contains the broadcast recording from the Newport Jazz Festival 1959 and the recording of a KQED television program (cf. **62.01.14**). The Compact Disc contains as bonus track "Ralph Gleason interviews Dave Brubeck" and "Some Brubeck Considerations on Classic Music and Jazz" (7:28). BANDSTAND (I) BDCD 1538 cf. **55.00.00**.

59.08.12   **Dave Brubeck Quartet**
New York City, New York.
Bill Smith cl; Dave Brubeck p; Gene Wright b; Joe Morello dr.

a.	CO62736	Hey Ho, Anybody Home?	5:14	COL CL 1454
b.	CO62737	The Twig	4:07	-
c.	CO62738	Blue Ground	5:34	-
d.	CO62739	Offshoot	2:33	-
e.	CO62740	Swingin' Round	7:23	-
f.	CO62741	Quiet Mood	5:51	-
g.	CO62742	The Riddle	3:52	-

Issues: COL CS 8248; **a,d** FON 467238 TE; FON TFE 17357; **d** COL C4K 52945.

Notes: COL CL 1454 is entitled "THE DAVE BRUBECK QUARTET: THE RIDDLE".
COL C4K 52945 cf. **46-48.00.00.**

59.08.13   **Dave Brubeck Quartet**
New York City, New York.
Bill Smith cl; Dave Brubeck p; Gene Wright b; Joe Morello dr.

a.	CO62743	Yet We Shall Be Merry	3:32	COL CL 1454

Issues: COL CS 8248; FON 467238 TE; FON TFE 17357.

Notes: COL CL 1454 is entitled "THE DAVE BRUBECK QUARTET: THE RIDDLE".

59.08.18   **Dave Brubeck Quartet**
New York City, New York.
Paul Desmond as; Dave Brubeck p; Gene Wright b; Joe Morello dr.

a.	CO62752	Blue Rondo A La Turk	6:45	COL CL 1397
b.	CO62752	Blue Rondo A La Turk (alt. take)		COL 4-41479
c.	CO62753	Pick Up Sticks	4:13	COL CL 1397

Issues: **a,c** CBS 460611-1/-2; COL CG 33666; COL CJ-40585; COL CK-40585; COL CK-52860; COL CS 8192; JW 77035; **a** CBS 1103; CBS 54490; CBS 54703; CBS 80776; CBS 453041-1; CBS 465192-1/-2; CBS 465429-2; CBS 467148-2; CBS EP 5528; CBS EP 5608; CBS S 67209; CBS/EMBA 31769; CBS/SONY 23 AP 663; CBS/SONY 23 AP 1321; CBS/SONY 32 DP 785; COL 4-33036; COL 13-33036; COL CK 45037; COL CK-47931; COL C4K 52945;

COL CL 1610; COL CL 2484; COL CS 8410; COL CS 9284; COL G 30625; COL J2C 45037; COL JS7-4S7 30720; COL KG 32761; COL SONP 50003; COL SONX 60138; COL SOPM 47; COL XSV 65036; COL XTV 65036; ELITE 009 CD; FON 271168 TF; FON 780013 TV; FON TFL 5136; MEL S60-07229/30; RMN 73004; SUP 015/115.1029; ZOUNDS 27200446B; b FON 271168 TF; FON H 339; c CBS EP 5523.

Notes: COL CL 1397 is entitled "THE DAVE BRUBECK QUARTET: TIME OUT". Entry b is given following Raben /3./. CBS S 67209 is a sampler with the title "SUPERB SUPER JAZZ PARTY" containing two records. COL CL 1610, COL CS 8410 are samplers with the title "JAZZ POLL WINNERS". COL XSV 65036, COL XTV 65036 are samplers from the "EXCLUSIVE WORLD JAZZ SERIES" expressly for The Lark automobile by Studebaker. RMN 73004 is a sampler on CD with the title "JAZZ ROUND MIDNIGHT VOL. 4". CBS 54703, COL KG 32761 cf. 56.07.06; CBS 453041-1, CBS 465429-2 cf. 59.07.01; CBS 54490, CBS 80776 cf. 54.03-04.00; CBS 465192-1/-2, COL CK 45037, COL J2C 45037 cf. 58.03.05; CBS 467148-2, ZOUNDS 27200446B cf. 54.10.12; CBS/EMBA 31769 cf. 58.07.28; CBS/SONY 23 AP 663 cf. 59.07.01; CBS/SONY 23 AP 1321 cf. 57.05.02; COL CG 33666 cf. 59.04.22; CBS 460611-1/-2, COL CJ-40585, COL G 30625, COL CK-40585, COL CK-52860, JW 77035 cf. 59.06.25; COL CK-47931 cf. 58.03.05; COL C4K 52945 cf. 46-48.00.00; COL CL 2484 cf. 56.04.18+19; ELITE 009 CD cf. 54.10.14; MEL S60-07229/30 cf. 56.03.12; SUP 015/115.1029 cf. 59.07.01.

59.09.10   Dave Brubeck Quartet
New York City, New York.
Paul Desmond as (b,c); Dave Brubeck p; Gene Wright b; Joe Morello dr (b,c).
a. CO62968   At The Darktown Strutters' Ball   1:36   COL CL 1439
b. CO62970   When It's Sleepy Time Down South   5:50   -
c. CO62973   Nobody Knows The Trouble I've Seen 5:55   -

Issues: COL CS 8235; a COL C4K 52945; COL JS7-4S7 30722; FON 467176 TE; FON TFE 17306; b FON 467225 TE; FON TFE 17363.

Notes: COL CL 1439 is entitled "DAVE BRUBECK QUARTET TRIO AND DUO: SOUTHERN SCENE". COL C4K 52945 cf. 46-48.00.00.

59.09.11   Dave Brubeck Quartet
New York City, New York.
Paul Desmond as; Dave Brubeck p; Gene Wright b; Joe Morello dr.
a. CO62972   Southern Scene   5:40   COL CL 1439

b. CO62975   Little Rock Getaway   3:17 -
c. CO62976   Darling Nellie Gray   5:15 -

Issues: COL CS 8235; **b,c** FON 467176 TE; FON TFE 17306; **b** COL JS7-4S7 30721; **c** FON 467225 TE; FON TFE 17363.

Notes: COL CL 1439 is entitled "DAVE BRUBECK QUARTET TRIO AND DUO: SOUTHERN SCENE".

59.10.29   Dave Brubeck Trio
Los Angeles, California.
Dave Brubeck p; Gene Wright b; Joe Morello dr (b-d).
a. HCO46373   Oh, Susanna   2:36   COL CL 1439
b. HCO46374   Deep In The Heart Of Texas   3:17 -
c. HCO46375   Jeanie With The Light Brown Hair   2:25 -
d. HCO46376   Happy Times   2:35 -

Issues: COL CS 8235; **a,c** COL JS7-4S7 30723; **b,c** CBS AGG 320026; COL PM 1; COL PMS-1; FON TFE 17307; **a** FON TFL 5136; COL JS7-4S7 30721.

Notes: COL CL 1439 is entitled "DAVE BRUBECK QUARTET TRIO AND DUO: SOUTHERN SCENE". COL PM 1, COL PMS-1 are samplers with the title "STARS FOR A SUMMER NIGHT".

59.12.12   Dave Brubeck Quartet With The New York Philharmonic
**   Conductor Leonard Bernstein**
New York City, New York, Carnegie Hall, Broadcast.
Paul Desmond as; Dave Brubeck p; Gene Wright b; Joe Morello dr; The New York Philharmonic, Leonard Bernstein cond.
a.   Dialogue(s) For Jazz Combo And Orchestra   OZO 14
              - Allegro
              - Andante - Ballad
              - Adagio - Ballad
              - Allegro - Blues

Notes: OZO 14 is entitled "DAVE BRUBECK - LEONARD BERNSTEIN: DIALOGUE FOR JAZZ COMBO & ORCHESTRA". Howard Brubeck's "Dialogues for Jazz Combo and

Orchestra" was first performed in a Philharmonic series on December 10, 11, and 13, 1959 in the Carnegie Hall, New York City. OZO 14 cf. **56.08.25**.

60.00.00   **Dave Brubeck Quartet**
Paul Desmond as; Dave Brubeck p; Gene Wright b; Joe Morello dr.
a.   Royalty Blues   COL GB-7, GS-7

Notes: COL GB-7, COL GS-7 are samplers entitled "THE HEADLINERS". They were released in 1960 for the 5th Anniversary of the Columbia Record Club.

60.01.29   **Dave Brubeck Quartet Featuring Jimmy Rushing**
New York City, New York.
Paul Desmond as; Dave Brubeck p; Gene Wright b; Joe Morello dr; Jimmy Rushing voc.

a.	Am I Blue	2:53	COL CL 1553
b.	There'll Be Some Changes Made	2:03	-
c.	Blues In The Dark	4:35	-
d.	Take Me Back, Baby		(unissued)

Issues: a-c COL CS 8353; FON TFE 17358; JW 77010; **a,c** ROJ 10055/56; **a** ATM 022; COL JS7-18S7 30903; ROJ 10016; **b** COL C4K 52945; COL JS7-18S7 30899; **c** COL C 30522.

Notes: COL CL 1553 is entitled "THE DAVE BRUBECK QUARTET FEATURING JIMMY RUSHING". COL C 30522 is a compilation album entitled "SUMMIT SESSIONS: DAVE BRUBECK WITH SPECIAL GUEST STARS" with recordings made between 1960 and 1967. The album contains one title "Our Time Of Parting" without participation of Dave Brubeck. The ATM releases are part of a series of 10 sampler CDs from All-Time Music with the title "16 ALL-TIME JAZZ SESSIONS". Volumes 3 to 8 each contain one tune only by the Dave Brubeck Quartet. ATM 022 is Vol. 5 of the series. ROJ 10016, ROJ 10055/56 are a sampler CD and 2-CD box, respectively, by a company called "Romance Of Jazz". COL C4K 52945 cf. **46-48.00.00**; JW 77010 cf. **58.07.03**.

60.01.30   **Dave Brubeck Quartet With The New York Philharmonic**
                        Conductor Leonard Bernstein
New York City, New York.
Paul Desmond as; Dave Brubeck p; Gene Wright b; Joe Morello dr; The New York Philharmonic, Leonard Bernstein cond.

a.	Dialogues For Jazz Combo And Orchestra	COL CL 1466
	- Allegro	6:55
	- Andante - Ballad	5:13
	- Adagio - Ballad	4:46
	- Allegro - Blues	5:34

Issues: CBS 61995; COL CS 8257; Adagio - Ballad, Andante - Ballad CBS EPCG 285541; Andante - Ballad COL 7-8257; Allegro - Blues COL C 30522; COL C4K 52945; FOLLET L 25.

Notes: COL CL 1466 is entitled "BERNSTEIN PLAYS BRUBECK PLAYS BERNSTEIN"; later issues were entitled "THE DAVE BRUBECK QUARTET PLAYS MUSIC FROM LEONARD BERNSTEIN'S WEST SIDE STORY: MARIA / I FEEL PRETTY / SOMEWHERE / TONIGHT AND A QUIET GIRL FROM WONDERFUL TOWN PLUS HOWARD BRUBECK'S DIALOGUES FOR JAZZ COMBO AND ORCHESTRA WITH THE NEW YORK PHILHARMONIC CONDUCTED BY LEONARD BERNSTEIN". The album contains four titles from the musical "West Side Story" (cf. **60.02.14**) as well as one more title from the musical "Wonderful Town" (cf. **60.02.17**). Both musicals are composed by Leonard Bernstein. CBS 61995 is an equivalent issue in the Series CBS / Classics. FOLLET L 25 is a 2 LP sampler with the title "THE ORIGINS AND DEVELOPMENT OF JAZZ", produced by Follet Publishing Co. in association with Columbia Special Products. COL C 30522 cf. **60.01.29**; COL C4K 52945 cf. **46-48.00.00**.

60.01.31   Dave Brubeck Trio
New York City, New York.
Dave Brubeck p; Gene Wright b; Joe Morello dr.

a.	CO63967	Zen Is When	2:47	COL CL 2212

Issues: COL CS 9012.

Notes: COL CL 2212 is entitled "THE DAVE BRUBECK QUARTET: JAZZ IMPRESSIONS OF JAPAN".

60.02.14   Dave Brubeck Quartet
New York City, New York.
Paul Desmond as; Dave Brubeck p; Gene Wright b; Joe Morello dr.

a.	CO64115	Tonight	3:48	COL CL 1466
b.	CO64116	I Feel Pretty	5:09	-

c.	CO64117	Maria	3:16	-
d.	CO64118	Somewhere	4:13	-

Issues: CBS 21065; CBS 61995; CBS 450410-1/-2; COL CJ-40455; COL CK-40455; COL CS 8257; **a-c** CBS EP 5530; FON 467242 TE; **a,c** CBS 1115; CBS 80776; CBS AAL 115; **b,c** COL 7-8257; **c,d** COL CK-47931; ELITE 009 CD; **a** FON 467225 TE; **b** ZOUNDS 27200446B; **c** CBS 21120; COL 3-42443; COL 4-42443; **d** CBS 450979-1/-2; CBS 465932-2; CBS 466690-2; COL CJ-40474; COL CK-40474; COL C4K 52945.

Notes: COL CL 1466 is entitled "BERNSTEIN PLAYS BRUBECK PLAYS BERNSTEIN"; later issues were entitled "THE DAVE BRUBECK QUARTET PLAYS MUSIC FROM LEONARD BERNSTEIN'S WEST SIDE STORY: MARIA / I FEEL PRETTY / SOMEWHERE / TONIGHT AND A QUIET GIRL FROM WONDERFUL TOWN PLUS HOWARD BRUBECK'S DIALOGUES FOR JAZZ COMBO AND ORCHESTRA WITH THE NEW YORK PHILHARMONIC CONDUCTED BY LEONARD BERNSTEIN". CBS 21065 is an album from the CBS series "I LOVE JAZZ" with the title "BRUBECK PLAYS WEST SIDE STORY / PREVIN PLAYS MY FAIR LADY". CBS 21120 is a sampler from the CBS series "I LOVE JAZZ" entitled "THE BEST OF I LOVE JAZZ", released in 1984. CBS 465932-2 is a sampler entitled "JAZZ FEELINGS VOL. III", released in 1989. CBS 466690-2 is a sampler released in Germany with the title "SCHMUSEJAZZ". CBS 450410-1/-2, COL CJ-40455 and COL CK-40455 are albums from the series "COLUMBIA / CBS JAZZ MASTERPIECES" with the title "THE DAVE BRUBECK QUARTET PLAYS MUSIC FROM WEST SIDE STORY AND ... (OTHER SHOWS AND FILMS)", released in 1986 with digitally remastered tapes. CBS 61995 cf. **60.01.30**; CBS 80776 cf. **54.03-04.00**; CBS 450979-1/-2, COL CJ-40474, COL CK-40474 cf. **59.07.01**; COL CK-47931 cf. **58.03.05**; COL C4K 52945 cf. **46-48.00.00**; ELITE 009 CD cf. **54.10.14**; ZOUNDS 27200446B cf. **54.10.12**.

60.02.16		**Dave Brubeck Quartet Featuring Jimmy Rushing**
New York City, New York.
Paul Desmond as; Dave Brubeck p; Gene Wright b; Joe Morello dr; Jimmy Rushing voc.

a.	My Melancholy Baby	3:55	COL CL 1553
b.	You Can Depend On Me	3:31	-

Issues: COL CS 8353; JW 77010; **a** COL JS7-18S7 30899; FON TFE 17358; **b** COL JS7-18S7 30903; FON 467 244 TE.

Notes: COL CL 1553 is entitled "THE DAVE BRUBECK QUARTET FEATURING JIMMY RUSHING". JW 77010 cf. **58.07.03**.

60.02.17   **Dave Brubeck Trio**
New York City, New York.
Dave Brubeck p; Gene Wright b; Joe Morello dr.
a.   CO64543   A Quiet Girl   2:23   COL CL 1466

Issues: CBS 21065; CBS 61995; CBS 450979-1/-2; COL 7-8257; COL CJ-40455; COL CK-40455; COL CS 8257.

Notes: COL CL 1466 is entitled "BERNSTEIN PLAYS BRUBECK PLAYS BERNSTEIN"; later issues were entitled "THE DAVE BRUBECK QUARTET PLAYS MUSIC FROM LEONARD BERNSTEIN'S WEST SIDE STORY: MARIA / I FEEL PRETTY / SOMEWHERE / TONIGHT AND A QUIET GIRL FROM WONDERFUL TOWN PLUS HOWARD BRUBECK'S DIALOGUES FOR JAZZ COMBO AND ORCHESTRA WITH THE NEW YORK PHILHARMONIC CONDUCTED BY LEONARD BERNSTEIN". CBS 61995 cf. **60.01.30**; CBS 450979-1/-2; COL CJ-40455; COL CK-40455 cf. **60.02.14**.

60.05-06.00   **Dave Brubeck Quartet**
New York City, New York.
Bill Smith cl; Dave Brubeck p; Gene Wright b; Joe Morello dr.

a.	1934	The Piper	2:43	FAN 3301
b.	1935	Soliloquy	3:24	-
c.		Dorian Dance	3:24	-
d.		Peace, Brother	3:50	-
e.		Invention	4:55	-
f.		Lydian Line	5:21	-
g.		Catch Me If You Can (Chilame)	1:43	-
h.		Frisco Fog	5:57	-
i.		One For The Kids	3:00	-
k.		Ballade	3:58	-

Issues: FAN 8047; FAN-OJCCD 200-2; **a,b** FAN 549-X; FAN F 1934; VOC V-F 2425.

Notes: FAN 3301 is entitled "BRUBECK A LA MODE FEATURING BILL SMITH". FAN-OJCCD 200-2 is a re-issue with the title "BRUBECK A LA MODE" released in 1990.

60.08.04   **Dave Brubeck Quartet Featuring Jimmy Rushing**
New York City, New York.

Paul Desmond as; Dave Brubeck p; Gene Wright b; Joe Morello dr; Jimmy Rushing voc.

a.	I Never Knew	2:28	COL CL 1553
b.	Ain't Misbehavin'	3:21	-
c.	Evenin'	4:09	-
d.	All By Myself	2:29	-
e.	River, Stay 'Way From My Door	4:21	-

Issues: COL CS 8353; JW 77010; **a,b,e** FON 467244 TE; **d,e** COL JS7-18S7 30902; **a** ATM 027; **b** ATM 037; **c** ATM 012; GDJ 28; **d** ATM 017.

Notes: COL CL 1553 is entitled "THE DAVE BRUBECK QUARTET FEATURING JIMMY RUSHING". GDJ 28 is a compilation album from the series "I GRANDI DEL JAZZ" with the title "JIMMY RUSHING" , released in 1968. ATM 012 = Vol. 3, ATM 017 = Vol. 4, ATM 027 = Vol. 6, ATM 037 = Vol. 8 cf. **60.01.29**; JW 77010 cf. **58.07.03**.

60.09.09   **Dave Brubeck Trio Featuring Carmen McRae**

New York City, New York.

Dave Brubeck p; Gene Wright b; Joe Morello dr; Carmen McRae voc.

a.	CO65315	Weep No More	2:49	COL CL 1609
b.	CO65316	Briar Bush	2:58	-
c.	CO65317	Paradiddle Joe	2:00	-
d.	CO65318	Strange Meadow Lark	2:38	-
e.		There'll Be No Tomorrow	4:35	COL CL 1678

Issues: a-d COL CS 8409; FON TFE 17384; **b,c** COL 3-42068; COL 4-42068; **a** COL C4K 52945; **c** COL XSV 86015; COL XTV 82029; **e** COL CS 8478.

Notes: COL CL 1609 is entitled "THE DAVE BRUBECK QUARTET WITH GUEST STAR CARMEN MCRAE: TONIGHT ONLY". COL CL 1678 is entitled "GOLD & FIZDALE PLAY DAVE BRUBECK'S JAZZ BALLET "POINTS ON JAZZ" / CARMEN MCRAE SINGS WITH THE DAVE BRUBECK TRIO THEME FROM POINTS ON JAZZ "THERE'LL BE NO TOMORROW". The selection "There'll Be No Tomorrow" was probably recorded at this session (Raben /3./). COL XTV 82029 is a sampler entitled "SWINGIN' SOUND!", released for W.A. Sheaffer Pen Co. COL C4K 52945 cf. **46-48.00.00**; COL XSV 86015 cf. **59.07.01**.

60.12.14   **Dave Brubeck Quartet**

New York City, New York.

Paul Desmond as; Dave Brubeck p; Gene Wright b; Joe Morello dr.

a.   Tristesse   4:58   COL CL 1609
b.   CO65711   Melanctha   9:58   -

Issues: COL CS 8409.

Notes: COL CL 1609 is entitled "THE DAVE BRUBECK QUARTET WITH GUEST STAR CARMEN MCRAE: TONIGHT ONLY".

60.12.15   Dave Brubeck Quartet
New York City, New York.
Paul Desmond as; Dave Brubeck p; Gene Wright b; Joe Morello dr.

a.   CO65709   Late Lament   6:17   COL CL 1609
b.   CO65710   Tonight Only   7:27   -
c.   CO65712   Talkin' And Walkin'   4:24   -

Issues: COL CS 8409; **b** FON TFE 17395.

Notes: COL CL 1609 is entitled "THE DAVE BRUBECK QUARTET WITH GUEST STAR CARMEN MCRAE: TONIGHT ONLY".

61.00.00   Arthur Gold & Robert Fizdale
New York City, New York.
Arthur Gold p; Robert Fizdale p.

a.   Points On Jazz   COL CL 1678
                     1. Prelude   3:57
                     2. Scherzo   1:49
                     3. Blues   5:30
                     4. Fugue   2:47
                     5. Rag   2:05
                     6. Chorale   2:31
                     7. Waltz   2:08
                     8. A La Turk   5:24

Issues: COL CS 8478.

Notes: COL CL 1678 is entitled "GOLD & FIZDALE PLAY DAVE BRUBECK'S JAZZ

BALLET "POINTS ON JAZZ" / CARMEN MCRAE SINGS WITH THE DAVE BRUBECK TRIO THEME FROM POINTS ON JAZZ "THERE'LL BE NO TOMORROW". "Points On Jazz" is a ballet suite composed by Dave Brubeck to be performed originally by the Metropolitan Opera Ballet. After the ballet presentation at the Met was cancelled, Dave Brubeck arranged the score for the piano duo of Gold and Fizdale. The orchestrated version of the ballet had its first performance in January 1961.

61.00.00   Dave Brubeck Quartet
Live Concert in Europe.
Paul Desmond as; Dave Brubeck p; Gene Wright b; Joe Morello dr.

a.	Castilian Drums	5:55	EUJ EJ 1032
b.	Three To Get Ready	5:44	-
c.	St. Louis Blues	9:04	-
d.	Forty Days	5:00	-
e.	Summer Song	5:08	-
f.	Someday My Prince Will Come	6:21	-

Issues: DRIVE 3510; CUR GJ-40; DEN CD 86.3.31; DEN 33C38-7681; DEN YX 7362-SL; a-d,f DEJA DVRECD 58; b-d GOJ LPJT 3.

Notes: EUJ EJ 1032 is entitled "THE QUARTET". DRIVE 3510 is a CD with the title "DAVE BRUBECK: THESE FOOLISH THINGS" released by Baur Music Production in 1989 in a series called "JAZZ CLUB". The album contains two more titles with the Dave Brubeck Trio featuring Gerry Mulligan (cf. **68.05.17**). CUR GJ-40 is entitled "DAVE BRUBECK * PAUL DESMOND * JOE MORELLO * GENE WRIGHT", released in 1981 as Vol. 40 from the series "I GIGANTI DEL JAZZ". DEN CD 86.3.31, DEN 33C38-7681, DEN YX 7362-SL are entitled "DAVE BRUBECK: THE QUARTET" released by Nippon Columbia in 1985. The CD issues contain two more titles, which must have been recorded at a later date (cf. **74.00.00**). The selection "Cassandra" is mis-titled "Castilian Drums". It is likely that this concert in Europe was recorded at a later time, probably 1966. DEJA DVRECD 58 cf. **51.12.15**; GOJ LPJT 3 cf. **54.10.12**.

61.03.20   Dave Brubeck Quartet
Los Angeles, California.
Bill Smith cl; Dave Brubeck p; Gene Wright b; Joe Morello dr.

a.	The Unihorn	5:13	FAN 3319
b.	Bach An' All	3:49	-
c.	Siren Song	5:35	-

d.	Pan's Pipes	4:10	-
e.	By Jupiter	3:54	-
f.	Baggin' The Dragon	6:46	-
g.	Apollo's Axe	3:19	-
h.	The Sailor And The Mermaid	4:13	-
i.	Nep-Tune	2:51	-
k.	Pan Dance	3:35	-

Issues: FAN 8063.

Notes: FAN 3319 is entitled "DAVE BRUBECK QUARTET: NEAR-MYTH / BRUBECK-SMITH".

61.05.03   Dave Brubeck Quartet
New York City, New York.
Paul Desmond as; Dave Brubeck p; Gene Wright b; Joe Morello dr.

a.	CO66978	Castilian Blues	2:31	COL CL 1775
b.	CO66979	Castilian Drums		(unissued)
c.	CO66980	It's A Raggy Waltz	5:15	COL CL 1690

Issues: a COL CS 8575; **c** CBS 1122; CBS 54703; CBS 80775; CBS 460494-1; CBS CA 281122; CBS EP 5534; CBS/EMBA 31769; CBS/SONY 23 AP 663; CBS/SONY 23 AP 1321; CBS/SONY 32 DP 785; COL 4-42228; COL CL 2484; COL CS 8490; COL CS 9284; COL G 30625; COL JS7-42S7 31312; COL KG 32761; COL SOPM 47; COM 6187382; FON 271174 TF; FON 467273 TE; JW 77035; MEL S60-07229/30; SUP 015/115.1029; ZOUNDS 27200446B.

Notes: COL CL 1690 is entitled "THE DAVE BRUBECK QUARTET: TIME FURTHER OUT". COL CL 1775 is entitled "THE DAVE BRUBECK QUARTET: COUNTDOWN TIME IN OUTER SPACE". CBS 460494-1 is a sampler entitled "JAZZ A TOUS LES ETAGES VOL. 3". CBS 54703, COL KG 32761 cf. **56.07.06**; CBS 80775 cf. **54.03-04.00**; CBS/EMBA 31769 cf. **58.07.28**; CBS/SONY 23 AP 663 cf. **59.07.01**; CBS/SONY 23 AP 1321 cf. **57.05.02**; COL CL 2484 cf. **56.04.18+19**; COL G 30625 cf. **59.06.25**; COM 6187382 cf. **57.06.29**; JW 77035 cf. **59.06.25**; MEL S60-07229/30 cf. **56.03.12**; SUP 015/115.1029 cf. **59.07.01**; ZOUNDS 27200446B cf. **54.10.12**.

61.05.04   Dave Brubeck Quartet
New York City, New York.

Paul Desmond as; Dave Brubeck p; Gene Wright b; Joe Morello dr.

a. CO66982   Three's A Crowd   2:41   COL CL 1775

Issues: COL CS 8575.

Notes: COL CL 1775 is entitled "THE DAVE BRUBECK QUARTET: COUNTDOWN TIME IN OUTER SPACE".

61.05.15   Dave Brubeck Quartet
New York City, New York.
Paul Desmond as; Dave Brubeck p; Gene Wright b; Joe Morello dr.

a. CO67013   Blue Shadows In The Street   6:29   COL CL 1690

Issues: CBS EP 5534; COL CS 8490; COL G 30625; COL JS7-42S7 31316 (?); FON 467273 TE; FON H 352.

Notes: COL CL 1690 is entitled "THE DAVE BRUBECK QUARTET: TIME FURTHER OUT". COL G 30625 cf. **59.06.25**.

61.05.25   Dave Brubeck Quartet
New York City, New York.
Paul Desmond as; Dave Brubeck p; Gene Wright b; Joe Morello dr.

a. CO67148   Charles Matthew Hallelujah   2:52   COL CL 1690
b. CO67149   Eleven Four   (unissued)
c. CO67150   Bluette   5:21   COL CL 1690

Issues: a,c COL CS 8490; COL G 30625; a CBS CA 281147; CBS EP 5535; CBS/SONY 23 AP 1321; COL 3-42443; COL 4-42443; COL C4K 52945; COL JS7-42S7-31313; c COL JS7-42S7 31312 (?); FON 467274 TE.

Notes: COL CL 1690 is entitled "THE DAVE BRUBECK QUARTET: TIME FURTHER OUT". CBS/SONY 23 AP 1321 cf. **57.05.02**; COL C4K 52945 cf. **46-48.00.00**; COL G 30625 cf. **59.06.25**.

61.06.02   Dave Brubeck Quartet
New York City, New York.

Paul Desmond as (a,c); Dave Brubeck p; Gene Wright b; Joe Morello dr.
a. CO66981   Far More Blue   4:35 COL CL 1690
b. CO66984   Bru's Boogie Woogie   2:24 -
c. CO66985   The Lawless Mike   COL GB-9

Issues: a,b CBS EP 5535; COL CS 8490; **a** COL 3-42446 (ed.); COL 4-42446 (ed.); COL JS7-42S7 31313 (?); FON 467274 TE; **b** CBS CA 281147; COL JS7-42S7-31315; **c** COL GS-9.

Notes: COL CL 1690 is entitled "THE DAVE BRUBECK QUARTET: TIME FURTHER OUT". COL GB-9, COL GS-9 are samplers entitled "THE HEADLINERS, VOL. 2", released by the Columbia Record Club in a limited edition. Raben /3./ gives two more unissued versions of "The Lawless Mike".

61.06.08   Dave Brubeck Trio and Quartet
New York City, New York.
Paul Desmond as (b); Dave Brubeck p; Gene Wright b; Joe Morello dr.
a. CO66983   Maori Blues   3:54 COL CL 1690
b. CO67149   Eleven Four   2:48 COL CL 1775
c. CO67195   Unsquare Dance   2:02 COL CL 1690
d. CO67537   Far More Drums   3:59 -

Issues: a,c,d COL CS 8490; COL G 30625; **a,d** COL JS7-42S7-31314 (?); **b,c** COL SOPM 47; **a** COL 4-42443; COL D 288; COL DS 288; **b** CBS CG 285529; CBS/SONY 23 AP 663; CBS/SONY 23 AP 1321; COL 3-42404; COL 4-42404; COL CS 8575; **c** ATM 007; ATM 402; CBS 4662; CBS 54703; CBS 80777; CBS 467148-2; CBS AAG 102; CBS CA 281102; CBS EP 5534; CBS/EMBA 31769; CBS/SONY 32 DP 785; COL 3-42228; COL 4-42228; COL C4K 52945; COL CL 2484; COL CS 9284; COL CSS 524; COL JS7-42S7 31315; COL KG 32761; COM 6187382; ELITE 009 CD; FON 271174 TF; FON 467273 TE; JW 77010; MEL S60-07229/30.

Notes: COL CL 1690 is entitled "THE DAVE BRUBECK QUARTET: TIME FURTHER OUT". COL CL 1775 is entitled "THE DAVE BRUBECK QUARTET: COUNTDOWN TIME IN OUTER SPACE". ATM 402 is a sampler 4-CD box with only two Brubeck tracks. The title is "75 ALL TIME JAZZ SESSIONS". COL CSS 524 is a sampler entitled "ZENITH SALUTES THE JAZZ WORLD". CBS 54703, COL KG 32761 cf. **56.07.06**; ATM 007 cf. **60.01.29**; CBS 80777 cf. **54.03-04.00**; CBS 467148-2 cf. **54.10.12**; CBS/EMBA 31769 cf. **58.07.28**; CBS/SONY 23 AP 663 cf. **59.07.01**; CBS/SONY 23 AP 1321 cf. **57.05.02**; COL C4K 52945 cf. **46-48.00.00**; COL CL 2484 cf. **56.04.18+19**; COL D 288, COL DS 288 cf. **58.07.25**; COL G

30625 cf. **59.06.25**; COM 6187382 cf. **57.06.29**; ELITE 009 CD cf. **54.10.14**; JW 77010 cf. **58.07.03**; MEL S60-07229/30 cf. **56.03.12**.

61.06.12+13   Dave Brubeck Quartet
New York City, New York.
Paul Desmond as; Dave Brubeck p; Gene Wright b; Joe Morello dr.

a.	CO69309	It's A Raggy Waltz	COL S7-31312
b.	CO69310	Bluette	-
c.	CO69311	Far More Blue	COL S7-31313
d.	CO69312	Far More Drums	COL S7-31314
e.	CO69313	Blue Shadows In The Street, Part 1	COL S7-31316
f.	CO69314	Blue Shadows In The Street, Part 2	-

Notes: This entry is given following Raben /3./, who denotes as source the Columbia files. It has not been verified whether these issues are different from the versions issued on COL CL 1690.

61.06.28   Dave Brubeck Quartet
New York City, New York.
Paul Desmond as; Dave Brubeck p; Gene Wright b; Joe Morello dr.

a.	CO67518	Why Phillis	2:15	COL CL 1775
b.	CO67595	Danse Duet	2:56	-

Issues: COL CS 8575; **a** COL C4K 52945; **b** CBS CG 285529.

Notes: COL CL 1775 is entitled "THE DAVE BRUBECK QUARTET: COUNTDOWN TIME IN OUTER SPACE". COL C4K 52945 cf. **46-48.00.00**.

61.07.03
London, Great Britain.
Bert Courtley tp; Johnny Scott as (a), fl (b); Dave Brubeck p; Kenny Napper b; Alan Ganley dr.

a.		It's A Raggy Waltz	3:28	FON TFL 5179
b.		Blue Shadows In The Street	4:24	-

Dave Brubeck p; Charles Mingus b.

c.		Non-Sectarian Blues	3:32	COL C 30522

Issues: a,b FON STFL 591; EPIC LA 16032; EPIC BA 17032; **c** COL C4K 52945.

Notes: FON TFL 5179 is entitled "ALL NIGHT LONG" and presents the soundtrack of the film with the same title of the Rank Organisation. Amongst many British musicians, Dave Brubeck serves as a walk-on actor and participates in two tunes. "All Night Long" is a modern jazz club version of Shakespeare's "Othello". COL C 30522 is a compilation album entitled "SUMMIT SESSIONS: DAVE BRUBECK WITH SPECIAL GUEST STARS".
COL C 30522 cf. **60.01.29**; COL C4K 52945 cf. **46-48.00.00**.

61.08.21   Dave Brubeck Quartet With Orchestra
New York City, New York.
Paul Desmond as; Dave Brubeck p; Gene Wright b; Joe Morello dr;
Symphony Orchestra, Concertmaster Max Pollikoff; Howard Brubeck arr, cond.

a.	CO67947	Kathy's Waltz	3:02	COL CL 1963
b.	CO67948	Summer Song	6:26	-
c.	CO67949	G Flat Theme	3:55	-

Issues: COL CS 8763; **a** COL C4K 52945; COL GB 11; COL GS 11; **b (ed.)** COL 3-42804; COL 4-42804.

Notes: COL CL 1963 is entitled "THE DAVE BRUBECK QUARTET WITH ORCHESTRA: BRANDENBURG GATE REVISITED". COL GB 11 and COL GS 11 are samplers with the title "THE HEADLINERS, VOL. 3", released by the Columbia Record Club in a limited edition.
COL C4K 52945 cf. **46-48.00.00**.

61.08.22   Dave Brubeck Quartet With Orchestra
New York City, New York.
Paul Desmond as; Dave Brubeck p; Gene Wright b; Joe Morello dr;
Symphony Orchestra, Concertmaster Max Pollikoff; Howard Brubeck arr, cond.

a.	CO67950	In Your Own Sweet Way	4:56	COL CL 1963
b.		Brandenburg Gate	19:55	-

       1. Brandenburg Gate
       2. Serenade
       3. Night Song
       4. Awakening
       5. Morning Song
       6. Pivot Dance
       7. Exhilaration Dance
       8. Movement

9. Triolet
10. Repercussion
11. Final Dance

Issues: COL CS 8763; **a** COL CL 1765; COL CS 8565; MEL S60-07229/30; SUP 015/115.1029; **b1** FOLLET L 25.

Notes: COL CL 1963 is entitled "THE DAVE BRUBECK QUARTET WITH ORCHESTRA: BRANDENBURG GATE REVISITED". COL CL 1765, COL CS 8565 are samplers with the title "WHO'S WHO IN THE SWINGING SIXTIES".
FOLLET L 25 cf. **60.01.30**; MEL S60-07229/30 cf. **56.03.12**; SUP 015/115.1029 cf. **59.07.01**.

61.09.00   Dave Brubeck Trio Featuring Carmen McRae
New York City, New York.
Dave Brubeck p; Gene Wright b; Joe Morello dr; Carmen McRae voc.

a.	Summer Song	2:32	COL 4-43032
b.	Easy As You Go	1:35	COL 4-42292
c.	Take Five		–

Issues: a,b CBS 467140-2; **b,c** COL 3-42292.

Notes: CBS 467140-2 is entitled "THE REAL AMBASSADORS: D. BRUBECK * L. ARMSTRONG * L(AMBERT). H(ENDRICKS). R(OSS). TRIO * C. MCRAE". (cf. **61.09.12**). Dave Brubeck and Carmen McRae recorded "Take Five" and "Easy As You Go" only twice, for the 45 rpm version and for the LP issue "LIVE AT BASIN STREET EAST" (W.H. Schrickel).

61.09.06   Dave Brubeck Trio Featuring Carmen McRae
New York City, New York, Basin Street East.
Dave Brubeck p; Gene Wright b; Joe Morello dr; Carmen McRae voc.

a.	CO85796	When I Was Young	2:45	COL CL 2316
b.	CO85797	In Your Own Sweet Way	2:56	–
c.	CO85798	Too Young For Growing Old	3:00	–
d.	CO85799	Ode To A Cowboy	3:05	–
e.	CO85800	There'll Be No Tomorrow	4:30	–
f.	CO85801	Melanctha	4:38	–
g.	CO85802	It's A Raggy Waltz	2:35	–
h.	CO85804	Oh, So Blue	2:27	–

i. CO85805   Lord, Lord   5:20   -
k. CO85806   Travellin' Blues   2:48   -

Issues: COL CJ-8192; COL CK-8192; COL CS 9116; **b,g,k** CBS EP 5659; **g,k** CBS 1913; CBS
SP A 9116; COL 4-43279; **g** FON 271181 TF; FON H 379; FON TFE 17395; **k** COL C 30522;
COL C4K 52945.

Notes: COL CL 2316 is entitled "CARMEN MCRAE WITH DAVE BRUBECK: TAKE FIVE *
RECORDED LIVE AT BASIN STREET EAST". COL C 30522 cf. **60.01.29**; COL C4K 52945
cf. **46-48.00.00**.

61.09.09   Dave Brubeck Quartet Featuring Carmen McRae
New York City, New York, Basin Street East.
Paul Desmond as (a); Dave Brubeck p; Gene Wright b; Joe Morello dr; Carmen McRae voc.
a. CO68565   Take Five   2:14   COL CL 2316
b. CO68691   Easy As You Go   1:32   -

Issues: CBS CA 281120; CBS SP A 9116; COL CJ-8192; COL CK-8192; COL CS 9116; FON
271180 TF; **a** CBS EP 5659; FON 271181 TF; FON H 379; FON TFE 17395; SSO 4.

Notes: COL CL 2316 is entitled "CARMEN MCRAE WITH DAVE BRUBECK: TAKE FIVE *
RECORDED LIVE AT BASIN STREET EAST". SSO 4 is a sampler with the title "JAZZ JUICE
2 - DEVILS MUSIC" released in 1985.

61.09.12   Dave Brubeck Trio Featuring Louis Armstrong,
**   Lambert, Hendricks And Ross**
New York City, New York.
Louis Armstrong tp (c), voc (a-d); Dave Brubeck p; Gene Wright b; Joe Morello dr; Howard
Brubeck tubular chimes (c); Dave Lambert voc; Jon Hendricks voc; Annie Ross voc.
a. CO67987   They Say I Look Like God   5:26   COL OL 5850
b. CO67988   Everybody's Comin'   1:46   -
c. CO68175   Swing Bells / Blow Satchmo / Finale   6:06   -
d. CO68176   The Real Ambassadors   3:06   -
e.   Blow Satchmo   0:44   -

Issues: CBS 467140-2; COL OS 2250; **b** COL JS7-69S7-31587; **c** COL JS7-69S7-31591; **d**
COL C4K 52945; COL JS7-69S7-31590.

Notes: COL OL 5850 is entitled "THE REAL AMBASSADORS: AN ORIGINAL MUSICAL PRODUCTION BY DAVE AND IOLA BRUBECK". CBS 467140-2 is an album from the CBS series "I LOVE JAZZ" with the title "THE REAL AMBASSADORS: D. BRUBECK * L. ARMSTRONG * L(AMBERT). H(ENDRICKS). R(OSS). TRIO * C. MCRAE: AN ORIGINAL MUSICAL PRODUCTION BY DAVE AND IOLA BRUBECK", released in 1990. The compact disc contains two unissued tracks (cf. **61.09.20**) and three more tracks (cf. **61.09.13, 61.09.19**) which were not on the original LP release. The exact recording dates for some of the titles of "THE REAL AMBASSADORS" are open to discussion. We crosschecked the Louis Armstrong discography "BOY FROM NEW ORLEANS" by Hans Westerberg.

The musical production composed by Dave Brubeck with lyrics by Dave and Iola Brubeck was performed for the first time at the Monterey Jazz Festival in Monterey, California on September 23, 1962 with the following cast:

Hero	Louis Armstrong
Girl Singer	Carmen McRae
Side Man	Trummy Young
The Chorus:	Dave Lambert; Jon Hendricks; Yolande Bavan
(Ambassadors, Priests, Citizens)	
Narrator	Iola Brubeck
Band I (Modern)	Dave Brubeck; Joe Morello; Eugene Wright
Band II (Traditional)	Louis Armstrong;Trummy Young; Joe Darensbourg; Billy Kyle; Willy Kronk; Danny Barcelona
Musical Coordinator	Howard Brubeck.

COL C4K 52945 cf. **46-48.00.00**.

**61.09.13   Dave Brubeck Trio Featuring Louis Armstrong And
                    Carmen McRae**

New York City, New York.
Louis Armstrong tp (c), voc; Dave Brubeck p; prob. Billy Kyle p (b); Gene Wright b; Joe Morello dr; Carmen McRae voc (a,c,d).

a.	CO67989	I Didn't Know Until You Told Me	2:58	COL OL 5850
b.	CO67991	Summer Song	3:14	-
c.	CO68177	You Swing, Baby	2:31	CBS FC 38508
d.	CO68178	One Moment Worth Years	4:18	COL OL 5850

Issues: CBS 467140-2; **a,b** COL OS 2250; **b** CBS 1508; CBS AAG 201; CBS EP 5698; COL 4-43032; COL C 30522; COL C4K 52945; COL JS7-69S7-31589; **c** BOMC 21-6547; CBS 88669; **d** CBS FC 38508.

Notes: COL OL 5850 is entitled "THE REAL AMBASSADORS: AN ORIGINAL MUSICAL PRODUCTION BY DAVE AND IOLA BRUBECK". CBS FC 38508 is a sampler with the title "SINGIN' TILL THE GIRLS COME HOME". BOMC 21-6547 is a 4 album set with the title "LOUIS ARMSTRONG: RARE AND UNRELEASED PERFORMANCES". CBS 88669 is a two album set with the title "RARE PERFORMANCES OF THE 50's AND THE 60's". COL C 30522 is a compilation album entitled "SUMMIT SESSIONS: DAVE BRUBECK WITH SPECIAL GUEST STARS". "You Swing, Baby" is "The Duke".
CBS 467140-2 **61.09.12**; COL C 30522 cf. **60.01.29**; COL C4K 52945 cf. **46-48.00.00**.

61.09.19   **Dave Brubeck Trio With Louis Armstrong All Stars And**
                   Lambert, Hendricks And Ross And Carmen McRae
New York City, New York.
Louis Armstrong tp, voc; Trummy Young tb, voc (a,e,f); Joe Darensbourg cl (b-g); Dave Brubeck p (b-g); Billy Kyle p (b-g); Gene Wright b (b-g); Irv Manning b (b-g); Joe Morello dr (b-g); Danny Barcelona dr (b-g); Dave Lambert voc (e); Jon Hendricks voc (e); Annie Ross voc (e); Carmen McRae voc (b).

a.	CO62590	King For A Day	3:41	COL OL 5850
b.	CO67990	Good Reviews	2:05	-
c.	CO68006	Since Love Had Its Way	2:31	-
d.	CO68007	Nomad	2:51	COL 4-43032
e.	CO68008	Cultural Exchange	4:38	COL OL 5850
f.	CO68009	Remember Who You Are	2:31	-
g.	CO68010	Lonesome	2:24	COL C 30522

Issues: CBS 467140-2; **a,c-e** COL OS 2250; **b,e** COL JZSP 58120/21; **c,g** CSP C3 10404; **d,g** CBS 88669; **a** COL JS7-69S7 31589; **b** CBS FC 38508; **c** CBS BPG 62034; COL CL 1765; COL CS 8565; COL (J) YS 222; COL JS7-69S7-31591; **d** CBS 1508; CBS 62902; CBS AAG 201; CBS EP 5968; **e** COL JS7-69S7-31587; **f** COL JS7-69S7-31588.

Notes: COL OL 5850 is entitled "THE REAL AMBASSADORS: AN ORIGINAL MUSICAL PRODUCTION BY DAVE AND IOLA BRUBECK". Jepsen /1./ and Raben /3./ indicate that the vocal parts of Armstrong and Young were most likely recorded at this session and dubbed in the trio part of "King For A Day" from the session **59.07.02**. COL C 30522 is a compilation album entitled "SUMMIT SESSIONS: DAVE BRUBECK WITH SPECIAL GUEST STARS". COL JZSP 58120/21 is a promotional 45-rpm.
CBS 88669, CBS FC 38508 cf. **61.09.13**; CBS 467140-2, COL OL 5850 cf. **61.09.12**; COL C 30522 cf. **60.01.29**; COL CL 1765 cf. **61.08.22**.

61.10.13   Dave Brubeck Quartet
New York City, New York.
Paul Desmond as (a); Dave Brubeck p; Gene Wright b; Joe Morello dr.
a. CO68596   It's A Raggy Waltz   COL 4-42228
b. CO68598   Countdown   2:23   COL CL 1775

Issues: a COL 3-42228; FON H 352; **b** CBS CG 285529; CBS/SONY 23 AP 1321; COL 3-42404; COL 4-42404; COL CS 8575; COL G 30625.

Notes: COL CL 1775 is entitled "THE DAVE BRUBECK QUARTET: COUNTDOWN TIME IN OUTER SPACE". CBS/SONY 23 AP 1321 cf. **57.05.02**; COL G 30625 cf. **59.06.25**.

61.12.12   Dave Brubeck Trio With Carmen McRae
New York City, New York.
Dave Brubeck p; Gene Wright b; Joe Morello dr; Carmen McRae voc.
a. CO68797   In The Lurch   2:28   COL OL 5850

Issues: CBS 467140-2; CBS FC 38508; COL OS 2250; COL JS7-69S7-31590.

Notes: COL OL 5850 is entitled "THE REAL AMBASSADORS: AN ORIGINAL MUSICAL PRODUCTION BY DAVE AND IOLA BRUBECK".
COL OL 5850, CBS 467140-2 cf. **59.07.02**; CBS FC 38508 cf. **61.09.13**.

61.12.15   Dave Brubeck Quartet
New York City, New York.
Paul Desmond as; Dave Brubeck p; Gene Wright b; Joe Morello dr.
a. CO66979   Castilian Drums   4:10   COL CL 1775
b.   Fast Life   3:46   -
c. CO68566   Someday My Prince Will Come   6:22   -
d. CO68597   Waltz Limp   4:16   -
e. CO68597   Waltz Limp (alt.take)   1:15   COL CL 1970

Issues: a-d COL CS 8575; **a,c** CBS 54703; COL KG 32761; **a,d** COL G 30625; **a** CBS/EMBA 31769; COL D 288; COL DS 288; **c** CBS/SONY 23 AP 663; CBS/SONY 23 AP 1231; COL 3-42444 (ed.) (?); COL 4-42444 (ed.) (?); COL SOPM 47; SUP 015/115.1029; ZOUNDS 27200446B; **d** CBS 52742; CBS 466447-2; **d** or **e** CBS 66425; **e** AMI 850.083; CBS 62141; COL CS 8770; SUP 015.2114.

Notes: COL CL 1775 is entitled "THE DAVE BRUBECK QUARTET: COUNTDOWN TIME IN OUTER SPACE". CBS 66425 is a 4 LP sampler entitled "JAZZ ANTHOLOGY: FROM KING OLIVER TO ORNETTE COLEMAN". CBS 52742 is a sampler with the title "JAZZ CONSTELLATION". CBS 62141, COL CL 1970 and COL CS 8770 are samplers entitled "THE GIANTS OF JAZZ". CBS 466447-2 is a sampler with the title "THE GIANTS OF JAZZ" from the series "I LOVE JAZZ".
CBS 54703, COL KG 32761 cf. **56.07.06**; CBS/EMBA 31769 cf. **58.07.28**; CBS/SONY 23 AP 663 cf. **59.07.01**; CBS/SONY 23 AP 1321 cf. **57.05.02**; COL D 288, COL DS 288 cf. **58.07.25**; COL G 30625 cf. **59.06.25**; SUP 015/115.1029 cf. **59.07.01**; ZOUNDS 27200446B cf. **54.10.12**.

61.12.19   **Dave Brubeck Trio With Carmen McRae**
New York City, New York.
Paul Desmond as (b); Dave Brubeck p; Gene Wright b; Joe Morello dr; Carmen McRae voc (a).
a. CO68799   My One Bad Habit   2:37   COL OL 5850
b. CO69504   Back To Earth   3:18   COL CL 1775

Issues: a CBS 467140-2; COL JS7-69S7 31588; COL OS 2250; **b** CBS CG 285529; COL CS 8575.

Notes: COL OL 5850 is entitled "THE REAL AMBASSADORS: AN ORIGINAL MUSICAL PRODUCTION BY DAVE AND IOLA BRUBECK". COL CL 1775 is entitled "THE DAVE BRUBECK QUARTET: COUNTDOWN TIME IN OUTER SPACE".
COL OL 5850, CBS 467140-2 cf. **59.07.02**.

62.01.03   **Dave Brubeck Quartet**
New York City, New York.
Paul Desmond as; Dave Brubeck p; Gene Wright b; Joe Morello dr.
a.   Vento Fresco (Cool Wind)   3:30   COL CL 1998
b.   Coraçao Sensivel (Tender Heart)   4:10   -
c.   Irmao Amigo (Brother Friend)   3:22   -
d.   Cantiga Nova Swing   2:46   -
e.   Lamento   4:45   -

Issues: COL CS 8798; **a,c,d** CBS EP 5558; **b** COL D 288; COL DS 288; COL KG 32761.

Notes: COL CL 1998 is entitled "THE DAVE BRUBECK QUARTET: BOSSA NOVA U.S.A.".
COL D 288, COL DS 288 cf. **58.07.25**; COL KG 32761 cf. **56.07.06**.

62.01.14   **Dave Brubeck Quartet**
San Francisco, California, KQED TV Program.
Paul Desmond as; Dave Brubeck p; Gene Wright b; Joe Morello dr.

a.	St. Louis Blues	5:36	MOR MLP 028-1
b.	Nomad	6:08	-
c.	Thank You	5:47	-
d.	Brandenburg Gate	4:24	-

Issues: MOR MCD 028-2.

Notes : MOR MLP 028-1, MOR MCD 028-2 are entitled "DAVE BRUBECK FEATURING PAUL DESMOND: ST. LOUIS BLUES". MOR MLP 028-1, MOR MCD 028-2 cf. **59.07.05**.

62.04.03   **Dave Brubeck Quartet**
Sydney, Australia.
Paul Desmond as; Dave Brubeck p; Gene Wright b; Joe Morello dr.

a.	The Craven "A" Theme	CRAVEN "A" unn.

Notes: This entry is given following Raben /3./.

62.06.11   **Dave Brubeck Quartet**
New York City, New York.
Paul Desmond as; Dave Brubeck p; Gene Wright b; Joe Morello dr.

a.	My Romance	6:50	COL CL 2437

Issues: CBS 450979-1/-2; COL CJ-40455; COL CK-40455; COL CS 9237.

Notes: COL CL 2437 is entitled "DAVE BRUBECK QUARTET: MY FAVORITE THINGS". CBS 450979-1/-2; COL CJ-40455; COL CK-40455 cf. **60.02.14**.

62.07.02   **Dave Brubeck Quartet**
New York City, New York.
Paul Desmond as; Dave Brubeck p; Gene Wright b; Joe Morello dr.

a.	CO75595	Angel Eyes	7:22	COL CL 2348
b.	CO75596	The Night We Called It A Day	6:11	-
c.	CO75597	Will You Still Be Mine	5:20	-
d.		I'm In A Dancing Mood	2:59	COL CL 2484

Issues: a-c COL CS 9148; **a** CBS SOPM 47; **c** COL CSP 291; **d** CBS/EMBA 31769; COL 3-42444 (?); COL 4-42444 (?); COL CS 9284; COL KG 32761; COL XTV 82029; COM 6187382; MEL S60-07229/30.

Notes: COL CL 2348 is entitled "DAVE BRUBECK QUARTET: ANGEL EYES". COL CL 2484 is a compilation album with the title "DAVE BRUBECK'S GREATEST HITS", released in 1964. COL CSP 291 is a sampler with the title "THE GOLDEN GREATS", produced by Columbia Special Products in conjunction with American Freedom from Hunger Foundation. CBS/EMBA 31769 cf. **58.07.28**; COL KG 32761 cf. **56.07.06**; COL CL 2484 cf. **56.04.18+19**; COL XTV 82029 cf. **60.09.09**; COM 6187382 cf. **57.06.29**; MEL S60-07229/30 cf. **56.03.12**.

62.07.05   **Dave Brubeck Quartet**
New York City, New York.
Paul Desmond as; Dave Brubeck p; Gene Wright b; Joe Morello dr.

a.		(The) Trolley Song	3:03 COL CL 1998
b.	CO75598	This Can't Be Love	6:50 -

Issues: COL CS 8798; **a** CBS BP 5558; CBS 21109; CBS 54703; CBS 80775; CBS S 66266; CBS/EMBA 31769; COL CL 2484; COL CS 9284; COL G 30217; COL KG 32761; COM 6187382; ELITE 009 CD; CBS/EMBA 31068; MEL S60-07229/30; **b** CBS 1148; COL 3-42651; COL 4-42651; .

Notes: COL CL 1998 is entitled "THE DAVE BRUBECK QUARTET: BOSSA NOVA U.S.A.". CBS 21109 is a sampler with the title "JAZZ & CINEMA" from the series "I LOVE JAZZ". CBS/EMBA 31068 is a sampler entitled "JAZZ GIANTS AT THEIR BEST". COL G 30217 is a sampler with two records and the title "FILL YOUR HEAD WITH JAZZ" , released in 1970. CBS 54703, COL KG 32761 cf. **56.07.06**; CBS 80775 cf. **54.03-04.00**; CBS/EMBA 31769 cf. **58.07.28**; COL CL 2484 cf. **56.04.18+19**; COM 6187382 cf. **57.06.29**; ELITE 009 CD cf. **54.10.14**; MEL S60-07229/30 cf. **56.03.12**.

62.07.12   **Dave Brubeck Quartet**
New York City, New York.
Paul Desmond as; Dave Brubeck p; Gene Wright b; Joe Morello dr.

a.	Theme For June	4:15	COL CL 1998
b.	There'll Be No Tomorrow	5:42	-
c.	The Most Beautiful Girl In The World	5:18	COL CL 2437

Issues: a,b COL CS 8798; **c** CBS 450979-1/-2; COL CJ-40455; COL CK-40455; COL CS 9237; ELITE 009 CD.

Notes: COL CL 1998 is entitled "THE DAVE BRUBECK QUARTET: BOSSA NOVA U.S.A.". COL CL 2437 is entitled "DAVE BRUBECK QUARTET: MY FAVORITE THINGS". CBS 450979-1/-2; COL CJ-40455; COL CK-40455 cf. **60.02.14**; ELITE 009 CD cf. **54.10.14**.

62.07.19   Dave Brubeck Quartet
New York City, New York.
Paul Desmond as; Dave Brubeck p; Gene Wright b; Joe Morello dr.
a.	Why Can't I	6:52	COL CL 2437
b.	(The) Circus (Is) On Parade	3:14	-

Issues: COL CS 9237.

Notes: COL CL 2437 is entitled "DAVE BRUBECK QUARTET: MY FAVORITE THINGS".

62.08.28   Dave Brubeck Quartet Featuring Tony Bennett
Washington, D.C.
Paul Desmond as; Dave Brubeck p; Gene Wright b; Joe Morello dr; Tony Bennett voc.
a.	That Old Black Magic	3:15	COL C 30522

Notes: COL C 30522 is a compilation album entitled "SUMMIT SESSIONS: DAVE BRUBECK WITH SPECIAL GUEST STARS". COL C 30522 cf. **60.01.29**.

62.10.25   Dave Brubeck Quartet
New York City, New York.
Paul Desmond as; Dave Brubeck p; Gene Wright b; Joe Morello dr, perc (b).
a.	Bossa Nova U.S.A.	2:24	COL CL 1998
b.	Santa Claus Is Coming To Town	3:40	COL CL 1893
c.	Over And Over Again	4:02	COL CL 2437
d.	Little Girl Blue	5:31	-

Issues: c,d COL CS 9237; **a** ATM 402; CBS 1148; CBS 54703; CBS/EMBA 31769; CBS/SONY 32 DP 785; COL 3-42651; COL 4-42651; COL 4-42675; COL C4K 52945; COL CL 2484; COL CS 9284; COL CS 8798; COL SOPM 47; JW 77010; MEL S60-07229/30; SUP

015/115.1029; **b** CBS A 21618; COL CK 40166; COL PC 36903; COL CS 8693; HAR KH 32529; SONY CSCS-5030; **c** COL CSP 298; COL CSP 345; COL CSS 654.

Notes: COL CL 1998 is entitled "THE DAVE BRUBECK QUARTET: BOSSA NOVA U.S.A.". COL CL 2437 is entitled "DAVE BRUBECK QUARTET: MY FAVORITE THINGS". COL CL 1893 is a sampler with the title "JINGLE BELL JAZZ". COL CK 40166, SONY CSCS 5030 are CD issues with the same title. CBS A 21618 is a sampler CD entitled "A JAZZ CHRISTMAS". COL CSP 345 and COL CSS 654 are samplers with the title "NOW IS THE TIME FOR ALL GOOD JAZZ", released by Columbia Special Products in a limited edition for Clairtone. COL CSP 298 is a sampler with the title "THE JAZZ SOUND". ATM 402 cf. **61.06.08**; CBS 54703 cf. **56.07.06**; COL C4K 52945 cf. **46-48.00.00**; COL CL 2484 cf. **56.04.18+19**; JW 77010 cf. **58.07.03**; MEL S60-07229/30 cf. **56.03.12**; SUP 015/115.1029 cf. **59.07.01**.

62.12.03   **Dave Brubeck Quartet**
Amsterdam, The Netherlands, Concertgebouw.
Paul Desmond as; Dave Brubeck p; Gene Wright b; Joe Morello dr.

a.	Bossa Nova U.S.A.	6:02	CBS EPCG 285553
b.	Take The "A" Train	5:09	-
c.	Since Love Had Its Way	5:57	COL CS 9897
d.	The Real Ambassador	6:31	-
e.	Dizzy Ditty	2:50	-
f.	Good Reviews	3:55	-
g.	King For A Day	3:00	-
h.	They Say I Look Like God	4:14	-
i.	Cultural Exchange	5:57	-
k.	Brandenburg Gate	11:55	-

Issues: b,d CBS 462403-1/-2; COL CK-44215; COL JC2-44215; **b** COL CJ-44380; COL CK-44380; **i** COL GB 13 (?); COL GS 13 (?).

Notes: COL CS 9897 is entitled "THE DAVE BRUBECK QUARTET: BRUBECK IN AMSTERDAM". COL CJ-44380 is a sampler with the title "COLUMBIA JAZZ MASTERPIECES SAMPLER VOLUME V" from the series "COLUMBIA JAZZ MASTERPIECES", released in 1988 with digitally remastered tapes. COL CK-44380 is the CD issue with the same title. COL GB 13 and COL GS 13 are samplers entitled "THE HEADLINERS '63", released as a Columbia Record Club Exclusive. CBS 462403-1/-2; COL CK-44215; COL JC2-44215 cf. **58.03.05**.

63.02.22   Dave Brubeck Quartet
New York City, New York, Carnegie Hall.
Paul Desmond as; Dave Brubeck p; Gene Wright b; Joe Morello dr.

a.	St. Louis Blues	11:05	COL CL 2036
b.	Bossa Nova U.S.A.	7:00	-
c.	For All We Know	9:30	-
d.	Pennies From Heaven	9:52	-
e.	Southern Scene (Briar Bush)	6:50	-
f.	Three To Get Ready	5:50	-
g.	Eleven-Four	3:00	COL CL 2037
h.	It's A Raggy Waltz	6:39	-
i.	King For A Day	6:35	-
k.	Castilian Drums	13:10	-
l.	Blue Rondo A La Turk	12:07	-
m.	Take Five	6:23	-

Issues: COL C2L-26; COL C2S-826; SONY (J) SRCS 7114-15; **a-f,l,m** GOJ CD 53031; **a-f** COL CS 8836; **g-m** COL CS 8837; **c,d,l,m** CBS 462403-1/-2; COL JC2-44215; COL CK-44215; **h,l,m** COL G 30625; DEJA DVCD 2036; **a,l** COL KG 32761; **f(ed.),m** CBS 460494-1; **h,m** FON TFE 17395; **l,m** GDJ 82; GOJ LPJT 3; ZOUNDS 27200446B; **c** ELITE 009 CD; **e** COL D 288; COL DS 288; **f** COL 3-42804 (ed.); COL 4-42804 (ed.); COL 4-43732 (ed.); **h** CBS 54490; **g** COL XLP 59400 (ed.) (?); **h** COL C4K 52945; **m** GOJ CD 53025.

Notes: COL CL 2036 and COL CL 2037 are entitled "THE DAVE BRUBECK QUARTET AT CARNEGIE HALL PART 1" and "THE DAVE BRUBECK QUARTET AT CARNEGIE HALL PART 2", respectively. COL C2L-26 is a combined release of the two previous albums. SONY (J) SRCS 7114-15 is the 2 CD box with the same title. COL XLP 59400 is a demo LP and contains disc jockey short cuts. GOJ CD 53025 is a sampler entitled "JAZZ PARADE 40's - 60's". GOJ CD 53031 is entitled "N.Y.C., CARNEGIE HALL, FEBRUARY 22, 1963 : THE DAVE BRUBECK QUARTET WITH PAUL DESMOND FEATURING GENE WRIGHT & JOE MORELLO" and was released in 1988 by the JOKER TONVERLAG AG in the series "IMMORTAL CONCERTS". CBS 54490 cf. **54.03-04.00**; CBS 460494-1 cf. **61.05.03**; CBS 462403-1/-2, COL JC2-44215, COL CK-44215 cf. **58.03.05**; COL C4K 52945 cf. **46-48.00.00**; COL D 288, COL DS 288 cf. **58.07.25**; COL G 30625 cf. **59.06.25**; COL KG 32761 cf. **56.07.06**; ELITE 009 CD cf. **54.10.14**; GDJ 82, GOJ LPJT 3, ZOUNDS 27200446B cf. **54.10.12**.

63.03.23   Dave Brubeck Quartet
New York City, New York.

Bill Smith cl; Dave Brubeck p; prob. Gene Wright b; prob. Joe Morello dr.
a. CO77751   Bag O' Heat   COL 4-43409

Notes: This entry is given following Raben /3./. Columbia published a promotion record with the same number containing the tune "I Don't Got To Show You No Stinkin' Badges" by Bill Smith instead of "Bag O' Heat" (W.L. White).

63.03.25   Dave Brubeck Quartet
New York City, New York.
Bill Smith cl; Dave Brubeck p; prob. Gene Wright b; prob. Joe Morello dr.
a. CO77743   Happy Bandito   COL 4-43409

Notes: This entry is given following Raben /3./.

63.07.07   Dave Brubeck Quartet
Newport, Rhode Island, Newport Jazz Festival.
Paul Desmond as; Dave Brubeck p; Gene Wright b; Joe Morello dr.
a.   It's A Raggy Waltz   COL C2-38262

Issues: CBS 88605.

Notes : COL C2-38262 is a sampler with the title "NEWPORT JAZZ FESTIVAL: LIVE".

63.10.15   Dave Brubeck Quartet
New York City, New York.
Paul Desmond as; Dave Brubeck p; Gene Wright b; Joe Morello dr.
a. CO79292   Cable Car   2:58   COL CL 2127
b. CO79293   Theme From "Elementals"   3:03   COL 4-42920

Issues: CBS 1385; a COL 4-42920 (ed.); COL CS 8927; COL CSP 217 M; COL CSP 217 S; COL D 288; COL DS 288; COL G 30625.

Notes: COL CL 2127 is entitled "THE DAVE BRUBECK QUARTET: TIME CHANGES". The selection **b** is given following Raben /3./. CBS 1385 is a 45 rpm single giving only the theme (3:03) from "Elementals". COL CSP 217 M, COL CSP 217 S cf. **59.07.01**; COL D 288, COL DS 288 cf. **58.07.25**; COL G 30625 cf. **59.06.25**.

63.11.20   Dave Brubeck Quartet
New York City, New York.
Paul Desmond as; Dave Brubeck p; Gene Wright b; Joe Morello dr.
a. CO79951   World's Fair   2:43   COL CL 2127

Issues: COL C4K 52945; COL CS 8927; COL G 30625.

Notes: COL CL 2127 is entitled "THE DAVE BRUBECK QUARTET: TIME CHANGES".
COL C4K 52945 cf. **46-48.00.00**;COL G 30625 cf. **59.06.25**.

63.12.03   Dave Brubeck Quartet
New York City, New York.
Paul Desmond as (b,c); Dave Brubeck p; Gene Wright b; Joe Morello dr.
a. CO79938   Iberia   2:58   COL CL 2127
b. CO79939   Unisphere   5:41   -
c. CO79940   Shim Wa   4:02   -

Issues: COL CS 8927; COL G 30625; **a** COL D 288; COL DS 288; **b** CBS 1541; COL 4-43091
(ed.).

Notes: COL CL 2127 is entitled "THE DAVE BRUBECK QUARTET: TIME CHANGES".
COL D 288, COL DS 288 cf. **58.07.25**; COL G 30625 cf. **59.06.25**.

63.12.12   Dave Brubeck Quartet With Symphony Orchestra
64.01.08   Dave Brubeck Quartet With Symphony Orchestra
New York City, New York.
Paul Desmond as; Dave Brubeck p; Gene Wright b; Joe Morello dr;
Symphony Orchestra, Rayburn Wright cond.
a. CO81411   Elementals   16:40   COL CL 2127

Issues: COL CS 8927.

Notes: COL CL 2127 is entitled "THE DAVE BRUBECK QUARTET: TIME CHANGES".
"Elementals" was composed by Dave Brubeck for the final concert of a course for arrangers at the
Eastman School of Music in Rochester, New York, where it was first performed on August 1,
1963.

64.00.00   Dave Brubeck and Ranny Sinclair
Dave Brubeck p; unknown g; unknown b; unknown dr; Ranny Sinclair voc.
a.   Something To Sing About   COL 4-43759
b.   Autumn In New York   -

Notes: This entry is given following Raben /3./.

64.02.07   Dave Brubeck
Dave Brubeck p; unknown musicians.
a.   Here's To Veterans

Notes: This entry is given following Willmon L. White (Cassette # 910).

64.06.00   Dave Brubeck Quartet
Chicago, Illinois.
Paul Desmond as; Dave Brubeck p; Gene Wright b; Joe Morello dr.
a.   The Old Folks At Home   7:36   JCO JC 003
b.   In Your Own Sweet Way   7:42   -
c.   Osaka Blues   8:50   -
d.   Koto Song   7:08   -
e.   You Go To My Head   12:20   -
f.   Cable Car   5:44   -

Notes : JCO JC 003 is entitled "DAVE BRUBECK QUARTET IN CONCERT 1964". "The Old Folks At Home" Is "Swanee River".

64.06.16+17   Dave Brubeck Quartet
New York City, New York.
Paul Desmond as; Dave Brubeck p; Gene Wright b; Joe Morello dr.
a. CO82307   Koto Song   3:00   COL CL 2212
b. CO82308   Osaka Blues   5:11   -
c. CO82309   Tokyo Traffic   5:48   -
d. CO82310   Fujiyama   5:04   -
e. CO82311   Toki's Theme   2:07   -
f. CO82312   The City Is Crying   6:00   -
g. CO82313   Rising Sun   4:40   -

Issues: COL CS 9012 **a** CBS 54490; **c** COL D 288; COL DS 288; **d** COL OC 44314; COL C4K 52945; **e** CBS 1541; COL 4-43091; COL 4-43133.

Notes: COL CL 2212 is entitled "THE DAVE BRUBECK QUARTET: JAZZ IMPRESSIONS OF JAPAN". COL OC 44314 is a sampler entitled "PIONEERS OF THE NEW AGE", released in 1988. "Toki's Theme" issued on COL 4-43133 is listed in the Columbia files with the recording date **64.08.17** and masternumber CO83649 according to Raben /3./. CBS 54490 cf. **54.03-04.00**; COL C4K 52945 cf. **46-48.00.00**; COL D 288, COL DS 288 cf. **58.07.25**.

64.06.18   **Dave Brubeck Quartet**
New York City, New York.
Paul Desmond as; Dave Brubeck p; Gene Wright b; Joe Morello dr.
a. CO82317   Winter Ballad   2:45   COL CL 2275

Issues: CBS 466971-2; COL CK-46189; COL CS 9075.

Notes: COL CL 2275 is entitled "DAVE BRUBECK: JAZZ IMPRESSIONS OF NEW YORK" and features the music from the CBS Television Network Series "MR. BROADWAY". CBS 466971-2; COL CK-46189 are CDs with the same title from the series "COLUMBIA / CBS JAZZ MASTERPIECES" released in 1990. The original tapes were digitally remastered at the CBS Records New York Studio.

64.06.24   **Dave Brubeck Quartet**
New York City, New York.
Paul Desmond as; Dave Brubeck p; Gene Wright b; Joe Morello dr.
a. CO82329   Lonely Mr. Broadway   4:20   COL CL 2275

Issues: CBS 466971-2; COL CK-46189; COL CS 9075.

Notes: COL CL 2275 is entitled "DAVE BRUBECK: JAZZ IMPRESSIONS OF NEW YORK". CBS 466971-2; COL CK-46189 cf. **64.06.18**.

64.06.25   **Dave Brubeck Quartet**
New York City, New York.
Paul Desmond as, mar (c); Dave Brubeck p; Gene Wright b; Joe Morello dr; Howard Brubeck perc (c); John Lee tom-tom (c); Teo Macero claves (c).

a.	CO82337	Something To Sing About	3:52	COL CL 2275
b.	CO82338	Broadway Bossa Nova	3:15	-
c.	CO82339	Upstage Rhumba	3:10	-

Issues: CBS 466971-2; COL CK-46189; COL CS 9075; **b** COL CSP 206; **c** COL C4K 52945.

Notes: COL CL 2275 is entitled "DAVE BRUBECK: JAZZ IMPRESSIONS OF NEW YORK". COL CSP 206 is a sampler entitled "THE SOUNDS THAT SWING", released in a limited edition for Philco, a division of Ford Motor Co.
CBS 466971-2; COL CK-46189 cf. **64.06.18**; COL C4K 52945 cf. **46-48.00.00**.

64.07.15   Dave Brubeck Quartet
New York City, New York.
Paul Desmond as; Dave Brubeck p; Gene Wright b; Joe Morello dr.

a.	CO83551	Theme From "Mr. Broadway"	2:25	COL CL 2275
b.	CO83552	Autumn In Washington Square	5:27	-

Issues: CBS 466971-2; COL CK-46189; COL CS 9075; **a** COL 4-43133; COL CL 2484; COL CS 9284; COL DJ-11; MEL S60-07229/30; SUP 015/115.1029.

Notes: COL CL 2275 is entitled "DAVE BRUBECK: JAZZ IMPRESSIONS OF NEW YORK". COL DJ-11 is a sampler entitled "LITTLE BITS OF JAZZ". "Theme From Mr. Broadway" issued on COL 4-43133 is listed in the Columbia files with the recording date **64.08.17** and master number CO83931 /3./. CBS 466971-2; COL CK-46189 cf. **64.06.18**; COL CL 2484 cf. **56.04.18+19**; MEL S60-07229/30 cf. **56.03.12**; SUP 015/115.1029 cf. **59.07.01**.

64.08.11   Dave Brubeck Quartet
New York City, New York.
Paul Desmond as; Dave Brubeck p; Gene Wright b; Joe Morello dr.

a.	CO83575	Spring In Central Park	2:27	COL CL 2275
b.	CO83576	Sixth Sense	6:55	-

Issues: CBS 466971-2; COL CK-46189; COL CS 9075.

Notes: COL CL 2275 is entitled "DAVE BRUBECK: JAZZ IMPRESSIONS OF NEW YORK". CBS 466971-2; COL CK-46189 cf. **64.06.18**.

64.08.19   Dave Brubeck Quartet
New York City, New York.
Paul Desmond as; Dave Brubeck p; Gene Wright b; Joe Morello dr.
a. CO83589   Summer On The Sound   2:40   COL CL 2275

Issues: CBS 466971-2; COL CK-46189; COL CS 9075.

Notes: COL CL 2275 is entitled "DAVE BRUBECK: JAZZ IMPRESSIONS OF NEW YORK".
CBS 466971-2; COL CK-46189 cf. **64.06.18**.

64.08.21   Dave Brubeck Quartet
New York City, New York.
Paul Desmond as; Dave Brubeck p; Gene Wright b; Joe Morello dr.
a. CO83596   Broadway Romance   5:50   COL CL 2275

Issues: CBS 466971-2; COL CK-46189; COL CS 9075.

Notes: COL CL 2275 is entitled "DAVE BRUBECK: JAZZ IMPRESSIONS OF NEW YORK".
CBS 466971-2; COL CK-46189 cf. **64.06.18**.

64.09.26+27   Dave Brubeck Quartet
Berlin, Germany, Philharmonie.
Paul Desmond as; Dave Brubeck p; Gene Wright b; Joe Morello dr.
a.   St. Louis Blues   12:05   CBS 62578
b.   Koto Song   7:44   -
c.   Take The "A" Train   8:30   -
d.   Take Five   6:30   -

Notes: CBS 62578 is entitled "DAVE BRUBECK IN BERLIN". This mono album was recorded during a concert at the "Berliner Jazztage 1964" (Berlin Jazz Days 1964) in cooperation with the Westdeutscher Rundfunk Köln (WDR) (West German Broadcasting Corporation Cologne).

65.02.15   Dave Brubeck Quartet
New York City, New York.
Paul Desmond as; Dave Brubeck p; Gene Wright b; Joe Morello dr.
a. CO85513   Little Man With A Candy Cigar   3:32   COL CL 2348

b.	CO85546	Let's Get Away From It All	3:57	-
c.	CO85547	Everything Happens To Me	5:45	-
d.	CO85420	Violets For Your Furs	5:49	-

Issues: COL CS 9148; **a** COL C4K 52945; **b** COL KG 32761; ZOUNDS 27200446B.

Notes: COL CL 2348 is entitled "DAVE BRUBECK QUARTET: ANGEL EYES". COL C4K 52945 cf. **46-48.00.00**; COL KG 32761 cf. **56.07.06**; ZOUNDS 27200446B cf. **54.10.12**.

65.08.22   **Dave Brubeck Quartet**
Stratford, Ontario, Canada, Stratford Music Festival.
Paul Desmond as; Dave Brubeck p; Gene Wright b; Joe Morello dr.

a.	St. Louis Blues	9:48	CAN-AM 1500
b.	Take The "A" Train	7:53	-
c.	Cultural Exchange	6:06	-
d.	Tangerine	6:08	-
e.	Someday My Prince Will Come	4:34	-
f.	These Foolish Things	10:28	-
g.	Koto Song	3:55	-
h.	Take Five (inc.)	1:47	-

Notes: CAN-AM 1500 is entitled "THE CANADIAN CONCERT OF DAVE BRUBECK". The album was recorded live at the Stratford Music Festival. The original issue RM 140 by the Canadian Broadcasting Corporation Co. was distributed to radio stations only (Raben /3./).

65.09.20   **Dave Brubeck Quartet**
New York City, New York.
Paul Desmond as; Dave Brubeck p; Gene Wright b; Joe Morello dr.

| a. | CO86589 | Lonesome | 7:10 | COL CL 2512 |
| b. | CO86590 | Cassandra | 4:19 | - |

Issues: COL CS 9312; **b** COL CSS 524; COL G 30625.

Notes: COL CL 2512 is entitled "DAVE BRUBECK: TIME IN".
COL CSS 524 cf. **61.06.08**; COL G 30625 cf. **59.06.25**.

65.09.22   Dave Brubeck Quartet
New York City, New York.
Paul Desmond as (b); Dave Brubeck p; Gene Wright b; Joe Morello dr.
a.   My Favorite Things   2:52   COL CL 2437
b.   This Can't Be Love   6:32   -

Issues: COL CS 9237; COL CSP 326; **a** CBS 54703; CBS/EMBA 31769; CBS/COL HOUSE 6P
6624; COL C4K 52945; COL KG 32761; COL XTV 88514.

Notes: COL CL 2437 is entitled "DAVE BRUBECK QUARTET: MY FAVORITE THINGS".
CBS/COL HOUSE 6P 6624 is a six LP boxed set entitled "ALL-STAR PIANO". COL CSP 326
is a Zenith stereo anthology entitled "JAZZ: RED HOT & COOL": COL XTV 88514 is a sampler
entitled "THE HOT ONES". CBS 54703, COL KG 32761 cf. **56.07.06**; CBS/EMBA 31769 cf.
58.07.28; COL C4K 52945 cf. **46-48.00.00**.

65.10.13   Dave Brubeck Quartet
New York City, New York.
Paul Desmond as (a-d,f); Dave Brubeck p; Gene Wright b; Joe Morello dr.
a. CO86584   He Done Her Wrong   2:15   COL CL 2512
b. CO86585   40 Days   4:38   -
c. CO86586   Softly,William,Softly   5:38   -
d. CO86587   Lost Waltz   3:52   -
e. CO86613   Time In   3:56   -
f. CO86616   Travellin' Blues   5:56   -

Issues: COL CS 9312; **a** COL G 30625; **d** COL C4K 52945; GDJ 82.

Notes: COL CL 2512 is entitled "DAVE BRUBECK: TIME IN".
COL C4K 52945 cf. **46-48.00.00**; COL G 30625 cf. **59.06.25**; GDJ 82 cf. **54.10.12**.

65.12.08   Dave Brubeck Quartet
New York City, New York.
Paul Desmond as; Dave Brubeck p; Gene Wright b; Joe Morello dr.
a. CO87360   Anything Goes   5:40   COL CL 2602
b. CO87361   All Through The Night   8:25   -
c. CO87363   Night And Day   4:55   -
d. CO87364   What Is This Thing Called Love 6:16   -

Issues: COL CS 9402; **c,d** CBS 450410-1/-2; COL CJ-40455; COL CK-40455; ZOUNDS 27200446B; **c** CBS 80775; COL KG 32761; **d** CBS 80777; COL C21 7926-2CD.

Notes: COL CL 2602 is entitled "THE DAVE BRUBECK QUARTET PLAYS COLE PORTER: ANYTHING GOES!". COL C21 7926-2CD is a sampler from the Columbia Music Collection entitled "THE GREAT AMERICAN COMPOSER: COLE PORTER".
CBS 450410-1/-2; COL CJ-40455; COL CK-40455 cf. **60.02.14**; COL KG 32761 cf. **56.07.06**; CBS 80775, CBS 80777 cf. **54.03-04.00**; ZOUNDS 27200446B cf. **54.10.12**.

66.01.26   **Dave Brubeck Trio**
New York City, New York.
Dave Brubeck p; Gene Wright b; Joe Morello dr.
a. CO89000   Love For Sale   5:18   COL CL 2602

Issues: CBS 80777; COL CS 9402.

Notes: COL CL 2602 is entitled "THE DAVE BRUBECK QUARTET PLAYS COLE PORTER: ANYTHING GOES!". CBS 80777 cf. **54.03-04.00**.

66.02.17   **Dave Brubeck Quartet**
New York City, New York.
Paul Desmond as; Dave Brubeck p; Gene Wright b; Joe Morello dr.
a. CO89061   I Get A Kick Out Of You   5:15   COL CL 2602
b. CO89062   Just One Of Those Things   6:19   -
c. CO89063   You're The Top   6:35   -

Issues: CBS 467148-2; COL CS 9402; a CBS 80777; COL C4K 52945.

Notes: COL CL 2602 is entitled "THE DAVE BRUBECK QUARTET PLAYS COLE PORTER: ANYTHING GOES!". CBS 80777 cf. **54.03-04.00**; CBS 467148-2 cf. **54.10.12**; COL C4K 52945 cf. **46-48.00.00**.

66.06.14+15   **Dave Brubeck Quartet**
Las Vegas, Nevada, Tropicana Hotel.
Paul Desmond as (a,b,d,e,h); Dave Brubeck p; Gene Wright b; Joe Morello dr.
a. HCO88021   Who's Afraid?   3:07   COL CL 2712

b.	CO93815	Ace In The Hole	6:44	-
c.	CO93817	Jackpot	10:59	-
d.	CO93818	Out Of Nowhere	6:49	-
e.	CO93819	You Go To My Head	10:21	-
f.	CO93821	Chicago	4:03	-
g.	CO93822	Rude Old Man	2:55	-
h.	CO93904	Win A Few, Lose A Few	4:51	-

Issues: COL CS 9152; **d,f** CBS 80776; **a** COL 4-43732.

Notes: COL CL 2712 is entitled "DAVE BRUBECK : JACKPOT * RECORDED LIVE IN LAS VEGAS". The 45-rpm issue COL 4-43732 does not have any applause while the LP issue COL CL 2712 has; this indicates that the master HCO88021 is from a Los Angeles studio recording with the applause added afterwards, Raben /3./. CBS 80776 cf. **54.03-04.00.**

66.10-11.00   Dave Brubeck Quartet
Karlsruhe, Germany.
Paul Desmond as; Dave Brubeck p; Gene Wright b; Joe Morello dr.

a.	Koto Song	8:04	COL C 30522

Issues: COL C4K 52945.

Notes: COL C 30522 is a compilation album entitled "SUMMIT SESSIONS: DAVE BRUBECK WITH SPECIAL GUEST STARS". For four more titles of this concert see the next section. COL C 30522 cf. **60.01.29**; COL C4K 52945 cf. **46-48.00.00.**

67.05.12   Dave Brubeck And Thelonious Monk
Puebla, Mexico, Puebla Arts Festival.
Dave Brubeck p; Thelonious Monk p; Larry Gales b; Ben Riley dr.

a.	C-Jam Blues	5:30	COL C 30522

Notes: COL C 30522 is a compilation album entitled "SUMMIT SESSIONS: DAVE BRUBECK WITH SPECIAL GUEST STARS". COL C 30522 cf. **60.01.29.**

67.05.12   Dave Brubeck Quartet & Guests
Puebla, Puebla, Mexico, Jazz Festival.

Paul Desmond as (a,c-i); Dave Brubeck p (a,c-i); Benjamin "Chamin" Correa g (a-d,f-i); Gene Wright b; Joe Morello dr; Salvador "Rabito" Agueros perc.

67.05.13   **Dave Brubeck Quartet**

Mexico City, Mexico, Palace Of Fine Arts.

67.05.14   **Dave Brubeck Quartet**

Mexico City, Mexico, National Auditorium.

Paul Desmond as; Dave Brubeck p; Gene Wright b; Joe Morello dr.

a.	CO93275	Cielito Lindo (Blue Sky) (Arr. Brubeck)	5:00	COL CL 2695
b.	CO93277	Alla En El Rancho Grande (My Ranch)	2:58	-
c.	CO93278	Poinciana (Song Of The Trees)	6:42	-
d.	CO93279	Besame Mucho (Kiss Me Much)	5:54	-
e.	CO93280	Estrellita (Little Star)	4:50	-
f.	CO93281	Sobre Las Olas (Over The Waves) (Arr. Brubeck)	3:16	-
g.	CO93282	Nostalgia De Mexico	3:16	-
h.	CO93283	La Bamba (Folk Dance From Veracruz) (Arr. Brubeck)	5:11	-
i.	CO93323	La Paloma Azul (The Blue Dove - Mexican Folk Song)(Arr. Brubeck)	6:18	-

Issues: CBS 465623-2; COL CS 9495; **c,d** CBS 80777; **a** GDJ 82; **c** CBS 467139-2; COL/SONY 471683-2; **e,i** COL C4K 52945.

Notes: COL CL 2695 is entitled "BRAVO! BRUBECK! RECORDED LIVE IN MEXICO". CBS 465623-2 is a CD with the same title from the series "I LOVE JAZZ" , released in 1989 with digitally remastered tapes. CBS 467139-2 is a sampler from the series "I LOVE JAZZ" with the title "LATIN JAZZ", released in 1990. COL/SONY 471683-2 is a compilation CD made in France with the title "THE ESSENTIAL LATIN JAZZ".
CBS 80777 cf. **54.03-04.00**; COL C4K 52945 cf. **46-48.00.00**; GDJ 82 cf. **54.10.12**.

67.07.22   **Dave Brubeck Quartet**

Juans-Les-Pins, France,

Paul Desmond as (a,b,d,e); Dave Brubeck p; Gene Wright b; Joe Morello dr.

a.		One Moment Worth Years	9:10	JMY 1001-2
b.		Mexican Folk Song	7:15	-
c.		Blues For Joe	7:55	-
d.		Take Five	4:45	-
e.		Take The "A" Train	6:30	-

Issues: a,d,e DEJA DVRECD 58; **a,e** ROC unn.

Notes: JMY 1001-2 is entitled "DAVE BRUBECK QUARTET FEATURING PAUL DESMOND: TAKE FIVE LIVE" , released in 1990 on Compact Disc only. It was recorded live at the Jazz Festival 1967 at Juans-Les Pins. "Mexican Folk Song" is "La Paloma Azul". DEJA DVRECD 58 cf. **51.12.15**; ROC unn. cf. **49.09.00**.

67.08.00
Wilton, Connecticut.
Dave Brubeck p, el-org; Gene Wright b; Joe Morello d; Palghat Raghu mridangam; Danny Brubeck finger cymbals.

a.	Raga Theme For Raghu	2:48	COL C 30522
b.	Do Not Fold, Staple, Spindle	1:57	COL 4-44345
	Or Mutilate		

Dave Brubeck p; Bill Crofut bjo, voc; Steve Addis g, voc; Gene Wright b; Joe Morello d.

c.	Men Of Old	2:48	COL C 30522

Dave Brubeck p; Gene Wright b; Joe Morello d; Peter Yarrow, Paul Stokey & Mary Travers g, voc.

d.	Because All Men Are Brothers	3:16	COL C 30522

Issues: a COL 4-44345.

Notes: COL C 30522 is a compilation album entitled "SUMMIT SESSIONS: DAVE BRUBECK WITH SPECIAL GUEST STARS". COL C 30522 cf. **60.01.29**.

67.11.13 **Dave Brubeck Quartet**
Paris, France, Salle Pleyel.
Paul Desmond as; Dave Brubeck p; Gene Wright b; Joe Morello dr.

a.	Swanee River (Arr. Brubeck)	8:47	COL CS 9672
b.	These Foolish Things	12:26	-
c.	Forty Days	6:45	-
d.	One Moment Worth Years	8:06	-
e.	La Paloma Azul (The Blue Dove)	6:58	-
	(Arr. Brubeck)		
f.	Three To Get Ready	5:12	-

Issues: c COL C4K 52945; **f** CBS 54490.

Notes: COL CS 9672 is entitled "THE DAVE BRUBECK QUARTET: THE LAST TIME WE SAW PARIS * RECORDED LIVE IN PARIS". CBS 54490 cf. **54.03-04.00**; COL C4K 52945 cf. **46-48.00.00**.

68.03.19+20   **Dave Brubeck**
Cincinnati, Ohio.
Cincinnati Symphony Orchestra, Erich Kunzel cond; Dave Brubeck p; Miami University A Cappella Singers, George Barron dir; William Justus baritone; Gerre Hancock org; Frank Proto b, del rhuba; David Frerichs dr, tablas.

a.   The Light In The Wilderness   DEC DXSA 7202
                  An Oratorio For Today
                  Music By Dave Brubeck
                  Text Adapted From The Scriptures
                  By Dave And Iola Brubeck.
                  1. The Temptations
                  2. Forty Days
                  3. Repent! Follow Me
                  4. The Sermon On The Mount
                  5. Repent! Follow Me / The Kingdom Of God
                  6. The Great Commandment
                  7. Love Your Enemies
                     Interlude
                  8. What Does It Profit A Man? /
                     Where Is God?
                  9. We Seek Him / Peace I Leave With You
                  10. Let Not Your Heart Be Troubled
                  11. Yet A Little While
                  12. Praise Ye The Lord

Issues: MIDLAND JAZZ FESTIVAL 1974.

Notes: DEC DXSA 7202 is entitled DAVE BRUBECK: THE LIGHT IN THE WILDERNESS * AN ORATORIO FOR TODAY * ERICH KUNZEL CONDUCTING THE CINCINNATI SYMPHONY ORCHESTRA * DAVE BRUBECK PIANO". "The Light In The Wilderness" was given its World Première by the Cincinnati Symphony Orchestra at its second annual Ecumenical Concert, February 29, Erich Kunzel conducting. MIDLAND JAZZ FESTIVAL 1974 is a non-commercial release. The re-release of "The Light In The Wilderness" on CD will be available through the Musical Heritage Society.

68.05.17　　　Dave Brubeck Quartet

New Orleans, Louisiana.

Gerry Mulligan bar; Dave Brubeck p; Jack Six b; Alan Dawson dr.

a.	Out Of The Way	8:00	OXF OX/3024
b.	These Foolish Things	10:00	-
c.	Jumpin' Beans	6:50	-
d.	St. Louis Blues	5:45	-

Issues: b,c DRIVE 3510.

Notes: OXF OX/3024 is entitled "GERRY MULLIGAN WITH DAVE BRUBECK QUARTET: LIVE IN NEW ORLEANS 1968". According to Bruyninckx /2./ the information on the record cover of OXF OX/3024 is partly incorrect; one tune is without the participation of Dave Brubeck. DRIVE 3510 cf. **61.00.00.**

68.05.23　　　Dave Brubeck Trio Featuring Gerry Mulligan

Mexico City, Mexico, National Auditorium.

Gerry Mulligan bar; Dave Brubeck p; Jack Six b; Alan Dawson dr.

a.	Jumping Bean	3:55	COL CS 9704
b.	Adios, Mariquita Linda	4:07	-
c.	Indian Song	7:07	-
d.	Tender Woman (Tierna Mujer)	6:35	-
e.	Amapola	7:55	-
f.	Lullaby De Mexico (Lullaby Of Mexico)	6:35	-
g.	Sapito	3:02	-
h.	Recuerdo (Remembrance)	5:28	-
i.	Theme For Jobim	4:20	COL C 30522

Issues: f,h GDJ 82; **g,h** COL C4K 52945.

Notes: COL CS 9704 is entitled "THE DAVE BRUBECK TRIO FEATURING GERRY MULLIGAN: BRUBECK * MULLIGAN: COMPADRES". COL C 30522 is a compilation album entitled "SUMMIT SESSIONS: DAVE BRUBECK WITH SPECIAL GUEST STARS". COL C 30522 cf. **60.01.29**; COL C4K 52945 cf. **46-48.00.00**; GDJ 82 cf. **54.10.12.**

68.10.04　　　Dave Brubeck Trio Featuring Gerry Mulligan

New York City, New York.

Gerry Mulligan bar; Dave Brubeck p; Jack Six b, el-b; Alan Dawson dr.

a.	Limehouse Blues	4:47	COL CS 9749
b.	Broke Blues	4:57	-
c.	Blues Roots	6:50	-
d.	Things Ain't What They Used To Be	7:21	-

Issues: b,c COL 4-44834; a COL CSP P 15949.

Notes: COL CS 9749 is entitled "THE DAVE BRUBECK TRIO FEATURING GERRY MULLIGAN: BLUES ROOTS". **b** Gerry Mulligan's part was recorded separately and later dubbed in. **c** Dave Brubeck plays Honky Tonk Piano. COL CSP P 15949 is entitled "MONTREUX - DETROIT JAZZ FESTIVAL".

68.12.13   **Dave Brubeck Trio Featuring Gerry Mulligan**

New York City, New York.

Gerry Mulligan bar; Dave Brubeck p; Jack Six b; Alan Dawson dr.

a.	Journey	8:56	COL CS 9749
b.	Cross Ties	11:07	-
c.	Movin' Out	5:33	-

Notes: COL CS 9749 is entitled "THE DAVE BRUBECK TRIO FEATURING GERRY MULLIGAN: BLUES ROOTS". **b** Gerry Mulligan's part was recorded separately and later dubbed in; **c** Dave Brubeck and Alan Dawson double tracked.

69.10.19

Cincinnati, Ohio.

The Cincinnati Brass Ensemble, Erich Kunzel cond; The Westminster Choir, Robert Carwithen dir; McHenry Boatwright bass-baritone; Cantor Harold Orbach tenor; Dave Brubeck p; Jack Six b; Alan Dawson dr; Robert Delcamp org.

a.	The Gates Of Justice	DEC DL 710175

Music By Dave Brubeck

Text Adapted by Iola and Dave Brubeck.

1. Lord, The Heaven Of Heavens Cannot Contain Thee
2. Oh, Come Let Us Sing A New Song Unto The Lord
3. Open The Gates / Chorale
4. Except The Lord Build The House
5. Lord, Lord (Spiritual)

6. Ye Shall Be Holy
7. Shout Unto The Lord
8. When I Behold Thy Heavens
9. How Glorious Is Thy Name
10. The Lord Is Good
11. His Truth Is A Shield
12. Oh, Come Let Us Sing A New Song

Notes : DEC DL 710175 is entitled "DAVE BRUBECK: THE GATES OF JUSTICE". "The Gates Of Justice" was written in response to a commission from the College-Conservatory of Music of the University of Cincinnati and the Union of American Hebrew Congregations through the auspices of the Corbett Foundation, and was first performed on the occasion of the dedication of Rockdale Temple in Cincinnati, on October 19, 1969.

70.03.01

The University of Minnesota Chorus, Brass & Percussion; Dave Brubeck p; Jack Six b; Alan Dawson dr.

a.   The Gates Of Justice   MARK UMC 2139

Notes: This entry is given following W. H. Schrickel.

**70.05.26   Dave Brubeck Trio With Gerry Mulligan And
                  The Cincinnati Symphony Orchestra**

Cincinnati, Ohio, Music Hall.
Gerry Mulligan bar; Dave Brubeck p; Jack Six b; Alan Dawson dr; Cincinnati Symphony Orchestra, Erich Kunzel cond.

a.	Happy Anniversary (Arr. Brubeck)	4:48	DEC DL 710181
b	The Duke (Arr. Proto)	6:45	-
c.	Blessed Are The Poor (Arr. Brubeck)	4:50	-
d.	Forty Days (Arr. Brubeck)	2:56	-
e.	Elementals (Arr. Brubeck)	15:35	-

Issues: MCA MCAD 42347.

Notes: DEC DL 710181 is entitled "BRUBECK / MULLIGAN / CINCINNATI: DAVE BRUBECK TRIO WITH GERRY MULLIGAN & THE CINCINNATI SYMPHONY ORCHESTRA ERICH KUNZEL CONDUCTOR TUES. MAY 26 8.00 P.M.". MCA MCAD

42347 is the CD issue with the title "BRUBECK / MULLIGAN / CINCINNATI: DAVE BRUBECK TRIO WITH GERRY MULLIGAN & THE CINCINNATI SYMPHONY ORCHESTRA".

70.10.29   Dave Brubeck Trio Featuring Gerry Mulligan
Warsaw, Poland, Congress Hall.
Gerry Mulligan bar; Dave Brubeck p; Jack Six b; Alan Dawson dr.

a.	Jumpin' Beans	7:15	MUZA XL 0696
b.	St. Louis Blues	11:09	-

Issues: MUZA SXL 0969.

Notes: MUZA XL 0696 is entitled "JAZZ JAMBOREE - 1970 (VOL. 1)". Dave Brubeck's part is only one side of MUZA XL 0696. The other side is by Andrzej Kurylewicz Contemporary Music Foundation and Wanda Warska.

70.11.07   Dave Brubeck Trio Featuring Gerry Mulligan
Berlin, Germany, Philharmonie, Berliner Jazz-Tage 1970.
Gerry Mulligan bar; Dave Brubeck p; Jack Six b; Alan Dawson dr.

a.	Limehouse Blues	6:00	CBS S 67261
b.	St. Louis Blues	6:30	-
c.	The Duke	7:33	-
d.	Blessed Are The Poor	9:46	-
e.	Things Ain't What They Used To Be	10:40	-
f.	New Orleans	14:05	-
g.	Indian Song	10:45	-
h.	Basin Street Blues	4:40	-
i.	Take Five	3:25	-
k.	Lullaby De Mexico (Lullaby Of Mexico)	4:30	-
l.	Out Of The Way Of The People	6:35	-

Issues: COL (CAN) GES 90100; **a,d,e,g,k** COL KC 32143; **b,i,k** CBS (J) SOPW 56; **b** COL C4K 52945; **h** CBS 54490.

Notes: CBS S 67261 is entitled "DAVE BRUBECK TRIO & GERRY MULLIGAN: LIVE AT THE BERLIN PHILHARMONIE". COL KC 32143 is entitled "DAVE BRUBECK TRIO & GERRY MULLIGAN: LIVE AT THE BERLIN PHILHARMONIC". This album was recorded live at the Berlin Jazz Days in 1970 in collaboration with the SFB Station Free Berlin. For two more titles see the next section. CBS 54490 cf. **54.03-04.00**; COL C4K 52945 cf. **46-48.00.00**.

71.07.03   **Dave Brubeck Quartet Featuring Gerry Mulligan**
Newport, Rhode Island, Newport Jazz Festival.
Gerry Mulligan bar; Dave Brubeck p; Jack Six b; Alan Dawson dr.

a.	23764	Blues For Newport	16:24	ATL SD 1607
b.	23765	Take Five	9:32	-
c.	23766	Open The Gates (Out Of The Way Of The People)	8:15	-

Issues: ATL 1607-2; **b (ed.)** ATL 20034; **b** ATL 20052; ATL 20269; CHA CTR 20092; MIDI MID 20092; WYN DVCD-2036.

Notes: ATL SD 1607 is entitled "THE DAVE BRUBECK QUARTET FEATURING GERRY MULLIGAN * ALAN DAWSON * JACK SIX: THE LAST SET AT NEWPORT". For the issue of ATL 1607-2 the tapes were digitally remastered. ATL 20052 is a sampler with the title "BLUES 'N' JAZZ -25- THE ATLANTIC YEARS". ATL 20034 is a sampler entitled "HEAVY AND ALIVE". ATL 20269, CHA CTR 20092 and MIDI MID 20092 are compilation albums with the title "DAVE BRUBECK" from the series "COLLECTION", released in 1975.

71.08.30+31
Cincinnati, Ohio, Corbett Auditorium, University of Cincinnati Conservatory Of Music.
Cincinnati Symphony Orchestra, Erich Kunzel cond; St. John's Assembly, Gordon Franklin dir; Charlene Peterson soprano; Dave Brubeck p, osc; Lowell Thompson perc;
New Heavenly Blue: Chris Brubeck tb, keyb, voc; Steve Dudash voc, viol, g; Peter Bonisteel perc; Chris Brown el-b, b, voc; Jim Cathcart tp, org, voc; Dave Mason g, viola, voc; Peter Ruth harm, fl, voc.

a.		Truth Is Fallen Music By Dave Brubeck. Text Selected And Adapted By Iola Brubeck With Original Words By Iola and Christopher Brubeck.		ATL SD 1606
	27780	1. Prelude	11:20	-
		2. Merciful Men Are Taken Away		
		3. Truth Is Fallen	8:15	-
	27781	4. Oh, That My Head Were Waters	8:20	-
		5. Speak Out / I Called And		

No One Answered
6. Yea, Truth Faileth   5:10   -
7. Truth (Planets Are Spinning)
8. Is The Lord's Hand Shortened?   7:58   -
9. Arise!

Notes: ATL SD 1606 is entitled "DAVE BRUBECK: TRUTH IS FALLEN". Dave Brubeck was commissioned by the Midland Symphony Orchestra to compose a piece to be performed at the dedication of the Midland Center For The Arts, Midland, Michigan. The world premiere of "Truth is Fallen" was performed by the Midland Symphony Orchestra and the Midland Music Society Chorale, Don Th. Jaeger, conducting, May 1 and 2, 1971. The cantata is dedicated to the slain students of Kent University and Mississippi State, and all other innocent victims, caught in the cross-fire between repression and rebellion.

72.10.26   **Dave Brubeck Trio Featuring Gerry Mulligan And Paul Desmond**
Paris, France, Olympia.
Paul Desmond as; Gerry Mulligan bar; Dave Brubeck p; Jack Six b; Alan Dawson dr.
a. 26141   Koto Song (no bar)   5:05   ATL SD 1641

Issues: ATL 1641-2; ATL 781707-1/-2.

Notes: ATL SD 1641 is entitled "DAVE BRUBECK * GERRY MULLIGAN * PAUL DESMOND * ALAN DAWSON * JACK SIX: WE'RE ALL TOGETHER AGAIN FOR THE FIRST TIME". For other titles of this concert see the next section. ATL 781707-1/-2 are samplers entitled "ATLANTIC JAZZ PIANO".

72.10.28   **Dave Brubeck Trio Featuring Gerry Mulligan And Paul Desmond**
Rotterdam, The Netherlands, De Doelen.
Paul Desmond as (a); Gerry Mulligan bar (a); Dave Brubeck p; Jack Six b (a); Alan Dawson dr (a).
a 26143   Rotterdam Blues   6:45   ATL SD 1641
b. 26144   Sweet Georgia Brown   1:00   -

Issues: ATL 1641-2; a ATL 20269; CHA CTR 20092; MIDI MID 20092; WYN DVCD-2036.

Notes: ATL SD 1641 is entitled "DAVE BRUBECK * GERRY MULLIGAN * PAUL DESMOND * ALAN DAWSON * JACK SIX: WE'RE ALL TOGETHER AGAIN FOR THE

FIRST TIME". For other titles of this concert see the next section.
ATL 20269, CHA CTR 20092, MIDI MID 20092, WYN DVCD-2036 cf. **71.07.03**.

72.11.04   Dave Brubeck Trio Featuring Gerry Mulligan And Paul Desmond
Berlin, Germany, Philharmonie.
Paul Desmond as; Gerry Mulligan bar; Dave Brubeck p; Jack Six b; Alan Dawson dr.

a.	26139	Truth	10:21	ATL SD 1641
b.	26140	Unfinished Woman	7:20	-
c.	26142	Take Five	16:00	-

Issues: ATL 1641-2.

Notes: ATL SD 1641 is entitled "DAVE BRUBECK * GERRY MULLIGAN * PAUL DESMOND * ALAN DAWSON * JACK SIX: WE'RE ALL TOGETHER AGAIN FOR THE FIRST TIME". For other titles of this concert see the next section.

73.07.17   Dave Brubeck Trio
New York City, New York, C. I. Studios.
Dave Brubeck p; Jack Six b; Alan Dawson dr.
                       Jimmy Van Heusen Medley:

a.	27487	Deep In A Dream	2:40	ATL SD 1684
b.	27488	Like Someone In Love	4:50	-
c.	27489	Here's That Rainy Day	4:28	-
d.	27490	Polka Dots And Moonbeams	3:59	-
e.	27491	It Could Happen To You	4:56	-

Issues: ATL 1684-2.

Notes: ATL SD 1684 is entitled "DAVE BRUBECK * ANTHONY BRAXTON * ALAN DAWSON * ROY HAYNES * LEE KONITZ * JACK SIX: ALL THE THINGS WE ARE". The recordings were remastered with the matrix numbers: 27487 = 31919; 27488 = 31920; 27489 = 31921; 27490 = 31922; 27491 = 31923.

73.08.06   Two Generations Of Brubeck
New York City, New York, C.I. Studios.
Dave Brubeck And The New Heavenly Blue:

Dave Brubeck p; Jim Cathcart el-p; Chris Brubeck el-b; Stephen Dudash viol; David Mason g;
Richie Morales dr; Peter Ruth harm.

a. 27169   Blue Rondo A La Turk   7:55   ATL SD 1645

Chris Brubeck tb (c), el-b (b); Jerry Bergonzi ss, ts; Perry Robinson cl; Dave Brubeck p; Darius
Brubeck p; David Dutemple el-b (b); Danny Brubeck dr; Randie Powell perc.

b. 27170   The Holy One   3:37   ATL SD 1645
c. 27171   Circadian Dysrhythmia   3:20   -

Issues: a ATL 3015 (ed.); ATL 20269; CHA CTR 20092; CITADEL 8860 (?); MIDI MID
20092; WYN DVCD-2036.

Notes: ATL SD 1645 is entitled "DAVE BRUBECK: TWO GENERATIONS OF BRUBECK".
CITADEL 8860 is a sampler CD entitled "THE BEST OF JAZZ". "Blue Rondo" on ATL 3015 is
an edited version (3:22). ATL 20269, CHA CTR 20092, MIDI MID 20092 cf. **71.07.03**.

73.08.07   **Two Generations Of Brubeck**
New York City, New York, C.I. Studios.
Dave Brubeck p; Darius Brubeck clav, el-p, org (b-d); Chris Brubeck el-b (b-d); Randie Powell
perc (b-d).

a. 27165   Thank You (Dziekuje)   5:30   ATL SD 1645
b. 27166   Three To Get Ready   4:16   -
c. 27167   Knives   4:19   -
d. 27168   Unsquare Dance   2:43   -
e. 27172   Band Call   (unissued)
f. 27173   Tin Sink   8:31   ATL SD 1645

Issues: b,d ATL 20269; CHA CTR 20092; MIDI MID 20092; WYN DVCD-2036; **b** ATL 3015.

Notes: ATL SD 1645 is entitled "DAVE BRUBECK: TWO GENERATIONS OF BRUBECK".
ATL 20269, CHA CTR 20092, MIDI MID 20092 cf. **71.07.03**.

73.08.20   **Two Generations Of Brubeck**
New York City, New York, C.I.Studios.
Chris Brubeck tb; Jerry Bergonzi ss, ts; Perry Robinson cl; Dave Brubeck el-p; Darius Brubeck p;
David Dutemple el-b; Danny Brubeck dr; Randie Powell perc.

a. 27176   Call Of The Wild   2:56   ATL   SD   1645

Notes: ATL SD 1645 is entitled "DAVE BRUBECK: TWO GENERATIONS OF BRUBECK".

74.00.00   **Dave Brubeck Group**

Dave Brubeck p; Darius Brubeck keyb; prob. Chris Brubeck el-b; prob. Danny Brubeck dr; prob. Perry Robinson cl (b).

a.	Brandenburg Gate	9:37	DEN 86.3.31
b.	In Your Own Sweet Way	7:46	-

Issues: DEN 33C38-7681.

Notes: DEN 86.3.31 is entitled "DAVE BRUBECK: THE QUARTET". The recording date and the personnel is not known, the information in the liner notes is incorrect (Paul Desmond cl!). "Brandenburg Gate" resembles the broadcasted version from the Cologne concert from March 6, 1974. For this session see the next section. DEN 86.3.31 cf. **61.00.00**.

74.06.27   **Two Generations Of Brubeck**

New York City, New York, C.I. Studios.

Perry Robinson cl; Jerry Bergonzi ss; Dave Brubeck p; Darius Brubeck el-p; Dave Powell el-b; Danny Brubeck dr.

a.	29079	Mr. Broadway	2:44	ATL SD 1660

Dave Brubeck p; Darius Brubeck el-p; Chris Brubeck el-b; Danny Brubeck dr.

b.	29080	Forty Days	7:20	ATL SD 1660
c.	29081	It's A Raggy Waltz	6:00	-

Dave Brubeck p.

d.	29082	The Duke	2:48	ATL SD 1660

Chris Brubeck tb; Jerry Bergonzi ts; Perry Robinson cl; Dave Brubeck p; Dave Powell el-b; Danny Brubeck dr; Peter Ruth harm.

e.	29086	Christopher Columbus	4:00	ATL SD 1660

Issues: a,c ATL 20269; CHA CTR 20092; MIDI MID 20092; WYN DVCD-2036; a COL C4K 52945.

Notes: ATL SD 1660 is entitled "DAVE BRUBECK: TWO GENERATIONS OF BRUBECK: BROTHER, THE GREAT SPIRIT MADE US ALL". The album ATL SD 1660 contains three more titles without participation of Dave Brubeck.
ATL 20269, CHA CTR 20092; MIDI MID 20092 cf. **71.07.03**; COL C4K 52945 cf. **46-48.00.00**.

74.10.03   **Dave Brubeck Groups**

New York City, New York, C.I. Studios.

Anthony Braxton as (b,c); Lee Konitz as (a,c,d); Dave Brubeck p; Jack Six b (a-c); Roy Haynes dr (a-c).

a.	29648	In Your Own Sweet Way	7:39	ATL SD 1684
b.	29649	Like Someone In Love	6:21	-
c.	29650	All The Things You Are	7:27	-
d.	29651	Don't Get Around Much Anymore	2:46	-

Issues: ATL 1684-2.

Notes: ATL SD 1684 is entitled "DAVE BRUBECK * ANTHONY BRAXTON * ALAN DAWSON * ROY HAYNES * LEE KONITZ * JACK SIX: ALL THE THINGS WE ARE". The recordings were remastered with the matrix numbers: 29648 = 31917; 29649 = 31916; 29650 = 31918; 29651 = 31924.

75.06.10   Dave Brubeck And Paul Desmond
SS Rotterdam.
Paul Desmond as; Dave Brubeck p.

a.		You Go To My Head	7:15	HOR SP 703

Issues: A&M 394915-2.

Notes: HOR SP 703 is entitled "BRUBECK & DESMOND 1975: THE DUETS". A&M 394915-2 is the CD issue with the same title.

75.09.15+16   Dave Brubeck And Paul Desmond
New York City, New York, C.I. Recording Studios.
Paul Desmond as; Dave Brubeck p.

a.	Alice In Wonderland	4:04	HOR SP 703
b.	These Foolish Things	5:06	-
c.	Blue Dove	4:32	-
d.	Stardust	4:39	-
e.	Koto Song	5:54	-
f.	Balcony Rock	2:15	-
g.	Summer Song	3:16	-

Issues: A&M 394915-2; **c** (ed.),**f** HOR HZ 102; **e,f** HOR HP-1.

Notes: HOR SP 703 is entitled "BRUBECK & DESMOND 1975: THE DUETS". A&M 394915-2 is the CD issue with the same title. HOR HP-1 is a sampler entitled "JAZZ IS ON THE HORIZON".

76.03.10   Dave Brubeck Quartet
Interlochen, Michigan, Interlochen Arts Academy.
Paul Desmond as; Dave Brubeck p; Gene Wright b; Joe Morello dr.

a.	St. Louis Blues	9:05	HOR SP 714
b.	Three To Get Ready And	6:07	-
	Four To Go		
c.	African Times Suite	8:02	-
	1st Movement : African Time		
	2nd Movement : African Breeze		
	3rd Movement : African Dance		
d.	Salute To Stephen Foster	6:25	-
e.	Take Five	9:50	-

Issues: A&M 396998-2; **e** HOR SP 8413.

Notes: HOR SP 714 is entitled "THE DAVE BRUBECK QUARTET: 25TH ANNIVERSARY REUNION". For the release of the CD issue A&M 396998-2 in 1989 the tapes were digitally remastered at Van Gelder Recording Studios, Englewood Cliffs, New Jersey. HOR SP 8413 is a sampler entitled "GET JAZZED".

76.03.12   Dave Brubeck Quartet
Fort Wayne, Indiana, Scottish Rite Auditorium.
Paul Desmond as; Dave Brubeck p; Gene Wright b; Danny Brubeck dr.

a.	Don't Worry 'Bout Me	6:48	HOR SP 714

Issues: A&M 396998-2.

Notes: HOR SP 714 is entitled "THE DAVE BRUBECK QUARTET: 25TH ANNIVERSARY REUNION". A&M 396998-2 cf. **76.03.10**.

77.07.17   New Brubeck Quartet
Montreux, Switzerland, Montreux International Festival.

Dave Brubeck p; Darius Brubeck synth, el-keyb; Chris Brubeck el-b; Danny Brubeck perc.

a.	(It's A) Raggy Waltz	10:00	TOM TOM-7018
b.	Brandenburg Gate	10:29	-
c.	In Your Own Sweet Way	4:30	-
d.	It Could Happen To You	10:16	-
e.	God's Love (Made Visible)	6:20	-
f.	Summer Music	6:00	-

Issues: TOM TOM 269613-2; c TOM TOM 269616-2.

Notes: TOM TOM-7018 is entitled "THE NEW BRUBECK QUARTET LIVE AT MONTREUX". Raben /3./ gives two more unissued titles "Unisphere" and "Take Five". TOM TOM 269613-2 is the CD issue with the same title. TOM TOM 269616-2 is a sampler CD entitled "THE TOMATO SAMPLER", released in 1991.

78.02.27+28   New Brubeck Quartet
Sound Stage Studios, Nashville, Tennessee.
Dave Brubeck p; Darius Brubeck el-p, keyb; Chris Brubeck el-b, b-tb; Danny Brubeck perc.

a.	Ellington Medley: The Duke/ C-Jam Blues / Don't Get Around Much Anymore / Caravan / Mood Indigo / Take The "A" Train / Cottontail	16:51	DD 106
b.	Forty Days / Sermon On The Mount	19:55	-
c.	Unisphere	5:37	-
d.	Three To Get Ready	4:00	-
e.	Blue Rondo A La Turk	6:57	-
f.	Unsquare Dance	5:43	-
g.	Take Five	11:40	-

Notes: DD 106 is a double album with the title "THE NEW BRUBECK QUARTET: A CUT ABOVE!". The album was recorded by Direct-Disk Labs, Nashville, Tennessee by the direct-to-disc recording process and issued in a special limited and numbered edition.

79.05.09
Minneapolis, Minnesota, Orpheum Theatre.
Phyllis Bryn-Julson soprano; Gene Tucker tenor; Jake Gardner baritone; John Stephens bass; Dave Brubeck p; Richard Davis b; Mel Lewis dr; Lee Arellano perc,voc; The Dale Warland

Singers; Edith Norberg's Carillon Choristers; The St. Paul Chamber Orchestra, Dennis Russell Davies cond.

a.   La Fiesta De La Posada   CBS IM 36662
                A Christmas Choral Pageant
                Music By Dave Brubeck / Text By Iola Brubeck.
                1. Prelude   17:50   -
                2. La Posada
                3. Processional
                4. In The Beginning
                5. Where Is He?
                6. Gloria
                7. We Have Come To See The Son Of God
                8. Behold! The Holy One
                9. Run,Run,Run
                10. Gold,Frankincense And Myrrh   19:23   -
                11. My Soul Magnifies The Lord
                12. Sleep,Holy Infant,Sleep
                13. In The Beginning
                14. Neither Death Nor Life
                15. God's Love Made Visible
                16. La Piñata

Issues: CBS (DIGITAL) 36662; CBS 73903.

Notes: CBS IM 36662, CBS 73903 are entitled "LA FIESTA DE LA POSADA". The composition was dedicated to the memory of Edith Norberg.

79.08.21   Dave Brubeck Quartet
Concord, California, Concord Jazz Festival 1979.
Jerry Bergonzi ts, el-b (e); Dave Brubeck p; Chris Brubeck el-b, tb (e); Butch Miles dr.

a.   Cassandra   5:24   CON CJ-103
b.   The Masquerade Is Over   8:13   -
c.   Hometown Blues   7:31   -
d.   Yesterdays   7:49   -
e.   Two-Part Contention   6:08   -
f.   Caravan   4:04   -

Issues: f COL C4K 52945.

Notes: CON CJ-103 is entitled "THE DAVE BRUBECK QUARTET: BACK HOME".
COL C4K 52945 cf. **46-48.00.00.**

80.00.00
Providence, Rhode Island.
Jerry Bergonzi as; Dave Brubeck p; Chris Brubeck el-b, tb; Randy Jones dr; Daisy Newman (cantor) soprano; Tim Noble (cantor) baritone; William McGraw (priest) baritone; The Cincinnati May Festival Chorus, John Leman dir; Mt. Washington (Ohio) Presbyterian Church Handbell Choir, Wylene Davis dir; Erich Kunzel cond.

a. To Hope! A Celebration   PAA DRP-8313
by Dave Brubeck. Text from the
Lectionary and Sacramentary for
Mass with selected text
by Iola Brubeck.

1. Shout Joyfully To God	2:40	-
2. Lord Have Mercy	4:55	-
3. The Desert And The Parched Land	1:23	-
4. The Peace Of Jerusalem	2:35	-
5. Alleluia	7:32	-
6. Father All Powerful	2:05	-
7. Holy Holy Holy	3:10	-
8. When He Was At Supper	3:06	-
9. When We Eat This Bread	1:13	-
10. Doxology And Great Amen	1:58	-
11. Our Father	2:45	-
12. Lamb Of God Litany	1:35	-
13. All My Hope	3:30	-
14. Finale: Glory To God	2:50	-

Notes: PAA DRP-8313 is entitled "TO HOPE! A CELEBRATION BY DAVE BRUBECK", released at the 1983 Convention in St. Louis, Missouri. "To Hope" was first performed at the 1980 Convention of the National Association of Pastoral Musicians in Providence, Rhode Island.

80.03.00   Dave Brubeck Quartet
Dallas, Texas, TM Productions.
Jerry Bergonzi ts, el-b (d); Dave Brubeck p; Chris Brubeck el-b, b-tb (d); Randy Jones dr.
a.   Brother, Can You Spare A Dime?   7:08   CON CJ-129

b.	Like Someone In Love	5:39	-
c.	Theme For June	7:27	-
d.	Lord, Lord	6:21	-
e.	Mr. Fats	3:12	-
f.	Tritonis	8:05	-

Notes: CON CJ-129 is entitled "THE DAVE BRUBECK QUARTET: TRITONIS".

81.09.00   **Dave Brubeck Quartet**
San Francisco, California, Coast Recorders.
Jerry Bergonzi ts, el-b (e); Dave Brubeck p; Chris Brubeck el-b, b-tb (e); Randy Jones dr.

a.	Music, Maestro, Please!	8:52	CON CJ-178
b.	I Hear A Rhapsody	6:02	-
c.	Symphony	5:05	-
d.	I Thought About You	5:17	-
e.	It's Only A Paper Moon	5:00	-
f.	Long Ago And Far Away	7:59	-
g.	St. Louis Blues (p-solo)	3:09	-

Issues: CON CCD-4178.

Notes: CON CJ-178 is entitled "THE DAVE BRUBECK QUARTET: PAPER MOON".

82.08.00   **Dave Brubeck Quartet**
Concord, California, Concord Jazz Festival 1982.
Bill Smith cl; Dave Brubeck p; Chris Brubeck el-b, b-tb; Randy Jones dr.

a.	Benjamin	5:38	CON CJ-198
b.	Koto Song	8:34	-
c.	Black And Blue	7:03	-
d.	Softly, William, Softly	7:24	-
e.	Take Five	8:50	-

Issues: CON CCD-4198; a CON CJ-278.

Notes: CON CJ-198, CON CCD-4198 are entitled "THE DAVE BRUBECK QUARTET: CONCORD ON A SUMMER NIGHT". CON CJ-278 is a sampler with the title "THE CONCORD SOUND VOL. 1", released in 1985.

82.09.01   **Dave Brubeck Quartet**
Osaka, Japan, Osaka Festival Hall, Aurex Jazz Festival 1982.
Michael Pedicin ts; Dave Brubeck p; Chris Brubeck el-b, b-tb; Randy Jones d.
a.   You Don't Know What Love Is   8:40   EAS EWJ 80239
b.   Take Five   12:10   -
c.   St. Louis Blues   10:05   -

Notes: EAS EWJ 80239 is entitled "THE DAVE BRUBECK QUARTET: AUREX JAZZ FESTIVAL '82".

82.09.02   **Dave Brubeck Quartet**
Tokyo, Japan, Budokan, Aurex Jazz Festival 1982.
Michael Pedicin ts; Dave Brubeck p; Chris Brubeck el-b; Randy Jones dr.
a.   Someday My Prince Will Come   8:40   EAS EWJ 80239

Notes: EAS EWJ 80239 is entitled "THE DAVE BRUBECK QUARTET: AUREX JAZZ FESTIVAL '82".

82.09.03   **Dave Brubeck Quartet**
Japan, Aurex Jazz Festival 1982.
Michael Pedicin ts; Dave Brubeck p; Chris Brubeck el-b, b-tb; Randy Jones dr.
a.   Fantasy No.1   7:47   EAS EWJ 80255
b.   Take The "A" Train   5:41   -

Notes: EAS EWJ 80255 is a sampler with the title "AUREX JAZZ FESTIVAL '82 : LIVE SPECIAL". The balance of this record is made up by Woody Herman and His Orchestra.

82.09.05   **Dave Brubeck Quartet**
Yokohama, Japan, Yokohama Stadium, Aurex Jazz Festival 1982.
Dave Brubeck p; Chris Brubeck el-b, b-tb; Randy Jones dr.
a.   Big Bad Basie   7:10   EAS EWJ 80239

Notes: EAS EWJ 80239 is entitled "THE DAVE BRUBECK QUARTET: AUREX JAZZ FESTIVAL '82". Michael Pedicin does not play in this tune.

83.01.28   **Dave Brubeck Quartet**
B.B.King and His Orchestra

Cannes, France, Palais Des Congres, MIDEM Festival.
Bill Smith cl; Dave Brubeck p; Chris Brubeck el-b, b-tb (c); Randy Jones dr; B.B. King g and His Orchestra (e).

a.	Lover Man	7:13	KIN 804 628-928
b.	Blue Rondo	6:59	-
c.	Ol' Bill Basie	6:03	-
d.	Tritonis	7:35	TOB B/2689
e.	Jam Session	12:45	MAS MA 281285

Issues: a-c CLEO CLCD 5006; JAZZ GALA KM 26001; KIN CD GATE 7017; PLAT PLP 17/24034; b,c,e SPEC 85013; b,c MAS MA 281285; a CLOUD INTERNATIONAL 380612-2; b CLOUD INTERNATIONAL 380608-2; c CLEO CLCD 5000; HRCD 6; e (ed.) TOB B/2689.

Notes: KIN 804 628-928 is a sampler with the title "PAT METHENY * THE HEATH BROS. * DAVE BRUBECK QUARTET * B.B. KING: LIVE IN CONCERT". PLAT PLP 17/24034 is a sampler with the title "PAT METHENY ABSOLUTELY LIVE". SPEC 85013 is a sampler with the title "GIANTS OF JAZZ & BLUES IN CONCERT: DAVE BRUBECK / PAT METHENY / HEATH BROTHERS / B.B. KING". CLEO CLCD is a sampler entitled "JAZZ FOR EVERYONE". CLOUD INTERNATIONAL 380608-2 is a sampler CD with the title "THE BEST OF THE NORTHSEA JAZZ FESTIVAL, VOLUME 1", released in 1992 in The Netherlands. CLOUD INTERNATIONAL 380612-2 is a sampler CD with the title "THE BEST OF THE NORTHSEA JAZZ FESTIVAL, VOLUME 2", released in 1993 in The Netherlands. HRCD 6 is a sampler entitled "THE JAZZ COLLECTION VOL. 2" marketed in Benelux by Disky B.V. TOB B/2689 is a sampler with the title "DAVE BRUBECK: ALL OVER AGAIN" from the series American Jazz & Blues History Vol. 189. "Blue Rondo" is "Blue Rondo A La Turk"; "Ol' Bill Basie" is "Big Bad Basie". "Jam" on TOB B/2689 is an edited version (9:20) of "Jam Session".

84.08.00   **Dave Brubeck Quartet**

Concord, California, Concord Pavillion.
Bill Smith cl; Dave Brubeck p; Chris Brubeck el-b, b-tb; Randy Jones dr.

a.	Polly	7:46	CON CJ-259
b.	I Hear A Rhapsody (Arr. D. Brubeck)	6:12	-
c.	Thank You	4:20	-
d.	Big Bad Basie	5:33	-
e.	For Iola	7:13	-

| f. | Summer Song | 5:00 | - |
| g. | Pange Lingua March | 8:56 | - |

Issues: CON CCD-4259.

Notes: CON CJ-259 and CON CCD-4259 are entitled "THE DAVE BRUBECK QUARTET: FOR IOLA"

84.10.05-12   Dave Brubeck And Marian McPartland
New York City, New York, Radio Broadcast.
Dave Brubeck p (a-g,i); Marian McPartland (a,c,d,g-i).

a.	St. Louis Blues	7:08	JAZZ ALLIANCE
b.	Thank You (Dziekuje)	3:17	TJA-12001
c.	The Duke	4:02	-
d.	In Your Own Sweet Way	5:01	
e.	Let's Be Fair And Square In Love (theme)		(unissued)
f.	There's Honey On The Moon Tonight (theme)		-
g.	One Moment Worth Years	2:37	TJA-12001
h.	Summer Song	4:33	-
i.	Free Piece	3:19	-
k.	Polytonal Blues	1:03	-
l.	Take Five	4:23	-

Notes: JAZZ ALLIANCE TJA-12001 is entitled "MARIAN MCPARTLAND'S PIANO JAZZ WITH GUEST DAVE BRUBECK", released in 1993. Dave Brubeck was guest star in Marian McPartland's radio show "Piano Jazz" for the South Carolina Educational Radio Show and U.S. National Public Radio. The given date is the broadcasting week.

85.06.27   Dave Brubeck Quartet
            Cincinnati Choral Society, Saint Edwards Parish Choir
Cincinnati, Ohio, Cincinnati Exposition Center.
Bill Smith cl; Dave Brubeck p; Chris Brubeck el-b; Randy Jones dr; Bill Justus baritone; The Cincinnati Choral Society; St. Edwards Parish Choir.

a.	Pange Lingua Variations
	1. Sing, My Tongue, Sing!
	2. To Us Is Given, To Us Is Born
	3. Thus, On The Night Of His Final Repast

                 4. The Word Made Flesh Transforms Bread

                 5. Let Us Bow Down And Do Homage

                 6. Praise To The Father! Praise To The Son!

b.   The Voice Of The Holy Spirit (Tongues Of Fire)

            Text and Music by Dave Brubeck

            Part I

            1. Preface

            2. Full Authority

            3. Witnesses

            4. Pentecost

            5. Tongues Of Fire

            6. New Wine

            7. Peter's Sermon

            Part II

            8. My Children

            9. Silver And Gold

           10. Greater Gifts

           11. Though I Speak With The Tongues Of Men And Angels

           12. When I Was A Child

           13. For Those Who Love God

           14. Be Strong In The Lord

           15. Benediction

Notes: The performance of these works, composed by Dave Brubeck, at the 8th Annual Convention of the National Association of Pastoral Musicians, was released on cassette only.

85.12.00   **Dave Brubeck Quartet**

East Norwalk, Connecticut, SounTec Studios.

Bill Smith cl; Dave Brubeck p; Chris Brubeck el-b, b-tb (d,e); Randy Jones dr.

a.	Reflections Of You	5:24	CON CJ-299
b.	A Misty Morning	6:22	-
c.	I'd Walk A Country Mile	6:23	-
d.	My One Bad Habit	4:57	-
e.	Blues For Newport	4:44	-
f.	We Will All Remember Paul	5:06	-
g.	Michael, My Second Son	5:20	-
h.	Blue Lake Tahoe	5:10	-

Issues: CON CCD-4299.

Notes: CON CJ-299 and CON CCD-4299 are entitled "THE DAVE BRUBECK QUARTET: REFLECTIONS".

86.11.00   Dave Brubeck Quartet
San Francisco, California, Russian Hill Recording.
Bill Smith cl; Dave Brubeck p; Chris Brubeck el-b, b-tb (g,h); Randy Jones dr.

a.	How Does Your Garden Grow?	5:55	CON CJ-317
b.	Festival Hall	5:55	-
c.	Easy As You Go	3:15	-
d.	Blue Rondo A La Turk	7:30	-
e.	Dizzy's Dream	4:08	-
f.	I See, Satie	3:45	-
g.	Swing Bells	3:30	-
h.	Strange Meadow Lark	5:05	-
i.	Elena Joy	5:13	-

Issues: CON CCD-4317.

Notes: CON CJ-317 and CON CCD-4317 are entitled "BRUBECK: BLUE RONDO * THE 1987 DAVE BRUBECK QUARTET".

87.03.00   Dave Brubeck Quartet
Moscow, USSR, Rossiya Concert Hall.
Bill Smith cl; Dave Brubeck p; Chris Brubeck el-b; Randy Jones dr.

a.	Give Me A Hit	8:27	MEL C60 3019 3007
b.	Theme For June	10:34	-
c.	Someday My Prince Will Come	7:05	-
d.	Blues For Newport	8:35	-
e.	King For A Day	3:35	-
f.	Unsquare Dance	6:30	MEL C60 3019 5001
g.	These Foolish Things	4:45	-
h.	Pange Lingua March	11:00	-
i.	Koto Song	9:35	-
k.	Take Five	12:40	-
l.	Three To Get Ready	8:30	CON CJ-353
m.	St. Louis Blues	9:50	-
n.	Unsquare Dance	5:02	-
o.	Tritonis	7:58	COL C4K 52945

Issues: a,b CON CJ-353; a,b,k(ed),l-n CON CCD-4353.

Notes: CON CJ-353, CON CCD-4353 are entitled "DAVE BRUBECK: MOSCOW NIGHT". MEL C60 3019 3007 is entitled "DAVE BRUBECK QUARTET: DAVE BRUBECK IN MOSCOW 1"; MEL C60 3019 5001 is entitled "DAVE BRUBECK QUARTET: DAVE BRUBECK IN MOSCOW 2". The Concord releases have probably been recorded on March 26 in co-operation with Melodiya, USSR. The two versions of "Unsquare Dance" seem to be different; probably more than one concert was recorded during the tour through the USSR. The bonus track "Take Five" on CON CCD-4353 is an edited version (7:15) of **k**. "Tritonis" was recorded March 30 in Moscow and was included in the Arts & Entertainment cable TV program "Moscow Night" (see the next section). COL C4K 52945 cf. **46-48.00.00.**

87.07.03   **Dave Brubeck Quartet with**
                 The Montreal Symphony Orchestra
Montreal, Quebec, Canada, Palais des Arts, Salle Wilfrid Pelletier.
Bill Smith cl; Dave Brubeck p, arr (d-g); Chris Brubeck el-b; Randy Jones dr; The Montreal Symphony Orchestra ("L'Orchestre Symphonique de Montréal"), Russell Gloyd cond, arr (c); Darius Brubeck arr (a,b).

a.	Summer Music	6:12	MM 5051-2
b.	Blue Rondo A La Turk	8:48	-
c.	Koto Song	10:13	-
d.	New Wine	6:07	-
e.	Lullaby	6:13	-
f.	Out Of The Way Of The People	9:56	-
g.	Take The "A" Train	4:23	-

Issues: g LIM 820844-2; MM 65064-2.

Notes: MM 5051-2 is entitled "THE DAVE BRUBECK QUARTET WITH THE MONTREAL INTERNATIONAL JAZZ FESTIVAL ORCHESTRA: NEW WINE". The album was recorded in performance during the Montreal International Jazz Festival and released in 1990. The concert was TV broadcasted with the title "DAVE BRUBECK: SYMPHONIQUE" (with the exception of the title "New Wine") produced by Spectel Video Inc. in 1987. LIM 820844-2, MM 65064-2 are sampler CDs entitled "MUSICMASTERS JAZZ COLLECTION VOL.II" , released in 1992.

88.08.03   **Erich Kunzel: Cincinnati Pops Big Band Orchestra**
Cincinnati, Ohio, Music Hall.

Doc Severinsen tp; Gerry Mulligan bar; Dave Brubeck p; Ray Brown b; Cincinnati Pops Big Band
Orchestra; Erich Kunzel cond.
a.   Take The "A" Train (Arr. Newsom)   4:27   TEL CD 80177
Doc Severinsen tp; Buddy Morrow tb; Gerry Mulligan bar; Eddie Daniels cl; Dave Brubeck p;
Ray Brown b; Ed Shaughnessy dr; Cab Calloway voc; Cincinnati Pops Big Band Orchestra; Erich
Kunzel cond.
b.   When The Saints (Arr. Tyzik)   9:31   -

Notes: TEL CD 80177 is entitled "ERICH KUNZEL CINCINNATI POPS BIG BAND
ORCHESTRA: THE BIG BAND HIT PARADE" , released in 1988. Dave Brubeck participates
in two of the sixteen tunes.

88.09.20-21   Dave Brubeck Group
San Francisco, California, Russian Hill Recording.
Bob Militello fl (a,c-e), as (f), ts (b,f); Dave Brubeck p; Chris Brubeck el-b (a-f), b-tb (f);
Matthew Brubeck cello (c); Randy Jones dr.
a.   Linus And Lucy   4:54   MM 65067-2
b.   When I Was A Child   6:31   -
c.   Quiet As The Moon   5:18   -
d.   Cast Your Fate To The Wind   5:32   -
e.   Benjamin   3:48   -
f.   Travellin' Blues   8:41   -

Issues: e COL C4K 52945; GRP-9596-1/-2.

Notes: GRP-9596-1/-2 is a sampler with the title "HAPPY ANNIVERSARY, CHARLIE
BROWN" released in 1989. MM 65067-2 is entitled "DAVE BRUBECK: QUIET AS THE
MOON" , released in 1991. COL C4K 52945 cf. **46-48.00.00.**

89.12.27   Dave Brubeck Group
West Hurley, New York, NRS Recording.
Dave Brubeck p; Matthew Brubeck cello; Chris Brubeck el-b; Danny Brubeck dr.
a.   Forty Days   6:52   MM 65067-2
b.   Unisphere   3:24   -

Notes: MM 65067-2 is entitled "DAVE BRUBECK: QUIET AS THE MOON" , released in
1991.

91.05.06+07   Dave Brubeck Quartet and Gregg Singers
San Francisco, California, Russian Hill Recording.
Bill Smith cl (a-k); Dave Brubeck p (a-k); Jack Six b (a-k); Randy Jones dr (a-k); The Gregg Smith Singers (l); Gregg Smith cond. (l).

a.	Once When I Was Very Young	3:54	MM 65083-2
b.	What Is This Thing Called Love	6:49	-
c.	Among My Souvenirs	4:06	-
d.	Dancin' In Rhythm	4:29	-
e.	Yesterdays	8:47	-
f.	In A Little Spanish Town	3:02	-
g.	Stardust	5:20	-
h.	Shine On Harvest Moon	5:08	-
i.	Gone With The Wind	7:09	-
k.	(This Is My First Affair So) Please Be Kind	5:30	-
l.	Once When I Was Very Young	3:34	-

Issues: g COL C4K 52945.

Notes: MM 65083-2 is a compact disc entitled "THE DAVE BRUBECK QUARTET: ONCE WHEN I WAS VERY YOUNG", released in 1992. Selection l is sung a capella by The Gregg Smith Singers in the Church of the Holy Trinity, New York City, New York.
COL C4K 52945 cf. **46-48.00.00.**

91.05.08   Dave Brubeck Group
San Francisco, California, Russian Hill Recording.
Bobby Militello fl (a,b,d); Dave Brubeck p; Matthew Brubeck cello (b,c); Jack Six b (a,b,d); Randy Jones dr (a,b,d).

a.	Bicycle Built For Two (Arr. Brubeck)	3:35	MM 65067-2
b.	Looking At A Rainbow	3:47	-
c.	The Desert And The Parched Land	5:22	-
d.	When You Wish Upon A Star	7:22	-

Notes: MM 65067-2 is entitled "DAVE BRUBECK: QUIET AS THE MOON" , released in 1991.

92.00.00   Dave Brubeck Trio
West Hurley, New York.

Dave Brubeck p; Chris Brubeck el-b, tb; Danny Brubeck dr.

a.	I Cried For You	5:10	MM 65102-2
b.	Broadway Bossa Nova	2:57	-
c.	King For A Day	5:43	-
d.	Autumn	6:32	-
e.	One Moment Worth Years	4:43	-
f.	Calcutta Blues	4:27	-
g.	Waltz Limp	3:41	-
h.	Jazzanians	7:57	-
i.	Over The Rainbow	4:58	-
k.	Bossa Nova U.S.A.	7:26	-
l.	Someday My Prince Will Come	5:37	-

Notes: MM 65102-2 is a compact disc entitled "TRIO BRUBECK", released in 1993.

Radio and Television Broadcasts, Live Concerts.

In this section Radio and Television Broadcasts as well as Live Concerts are included only if we have tapes or copies of audiovisual media in our collection (with a few exceptions). The notation "ann(ouncer)." indicates a verbal announcement over the music. We do not list interviews and introductions.

53.03.18   Dave Brubeck Quartet
Chicago, Illinois, Blue Note, Radio Broadcast.
Paul Desmond as; Dave Brubeck p; Ron Crotty b; Lloyd Davis dr.

a.	Lyons Busy (Theme) (ann.)
b.	Somebody Loves Me
c.	On A Little Street In Singapore
d.	Mam'selle (inc., ann.)

54.07.17   Dave Brubeck - Gerry Mulligan Quartet
Newport, Rhode Island, Newport Jazz Festival, Radio Broadcast.
Gerry Mulligan bar; Dave Brubeck p; prob. Bob Bates b; Joe Dodge dr.

a.	The Lady Is A Tramp
b.	Lullaby Of The Leaves
c.	Bernie's Tune

54.10.01   **Dave Brubeck Quartet**
New York City, New York, Basin Street, Radio Broadcast.
Paul Desmond as; Dave Brubeck p; Bob Bates b; Joe Dodge dr.
a.   Take The "A" Train (ann.)
b.   Fare Thee Well, Annabelle
c.   Here Lies Love (inc., ann.)

55.03.16   **Dave Brubeck Quartet**
New York City, New York, Radio Central, Radio Broadcast.
Paul Desmond as; Dave Brubeck p; Bob Bates b; Joe Dodge dr.
a.   Brother, Can You Spare A Dime?
b.   The Trolley Song

55.04.03   **Dave Brubeck Quartet**
New York City, New York, Radio Central, Radio Broadcast.
Paul Desmond as; Dave Brubeck p; Bob Bates b; Joe Dodge dr.
a.   The Trolley Song

55.06.26   **Dave Brubeck Quartet**
Carmel, California, Sunset Auditorium.
Paul Desmond as; Dave Brubeck p; Bob Bates b; Joe Dodge dr.
a.   Gone With The Wind
b.   Jeepers Creepers
c.   I'll Never Smile Again
d.   Brother, Can You Spare A Dime?
e.   The Trolley Song
f.   Little Girl Blue
g.   Take The "A" Train

55.07.16   **Dave Brubeck Quartet**
Newport, Rhode Island, Newport Jazz Festival, Radio Broadcast.
Paul Desmond as; Dave Brubeck p; Bob Bates b; Joe Dodge dr.
a.   Gone With The Wind
b.   Take The "A" Train

Notes: This set closes with the title "Tea For Two" (see the preceding section).

55.07.17   **Dave Brubeck Quartet**
Newport, Rhode Island, Newport Jazz Festival, Radio Broadcast.

Paul Desmond as; Dave Brubeck p; Bob Bates b; Joe Dodge dr.

a.   Balcony Rock

b.   The Trolley Song

c.   Unknown Title

d.   Crazy Chris (inc.,ann.)

e.   Don't Worry About Me

Notes: The last two entries are given according to private tapes of M. Frohne.

55.07.23   **Dave Brubeck Quartet**

New York City, New York, Basin Street, Radio Broadcast.

Paul Desmond as; Dave Brubeck p; Bob Bates b; Joe Dodge dr.

a.   Fare Thee Well, Annabelle (ann.)

b.   Lover Come Back To Me

c.   Love Walked In (inc.,ann.)

55.08.27   **Dave Brubeck Quartet**

New York City, New York, Basin Street, Radio Broadcast.

Paul Desmond as; Dave Brubeck p; Bob Bates b; Joe Dodge dr.

a.   Audrey (inc.)

b.   Love Walked In (inc.)

55.08.28   **Dave Brubeck Quartet**

New York City, New York, Basin Street, Radio Broadcast.

Paul Desmond as; Dave Brubeck p; Bob Bates b; Joe Dodge dr.

a.   I'll Never Smile Again

b.   In Your Own Sweet Way

55.08.29   **Dave Brubeck Quartet**

New York City, New York, Basin Street, Radio Broadcast.

Paul Desmond as; Dave Brubeck p; Bob Bates b; Joe Dodge dr.

a.   Back Bay Blues

b.   Jeepers Creepers

55.09.04   **Dave Brubeck Quartet**

New York City, New York, Basin Street, Radio Broadcast.

Paul Desmond as; Dave Brubeck p; Bob Bates b; Joe Dodge dr.

a.   Out Of Nowhere

b.   The Trolley Song (inc., ann.)

55.09-12.00   Dave Brubeck Quartet
New York City, New York, Basin Street, Radio Broadcast.
Paul Desmond as; Dave Brubeck p; Bob Bates b; Joe Dodge dr.
a.   I'll Never Smile Again
b.   Lover
c.   On The Alamo (inc., ann.)

55.10.01   Dave Brubeck Quartet
Chicago, Illinois, Blue Note, Radio Broadcast.
Paul Desmond as; Dave Brubeck p; Bob Bates b; Joe Dodge dr.
a.   Out Of Nowhere
b.   Stompin' For Mili
c.   Lover (inc., ann.)

55.10.15   Dave Brubeck Quartet
New York City, New York, Basin Street, Radio Broadcast.
Don Elliott mell (b); Paul Desmond as; Dave Brubeck p; Bob Bates b; Joe Dodge dr.
a.   Here Lies Love (ann.)
b.   Pennies From Heaven (inc., ann.)

55.10.16   Dave Brubeck Quartet
New York City, New York, Basin Street, Radio Broadcast.
Paul Desmond as; Dave Brubeck p; Bob Bates b; Joe Dodge dr.
a.   Lover
b.   Jeepers Creepers

56.02.18   Dave Brubeck Quartet
New York City, New York, Basin Street, Radio Broadcast.
Paul Desmond as; Dave Brubeck p; Norman Bates b; Joe Dodge dr.
a.   The Duke (ann.)
b.   In Your Own Sweet Way
c.   The Trolley Song (inc., ann.)

56.02.22   Dave Brubeck Quartet
New York City, New York, Basin Street, Radio Broadcast.
Paul Desmond as; Dave Brubeck p; Bob Bates b; Joe Dodge dr.
a.   In Your Own Sweet Way
b.   Interview (with musical examples)

c.   All The Things You Are
d.   The Duke

56.02.25   Dave Brubeck Quartet
New York City, New York, Basin Street, Radio Broadcast.
Paul Desmond as; Dave Brubeck p; Norman Bates b; Joe Dodge dr.
a.   The Duke (ann.)
b.   Audrey
c.   Brother, Can You Spare A Dime? (inc., ann.)

56.08.18   Dave Brubeck Quartet
New York City, New York, Basin Street, Radio Broadcast.
Paul Desmond as; Dave Brubeck p; Norman Bates b; Joe Dodge dr.
a.   Two-Part Contention (inc., ann.)

56.08.21   Dave Brubeck Quartet
New York City, New York, Basin Street, Radio Broadcast.
Paul Desmond as; Dave Brubeck p; Norman Bates b; Joe Dodge dr.
a.   Makin' Time
b.   I'm In A Dancing Mood

56.09.01   Dave Brubeck Quartet
New York City, New York, Basin Street, Radio Broadcast.
Paul Desmond as; Dave Brubeck p; Norman Bates b; Joe Dodge dr.
a.   I'm In A Dancing Mood (ann.)
b.   You Go To My Head (inc., ann.)

57.03.00   Dave Brubeck Quartet
Chicago, Illinois, Blue Note, Radio Broadcast.
Paul Desmond as; Dave Brubeck p; Norman Bates b; Joe Morello dr.
a.   The Duke (ann.)
b.   I'm In A Dancing Mood
c.   The Song Is You
d.   Plain Song (ann.,inc.)

Notes: The first three titles of this session were issued on JBR EB 402, JBR EBCD 2102-2.

58.02.00   Dave Brubeck Quartet
Manchester, Great Britain, Free Trade Hall.

Paul Desmond as; Dave Brubeck p; Gene Wright b; Joe Morello dr.
a.   Gone With The Wind
b.   One Moment Worth Years
c.   Watusi Drums
d.   For All We Know
e.   In Your Own Sweet Way
f.   The Wright Groove
g.   The Duke
h.   Take The "A" Train
i.   St. Louis Blues
k.   Audrey (inc.)
l.   God Save The Queen

58.02.22   Dave Brubeck Quartet
Berlin, Germany, Sportspalast.
Paul Desmond as; Dave Brubeck p; Gene Wright b; Joe Morello dr.
a.   The Duke
b.   Take The "A" Train
c.   Two-Part Contention
d.   These Foolish Things
e.   St. Louis Blues

Notes: The selections b - e were issued on PHIL W 72-2 (see the preceding section).

58.02.28   Dave Brubeck Quartet
Hannover, Germany, Niedersachsenhalle.
Paul Desmond as; Dave Brubeck p; Gene Wright b; Joe Morello dr.
a.   Out Of Nowhere
b.   Two-Part Contention
c.   I'm In A Dancing Mood
d.   These Foolish Things

Notes: The selections a and d were issued on PHIL W 72-2 (see the preceding section).

58.06.00   Dave Brubeck Quartet
Radio Broadcast "The Navy Swings", Transcriptions # 44/45.
Paul Desmond as; Dave Brubeck p; Joe Benjamin b; Joe Morello dr.
a.   The Duke (ann.)
b.   Take The "A" Train

c.	I'm In A Dancing Mood
d.	St. Louis Blues
e.	The Duke (ann.)
f.	Gone With The Wind
g.	For All We Know
h.	Sounds Of The Loop
i.	The Duke (ann.)
k.	Watusi Drums
l.	Thank You (Dziekuje)
m.	Nomad
n.	The Duke (inc., ann.)
o.	The Duke (ann.)
p.	Someday My Prince Will Come
q.	In Your Own Sweet Way
r.	Tangerine
s.	The Duke (inc., ann.)

58.07.03   Dave Brubeck Quartet
Newport, Rhode Island, Newport Jazz Festival, Radio Broadcast.
Paul Desmond as; Dave Brubeck p; Joe Benjamin b; Joe Morello dr.
a.   Take The "A" Train

Notes: For other titles of this session see the preceding section.

58.08.11   Dave Brubeck Quartet
Hollywood, California, Radio Broadcast.
Paul Desmond as; Dave Brubeck p; Joe Benjamin b; Joe Morello dr.
a.   The Duke (inc., ann.)
b.   St. Louis Blues
c.   Someday My Prince Will Come
d.   I'm In A Dancing Mood
e.   The Duke (inc., ann.)

59.09.00   Dave Brubeck Quartet
London, Great Britain, B.B.C. Radio Broadcast.
Paul Desmond as; Dave Brubeck p; Gene Wright b; Joe Morello dr.
a.   St. Louis Blues
b.   Swanee River
c.   Lonesome Road

d.   Take The "A" Train (inc.)
e.   I'm In A Dancing Mood
f.   Blue Rondo A La Turk
g.   These Foolish Things

Notes: This concert was part of the first European presentation of the Newport Jazz Festival.

60.00.00   Dave Brubeck Quartet
Detroit, Michigan, Detroit Jazz Festival, Radio Broadcast.
Paul Desmond as; Dave Brubeck p; Gene Wright b; Joe Morello dr.
a.   Swanee River
b.   Andante From "Dialogues For Jazz Combo And Orchestra"
c.   Unknown Title (Jam Session)

60.04.00   Dave Brubeck Quartet
Germany, Radio Broadcast.
Paul Desmond as; Dave Brubeck p; Gene Wright b; Joe Morello dr.
a.   St. Louis Blues
b.   Gone With The Wind
c.   One Moment Worth Years

60.04.02   Dave Brubeck Quartet
Essen, Germany, Grugahalle, Essen Jazz Festival 1960, WDR Radio Broadcast.
Paul Desmond as; Dave Brubeck p; Gene Wright b; Joe Morello dr.
a.   St. Louis Blues
b.   One Moment Worth Years
c.   Blue Rondo A La Turk
d.   These Foolish Things
e.   Sounds Of The Loop
f.   I'm In A Dancing Mood

60.06.30   Dave Brubeck Quartet
Newport, Rhode Island, Newport Jazz Festival, Radio Broadcast.
Paul Desmond as; Dave Brubeck p; Gene Wright b; Joe Morello dr.
a.   I'm In A Dancing Mood

61.00.00   Dave Brubeck Quartet
San Francisco, California, KQED Television Broadcast.
Paul Desmond as; Dave Brubeck p; Gene Wright b; Joe Morello dr.

a.   Take Five
b.   It's A Raggy Waltz
c.   Castilian Blues
d.   Waltz Limp
e.   Blue Rondo A La Turk (inc.)

Notes: This television production for KQED TV, San Francisco, by Ralph J. Gleason and Dick Christian is entitled "JAZZ CASUAL: DAVE BRUBECK QUARTET AND RALPH J. GLEASON".

61.00.00   Dave Brubeck Quartet
Hilversum, The Netherlands, A.V.R.O. Television Broadcast.
Paul Desmond as; Dave Brubeck p; Gene Wright b; Joe Morello dr.
a.   St. Louis Blues
b.   Brandenburg Gate
c.   It's A Raggy Waltz
d.   Blue Shadows In The Street
e.   Take Five

61.07.00   Dave Brubeck Quartet
Newport, Rhode Island, Newport Jazz Festival, Radio Broadcast.
Paul Desmond as; Dave Brubeck p; Gene Wright b; Joe Morello dr.
a.   Pennies From Heaven

61.11.00   Dave Brubeck Quartet
Essen, Germany, Grugahalle, WDR Radio Broadcast.
Paul Desmond as; Dave Brubeck p; Gene Wright b; Joe Morello dr.
a.   It's A Raggy Waltz
b.   Waltz Limp
c.   Take The "A" Train
d.   Nomad
e.   The Wright Groove
f.   You Go To My Head
g.   Brandenburg Gate
h.   Out Of Nowhere
i.   I'm In A Dancing Mood

61.11.06   Dave Brubeck Quartet
Zürich, Switzerland, Volkshaus, SRG Radio Broadcast.

Paul Desmond as; Dave Brubeck p; Gene Wright b; Joe Morello dr.
a.   St. Louis Blues (inc.)
b.   Gone With The Wind
c.   Someday My Prince Will Come
d.   It's A Raggy Waltz
e.   These Foolish Things
f.   I'm In A Dancing Mood
g.   Out Of Nowhere (inc.)
h.   Waltz Limp
i.   The Wright Groove
k.   Take Five
l.   Blue Rondo A La Turk

61.11.08   **Dave Brubeck Quartet**
Berlin, Germany, Berliner Sportpalast, Radio Broadcast.
Paul Desmond as; Dave Brubeck p; Gene Wright b; Joe Morello dr.
a.   Gone With The Wind
b.   It's A Raggy Waltz
c.   Brandenburg Gate
d.   Three To Get Ready And Four To Go
e.   The Wright Groove
f.   I'm In A Dancing Mood
g.   Take Five
h.   Blue Rondo A La Turk
i.   Waltz Limp
k.   Southern Scene

62.07.00   **Dave Brubeck Quartet Featuring Gerry Mulligan**
Newport, Rhode Island, Newport Jazz Festival.
Paul Desmond as; Gerry Mulligan bar; Dave Brubeck p; Gene Wright b; Joe Morello dr.
a.   All The Things You Are

62.10-11.00   **Dave Brubeck Quartet**
Manchester, Great Britain.
Paul Desmond as; Dave Brubeck p; Gene Wright b; Joe Morello dr.
a.   Dizzy Ditty
b.   Waltz Limp
c.   Take Five
d.   St. Louis Blues

e.	This Can't Be Love
f.	The Real Ambassadors
g.	King For A Day
h.	These Foolish Things
i.	Castilian Drums
k.	Take Five

63.07.07   Dave Brubeck Quartet
Newport, Rhode Island, Newport Jazz Festival, Radio Broadcast.
Paul Desmond as; Dave Brubeck p; Gene Wright b; Joe Morello dr.
a.   Waltz Limp

63.07.12
Rock Rimmon Festival.
Bobby Hackett corn; Benny Goodman cl; Paul Desmond as; Dave Brubeck p; Gene Wright b; Joe Morello dr.
a.   Poor Butterfly
b.   Sweet Georgia Brown
c.   On The Sunny Side Of The Street

Notes: This entry is given on the basis of a private tape of Benny Goodman (M. Frohne).

63.09.28   Dave Brubeck Quartet
Basel, Switzerland, Casino-Konzerthalle, SRG Radio Broadcast.
Paul Desmond as; Dave Brubeck p; Gene Wright b; Joe Morello dr.
a.   Take The "A" Train (inc.)
b.   Audrey
c.   Cable Car
d.   You Go To My Head
e.   Take Five
f.   Koto Song
g.   Pennies From Heaven
h.   Shim Wha
i.   Thank You (Dziekuje) (p-solo)

64.05-06.00   Dave Brubeck Quartet
London, Great Britain, B.B.C. Radio Broadcast.
Paul Desmond as; Dave Brubeck p; Gene Wright b; Joe Morello dr.
a.   Tokyo Traffic (inc.)

b.   Koto Song
c.   Pennies From Heaven
d.   Andante From "Dialogues For Jazz Combo And Orchestra"
e.   Unisphere
f.   Cable Car

64.05-06.00   Dave Brubeck Quartet
Manchester, Great Britain, Free Trade Hall.
Paul Desmond as; Dave Brubeck p; Gene Wright b; Joe Morello dr.
a.   Gone With The Wind
b.   Bossa Nova U.S.A.
c.   Since Love Had Its Way
d.   In Your Own Sweet Way
e.   King For A Day
f.   Tangerine
g.   Theme From "Mr. Broadway"
h.   All The Things You Are
i.   Audrey
k.   Swanee River

64.06.09   Dave Brubeck Quartet
London, Great Britain, "Jazz 625", B.B.C. Television Broadcast.
Paul Desmond as; Dave Brubeck p; Gene Wright b; Joe Morello dr.
a.   Danny's London Blues
b.   Andante From "Dialogues For Jazz Combo And Orchestra"
c.   The Wright Groove
d.   Take Five
e.   Sounds Of The Loop
f.   In Your Own Sweet Way (inc.)

64-65.00.00   Dave Brubeck Quartet
London, Great Britain, "Jazz 625", B.B.C. Television Broadcast.
Paul Desmond as; Dave Brubeck p; Gene Wright b; Joe Morello dr.
a.   Tokyo Traffic
b.   Koto Song
c.   Cable Car
d.   Shim Wha
e.   In Your Own Sweet Way (inc.)

65.07.00   **Dave Brubeck Quartet**
Newport, Rhode Island, Newport Jazz Festival, Radio Broadcast.
Paul Desmond as; Dave Brubeck p; Gene Wright b; Joe Morello dr.
a.   Take The "A" Train
b.   Brandenburg Gate
c.   Take Five

66.00.00   **Dave Brubeck Quartet**
London, Great Britain, "Jazz Goes To College", B.B.C. Television Broadcast.
Paul Desmond as; Dave Brubeck p; Gene Wright b; Joe Morello dr.
a.   Brandenburg Gate
b.   Take Five (inc.)

66.10-11.00   **Dave Brubeck Quartet**
Karlsruhe, Germany, Radio Broadcast.
Paul Desmond as; Dave Brubeck p; Gene Wright b; Joe Morello dr.
a.   Take The "A" Train
b.   Forty Days
c.   I'm In A Dancing Mood
d.   Take Five

Notes: For another title "Koto Song" see the preceding section.

66.11.00   **Dave Brubeck Quartet**
London, Great Britain, B.B.C. Radio Broadcast.
Paul Desmond as; Dave Brubeck p; Gene Wright b; Joe Morello dr.
a.   Out Of Nowhere
b.   One Moment Worth Years
c.   I'm In A Dancing Mood
d.   Three To Get Ready
e.   Cultural Exchange
f.   Forty Days
g.   Softly, William, Softly
h.   Tangerine
i.   Take Five
k.   Take The "A" Train

66.11.00   **Dave Brubeck Quartet**
Manchester, Great Britain, Free Trade Hall.

Paul Desmond as; Dave Brubeck p; Gene Wright b; Joe Morello dr.
a.   Pennies From Heaven
b.   Theme For June
c.   Forty Days
d.   Tangerine
e.   Take Five
f.   Cielito Lindo
g.   Balcony Rock
h.   Swanee River
i.   Someday My Prince Will Come
k.   These Foolish Things
l.   Take Five
m.   Unknown Title (inc.)

66.11.05   **Dave Brubeck Quartet**
Berlin, Germany, Berlin Jazz Days, Television and Radio Broadcast.
Paul Desmond as; Dave Brubeck p; Gene Wright b; Joe Morello dr.
a.   Take The "A" Train
b.   I'm In A Dancing Mood
c.   Take Five
d.   Someday My Prince Will Come (inc.)
e.   Brandenburg Gate
f.   Forty Days
g.   One Moment Worth Years
h.   Blues (inc.)

Notes: The titles **a-c** were broadcasted in 1990 within the German Television series (WDR) "JAZZ FOR FUN".

66.11.06   **Dave Brubeck Quartet**
Rotterdam, The Netherlands, "De Doelen", Newport Jazz Festival Tour 1966, Radio Broadcast.
Paul Desmond as; Dave Brubeck p; Gene Wright b; Joe Morello dr.
a.   Swanee River
b.   Tokyo Traffic
c.   One Moment Worth Years
d.   Forty Days
e.   Take The "A" Train
f.   Softly, William, Softly
g.   Three To Get Ready

h.	Cultural Exchange
i.	Blues
k.	Take Five
l.	It Could Happen To You
m.	Someday My Prince Will Come

66.11.12   Dave Brubeck Quartet
Paris, France, Salle Pleyel, O.R.T.F. Radio Broadcast.
Paul Desmond as; Dave Brubeck p; Gene Wright b; Joe Morello dr.

a.	Somebody Loves Me
b.	Brandenburg Gate
c.	Cassandra
d.	Take The "A" Train
e.	Pennies From Heaven
f.	These Foolish Things

67.03.13   Dave Brubeck Quartet
Norwich, Great Britain, University of East Anglia, B.B.C. Television Broadcast.
Paul Desmond as; Dave Brubeck p; Gene Wright b; Joe Morello dr.

a.	Take Five
b.	St. Louis Blues
c.	Brandenburg Gate
d.	Take The "A" Train
e.	Take Five (inc., ann.)

67.07.00   Dave Brubeck Quartet
Antibes, France, Jazz Festival, Antibes Session O.R.T.F. Radio Broadcast.
Paul Desmond as; Dave Brubeck p; Gene Wright b; Joe Morello dr.

a.	One Moment Worth Years
b.	Take Five (inc.)

67.07.00   Dave Brubeck Quartet
Paris, France, O.R.T.F. Radio Broadcast.
Paul Desmond as; Dave Brubeck p; Gene Wright b; Joe Morello dr.

a.	Cultural Exchange
b.	La Bamba
c.	St. Louis Blues
d.	La Paloma Azul

67.10.21   Dave Brubeck Quartet
London, Great Britain, B.B.C. Radio Broadcast.
Paul Desmond as; Dave Brubeck p; Gene Wright b; Joe Morello dr.
a.   St. Louis Blues
b.   Cielito Lindo
c.   Blues
d.   Swanee River
e.   Someday My Prince Will Come

67.10-11.00   Dave Brubeck Trio
Vienna, Austria, Kunstvereinssaal, Radio Broadcast.
Dave Brubeck p; Gene Wright b; Joe Morello dr.
a.   St. Louis Blues
b.   One Moment Worth Years
c.   Swanee River
d.   La Paloma Azul (The Blue Dove)
e.   Someday My Prince Will Come
f.   Take The "A" Train (inc.)

67.12.26   Dave Brubeck Quartet
Pittsburgh, Pennsylvania.
Paul Desmond as; Dave Brubeck p; Gene Wright b; Joe Morello dr.
a.   I'm In A Dancing Mood (inc.)   KAY 016 KJ

Notes: KAY 016 KJ is a video tape with the title "JAZZ THE INTIMATE ART" released in 1969. It contains four contributions of about 15 minutes length on the jazz musicians Louis Armstrong, Dizzy Gillespie and Charles Lloyd besides Dave Brubeck. Shown as a main part of the Brubeck set are parts of the rehearsal and performance of "The Light In The Wilderness" at the University of North Carolina.

68.07.00   Dave Brubeck Quartet
Newport, Rhode Island, Newport Jazz Festival, Radio Broadcast.
Gerry Mulligan bar; Dave Brubeck p; Jack Six b; Alan Dawson dr.
a.   Lullaby De Mexico
b.   Someday My Prince Will Come
c.   Jumpin' Beans

Notes: The concert was broadcasted from the "Newport Jazz Festival" through the radio program "Jazz Rondo" by V.P.R.O., Hilversum, The Netherlands.

68.10.00   **Dave Brubeck Trio Featuring Gerry Mulligan**
Rotterdam, The Netherlands.
Gerry Mulligan bar; Dave Brubeck p; Jack Six b; Alan Dawson dr.
a.   Basin Street Blues (inc.)

68.10.26   **Dave Brubeck Trio Featuring Gerry Mulligan**
Basel, Switzerland, Kasino Basel.
Gerry Mulligan bar; Dave Brubeck p; Jack Six b; Alan Dawson dr.
a.   New Orleans (inc.)
b.   Blessed Are The Poor
c.   Unknown Title
d.   Jumpin' Beans
e.   Limehouse Blues
f.   Someday My Prince Will Come
g.   Indian Song
h.   Basin Street Blues (inc.)

68.10.31   **Dave Brubeck Trio Featuring Gerry Mulligan**
London, Great Britain, "Jazz At The Maltings", B.B.C. Television Broadcast.
Gerry Mulligan bar; Dave Brubeck p; Jack Six b; Alan Dawson dr.
a.   Lullaby De Mexico (Lullaby Of Mexico)
b.   Jumpin' Beans
c.   Sapito
d.   Blues (inc.)

69.02.13   **Dave Brubeck Trio Featuring Gerry Mulligan**
London, Great Britain, "Jazz At The Maltings", B.B.C. Television Broadcast.
Gerry Mulligan bar; Dave Brubeck p; Jack Six b; Alan Dawson dr.
a.   Out Of Nowhere
b.   New Orleans
c.   Blessed Are The Poor (inc.)

69.04.29
Washington, D.C., White House, Radio Broadcast "Voice Of America".
Paul Desmond as; Gerry Mulligan bar; Dave Brubeck p; Milt Hinton b; Louis Bellson dr.
a.   Things Ain't What They Used To Be

Notes: This concert at the White House was given for the commemoration of the 70th birthday of Duke Ellington.

70.01.13   **Dave Brubeck Trio Featuring Gerry Mulligan**
New York City, New York, "Today Show", Television Broadcast.
Gerry Mulligan bar; Dave Brubeck p; Jack Six b; Alan Dawson dr.
a.   The Duke (inc., ann.)
b.   Lullaby De Mexico (Lullaby Of Mexico)
c.   Out Of The Way Of The People

70.10.24   **Dave Brubeck Trio Featuring Gerry Mulligan**
Milan, Italy.
Gerry Mulligan bar; Dave Brubeck p; Jack Six b; Alan Dawson dr.
a.   Out Of Nowhere
b.   The Duke
c.   Out Of The Way Of The People
d.   These Foolish Things
e.   Jumpin' Beans
f.   St. Louis Blues
g.   Sweet Georgia Brown

70.10.27   **Dave Brubeck Trio Featuring Gerry Mulligan**
Paris, France, Palais De Chaillot, O.R.T.F. Radio Broadcast.
Gerry Mulligan bar; Dave Brubeck p; Jack Six b; Alan Dawson dr.
a.   New Orleans
b.   Basin Street Blues
c.   Out Of Nowhere
d.   Jumpin' Beans (ann.)

70.10.30   **Dave Brubeck Trio Featuring Gerry Mulligan**
Rotterdam, The Netherlands, De Doelen, Newport Jazz Festival Tour 1970, Radio Broadcast.
Gerry Mulligan bar; Dave Brubeck p; Jack Six b; Alan Dawson dr.
a.   The Duke (inc.)
b.   Jumpin' Beans
c.   Things Ain't What They Used To Be

70.10.31   **Dave Brubeck Trio Featuring Gerry Mulligan**
London, Great Britain, Odeon Theatre, Hammersmith.
Gerry Mulligan bar; Dave Brubeck p; Jack Six b; Alan Dawson dr.
a.   Out Of Nowhere
b.   The Duke
c.   Out Of The Way Of The People

d.	These Foolish Things
e.	Jumpin' Beans
f.	New Orleans
g.	St. Louis Blues
h.	Lullaby De Mexico
i.	Indian Woman
k.	Things Ain't What They Used To Be

70.11.07   Dave Brubeck Trio Featuring Gerry Mulligan

Berlin, Germany, Philharmonie, Television Broadcast.
Gerry Mulligan bar; Dave Brubeck p; Jack Six b; Alan Dawson dr.

a.	Out Of Nowhere
b.	(Mexican) Jumpin' Beans

Notes: The concert was issued on CBS S 67261 (see the preceding section).

71.07.25   Dave Brubeck with The Boston Pops Orchestra

Boston, Massachusetts, Radio Broadcast.
Paul Desmond as (c,g,h); Gerry Mulligan bar (b,f,h); Dave Brubeck p; Jack Six b; Alan Dawson dr; Boston Pops Orchestra: Arthur Fiedler cond (a-d,h).

a.	Forty Days
b.	Blessed Are The Poor
c.	Summer Song
d.	Out Of The Way Of The People
e.	The Duke
f.	Lullaby De Mexico
g.	Take Five
h.	Kingdom Of Heaven

72.09.00   Dave Brubeck Trio Featuring Gerry Mulligan And Paul Desmond

Sydney, Australia.
Paul Desmond as; Gerry Mulligan bar; Dave Brubeck p; Jack Six b; Alan Dawson dr.

a.	Things Ain't What They Used To Be
b.	Blessed Are The Poor
c.	Out Of Nowhere
d.	Someday My Prince Will Come

72.10.22   Dave Brubeck Quartet

New York City, New York, Lincoln Center, Television Broadcast.

Paul Desmond as; Dave Brubeck p; Jack Six b; Alan Dawson dr.
a.   Take Five

Notes: The above title was recorded during the rehearsal for the B.B.C. Television show "Timex All-Star Swing Festival". Raben /3./ gives the non commercial source Timex TX-1129. The given date seems rather improbable.

72.10.26   **Dave Brubeck Trio Featuring Gerry Mulligan And Paul Desmond**
Paris, France, Olympia, Radio Broadcast.
Paul Desmond as; Gerry Mulligan bar; Dave Brubeck p; Jack Six b; Alan Dawson dr.
a.   Things Ain't What They Used To Be
b.   Jumpin' Beans
c.   Truth
d.   Someday My Prince Will Come
e.   Sermon On The Mount
f.   Take Five (inc., ann.)
g.   Segovia (inc.)
h.   Thank You (Dziekuje)
i.   Line For Lyons
k.   Venus Armee (inc.)
l.   All The Things You Are

Notes: For one other title of this concert see the preceding section.

72.10.27   **Dave Brubeck Trio Featuring Gerry Mulligan And Paul Desmond**
London, Great Britain, Odeon Theatre, Hammersmith.
Paul Desmond as; Gerry Mulligan bar; Dave Brubeck p; Jack Six b; Alan Dawson dr.
First Concert:
a.   Blues For Newport
b.   Truth
c.   New Orleans
d.   Someday My Prince Will Come
e.   Thirteen (Japanese Theme)
f.   Out Of Nowhere
g.   Repent
h.   All The Things You Are
i.   Take Five
Second Concert:
k.   Things Ain't What They Used To Be

l. Truth
m. Sermon On The Mount
n. Jumpin' Beans
o. Someday My Prince Will Come
p. Andante From "Dialogues For Jazz Combo And Orchestra"
q. All The Things You Are
r. These Foolish Things
s. Lullaby De Mexico
t. Thank You (Dziekuje)
u. Line For Lyons
v. Take Five
w. Take The "A" Train

72.10.28 Dave Brubeck Trio Featuring Gerry Mulligan And Paul Desmond
Rotterdam, The Netherlands, De Doelen, Newport Jazz Festival Tour 1972, Radio Broadcast.
Paul Desmond as (a-d); Gerry Mulligan bar (a-d); Dave Brubeck p; Jack Six b (a-d); Alan Dawson dr (a-d).
a. Line For Lyons (inc.)
b. Thank You (Dziekuje)
c. Take The "A" Train
d. Blues
e. Sweet Georgia Brown

Notes: For two more titles of this concert see the preceding section.

72.10.30 Dave Brubeck Trio Featuring Gerry Mulligan And Paul Desmond
Upsala, Sweden, Radio Broadcast.
Paul Desmond as; Gerry Mulligan bar; Dave Brubeck p; Jack Six b; Alan Dawson dr.
a. These Foolish Things (inc.)
b. Things Ain't What They Used To Be
c. Truth
d. Unfinished Woman
e. Summer Song (inc.)

72.10-11.00 Dave Brubeck Trio Featuring Gerry Mulligan And Paul Desmond
Newport Jazz Festival Tour in Europe.
Paul Desmond as; Gerry Mulligan bar; Dave Brubeck p; Jack Six b; Alan Dawson dr.
a. Segovia
b. Things Ain't What They Used To Be

c.   Truth
d.   Sermon On The Mount
e.   Jumpin' Beans
f.   For All We Know
g.   Someday My Prince Will Come
h.   Thank You (Dziekuje)
i.   These Foolish Things
k.   All The Things You Are
l.   Line For Lyons
m.   Take Five (inc.)

72.11.04   Dave Brubeck Trio Featuring Gerry Mulligan And Paul Desmond
Berlin, Germany, Philharmonie, Berlin Jazz Days; Television and Radio Broadcast.
Paul Desmond as; Gerry Mulligan bar; Dave Brubeck p; Jack Six b; Alan Dawson dr.
a.   Blues For Newport
b.   All The Things You Are
c.   Blues
d.   Take The "A" Train
e.   Line For Lyons
f.   Jumpin' Beans
g.   Little Girl Blue
h.   Someday My Prince Will Come
i.   Koto Song

Notes: For three more titles of this concert see the preceding section. **b** and **d** were broadcasted in 1990 part of a German Television series (WDR) "JAZZ FOR FUN".

72.11.10   Dave Brubeck Trio Featuring Gerry Mulligan And Paul Desmond
Bologna, Italy.
Paul Desmond as; Gerry Mulligan bar; Dave Brubeck p; Jack Six b; Alan Dawson dr.
a.   Things Ain't What They Used To Be
b.   All The Things You Are
c.   Take Five
d.   Truth

74.03.06   Two Generations Of Brubeck
Cologne, Germany, Gürzenich, WDR Radio Broadcast.
Jerry Bergonzi ts (e); Perry Robinson cl (e); Dave Brubeck p; Darius Brubeck el-p; Chris Brubeck el-b, tb (e); Danny Brubeck dr; prob. Peter Ruth harm (e).

a.   Brandenburg Gate
b.   It Could Happen To You
c.   Forty Days
d.   Out Of The Way Of The People
e.   Blues (inc., ann.)

74.03.09   **Two Generations Of Brubeck**
Rotterdam, The Netherlands, De Doelen, Radio Broadcast.
Jerry Bergonzi ts (f,g,h,i); Perry Robinson cl (f,g,h,i); Dave Brubeck p; Darius Brubeck el-p; Chris
Brubeck el-b, tb (f,g,h,i); David Powell b (f,g,h,i); Danny Brubeck dr; Peter "Madcat" Ruth harm
(f,g,h,i).
a.   It's A Raggy Waltz
b.   Brandenburg Gate
c.   It Could Happen To You
d.   Three To Get Ready
e.   Out Of The Way Of The People
f.   Rotterdam Blues
g.   Call Of The Wild
h.   Christopher Columbus
i.   Jesus Christ - Superstar
k.   Tin Sink
l.   Blue Rondo A La Turk
m.   Circadian Dysrhythmia
n.   Take Five

76.00.00
Television production.
a.   They All Sang Yankee Doodle

Notes: The different variations of this American folk song were composed by Dave Brubeck for
the bicentennial commemoration of the United States of America. They give musical impressions
of the different people and races who immigrated to the U.S.A.

76.00.00   **Dave Brubeck**
Wilton, Connecticut, B.B.C. Television production.
Dave Brubeck p.
a.   Thank You (Dziekuje)   BBCV 3014
b.   Koto Song (theme)   -
c.   Brandenburg Gate (theme)   -

d.	Theme From "Mr. Broadway" (theme)	-
e.	La Paloma Azul (The Blue Dove)	-

Notes: BBCV 3014 is a B.B.C. Television production by Margaret McCall commemorating the "Silver Anniversary 1976" of The Dave Brubeck Quartet. In the Television production more musical examples are given, played by Dave Brubeck, relating to different aspects in the interview.

76.01.21   Dave Brubeck Quartet Plus Guests

New York City, New York, Friars Club, B.B.C. Television production.

Paul Desmond as; Dave Brubeck p; Gene Wright b; Joe Morello dr; Darius Brubeck keyb (a); Chris Brubeck el-b (a); Danny Brubeck dr (a).

a.	Unsquare Dance	BBCV 3014
b.	St. Louis Blues (inc.)	-

Notes: In the television production, fragments of more tunes are presented that were performed at this concert.

76.02.27   Dave Brubeck Quartet Plus Guests

Boston, Massachusetts, Symphony Hall, B.B.C. Television production.

Paul Desmond as (b,d,e,h); Dave Brubeck p; Gene Wright b (d-h); Joe Morello dr (d-h); Darius Brubeck keyb (a,c); Chris Brubeck el-b (a), tb (c); Danny Brubeck dr (a,c); Rick Kilburn b (c).

a.	It Could Happen To You	BBCV 3014
b.	Balcony Rock	-
c.	Sermon On The Mount	-
d.	Take Five	-
e.	Three To Get Ready	-
f.	Salute To Stephen Foster	-
g.	African Breeze	-
h.	Take The "A" Train	-

Notes: In the television production, fragments of more tunes are presented that were performed at this concert.

76.08.28   Dave Brubeck Quartet

Rochester, New York, Eastman Theatre (At The Top).

Paul Desmond as (a-c,e,f); Dave Brubeck p; Gene Wright b; Joe Morello dr.

a.	St. Louis Blues
b.	Three To Get Ready
c.	It's A Raggy Waltz

d.   African Times Suite
e.   Salute To Stephen Foster
f.   Take The "A" Train
g.   Take Five

Notes: Parts of this concert were recorded on tape. This entry is given following Mathias C. Hermann.

77.04.09   Dave Brubeck and Sons with Jimmy Giuffre
New York City, New York, private tape.
Jimmy Giuffre ts (e), cl (d,e), fl (e); Perry Robinson cl (d,e); Dave Brubeck p; Darius Brubeck synth; Chris Brubeck el-b, b-tb (d); Danny Brubeck dr.
a.   It's A Raggy Waltz
b.   Summer Music
c.   God's Love Made Visible
d.   Ellington-Medley: The Duke / Things Ain't What They
          Used To Be / Don't Get Around Much Anymore / Caravan /
          Mood Indigo / Take The "A" Train / Cottontail
e.   St. Louis Blues

79.07.00   Dave Brubeck Quartet
Newport, Rhode Island, Newport Jazz Festival.
Jerry Bergonzi ts (a,b,d,e) el-b (c); Dave Brubeck p; Chris Brubeck el-b (a,b,d,e), b- tb(c); Butch Miles dr.
a.   Brother, Can You Spare A Dime?   FHV 19041V
b.   Tritonis   -
c.   Big Bad Basie   -
d.   Take Five   -
e.   St. Louis Blues   -

Notes: FHV 19041 V is entitled "DAVE BRUBECK", released by Forum Home Video in 1989.

79.07.00   Dave Brubeck Quartet
Den Haag, The Netherlands, North Sea Jazz Festival.
Jerry Bergonzi ts (a,b), el-b (c); Dave Brubeck p; Chris Brubeck el-b (a,b), b-tb (c); Randy Jones dr.
a.   Like Someone in Love
b.   It's A Raggy Waltz
c.   Big Bad Basie

79.11.01   Dave Brubeck Quartet
Stuttgart, Germany, Radio Broadcast.
Jerry Bergonzi as; Dave Brubeck p; Chris Brubeck el-b, tb (f,i); Butch Miles dr.

a.	Summer Music
b.	St. Louis Blues
c.	Brother, Can You Spare A Dime?
d.	In Your Own Sweet Way
e.	Tritonis
f.	Big Bad Basie
g.	Cassandra
h.	Like Someone In Love
i.	Hometown Blues
k.	God's Love Made Visible
l.	It Could Happen To You
m.	Ellington-Medley: The Duke / Things Ain't What They Used To Be / C-Jam Blues / Don't Get Around Much Anymore / Caravan
n.	Someday My Prince Will Come
o.	Take Five

80.00.00   Dave Brubeck Quartet
Salt Lake City, Utah, University of Utah, KUED Television Broadcast.
Jerry Bergonzi ts; Dave Brubeck p; Chris Brubeck el-b; Randy Jones dr.

a.	Brother, Can You Spare A Dime?
b.	I Hear A Rhapsody
c.	Tritonis
d.	Lord, Lord
e.	Summer Music
f.	Take Five

Notes: The production by KUED TV, University of Utah is entitled "DAVE BRUBECK AT SNOWBIRD".

80-81.00.00   Dave Brubeck Quartet
The Vineyards, Television Broadcast.
Jerry Bergonzi ts, el-b (e-f); Dave Brubeck p; Chris Brubeck el-b, b-tb (e-f); Randy Jones dr.

a.	Music, Maestro, Please
b.	The Peace Of Jerusalem (inc.)
c.	Tritonis (inc.)

d.   It's Only A Paper Moon (inc.)
e.   Black And Blue
f.   St. Louis Blues (inc.)
g.   I Hear A Rhapsody (inc.)
h.   Take Five

Notes: The production of Vintage Sounds is entitled "DAVE BRUBECK LIVE AT THE VINEYARDS". It Includes a 1961-version of "Take Five" by the Original Dave Brubeck Quartet. Some Tracks are incomplete because of interview statements by Dave Brubeck.

82.06.20   Dave Brubeck Quintet
Los Angeles, California, Hollywood Bowl, 4th Annual Playboy Jazz Festival.
Michael Pedicin ts; Bill Smith cl; Dave Brubeck p; Chris Brubeck el-b, tb; Gene Wright b; Randy Jones dr.

a.   Take Five (inc.)   PONY VIDEO G 88 M0015
b.   Tritonis   -
c.   Symphony   -

Notes: PONY VIDEO G 88 M0015 is a laser video disc, entitled "PLAYBOY JAZZ FESTIVAL, VOL. 2".

83.04.21   Dave Brubeck Quartet
Amersfoort, The Netherlands, De Flint, "Sesjun" Radio Broadcast by T.R.O.S.-Radio.
Bill Smith cl; Dave Brubeck p; Chris Brubeck el-b, b-tb (c,d); Randy Jones dr.

a.   Three To Get Ready
b.   In Your Own Sweet Way
c.   Big Bad Basie
d.   Black And Blue
e.   I Hear A Rhapsody
f.   God's Love Made Visible
g.   The Duke / Things Ain't What They Used To Be /
            Don't Get Around Much Anymore
h.   Take Five (inc.)

84.00.00   Dave Brubeck Quartet
San Francisco, California, Russian Hill Recording.
Bill Smith cl, sax, recorder; Dave Brubeck p; Chris Brubeck el-b, b-tb; Randy Jones dr.
a.   Ordeal By Innocence   MGM / UA ML 100618

Notes: MGM / UA ML 100618 is a movie laser disc. The Dave Brubeck Quartet plays the background music to the MGM movie "ORDEAL BY INNOCENCE" based on an Agatha Christie mystery novel.

84.06-07.00   Dave Brubeck Quartet
Newport, Rhode Island, JVC Jazz Festival, Television Broadcast.
Bob Militello as; Dave Brubeck p; Chris Brubeck el-b; Randy Jones dr.
a.   Blue Rondo A La Turk
b.   Take Five

Notes: The production of Roskoff Productions Ltd. is entitled "JAZZ COMES HOME TO NEWPORT" and includes other tracks by the Michel Petrucciano Trio, the Dizzy Gillespie All Stars, and the Stan Getz Quintet.

87.03.30   Dave Brubeck Quartet
Moscow, USSR, Rossiya Concert Hall.
Bill Smith cl; Dave Brubeck p; Chris Brubeck el-b; Randy Jones dr.
a.   St. Louis Blues
b.   Tritonis
c.   Koto Song
d.   Take Five
e.   Blue Rondo A La Turk

Notes: The production of Arts & Entertainment Productions is entitled "Moscow Night". For other titles of concerts of the Russian tour of the Dave Brubeck Quartet see the preceding section.

87.10.15   Dave Brubeck Quartet
Scheveningen, The Netherlands, Circus Theater.
Bob Militello as, fl; Dave Brubeck p; Gene Wright b; Randy Jones dr.
a.   Three To Get Ready
b.   St. Louis Blues (inc.)
c.   Thank You (Dziekuje)
d.   Someday My Prince Will Come
e.   Out Of The Way Of The People
f.   Swing Bells / The Duke / Things Ain't What They
          Used To Be / Don't Get Around Much Anymore
g.   Koto Song
h.   The Wright Groove
i.   Take Five

k.   Take The "A" Train

88.07.15   Dave Brubeck Quartet
Nice, France, Radio Broadcast.
Bill Smith cl; Dave Brubeck p; Chris Brubeck el-b, b-tb (c); Randy Jones dr.
a.   Bossa
b.   Open The Gates (Out Of The Way Of The People)
c.   Big Bad Basie

88.07.15   Dave Brubeck Quartet
Montreux, Switzerland, Montreux Jazz Festival, Television Broadcast.
Bill Smith cl; Dave Brubeck p; Chris Brubeck el-b; Randy Jones dr.
a.   Unsquare Dance

89.09.16-17   Dave Brubeck Quartet and Friends
Saratoga, California, Paul Masson Mountain Winery.
Bill Smith cl; Dave Brubeck p; Charles Matthew Brubeck cello (h,i,k); Jack Six b; Randy Jones dr;
Maruga perc (l).
a.   Look For The Silver Lining
b.   Benjamin
c.   The Peace Of Jerusalem / New Wine
d.   I Hear A Rhapsody
e.   Here's That Rainy Day
f.   St. Louis Blues
g.   These Foolish Things
h.   Charles Matthew Hallelujah
i.   Blue Rondo A La Turk
k.   Take The "A" Train
l.   I Got Rhythm

89.11.02   Dave Brubeck Quartet
Ludwigsburg, Germany, Bürgersaal im Forum, Schloßpark.
Bill Smith cl; Dave Brubeck p; Jack Six b; Randy Jones dr.
a.   St. Louis Blues
b.   Theme For June
c.   The Peace Of Jerusalem
d.   I Hear A Rhapsody
e.   Once When I Was Very Young
f.   It's A Raggy Waltz

g.   Take Five
h.   Take The "A" Train

90.07.07   Dave Brubeck Quartet
Nice, France, Radio Broadcast.
Bill Smith cl; Dave Brubeck p; Jack Six b; Randy Jones dr.
a.   Ellington-Medley: Swing Bells / The Duke /
                Things Ain't What They Used To Be / Take The
                "A" Train / Don't Get Around Much Anymore
b.   Cassandra
c.   Once When I Was Very Young
d.   The Peace Of Jerusalem
e.   Pangue Lingua March
f.   Blue Rondo A La Turk
g.   Take The "A" Train

90.07.09   Dave Brubeck Quartet
Nice, France, Grande Parade du Jazz, Radio Broadcast.
Bill Smith cl; Dave Brubeck p; Jack Six b; Randy Jones dr.
a.   Blues For Newport
b.   Yesterdays
c.   The Peace Of Jerusalem
d.   Summer Music
e.   I Hear A Rhapsody
f.   I Got Rhythm

90.07.13   Dave Brubeck Quartet plus Carmen McRae
The Hague, The Netherlands, North Sea Jazz Festival.
Bill Smith cl; Dave Brubeck p; Jack Six b; Randy Jones dr; Carmen McRae voc
(e-i).
a.   Blues For Newport (inc.)
b.   Once When I Was Very Young
c.   The Peace Of Jerusalem
d.   Pange Lingua March
e.   In Your Own Sweet Way
f.   Strange Meadow Lark
g.   Easy As You Go
h.   I Didn't Know
i.   Take Five

90.11.12-17   **Dave Brubeck Quartet with Metropole Orkest**
The Netherlands, A.V.R.O. Radio Broadcast.
Bill Smith cl; Dave Brubeck p; Jack Six b; Randy Jones dr; Metropole Orkest, Russell Gloyd
cond.

a.	God's Love Made Visible
b.	In Your Own Sweet Way
c.	Three To Get Ready
d.	Blue Rondo A La Turk
e.	Softly, William, Softly
f.	Brandenburg Gate, Revisited
g.	Back In Town

Notes: During Dave Brubeck's 70th Birthday Anniversary tour through The Netherlands in
November, 1990 five concerts were organized. Four of them were performed together with the
Metropole Orchestra in Amsterdam, Rotterdam, 's-Hertogenbosch and Bergen op Zoom. The fifth
in Sittard was performed only by the Quartet. f and g were not broadcasted.

90.11.27+28   **Dave Brubeck Quartet with Special Guests**
                      London Symphony Orchestra
London, Great Britain, Barbican Hall, Barbican Centre.
Bill Smith cl; Dave Brubeck p, arr (l); Jack Six b; Randy Jones dr; Stephane Grappelli viol (f,g);
Darius Brubeck p, arr (b,h,m); Chris Brubeck tb (d), el-b, arr (a,d); Matthew Brubeck cello;
Danny Brubeck dr; The London Symphony Orchestra, Russell Gloyd cond, arr (c); Howard
Brubeck arr (f,k).

a.	Cassandra
b.	Summer Music
c.	Softly, William, Softly
d.	Big Bad Basie
e.	God's Love Made Visible
	(From "La Fiesta De La Posada")
f.	In Your Own Sweet Way
g.	A Tribute To The Duke Of Ellington
h.	Three To Get Ready
i.	Three Excerpts From "The Light In The Wilderness"
	Forty Days / The Sermon On The Mount /
	The Kingdom
k.	Brandenburg Gate, Revisited
l.	Take Five
m.	Blue Rondo A La Turk

n.   When The Saints
o.   Take The "A" Train

Notes: These Concerts were the highlights of Dave Brubeck's tour through Europe under the heading "DAVE BRUBECK 70TH BIRTHDAY CONCERT".

90.12.06   Dave Brubeck
New York City, New York, "Today Show", Television Broadcast.
Dave Brubeck p; Chris Brubeck (a) el-b, b-tb.
a.   Big Bad Basie
b.   Happy Birthday To You

91.10.09+10   Dave Brubeck Quartet And The RIAS Tanzorchester
Berlin, Germany, 3SAT Television Broadcast.
Bill Smith cl; Dave Brubeck p; Jack Six b; Randy Jones dr; RIAS Tanzorchester (Horst Jankowski cond): Russell Gloyd cond (c).
a.   Three To Get Ready
b.   In Your Own Sweet Way
c.   Cassandra
d.   Take Five

91.10.21   Dave Brubeck Quartet
Leverkusen, Germany, Forum, 12. Leverkusener Jazz Tage.
Bill Smith cl; Dave Brubeck p; Jack Six b; Randy Jones dr.
a.   Love For Sale
b.   Dancin' In Rhythm
c.   Once When I Was Very Young
d.   Pange Lingua March
e.   Lover Man
f.   Unsquare Dance
g.   Shine On Harvest Moon
h.   Take The "A" Train
          Dave Brubeck & Sons (Home Cooking Quartet)
Dave Brubeck p; Matthew Brubeck cello; Chris Brubeck el-b, tb (o); Danny Brubeck dr.
i.   Three To Get Ready And Four To Go
k.   Forty Days
l.   It Could Happen To You
m.   The Desert And The Parched Land
n.   Cable Car

o.   The Sermon On The Mount
                      Dave Brubeck & Sons & The Dolphins
Chris Brubeck tb; Dave Brubeck p; Vinnie Martucci synth, keyb; Mike DeMicco el-g; Matthew
Brubeck cello; Rob Leon el-b; Danny Brubeck dr.
p.   Jazzanians
                      Dave Brubeck Quartet & Sons & The Dolphins
Chris Brubeck tb; Bill Smith cl; Dave Brubeck p; Vinnie Martucci synth, keyb; Mike DeMicco el-
g; Matthew Brubeck cello; Rob Leon el-b; Jack Six b; Danny Brubeck dr; Randy Jones dr.
q.   Blue Rondo A La Turk
r.   Take Five

Notes: The Concert at the 12th Leverkusen Jazz Days was video taped by the WDR (West
German Radio Broadcasting Company) and was broadcasted in parts.

92.11.05   Dave Brubeck Quartet and Matthew Brubeck
Bologna, Italy, Teatro Medico.
Bill Smith cl; Dave Brubeck p; Matthew Brubeck cello (h-l); Jack Six b; Randy Jones dr.
a.   Things Ain't What They Used To Be / Take The
                      "A" Train / Don't Get Around Much Anymore
b.   Once When I Was Very Young
c.   Theme For June
d.   The Peace Of Jerusalem
e.   Softly, William, Softly
f.   Open The Gates (Out Of The Way Of The People)
g.   St. Louis Blues
h.   Three To Get Ready
i.   Yesterdays
k.   Take Five
l.   Take The "A" Train